NIGHTBLOOM

NIGHTBLOOM

HERBERT LIEBERMAN

G.P. Putnam's Sons / New York

Designed by Richard Oriolo

Library of Congress Cataloging in Publication Data

Lieberman, Herbert H., date.
Nightbloom.

I. Title.
PS3562.I4N55   1984   813'.54   83-13742
ISBN 0-399-12904-9

Printed in the United States of America

Many thanks to Dr. Len Rubin of Chappaqua, New York, whence, one summer night, the idea sprang.

For Judy

APRIL / '79

1

The man stood at the edge of the rooftop, hands clasped, elbows pressed into the concrete ledge. The balmy spring breeze rustled the cuffs of his trousers and stirred his lapels. There was an imminence of rain, something one smelled in the exhalations from the sparse foliage and the full trash cans—something dank and sweetish wafting upward through the shafts below.

Periodically a gash of lightning rent the western sky. At that elevation, seven stories up, the city had the look of a dirty carpet onto which a billion gaudy sequins had been strewn. Neon and prismatic, the lights from the teeming theater district cast a glow of lurid red on the sky above, as if at that one point some vengeful, purging Old Testament fire were raging below.

In the palm of his hand the man rattled pebbles and a few chips of schist he'd gathered up off the tarred rooftop. He shook them in his hand as if he were telling beads or reading auguries from them. Then, with an air of dreamy abstraction, he would pitch one or two down into the warm pools of shimmering light where crowds of people streamed from the emptying theaters into the warm orange glow of café windows.

Of his actions the man appeared to be oblivious. On his face he wore a sweet, placid expression as if at that moment he was deep in the midst of recalling something infinitely pleasing, some point at which he existed in a dim, scarcely remembered past. Gently, and with an air of exquisite restraint, his arm rose and another pebble arched outward from his hand over the ledge top down into the void below.

❊　❊　❊

Francis Mooney grunted and stooped his 240-pound frame above the mound of dirty tarpaulin that lay heaped on the corner of Forty-ninth Street, just west of Eighth Avenue. It was now well past midnight, but still crowds of people gathered silent and watchful in a circle round him.

At the curbside, the radio from a police patrol car sputtered and crackled sporadic reports of the evening's crimes in progress.

Hunkered on his knees, Mooney lifted a corner of the tarpaulin and held it between thumb and forefinger, rather fastidiously, the way one might lift a lace doily. It was an incongruous gesture in someone of Mooney's girth. Beneath the tarpaulin was a man, slight, fortyish, with wide staring eyes. At the side of his head a pink, bulb-like excrescence like a newly bloomed hydrangea sprung whole from his skull. Mooney was careful to keep the soles of his scuffed black oxfords well back out of the way of the red puddle trickling over the pavement from beneath the tarpaulin.

Not far from the tarpaulin itself, a slab of concrete cinderblock lay, twelve inches across, four inches thick, weighing approximately forty pounds. At the elevation from which it had fallen, he judged, it had on impact reached a velocity of nearly two hundred miles an hour and had broken into four clean, nearly equal quarters.

"Hit him like a brick shithouse," Mooney muttered, more to himself than to the reporting patrolman hovering above him. A vision of the shattered, pulpy skull beneath the tarpaulin flashed in his head.

"Looks like it just fell from the roof," the patrolman responded. Mooney gaped upward. His slightly protuberant eyes ascended the brick facade of the building. "Probably broke off the coping up there."

"Any identification?"

"Name's Ransom," the patrolman answered, flipping pages in a little note pad. "John R., age forty-three. Musician. Address given here on his union card is 443 West Forty-seventh. A few blocks down. Probably just on his way home."

"Anyone see it?" Mooney asked without looking up.

"The kid over here," someone in the crowd said.

Mooney couldn't tell if the black child suddenly materializing before him had come forward voluntarily or was pushed. He was simply just there.

"What's your name, friend?"

"Cleveland."

"Cleveland what?"

The boy uttered a surname that got lost somewhere between the noise of the street and the fright constricting his throat.

"I can't hear you, Cleveland. Don't talk with your hands in your mouth. What's your last name?"

The boy swallowed hard. "Gaynes."

Mooney gazed up at him. What he saw was a scrawny, bug-eyed kid who was clearly frightened. "How old are you, Cleveland?"

"Sixteen."

Mooney estimated his real age to be somewhere closer to eleven or twelve, a part of one of the dog packs of homeless waifs who foraged regularly through the Times Square area. Bug life, Mooney thought. Lice. "You from round here, Cleveland?"

The boy's eyes widened. He appeared blank.

"Where do you live? Where do you crash?"

There was a pause while the crowd pushed forward and the boy stalled for time. "A hundred and thirty-eighth."

"And where?"

"St. Nicholas."

"You got a pad up there?"

"My cousin got a pad up there."

Mooney regarded the child skeptically.

"You see what happened here tonight, Cleveland?"

The boy gazed down at the sticky red puddle and the impersonal humped thing lying beneath the tarpaulin with the shoes sticking out from beneath. The crowds inched forward while Mooney, still stooping on cramped legs, waited.

"You see what happened, Cleveland?" he asked again.

The boy pointed to the slab of concrete. "That come down off the roof."

"From where? Point to it. The exact spot."

The boy's head turned and his eye wandered back up the gray brick facade of the building where inquisitive occupants in nightclothes leaned out over sills through lighted windows open to the street. "From there."

Mooney's eyes followed the boy's finger to the top of the building to a point just above and to the left of the uppermost fire escape. "You see someone throw it?"

The boy looked around uneasily.

"You see someone up there, Cleveland?"

"Uh-huh."

Mooney's interest perked. "Anyone you know?"

Dead-panned, the boy slowly shook his head right and left. "Nope."

"But you say you saw someone drop it?"

"Uh-huh."

"How come you saw that?"

13

The boy shrugged and made a face. "Just look up and seen him there. Then seen it comin' down."

"From that spot you showed me?" Mooney thrust a pudgy finger skyward.

"Uh-huh. From there."

By that time a sizable crowd had gathered. Two more patrol cars had joined the first. Their red dome lights spun while a gray forensic van from the medical examiner's office nosed its way slowly through the crowds, coming to collect the remains.

"No one threw it, Mooney." The cop scribbled in his pad. "Take it from me. It just broke off from the building. All of these old fleabags round here are falling apart."

"Probably," Mooney sighed. His leg had started to cramp from where he'd been kneeling above the tarpaulin. His nose made a high whistling sound as he wobbled to his feet. "I guess we oughta go up and have a look anyway."

Frank Mooney was an overweight, failed detective. Overweight because he was a compulsive eater with a predilection for beer and fried foods; failed because he was a malcontent, antisocial creature in an organization that bonded men on the principles of teamwork and compulsory fraternal loyalties. Like all misanthropes, he was not much on fraternal loyalties. In fact, Mooney had very little good to say about mankind in general and about cops, nothing whatever. He counted no man his brother. Moreover, he was given to a whole medley of habits that policemen have no business cultivating. He loved the ponies to the point of impecuniosity. Also, he had never married nor sought the company of any woman with serious regularity. On off-hours he was not averse to alleviating loneliness in sleazy West Side dives where professional women were known to ply their trade.

Twice he had made detective first grade—a captaincy—and twice he had been broken back down to detective second grade; this for (a) "acting unprofessionally," (b) "exceeding his authority," and (c) "comporting himself in a manner unbecoming a police officer."

Now his misanthropy was such that he took a kind of perverse delight in his demotions, and seized any opportunity to flaunt them jubilantly in the faces of junior colleagues, as if daring them to follow his example.

He was fifty-nine, a veteran of nearly forty years with the force, and thrice decorated for bravery. With four years away from retirement, no one, not even the commissioner, would have had the stomach to fire him. On several occasions, pressure had been brought to bear to make Mooney take early retirement. But he would not truckle before the chief. He would not be intimidated. Though there was no love lost between them and Mooney, the Policemen's Benevolent Association and the Detectives Endowment League both made it emphatically clear they would not brook any forced retirement in his case. But even more compelling, Mooney left little doubt that in forty years of service he had learned where all the department skeletons had been buried, and that if the situation warranted, he wouldn't hesitate to disinter them.

Mooney was therefore, in all respects, a survivor, a master at the art of staying afloat in the treacherous swamps of municipal bureaucracy. His ordeal, however, had not particularly ennobled him. As a youth he'd been striking and tall, in the blue-eyed, dark-haired Gaelic mold. But now age and chronic dissatisfaction had transformed the once alert, agreeably regular features into something flaccid and unshaped through which one might still glimpse the ruins of a more comely past.

The overall effect was heightened by a strangely cultivated voice that clashed with the stream of vileness steadily leaching from his mouth. He was emphatically a thorn in the department's side, a wart on the spanking-clean image they were always at such pains to promote.

Catalonia, Alonzo. Went out in April '75. Thirty-pound chunk of tile pried or fallen from a rooftop, 308 West 51. Busted his head. No witnesses. No suspects. Cause subsequently determined to be accidental. Case closed August '75. O'Meggins, Harold. May '76. Age 48. Locksmith. Skull crushed by 80 pounds of limestone chimney capping dropped or fallen from construction site, 423 West 47. No witnesses. No suspects. Cause subsequently determined to be accidental. No further investigation. Case closed July 4, 1976. Quigley, Wayne. Decapitated—Jesus, decapitated—May 12, 1977, by flying slate believed to have dropped or fallen from rooftop, 315 West 48. No witnesses. No suspects. Cause subsequently determined to be accidental. Case closed, June 14, 1977. Kim, Chai Soong—Christ—what the fuck kinda name is that? Oh, here it is. Korean. Waiter. Age 19. Death from falling concrete slab, April 13, 1978. That's a year ago today. Causes subsequently determined to be . . . Case dropped. Case dropped. Case dropped. Bullshit.

Mooney flung the precinct files aside with an air of disgust. Tilting his sizable girth backwards in the chair, he rummaged deep within his jacket pockets for a cigarette.

"Five people die over a space of five years, from bricks or slabs, or

15

flying objects falling from rooftops, all of 'em around the West Forties or low Fifties, or generally the theater district. All of 'em round ten or eleven at night. Two in May, three in April. But that roof was clean tonight. At least when I seen it. And nobody in the building, on the top floor, heard anybody movin' at that hour around up there. Can all the rest be coincidence? No witnesses. No suspects. Bullshit."

It was getting well on to 3:00 A.M. and he was still at the station house. He had filed his initial reports and he pondered now the wisdom of going home. He lived in a large, nearly unfurnished apartment up in the West Bronx around the Yankee Stadium. All he had in the way of household possessions was a large-screen color television, a couple of canvas director chairs, a Formica kitchen table, a couple of pots and pans, a few dishes, and a permanently unmade bed. His neighbors were all Puerto Ricans and Blacks, with a sprinkling of terrified geriatric Jews. Everyone in the building, except Mooney, was collecting one form of welfare assistance or another. Mooney never spoke to any of them.

Though he was bone-tired, he had no wish to go home. Home terrified him. He knew that if he went there now he would not sleep. Instead, he would merely lie in bed half-undressed in the sour rumplement of his sheets, toss and turn and stare at the nightmarish shadowshow that never ceased to play across his ceiling.

His mind was far too active for sleep. Disquieting images flashed across his fretful eye. Images of violence and carnage, tawdry and bizarre. Generally, they depicted the apocalypse of the urban night. Murder and mayhem. He could neither avert his eyes nor turn them off. Then came the images of lust. Vibrantly, pulsatingly pornographic. Dreams of murder and lust in the nighttime doodles of a lapsed Roman Catholic. He had not been to Confession for fifteen years. He was too haughty to go down on his knees before a priest and beg forgiveness. He was not a penitent. He had other ways, more circuitous but less demeaning, for assuaging guilt.

As always, after mental work he was famished. If he could not sleep then at least he would eat. The thought of hamburgers came to him, greasy fries and sweet, black coffee. A groan issued from the great vacant cavern of his stomach and shortly he was in his battered '70 Buick Skylark, heading crosstown toward the FDR Drive.

At Forty-fifth, in the shadow of the UN, he would get on the FDR Drive heading north. Despite the temperature or the time of year, he would drive with all the windows open, gulping frigid air for dear life, cooling his overheated body, freshening his clogged, drowsy brain.

Though it was the longer route, he would take the Willis Avenue Bridge which had no toll as opposed to the Triborough which tithed him a dollar. From Willis Avenue he would swing left onto the Major Deegan, tearing up the thruway to 161 Street, where he knew he could depend on an all-night White Tower to be open.

There were other all-night eateries in the area, establishments where he knew the food to be superior. There was the Bun & Burger on 168, Arthur Treacher's, the Taco Gaucho and the Chicken Shack. All stayed open the night. All served a credible hamburger, most of them better than the thin, leathery thing about the size of a half dollar the White Tower still foisted off on its unwitting clientele.

But to Mooney all of these places were parvenus, upstarts, spoilers. He didn't like the class of people that frequented them. Undesirable ethnic types, he reasoned, whereas the White Tower catered to the older, more established folks in the neighborhood.

But, more importantly, it had been the White Tower he knew as a moody youth growing up around the West Bronx. It was the place he haunted as a chronic truant, a friendless, sullen child whose premature obesity had doomed him to mostly solitary pleasures. He had been the neighborhood "fat kid," ridiculed by his peers into a sharp antipathy for all adolescent tribal codes of bonding. Gangs, teams or clubs he had no use for. Instead, he had made a fetish of aloofness, grew up distrusting the world in general and any number of things specifically. He sought the solace of isolation, finding it, oddly enough, in the high places—the rooftops of those onetime benign West Bronx polyglot neighborhoods where of a summer night he contemplated the evening sky and taught himself the stars, while the baking pavements of July and August suffocated all the sweltering life below.

His love of stargazing persisted well into adulthood. As a passion he kept it very much to himself, certain that among his colleagues at the station house it would become the butt of much amusement to be used against him. Astronomy was no doubt an improbable passion for such a man but, then again, Mooney was an improbable man. The son of strict Roman Catholic parents whose notions of faith fastened on the punitive, whatever intimations of divinity might have been lurking about in his boyish heart were quickly throttled. Why bother with a god if this is what it got you?

He pushed the swinging glass doors open and entered once more into that familiar harsh blue fluorescence. Warm, doughy, meaty odors came at him in waves—meat patties sizzling on a griddle, the smell of coffee in a large aluminum urn, sodden pickles in a plastic counter bowl, stale pound cake in cellophane encased in a thumb-stained cake-saver, all evoking in him the pleasant sensation of home-coming.

The place was empty except for the black counterman who instantly recognized the lumbering figure looming in the doorway. Quickly he tossed a number of frozen patties onto the grill and turned up the coffee.

Before the detective left that morning, somewhere near 5:00 A.M., having excoriated the police, harangued the judges, and denounced the entire penal system in general, he had consumed four hamburgers, three plates of fries saturated in packet ketchup, and four cups of a lethally treacly coffee.

2

"I will in a minute if you just give me a chance."

"I don't have a minute."

"I have a perfectly good excuse."

"You always do."

"What's wrong with that?"

"What's good about being gone four days? No call. No communication. What could be good about that?"

Her voice grew increasingly shrill. As she spoke she flung clothing into the yawning mouth of a Gladstone bag.

"Where do you think you're going at four in the morning?"

"Anywhere. It can't be far enough for me."

Watford watched her with an air of quiet amazement. The lurches and charges, the sweeping, scythelike motion of her arm chucking clothing, as if she were fencing with some invisible adversary. "Put the bag away, Inez. Let's try and talk." When he made a gesture toward the bag, she darted, snatched a lead paperweight, and brandished it above her head. "Put your hand on that again and so help me, I'll bash you."

"Inez—"

"Don't touch it. I warn you. Don't touch it."

"Okay, okay. Just stop shouting. It's four A.M."

"Shouting?" She was ashen, her body so taut she appeared to vibrate like a plucked string. "You want shouting. I'll give you shouting."

"Inez, the neighbors . . ."

"Fuck the neighbors. You just stay where you are. Not a step closer or, so help me, I'll brain you."

He watched her fling clothing with an air of quiet awe. The energy level she'd achieved inspired wonder in one for whom lassitude was virtually a way of life. "Won't you just let me try to explain?"

"I don't want explanations. I've heard all of them by this time. I told you, I'm nobody's nigger. I don't sit around the house. I don't twiddle my thumbs. I wait for no one."

"I said there'd be times when I'd go off like this."

"You did. You sure did." A spray of spittle arched outward from between her snarling lips. "But I'm dumb, you see. Slow on the uptake. I didn't realize what it really meant."

"That was all part of the arrangement."

"Agreed. It was. Only now I'm finished with the arrangement. Finito. Kaput. Up the arrangement." She jammed a toilet kit into the overflowing lip of the bag and, breathless, panting, pushed down with the full weight of her drab, frail body. Grunting, as if for punctuation, she wrestled the bag's zipper closed. "What kind of fucking arrangement, for God's sake? I sit around here. Clean your house. Cook your supper. Do your stinking wash. I was better off on my own. At least I was independent. What I made I kept. And I was beholden to no one. Least of all, some weirdo screw who thinks I should be grateful to him just for taking me in off the streets. You lost your job again, didn't you?" She laughed at the stunned, rather hurt expression in his eyes. The laugh was more a cackle. It rose shrill out of a slightly crooked, heavily painted mouth.

"Who said so?"

She laughed again, cheerlessly, forcing it, using the laughter like a goad. "Your office called wanting to know where you were. That was yesterday. They said you hadn't been in for five days. I said you were away on personal business. Just like you told me. That I'd have you call the moment you got back. They said not to bother. They'd be sending your severance check along in the next day or so, along with the junk in your desk. Whadya think of them apples, Charley?"

Watford was a fairly good-sized man, easily six foot, who contrived somehow to convey the impression of someone smaller. His stride was tentative, his shoulders stooped, and he went along at something of a crouch. Standing still, he could achieve a sense of motionlessness that was extraordinary in a human being, as if all his vital signs had closed down and he was in a state of suspended animation.

In a room full of people one had to look hard to see Watford. He

19

had the gift of assimilating himself perfectly into the surrounding landscape.

Now he could feel something starting to stir and swell within him. For a moment his vision dimmed and there was no air left in the room to breathe. The sensation that he was on the brink of blowing apart passed, followed by a strangely impressive calm. "You can go now, Inez."

That wasn't exactly the reply she'd been expecting. Her eyes opened and she gaped at him. Then once again that shrill, grating laughter. "Oh, may I? Well, thank you. I'm so grateful to you for permitting me to leave. 'Cause I can't breathe in this place any-more—this house with its doilies and lace and the funny little chintz chairs. All of that goddamned ditsy old-lady porcelain locked up in cabinets and your precious cranberry glass. It all smells of old lady. Camphor and mustiness and rubber stockings."

"It was my mother's glass."

"I know very well whose glass it was." She peered hard at him. Whatever coarse, slatternly attractiveness there was in her had now turned pinched and haggish. "So I'm very glad it's okay for me to leave this house now; leave you here with your antiques and your art-i-facts." She pronounced the word in mocking imitation of him, then watched him walking slowly toward her. She watched him warily, the way a rabbit, paralyzed and quivering, is transfixed by the approaching snake.

"You better go now, Inez."

"I don't need no second invitations, Buster," she murmured under her breath, grabbed the Gladstone, then lunged for the door, yanking it open so hard that it banged against the wall. In the next moment she was clattering down the stairs to the outside door.

Following her out to the head of the stairs, he stood there weaving, slightly dizzy, peering down at her, his legs trembling and nauseous the way ugly scenes had always made him nauseous.

At the bottom of the stairs, standing in the open frame of the door, with the damp chill of early morning rushing in, she glared up at him, all pinched and mean. "Fucking creep," she jeered, then slammed the door and was gone.

Long after she'd gone he stood at the top of the stairs, peering down at the place she'd just vacated. He half expected her to reappear, weeping and contrite. And if she had, he'd have taken her back, even though he didn't want her any longer. But Charles Watford was basically a generous man with a streak of antique chivalry—that same kind of fatuous comic gallantry that had done so much to turn a serious talented father into a music-hall buffoon. Old Cyril Watford, horologist, master clockmaker, a man of awesome reputation within the narrow compass of a small rarefied field, who as late as 1949 was still delighting the neighbors by attiring himself with spats and a boutonniere.

In his time Cyril had been summoned across oceans by kings, ministers, archbishops and heads of state, invited to climb dizzying towers and there enter the multichambered steel hearts of cathedral clocks, parliamentary spires, university belfries.

Like the anatomist or the great physician, Cyril Watford's whole being existed solely for the purpose of charting the inner workings of exquisitely complicated time machines. Cardiologist, pathologist, even psychoanalyst to the great clocks of the world, he could chart their diseases and effect their cures. Sprockets, gears, springs, spinwheels, balances were the vital organs he could transplant. His long, delicate fingers could probe their way through the lead-copper vascular system of a giant tower clock, locating stenosis and occlusion. Rooting out rust, he could restore a sixteenth-century masterwork to all of its former glory.

For this rare gift he was paid handsomely. His services were in great demand. But quixotic to his lyric Gaelic core, he gave away every penny he earned; emptied his pockets to strangers encountered in saloons or railway stations in foreign cities, subsequently reducing his family to the brink of penury. The sum effect of this on Cyril's wife, never strong in either body or spirit, was that she took to her bed with a vague disorder one day, and then later, to a bottle of barbiturates which ultimately proved her undoing.

Unable to sleep, Watford sat outside in the small backyard garden on a plastic chaise in what remained of the dampish misty night. Savoring the darkness, he thought of old Cyril, dead now some twenty years. The memory of the man was still a rancorous thing, fraught with a kind of terror.

Badly rattled from his encounter with Inez, he let the darkness roll over him, lap at him, quietly engulfing him. Watford enjoyed darkness, for in darkness he became most himself. In the brilliant light of day he tended to be other people. People he saw and for a while imitated. He wore a mask of cheerful amiability. Outwardly, a model human being.

But that was not the real Watford. The real Watford was a nocturnal creature. Like an owl or a cat, he came out only at night. Solitude and darkness were his métier. Mostly he was happy to sit all night in the garden on his chaise beneath the noble old tulip tree, vigilant, watchful, held in the exquisite tension of some forever nameless expectation. Muscles coiled, yet strangely calm, he dozed, but even then he remained keenly conscious of himself, aware of all the burrowing, digging, grubbing, stalking nocturnal life about him.

At dawn he rose, brushed the residue of night from his clothing, the accumulation of dew and fallen insect life, then went upstairs to shower and shave and prepare for work. No need for that now. He had no work to go to this morning and Inez, his companion of the last several months, the last of his remaining responsibilities, was gone.

3

The young man, whose name was Kramer, pressed the lower lid of Watford's eye down with his thumb, studying the pale pinkish pocket of inner flesh. From there his fingers strayed up behind Watford's ears, then down beneath the fleshy folds under the mandible, palpitating as he went, seeking for areas of enlargement.

"Stomach? Waterworks?" the intern asked.

"Fine. All fine."

"Lie back a minute." The young man gently guided Watford down on the bed till he lay flat, then ran his hands up under the hospital smock and completely explored the stomach and pelvic area.

"That hurt?" He pressed the area above the appendix.

"No."

"Have we had a BP on him?" the doctor asked the nurse hovering behind him, scribbling onto Watford's chart.

"One forty over seventy. On the low side, actually."

The internist appeared perplexed. "Okay. Want to pull up your shirt a minute?"

Docile as a child, Watford hauled the robe up around his shoulders. "Last night directly after supper it just came on me. I got extremely warm and faint. And my head—" He groaned. "Is the fever high?"

"Forty degrees centigrade. About a hundred and three Fahrenheit. That's high."

"What about the leukocytic count?" Watford asked suddenly.

The young man looked up from the chart on which he'd been scribbling. "Beg pardon?"

"The leukocytes." Watford smiled back archly. "The white blood cells. They ran some blood tests on me last night."

"Since you ask," the tired young man sighed, "it was close to 200,-000 cubic millimeters. That's high too. And I hear a slight tachycardia in your chest."

Watford smoothed his smock back down around his spindly milk-colored thighs and lay back on the bed.

"It's obvious," the young man went on, "you're working some kind of infection. I can't find the source of it. No focus of sepsis. I think you'd better plan to stay around a couple of days. I'd like to do some more blood workups. An IVN and a CAT scan. Will you get him set up for radiology first thing in the morning?" He addressed the nurse over his shoulder. "And let's try him on a half gram of Valium for that headache." The intern rose and was about to start out.

"Doctor," Watford called weakly from the bed. The young man turned. "The Valium won't do it."

"Why won't it?"

"I'm an old friend of these headaches."

"You get them often, do you?"

"At least one a month. They're migraine. Valium won't even make a dent in it."

The physician looked down at him, pondering. "Okay. We'll try you on some ergotamine." He took out his prescription pad.

"Actually, I've had much better luck with meperidine."

The young man's pen paused in midair. "Oh? How much?"

Watford reflected a moment. "I'd say about seven hundred milligrams taken intravenously."

Outside in the hall, the young intern paused to chat with the nurse. "When did he come in?"

"Last night. Around ten o'clock. Severe headache. Nausea. High fever. Claimed he was going to black out."

"You ever see him in here before?"

"No."

Something in the doctor's manner conveyed uneasiness. "Aside from the high leukocyte count and the tachycardia, which comes from the fever," he went on, "his life signs are fine. Heart. Blood pressure. Lungs. Can't find a thing wrong with him." He shrugged and started off, then turned abruptly. "If he asks you for any more Demerol, you let me know."

In Watford's room they had turned the lights down, with only the coin-slot operated TV casting a pale violet glow over the semiprivate room. He was glad that the bed opposite him was unoccupied. He sipped a bit of cranberry juice through a plastic straw and wiggled his toes cozily beneath the blankets.

Outside it had started to rain. The hard drizzle made a pleasant frying sound on the large panes. With a deliciously drowsy sense of well being, he watched the eleven o'clock news.

Shortly the nurse came back with a small phial and a hypodermic. "All right, Mr. Watford, will you please turn over."

The soul of compliance, Watford rolled on his side and hiked his smock. In the next instant he felt the punch of the needle and the quick cold contraction round the point of entry. "That ought to take care of the headache for now."

"I hope so," he sighed miserably. "I do hope so."

He let her pull the blankets up about him and tuck him in for the night.

"Want me to turn off the TV?"

"Leave it on, please. I like to fall asleep with it going. You can just turn the sound down."

After she left he finished his juice and watched the end of the news, feeling the Demerol slowly overtake him. In moments he was removed bodily from his immediate environment. Transported elsewhere, he savored the sense of unanchored weightlessness, of imminent levitation. There was the extra bonus, too, in that for Watford, Demerol taken intravenously was invariably attended by a surging penile erection.

His skin was suddenly very cool and he could feel the darkness of the room slipping over him like a black silk gauntlet. It snuggled against him like an old cat as he smiled mischievously into the encroaching shadows.

He dropped off, dreaming of a small child lying naked on an operating table. No more than possibly eight or so, the child was bathed in harsh white lights. Above him stood a surgeon with a gauze mask which tended to emphasize a pair of extremely kind eyes.

Next to the surgeon stood the anesthesiologist, joking broadly, holding up a small rubber mask for the child to see. At one point he put the mask over his own face while several nurses, starched and immaculate, clapped and laughed. One of them, a gray-haired, rosy-cheeked eminence, held his hand and patted it energetically.

"I'm going to slip the mask over your face now, Charles," the anesthesiologist stooped slightly and spoke into his ear. "When I tell you to start counting . . ."

Sometime later that evening Watford awoke. Someone, a nurse, no doubt, had turned off the television. The only illumination in the room now came from the corridor outside. Awake and keenly alert, like some small feral creature aware suddenly of a nearby predator, he listened to the nighttime squeak of cork-soled shoes hastening down the corridor, the rattle of a trolley full of medications, a moan from an adjacent room. Then silence.

A short while later he was up and moving. He crossed the room to the lavatory. Once there he zipped open the small plastic toilet kit into which he'd packed toothbrush and shaving equipment. Within that kit was a shallow, zippered inner pocket designed to keep a mirror, or possibly a needle and thread. From out of that pocket, Watford withdrew a hypodermic syringe and laid it carefully on the side of the sink.

In the next moment, he sat on the toilet and forced himself to have a bowel movement. When he'd finished, he took the hypodermic, plunged it into the bowl beneath him and filled the syringe with a solution of water and fecal matter. Then, still seated on the toilet, he lay back, pulled the hospital smock up above his pale, drooping belly and plunged the needle deep into the skin of the abdominal wall. So deftly had it been done that he scarcely felt the needle pinch or the fluid being injected into his system. Even the puncture was barely discernible.

In the next hour he would rise again and take two one-ounce phials of ipecac he'd brought along with him in his bag. Then in another twenty minutes or so, he knew, the retching and vomiting would commence.

4

By 9:00 A.M. Mooney, along with a detachment of forensic specialists, was standing on the spot above the alleyway where John Ransom had the sad misfortune of strolling the night before. From where he stood, Mooney gazed straight down eight stories into a narrow alleyway, a simple gash between two buildings, at the bottom of which he could see a kidney-shaped silhouette scrawled in chalk by the crime unit on the littered pavement to designate the exact spot where the victim lay after he'd been struck.

Dozens of buildings had been crammed cheek by jowl into that tiny half block above which they now stood. They adjoined and backed up to each other forming a vertiginous grid of fire escapes, catwalks, parapets and ramps. Sooty windows and rooftops looked down onto the street. The backs of the theater buildings were like a maze and the fire escapes permitted one to climb from one building to the next. More perplexing even were the steel doors in the yards and alleyways that anyone would have assumed would have been locked but, nevertheless, were open because vandals had ravaged the hinges. Not only did the phantom Bombardier appear to know every doorway, ramp and rusted railing, but he was able to clamber round from roof to roof in the dark, carrying his concrete bombs.

Clattering down the fire escape just below the ledge, they threaded their way across a rickety catwalk and entered one of those many disconcerting steel doors, opening onto a dark, rank, trash-littered stairway. A cat squealed and scurried out as they proceeded to descend several flights through the thick, murky, dark reeking of urine.

At the bottom they entered another door and found themselves beneath the proscenium of a theater swathed in silence. An eerie half-light filtered downward from some point above. Looking about they saw steel ladders, walls lined with complex electrical cable and circuit boxes, heavy guy lines ascending upward through to the wings and serving, no doubt, to raise and lower the curtain. There was a dumbwaiter that went up through an open shaft to a trap door, Mooney judged, just below the orchestra pit and stage. They were at the very bottom of the theater.

Musty old period costumes had been stored there in toppling piles; parts of dismantled stage sets stood about like ghostly wreckage—a pair of wooden carousel swans drowsed in the shadows, an Edwardian gasolier, and a mural of pinkish mermaids from above a nautical bar. A dozen or so faceless mannequins made of muslin stood about on steel pipe-stands with a curious air of expectation—as if awaiting assignations in the thick, gray silence.

When they came up again they had a call to go over to a building on Fiftieth Street. Something had been found on a rooftop there.

The building backed up directly to the one on Forty-ninth Street, where the cinder block had been dropped. It was a seedy, five-story office building with an air about it of something faintly louche. Its residents were largely small-time theatrical managers and booking

26

agents, plus a handful of film and record companies of the most dubious accreditation.

The elevator, a narrow, cagelike box, swayed creakingly upward to the fifth floor and lurched to a halt. From there they got out and walked up the remaining three flights to the roof. It was nearly noon now and the sun was high. Mooney, sweating and panting behind three others, climbed up through a partially open steel door and out onto the littered tar rooftop.

Two patrolmen and a plainclothes detective were waiting there for them. They were standing about beneath one of those large, pyramidal, peaked water towers that were a benchmark of all New York commercial architecture during the twenties and thirties.

Mooney's breath whistled as he came up to them. "Whatcha got?"

One of the patrolmen stood aside and spoke. "We found this."

At first sight it looked like some kind of undifferentiated mess—a kid's joke. Oil cloths, canvas and an old shower curtain tacked to the tower pylons to keep out wind and rain. Inside, cardboard cartons and old magazines had been rigged up to serve as a mattress. There were cups and water bottles, knives and forks. An empty can of corn had been discarded there along with other rubbish.

"Any idea who it was?" Mooney asked.

"Nope," said the plainclothesman, whose name was Aiello. "Thought you should see it, anyway."

"Did you talk to the building superintendent?"

"He knows nothing about it," Aiello replied.

"You can get in and out of this rattrap through half a dozen different exits," the other patrolman offered. "Place is wide-open twenty-four hours a day."

"Looks like whoever it was ain't been around for a while." Aiello knelt down to inspect the curious debris. "The litter is old. Cutlery is rusty."

"Probably a squatter." Mooney gazed round distastefully. "Probably lit out when the weather got warm. Take some pictures and send the cup and silverware down for analysis."

While some others took notes and gathered articles for analysis, Mooney, unimpressed, strolled across the roof to the ledge and stared out west over Forty-ninth Street. It had the look of a playground jungle gym—all chaos and entanglement. Steel-girded superstructures surmounted by marquees and gray, unlit neon lights—giant letters that hung like gauzy tracery painted against the gunmetal city sky.

Down below thousands swarmed into office buildings, scurrying along from every direction. Mooney stared down at the scene impassively. He had a sudden image of himself hoisting forty pounds of cement above his head, holding it out above the ledge—then letting go. Just letting go. Looking down on all that avid, lurching bug life, he could understand that. He well knew the feeling of contempt. He could see why.

5

"... and at the post in starting position number five, Honor Bound. In six, Dynaflow. At seven, Alternative, ridden by Velasquez, out of Darbyshire. Eight, Dogdays. . . ."

Standing amid the excited press at the rail, Frank Mooney ran the stump of his pencil up and down the columns of the *Racing Form.* Periodically he'd glance up at the tote board to check odds against the PP's of horses he'd been following. As usual, he'd had no compunction whatever about using his shield to get himself down directly on the field with the press and the big spenders.

As racing days went this one was perfect—bright, clear skies, and though it was cool, in the mid-fifties, Mooney was already sweating profusely. The Sunday capacity crowds at Aqueduct had turned the stands behind him into a crazy quilt of undulating color. Gaudy pennants on the roof of the stands snapped briskly in the gusty breeze and the jockeys and horses in the post parade caparisoned in their flashing silks made the heart leap with excitement.

Mooney had been there since early morning. He'd come out around 10:00 A.M. to walk through the paddocks, talk to the grooms and watch the workouts. More than anything, he loved the morning prowls before the race—the big bays and chestnuts browsing in the spanking white paddocks, the grooms and trainers moving through the stables, the profoundly satisfying smell of sawdust, leather and manure.

Well into the fourth race now, Mooney had made no score. Moreover, he had dropped several hundred dollars and had also missed by a hair the quinella, paying $52.40. The winning horse he'd picked, Piston, performed precisely as he'd expected. His second choice, a filly, Ball Point, a 3-to-1 odds-on favorite to finish in the money, had been brilliant for ninety-five percent of the run, then limped across in fifth position, as if she simply could not bear being that good.

If Mooney was sweating in fifty-degree weather, he had good reason to. He'd already dropped three hundred dollars. The fifth race was a $3500 maiden claiming race, full of horses so bad and so cheap their trainers were not afraid to lose them. Scouring the past performance charts in the Form, Mooney's eye had fastened on a three-year-old gelding called Indicator. Superficially, his record was dismal. Always a bad sign, he'd been running route races on a regular basis, and his last six times out he'd not run any better than fifth while competing with the dogs of horsedom. His trainer, however, was E. Y. Caldecott, who'd had an estimable record with maiden horses, and Indicator's last two times out he had done something completely out of character. He had broken slowly and rallied strongly, passing six horses and making up nine lengths in the last quarter mile. This was over six furlongs and that appeared to be Indicator's optimum distance. He would expire going an inch farther.

Indicator's recent running lines indicated that Caldecott was transforming the gelding into a strong stretch runner, particularly at six furlongs. The fifth race happened to be posted at six furlongs and the fact that the horse was blinkered and wearing mud caulks spoke tellingly of the trainer's game plan.

Mooney knew this track to be plaster hard, particularly during April when the ground was not yet entirely thawed, therefore, heavily biased toward stretch runners and outside post positions.

The bandages on Indicator's forelegs, however, gave Mooney pause. Bandaged forelegs on a hard track had negative implications, such as injury. Also the fact that Indicator, looking like a solid $6500 animal, was now slumming in a $3500 claiming race served to heighten Mooney's uneasiness. With a dropdown of $3000 something had to be wrong with the horse, for neither trainer, nor any other businessman, gives away $6500 merchandise for $3500.

Still, the trainer and the running lines had just about swayed Mooney. And besides, the competiton appeared weak. Carrerito was a turf horse. Dark Encounter was a sprinter with no guts much beyond the halfway. Zero Hour's figure in his last 5½-length victory was atrocious. And now the tote board beside Indicator's name was blinking 23–1.

Mooney rummaged deep within his jacket pocket and shredded the losing voucher tickets residing there. Four defeats had finally deprived him of his early-morning exhilaration.

It was several minutes before post time. He glanced once again at the tote board, still flashing 23–1, a mystic beacon that seemed pointed directly at him. In the next moment he turned, walked directly to the $50 window and bet his last $200 to win.

The gates opened with a roar. Indicator broke quickly and was running second when the field reached the first turn. Then he started dropping back. And back. And back. By the time the pack thundered past where Mooney stood stonyfaced, chewing the corner of his lip, the horse was in ignominy, running ninth. As they pounded past, Mooney felt the blast of heat from their exertions. As Indicator crossed before him he tried to peer directly into the gelding's eye, and from there into its great throbbing heart, willing the creature to win.

After three-quarters of a mile, Indicator was fourteen lengths out. Mooney watched the great clots of powder flung from the gelding's hooves, splatter dismally onto the track. With resignation, he lowered his binoculars.

But even as Mooney conceded defeat, Indicator had begun to gain ground on the final turn, running so wide that his jockey had to lean left in the saddle to keep him from going to the outside fence. Coming into the stretch he was still an impossible nine lengths behind the leader, Saddle Sore. The gelding continued to gather momentum through the stretch and suddenly he was in fifth position, coming up hard on fourth. If Mooney heard the wild roar of mankind gone mad in the stands behind him, he showed no outward sign. Encapsulated in a cold, cryptlike silence, he watched deadpan the blur of gray motion on the far track. He would permit nothing to break the line of communication between his own fierce will and that of the horse.

With only a sixteenth of a mile to run and in third position, Indicator still did not appear to have much of a chance. In those final yards, however, Saddle Sore began to tire perceptibly, and suddenly the gelding had pounded up abreast of him. The finish was too close to call.

During the agonizing moments while the photo was being developed, Mooney chewed his lower lip and consoled himself that even if the horse lost, he had not been disgraced. His own judgment was vindicated, even if it had cost him his last two hundred dollars.

On the board above the track the number 6 flashed—Saddle Sore, the winner by a nose. But a second later a red sign that said OBJECTION went up. It was a steward's inquiry against the winner. Moments later, the track announcer reported that Indicator's jockey, Angel Guzman, had also claimed foul against the winner.

Mooney sat numb beside the tote board where the numbers six and three, Indicator's number, were flashing, while the stewards pondered their decision. A man beside him was holding a $2 ticket on

Saddle Sore. He looked grim. "Forget it," he said forlornly. "They'll bust him." And he was right. They did. Saddle Sore was disqualified for crowding Indicator on the first turn, forcing Guzman to check his horse sharply so he wouldn't collide with Saddle Sore. The result was now official and the tote board flashed 3. Indicator was the winner and paid $43.20 to win. Mooney had won slightly more than four thousand dollars.

6

He had found her in a bar on Forty-ninth Street, the Spanish girl who disrobed for him, then took off his clothing, washed him, sat on his lap and dangled her breasts in his face. Laughing, she darted her tongue in and out of his ear, and squeezed him. Mooney lay back, accepting these attentions with an odd, almost gloomy reserve.

She was no more than eighteen or nineteen. Sweet and quite affectionate. Sympathetic to his size, and quickly grasping his problem, she knew how to make it all easy for him. Setting atop his pelvis, graceful and pert like a sparrow primping in a birdbath, she aroused him with her hands and mouth.

The embarrassment she sensed he felt, gross and naked before her made her doubly solicitous. She called him "Poppy" and kissed him over and over again, as if she truly meant it. Determined to please him, she was still young enough in the trade not to have had the last ounce of human tenderness flayed out of her.

As last, when it came time to culminate his pleasure, she sat astride him, then proceeded to move up and down, rotating her hips as she went. Eyes closed, Mooney lay dazed and panting in the overheated room that reeked of perspiration and cheap incense.

Slowly the motion continued, gathering momentum, peaking finally for Mooney with a long rush of release. The girl, sighing and moaning, might have been merely simulating passion, making him feel as though he'd given her more pleasure than she'd ever known. He may have half-suspected this was the case. In any event, when he left there somewhere in the early part of Sunday evening, several thousand dollars bulging in his pockets, he was, for the moment at least, at peace.

Mooney had little in the way of religious feelings. Spiritual intimations were not his strong suit. Only in the presence of the evening sky did he feel some vague, troublesome notion of things stirring outside himself. Call it wonder. If it was, he did not perceive it as such. He did not consciously go out on evenings to encounter deities. All he knew was that on rare occasions when he found himself gazing upward at the starry vault of heaven, he experienced a sharp anger in the face of stubborn puzzles intimating things that, in more guarded moments, he brusquely discounted. And of course it is axiomatic that detectives loathe insoluble puzzles.

Still, wonder notwithstanding, he watched the stars, knew the evening sky and could read it like his own newspaper. On the rooftop, where he stood now, leaning on the brick parapet, he watched Virgo recumbent in the southeastern sky; Draco looped and coiled above his head with Boötes, the Plowman, just to the left, and Arcturus glowing like a beacon in its tail. Mooney patted the bulge of dollars swelling in the pocket above his breast, leaned far out over the edge, and peered down into the teeming nighttime life swarming below him.

It was nearly 11:00 P.M. Theaters were just beginning to let out, disgorging their audiences onto the street. Horns blared, Taxis streamed crosstown and up Eighth Avenue. The marquees were still lit, setting the sky above the theater district ablaze. Even at the seven-story elevation, Mooney could feel the bustle and heat of mortal nervous energy emanating from below. From where he stood, he reasoned another man had stood six nights ago, at the same time and in that precise spot. No doubt, that man had stood at the ledge, just as Mooney did now, and peered down into the swarming dizzy tide of life below.

What occupied the detective's attention was a shallow pit in the outside wall just below him, where a slab of concrete had either fallen of its own accord or was chiseled out of the brick facade. Mooney leaned way over, hanging head down from the waist, as if nailed inverted to the wall and probed the damaged area with his stubby fingers.

The forensic unit that had examined the spot two days before had determined that the slab had come dislodged of its own accord. Indeed, he could see no sign of any tool that may have been used to pry the section loose. Had a chisel been used, it would certianly have left a cleaner, more uniform, defacement than the big ragged scar that gaped there now. Also, his fingers probing the area had encountered a good deal of moisture within the open fissure—moisture from rotting, leaky gutters that had no doubt over the years undermined the laths and joists below.

Grunting, red-faced, Mooney hauled himself upright and stood panting in the shadows. Shortly, he stooped and scooped up several bits of stone and pebble off the tarred rooftop. Back at the ledge he stood rolling the pebbles in his palm with the icy intensity of a crapshooter.

Standing alone amid the transoms and chimney pots, antennas and sheets hung on laundry lines flapping ghostly in the light breeze, Mooney made an effort to re-create in his own mind the scene of the murder. Initially, the man he saw was young, Hispanic—although he couldn't say why, except that the hallway and staircase leading to the roof had been liberally scored with graffiti clearly of Spanish origin. PUMO 134, GAETANO 108, HONCHO 128, indicating that the roof was heavily trafficked; used for assignations. In his mind he suddenly saw two young Spanish males. They'd been drinking up there on the roof. From a vision of two, he was able to posit a third. Possibly a girl. Sixteen or seventeen years old. All of them potheads, soaked in grass. One of them had found the slab of cinder block, or inadvertently found the damaged area, and was able to pry it out of the mortar below. Mooney visualized one of the youths—hypothetically, he called him Pumo, because of the graffiti on the stairway wall—eighteen, full of junk; swaggering in black leather studded with cheap chrome points; possibly a tattoo or so—skulls, swastikas, whatever. The typical nickel-dime Halloween costume of gang cultures.

The boy is now hefting the slab of mortar, holding it out over the ledge, defying the others. The presence of the girl makes him cocky, more reckless. He swaggers for her benefit, but deep down he does not intend to drop the slab.

The other youth jeers and taunts him. The girl laughs. She senses that her presence there makes Pumo's position doubly difficult. She enjoys his dilemma.

"Hey, Pumo. Drop it man. Gawhead—Drop it. Drop it. *Cobarde maricón.*"

Mooney could hear the taunts as clearly as if they were occurring at that moment. "Drop it, man. Drop it. Gawhead." The voices reverberated across the ghostly vacancy of the roof.

Leaning far out over the ledge, trying to follow the progress of their downward descent, one by one, Mooney let the pebbles fall from his hand.

But there was something profoundly unsatisfying about this vision.

33

It was a set piece. It lacked authority or any ring of truth. For one thing, he found no sign that a gang of youths had been up there. Gangs, in Mooney's experience, tended to leave behind their spoor—beer cans, wine bottles, reefer stubs, condoms. He found no such signs there.

But why should he persist? The forensic unit had been thorough enough. They had pored over the area. They had not been able to find a single piece of evidence, or lift a single fingerprint from the area where the slab had broken off. And other than three or four similar incidents that had occurred over the past four years, and the somewhat dubious testimony of an eleven-year-old street rat, there was absolutely no compelling reason to believe that last week's crushed skull was anything more than an accident. No perceivable human cause.

It was 11:00 P.M. Spica glared in the tail of Virgo; Castor and Pollux, the twins, glittered out of Gemini. Both Venus and Mars were in Pisces. Love and contention within the fish. He had won money that day and known love of a sort. What more was there? Mooney patted the bulge of cash above his breast and turned to go.

7

"I don't believe a word of it."

"It's true. See for yourself."

"All I can see is that the boy is faking. He doesn't want to go to school."

"Be sensible, Cyril. How could the boy be faking? Look at the flush on his cheek."

"A hundred and two degrees. Very convenient. Sickness invariably occurs on the morning of school examinations."

"That's unfair. Can't you see he's sick? I wouldn't send a dog out in this weather, little less my own child. He'd be back in an hour with pneumonia."

"You're ruining the boy, Mary. Mark my words, you're bringing him up to be a welcher. Well, Charles, congratulations. You win again."

The door slammed and his father was gone, leaving in his wake the odor of leather and cologne. He loathed that odor and would always loathe it. It filled his bathroom. It was in his clothing and his drawers. Sometimes he could even smell it on his mother when she'd been with him.

Now he'd gone, yet the odor lingered. His mother's cool hand was on his brow. It rested there ever so lightly, with an air of quiet anticipation.

"Charley?"

He didn't answer.

"Charley? Are you sleeping, dear?"

She leaned over him, rested her head on the pillow near his and whispered into his ear. "It's all right, dear. Your father's gone now. He doesn't mean what he says. It's just that sometimes he'd like to see you up and ever so much more active. Football. Hockey. Boy Scouts. You know. Charley—Charley—do you hear me?"

He nodded and felt the dammed-up tears start to spring at the corners of his eyes and track down his cheeks.

"I'll call Mr. Mortimer at school." She fussed over him. "We'll arrange to have you make up your test when you're feeling better. But, you know, dear, your father is right. I know for a fact that you've been neglecting your Latin. Skipping your homework. How could you possibly be prepared for an examination this morning? Now come, we won't discuss this any further. It's just between you and me, but we both know that there must be an improvement. Is that understood? Very good. Well then, Doctor says you must have plenty of fluids and rest. Meanwhile, just roll down your pajama trousers and let me take your temperature."

After she'd gone he listened to her puttering out in the kitchen. Soon she'd be back with soft eggs and toast. Just the way he liked them. Quickly he switched the thermometer she'd stuck in him for the one he kept wrapped in an old sock beneath the hissing radiator beside his bed.

"Charley." She reappeared, smiling at the door. "Charley, darling. Here are your eggs and there's some nice hot . . ."

"Mr. Watford . . ." He felt himself gently prodded. "Wake up, Mr. Watford. Dr. Kramer is here."

Watford cracked an eye and looked up into the solemn, doleful features of the young internist.

35

"Good morning, Mr. Watford." The doctor perused his chart. "How are we doing this morning?"

Watford started up, winced conspicuously, then lay back in bed. "That head still bothering you, is it?"

"It's awful, Doctor. Like a sledgehammer. And my stomach . . ."

"Hurting you?"

"Something fierce. And the vomiting . . ."

"When did that start?"

The intern, standing above him, arms akimbo, watched him with an air of consternation. "We'd better have a look." As he drew the covers down from Watford's chest, Watford raised the gown above his hips while the nurse slowly encircled them in a floor-to-ceiling curtain hung on tracks.

"Ow."

"That hurts, does it?" The doctor probed Watford's pelvis with a finger. "Is the pain generalized or at a certain spot?"

"It's right here, Doctor," Watford groaned and guided the intern's hand to an area just above the navel.

"Ow," he squealed again and sat bolt upright, suggesting exquisite tenderness.

The physician pulled Watford's gown back down over his knees and drew the covers up over him. "There's a great deal of tenderness there. Your fever is still high and your leukocytic count is way up over two hundred thousand. Could be an abscess or possibly peritonitis. In any case, I think you ought to plan on being here a few more days till we can get to the bottom of this." The young man turned to the nurse. "Will you have them get Mr. Watford ready for radiology within the hour." The doctor turned back to Watford, smiling. "See you shortly."

As he started out, Watford called feebly to him. "Doctor. My head."

"Oh, yes. Of course. Demerol, wasn't it?" The doctor picked up the house phone beside Watford's bed and dialed the hospital dispensary. "Hello. Dr. Kramer here. Will you send up eighty milligrams meperidine, parenteral dosage. Room 815, please. Thank you."

Left suddenly to himself, enclosed in the hushed white sanctity of the privacy curtian, encased in the starched antiseptic dignity of hospital linen, Charles Watford, smiling to himself, quite peacefully awaited the hospital attendants who would shortly come to wheel him to the radiology room. Stretching beneath the blankets he experienced the most wonderfully comforting sense of languor and well-being. In this briskly efficient, deeply caring temple of healing, he felt as if nothing again could ever possibly harm him.

36

MAY / '80

8

The calliope wheezes sad little tunes into the torrid air. The lion roars and paces its cage. The gorilla with its gray-green human eyes sucks grapes and picks its nose. Monkeys jabber and vault about on trapeze bars. A row of elephants tethered at stakes fork bales of straw into their mouths with swaying trunks.

The menagerie was particularly good that day. Festive Sunday crowds jammed into the big hall of the Pittsburgh Sports Arena. Squealing, laughing children wolfed frankfurters and cotton candy in a warm haze of sawdust and fresh manure.

Watford sauntered through the holiday crowds, a look of dreamy abstraction on his boyish face. The little girl beside him clasped his hand and edged closer to his leg. She winced as the shriek of a cockatoo rent the air.

"Shouldn't we go in and sit down now?" she asked. She held in her hand an untouched paper cone of pinkish cotton candy.

"Not yet. The show doesn't start for another twenty minutes. And, besides, we haven't seen the freaks yet."

They entered a large room adjoining the menagerie. It had high ceilings and long galleries down which people slowly ambled. By contast to the menagerie, this room was quiet. People moved through a wide aisle and tended either to stand silent or to whisper before the exhibits.

Watford had always loved the freak show. For him it had some special draw, an opportunity to relish a slight dread along with a sense of awe he could not quite articulate. About it all was an air of reverence. He walked like one in a church. There was the curious divinity of freaks. He could see the face of Christ in all the tired de-

formities. The infinite sadness of the fat man's eyes. The armless, leg-
less lady, an unappendaged torso propped up on a crate draped with
black imitation velvet, a marble bust of immobile torment. The tat-
tooed man, stigmata stenciled over every inch of his pelt. And the
self-immolation of the fire-eater staging hourly the bogus miracle of
an auto-da-fé.

They paused for a while amid a sweating, jostling crowd to watch
the human torso do tricks. She lit cigarettes and signed autographs by
means of a pencil tucked beneath her chin. Illuminated by a single
klieg light, her frizzy, carrot-colored hair, her thickly rouged and
lipsticked face transformed itself into a ghastly maquillage.

"How does she go to the bathroom?" someone whispered behind
them and there was giggling.

Wide-eyed and visibly uneasy, not certain whether to laugh or
close her eyes, the small child pressed closer to Watford when the
red gash of the torso's mouth cracked into a smile and greeted her in
a shrill harpy voice.

"Can't we go now?" six-year-old Millicent Rhodes whispered, her
eyes still fixed on the grinning torso nodding at her.

"We've got time. We still haven't seen everything. Don't you want
to see the fire-eater?"

At last she succeeded in steering him away from the freaks to out
under the big top where the overture and promenade were just
starting up.

Tubas, drums, xylophones, glockenspiels, the trombones and the
clash of cymbals swelled the tent. Colored floodlights swerved dizzy-
ingly round the triple arenas.

Up above the silver-threaded guylines and high wires, trapeze
bars awaited the aerialists and tightrope cyclists. Clowns and midg-
ets tumbled on the cinder footpath circling the main arenas. Behind
them came a man on stilts, followed by the elephants, a dancing
bear, and a brace of prancing Lippizaners with bright red feathers in
their ears.

And always the clowns, sad and ludicrous, and the hobos with their
baggy pants collapsing round their big, floppy shoes, cakewalking
through the promenade.

Watford observed the small child beside him, twirling the little
pencil flashlight he'd bought her outside at one of the concession-
aires. As he watched the floodlight reflected in her glowing eyes, he
was suffused with such a sense of tenderness that he had to choke
back tears.

They watched the aerialist scramble up the ladder and into the
labyrinth of silver wires strung like cobwebs at the peak of the tent.
The child watched intently a young girl, no more than seventeen or

eighteen, with the face of a quattrocento Madonna, effortlessly ascend a rope, then step outward onto a tiny platform one hundred and fifty feet above the roaring, taunting crowds. Fearless, imperturbable, she spread her arms out sidewards as though they were wings. There was a gasp as she stepped outward into space.

"You've got some hell of a nerve, Charley. Edgar's furious. Fit to be tied."

"It's only nine-thirty."

"Nine-thirty? You've been gone the whole day, for God's sake. Where the hell have you been?"

"I told you I was going to take her to the circus, didn't I?"

"The circus? Are you mad?"

"Didn't I tell you? I told you—I know I told you."

"About three weeks ago you mentioned something about taking her. But, of course, you neglected to tell us what day, or when. We wake up this morning. You're gone. She's gone. How the hell are we supposed to put all that together? We called the police."

"The police?"

"We thought she was kidnapped. We thought she ran away. God knows what we thought."

"Well, for Chrissake, if that isn't the dumbest—now don't—for God's sake, go and start bawling."

Watford made a motion toward his younger sister—a raised hand, a gesture half warning, half placatory—"Now don't, Renee—Please. There's no need for that. I can't stand when you do that."

Almost imperceptibly, his hand prodding gently at the small of her back, he nudged the child forward to plead his cause.

"Don't cry, Mommy. I'm fine. Uncle Charley and I had so much fun."

"Never mind the fun, young lady. Your father is nearly out of his mind with worry. He's been calling from the office all day."

Her taut, tired body was suddenly shaken with sobs. "You go wash up, Millicent. Get ready for bed. I've got to call your father."

Together, they watched the little girl walk out.

"Jesus, Charley. God damn you, anyway."

Watford flung his hand up in despair. "Well, what the hell did I do that was so gosh damned awful anyway? Will you kindly tell me that?"

"Charley Watford— you are a thoughtless, stupid—"

"I take a kid to the gosh damned circus—big deal—"

"It's not that you took her. It's how you took her. You stole her. You sneaked out of here at six A.M. like a thief, while everyone was still asleep. Not so much as a call all day, or a by-your-leave, to let us

41

know where you are. What are we supposed to think? It never crosses your stupid mind that we'd be worried sick. . . ."

"It was supposed to be a surprise," Watford whined pathetically. "Not only for her but for you, too. I thought I was doing you a big favor, taking her off your hands for the day. Giving you a vacation. I thought you and Edgar would be delighted. I thought you'd find it funny. A big joke. Ha, ha."

"Oh, God," she blanched and covered her mouth with her hands. "I still haven't called Edgar."

She bolted from the room, and in the next moment, he could hear the hasty, clicking sound of the dial, and her low, husky voice speaking rapidly into the phone. When she came back she looked ashen. "Look, Charley—"

"Renee—Don't . . ."

"Please don't interrupt me, Charley. Just let me get this off my chest. Edgar's about ready to wring your neck. He's furious. He has been for months. How long has it been now? Eight months? Nine months?"

"Sissy, look. Just . . ."

"No Sissy stuff, Charley. Not now. Please." She backed away as he slowly approached her, that look of puzzlement and hurt on his face. "I didn't mind taking you in after the hospital. You were recuperating. You were still weak. Also, I didn't want to see you go back to the house all by yourself."

"Listen, Renee. I wasn't going to say anything until it was certain. I think I've got a job lined up. . . ."

She paused, hooked in midsentence, her head cocked to one side. "How long?"

"A couple of days. A week at the most." He watched her closely, dangling more bait before her wary eyes. "It's a traveling job. Sales. Hardware. Machinery. That sort of thing. This guy, the manager . . . he's just got to clear it with home office." Sensing her growing skepticism, Watford's speech quickened and grew slightly frantic.

She wavered a moment, indecisively, torn between loyalty to both brother and husband. At last she shook her head back and forth, first slowly, then with gathering momentum. "No. No—Charley. Not this time. We've been down this road before. The last time . . ."

"I couldn't help that, Sissy."

"No Sissy stuff, I told you."

"Irene— You know yourself I couldn't help that. The guy promised me. It just fell through. I can't help that."

"I can't help it either, Charley. Not anymore. You've got to go now. It's not only your welfare that's at question. It's now a question of my family, my marriage, my life. Edgar simply won't stand for another day of this. We're all stretched to the . . ."

"Well, for gosh sakes," Watford laughed bitterly. "I take my niece to the circus, and for that I get tossed out into the cold."

"It's not cold, Charley. It's May. Spring. The lilacs are blooming outside in the yard." Her voice suddenly went soft and she spoke very slowly as though she were cajoling a child. "You can stay here tonight, but that's it. Tomorrow, out. Go home. Go back to the house. It ought to be lovely up that way now."

His fingers fumbled with a jacket button and he started to speak. But before he could she waved him to silence. "Don't, for God's sake, say another word, Charley. Don't try to play on my feelings 'cause I'm just about ready to bust." Her eyes were red and glistening."

"But I don't have . . ."

"Don't worry about that," her hands fluttered at him again. "I've got a few hundred stashed away. You can have it all. But you've got to go."

She watched him slump down into a chair. "Don't think I enjoy kicking my only brother out. I'm sorry, sweetie. I'm sorry for everything. I'm sorry about Mom and Dad. I'm sorry about you. You've had nothing but rotten luck. Don't think I haven't noticed. But I can't help it. I'm trying to make some kind of life for myself out here, and I'm afraid it just doesn't . . . can't possibly include you."

She blew her nose into her apron, then cocked an ear at a sound coming from the direction of her daughter's bedroom. "Coming, honey. Mommy'll be right up to tuck you in."

Her scrubbed, girlish features appeared suddenly hard and pinched. "Tonight, Charley. That's it. Tomorrow, out. And for God's sake, stay out of Edgar's way."

She started out, then turned abruptly. "Charley. Edgar knows all about those pills you take. What the hell are they for anyway?

"For my headaches. They're pain-killers."

"I realize that. But why so many? Every day, like that? And what in God's name are you doing with that doctor's bag with all those instruments?"

"Things." He looked away evasively. "It's for my medications. Would you prefer I live with this hammer banging around in my skull all day?"

"No. Of course not." She was suddenly contrite. "If you need it, you need it. It's only that Edgar . . ."

"Disapproves."

"Of course he disapproves of things like that. Wouldn't you?"

"Things like what?"

"Like that. You know. Pills. Drugs. Things like that. Edgar doesn't like that."

9

E. K. SHAVERS, UROLOGY, M.D., P.C., F.A.C.S., DIPLOMATE AMERICAN
BOARD OF UROLOGY, the directory in front of the building read. Along
with it were listed the names of a dozen other physicians all with interminable rows of letters following their names.

Above the directory on a thin plaque of marble and indited in im-
posing typography was a sign reading GRAMERCY MEDICAL ARTS
BUILDING. Watford had found the place in the Yellow Pages. Though
it was seven o'clock of a Saturday evening and at that hour no self-
respecting physician could expect to be found there, he had still
made a point of coming personally to the address. He wanted to be
certain that it was a medical group he had not had recourse to in the
past. And he'd had recourse to many.

One block from the Medical Arts Building he found precisely what
he needed—a large, late-night pharmacy. The Gramercy Drug
Mart's proximity to the Medical Arts Building virtually assured him
that the group there wrote many prescriptions and consequently enjoyed special privileges with the pharmacy.

The place was crowded. People at the soda fountain were drinking
coffee and malteds; shoppers moved up and down the crowded aisles
purchasing cosmetics and toiletries. In a corner of the store, not far
from where the pharmacists worked behind a large glass counter,
Watford found a public phone booth and quickly let himself in.

Closing the accordion glass doors behind him, he thumbed deftly
through a badly frayed Manhattan directory and found the telephone
number of the Gramercy Drug Mart. He dialed the number and
asked to be connected to the pharmacy. With a small shiver of delight he watched the young pharmacist, no more than thirty feet
from where he stood, reach for the phone.

44

"Hello—This is Dr. Shavers—"

"Good evening, Doctor."

"I'm calling from out of town. On a fishing trip. I'm sending over a patient of mine. Mr. Charles Watford. I'm admitting him to N.Y.U. Medical Center tonight with a renal colic. He'll be needing something for the pain until we can do urine strains and a blood workup. I think about seven hundred milligrams of meperidine ought to do him till I get back."

"Tablets, or the liquid, Doctor?"

"Liquid, I should think. Much faster. Get him through the night more comfortably. Dr. Rashower will be at the hospital tomorrow to do tests. He'll send over the prescription for you first thing in the morning."

"Very good, Doctor. What was the name again?"

"Watford. Charles Watford. He ought to be along any minute. He's not far from you. Started out, I believe, about twenty minutes ago."

"I'll see to it that he gets it. Good fishing, Doctor."

Watford hung up the phone, watching the pharmacist as he did so. He lingered an additional three minutes in the booth, then checked the directory again, this time for the telephone number of the admitting office at New York University Medical Center.

"Hello," he barked into the phone a moment later. "Dr. Shavers here. I'm calling from out of town. A patient of mine, Charles Watford, will be admitting himself in the next half hour. He has recurrent renal colic, and I suspect he may require catheterization. I'd like him admitted as an outpatient and put right to bed. My associate, Dr. Rashower, will be up first thing in the morning to do the blood work. The patient will be bringing in urine samples. Poor chap's in a great deal of pain so he'll require analgesics over the next forty-eight hours. Until I get back, I'd like him started on meperidine—seven hundred milligrams, liquid, limit his fluids and sodium; no coffee, tea or other stimulants. I'd like an IVN too, and we ought to set him up with radiology for a series of KVR scans. He's quite important. Diplomatic. State Department. That sort of thing. Please see to it that every step is taken to make him as comfortable as—"

"What did you say your name was, Doctor?" a nurse inquired politely on the other side.

"Shavers," Watford snapped at once, but his heart skipped a beat. "Dr. E. K. Shavers."

He realized suddenly that if she asked him what the *E* stood for, he couldn't say. But she never did.

"I'm sorry. We have no Dr. Shavers affiliated here. Could you please—"

"Sorry," Watford murmured—

45

"Wait. Don't hang up," he heard the voice say, but by that time he had judiciously clicked off.

In the next moment, he was scanning the directory for Beth Israel, another hospital he knew to be in the vicinity, and a likely candidate for affiliation with Dr. E. K. Shavers, Urology, M.D., P.C., F.A.C.S. In no time, he was on the phone with the admitting office of Beth Israel, recounting almost word for word the same scenario he had used a few moments before with N.Y.U. Medical Center. This time it worked like a charm.

He stepped out of the phone booth and wended his way slowly toward the counter. The pharmacist standing there was adding a column of figures. He looked up as Watford reached the counter.

"Hello—I'm Charles Watford."

"Ah, yes. Mr. Watford. Dr. Shavers called in your prescription a few minutes ago. It's waiting right here for you."

10

"Come up."

"It's too high."

"It's not high. You're being ridiculous. Come up here, I said."

"I'm going down."

"Don't be a fool."

"I'm dizzy. I'm—"

"Don't you dare go down."

In the empty steeple, the voices had a terrifying metallic resonance. A sharp brutal jolt from above. The boy looked up at the stern, gray presence on the stair—an august figure in his late sixties with a mane of flowing white hair and an eye that gave his gaze a beady, slightly walleyed cast.

46

"Come up, I tell you," the man fumed through clenched teeth, struggling to yank the boy bodily up the spiral stair that corkscrewed its way up through the center of the steeple. Against that force, the boy sank to his knees and pulled down hard against the upward drag.

"You're coming up, I said."

"No, I'm not," the boy bawled. He had a sinking sense of all defiance oozing out of him. They hung there that way in midair, as it were, locked to each other by the grasp of hands, unable to resolve their struggle one way or another. Gasping and grunting, the man hauled and tugged the boy inchingly upward. His terrified gaze caught sight of the upward reaches of the steeple, beyond the shoulder of the man, the high dark place where he was being dragged. There were beams, rafters and thick hanging ropes surrounding a labyrinth of immense mechanisms where the clock and the great chimes were housed. It was very high up there, and blindingly bright. Mote-filled sunbeams poured through the clerestory windows encircling the steeple.

The boy had already reached a height above the ground that had paralyzed his ability to look either up or down. Instead, he clamped his eyes shut and struggled against the powerful, ironlike tug of the hand.

"Up. Up."

"No. Please. I can't. I can't."

"You will."

"I can't."

"You will, damn you."

The boy felt his shoulder being torn from its socket. He struggled to dig his fingers and heels into the hard, unyielding oak of the stair. But, inch by inch, he could see himself losing ground, drawn irresistibly into the heights of the tower. There were no more words between the two adversaries. Only the panting and grunting of a grim struggle. Then the boy heard the loud ratcheting click-clack of the tower clock flywheel rotating slowly round above them.

Suddenly the hot dusty air in the steeple appeared to shudder, to break outward like some huge cloth rending. A pigeon fluttered wildly upward and something enormous exploded inside the boy's head as the chimes of noon began to bong.

"Wake up. Wake up, Mr. Watford."

Watford sat bolt upright in bed shaking his head. "My gosh. What happened?"

"I don't know. You must've been dreaming." The stout lady in the starched white uniform pushed him gently back down onto his pillows. "Just a dream, Mr. Watford. Nothing more."

"S'funny. I can't recall a blessed thing about it." Watford started to sit back up, then clutched his head.

"Still that headache?" the nurse asked, speaking in her warm Gaelic lilt.

"I wish you could let me have a bit more medication."

"I really can't, Mr. Watford. Not until either Dr. Shavers or Dr. Rashower sees you."

"But Dr. Shavers left instructions about my medication."

"Yes, he did. But we really can't give you any more Demerol without your physician first seeing you and approving it. Now if you're good, perhaps I can let you have some Empirin with a wee bit of codeine."

Watford groaned and held his head.

"Hush." The nurse pressed a finger to his lips and gestured with her head to the bed beside him. It was the first time he'd noticed someone else was there.

Momentarily distracted from his own discomfort, Watford peered hard at the pale shape slumbering there beneath white sheets. In profile he could discern sharply defined features, surmounted by a wreath of white hair. Except for an occasional flutter of eyelids, the expression on the pallid, waxen face was one of peaceful repose. Staring at the new patient, Watford felt a pang of resentment.

"Who's he?"

The nurse shrugged. "Name's Boyd, I think. He came in last night. Some kind of accident. Hurt his leg. They put twenty stitches in his thigh. Quite a mess, I hear. Ought to be coming out of the anesthesia any time now. Be nice company for you, I should think." She handed Watford an empty jar. "We'll be needing a specimen from you. No rush. I'll be back in fifteen minutes."

"Won't you please just see if you can't find me a bit more medication?"

"Absolutely not." The nurse beamed benevolently. "Not another drop until Dr. Rashower sees you. Now be sure to give your supper order to the nurse, like a good fellow."

She departed on a wave of rattling trays and the odor of starch and antiseptics. Watford turned and stared disapprovingly at the sallow, waxen mask lying on the pillow across the way. Several rubber tubes had been inserted in the man's nostrils and coiled upward like ivy tendrils into large hanging glassine bags of fluid nutriment.

Watford stared at the man, following with his eye the rhythm of his respiration. His sleep appeared to be deep. In the next moment Watford picked up the phone by his bedside and asked to be connected with the hospital dispensary.

"Dispensary," he snapped smartly into the phone. "This is Dr. Rashower in 418. Would you please send up a seven-hundred-milligram packet of meperidine? Patient's name is Charles Watford. If you don't have the liquid, the tablets will do fine. Soon as possible, please. He's experiencing a great deal of discomfort."

Watford hung up the phone and glanced across once more at his neighbor. The gentleman's head moved on the pillow, rolling slowly from side to side, dry lips sucking air, mumbling sounds; he appeared to be regaining consciousness.

Watford leaned over the better to hear the mumbling. "It's all right. You're going to be all right now."

Again the man mumbled.

"What? What's that?"

More indecipherable garble.

"I'm sorry. You'll have to speak more clearly. I can't—" Just then his eye caught sight of the jar the nurse had left behind. In the next moment he rose, took the jar, plus a breakfast fork left behind on his night table and went directly to the lavatory in the corner of the room and closed the door. Once there he urinated freely into the jar, set it down on the sink top, then taking the fork up, unhesitatingly punched one of the prongs into his thumb. Instantly a bubble of red swelled outward from the wound, followed by a steady flow of blood.

Watford permitted a number of droplets to drip into the urine sample, then swirled it about until it had achieved an even mixture. Next he ran cold water over the bleeding thumb until the wound had been sufficiently stanched. Finding a bit of gauze and adhesive in the medicine cabinet above the sink, he bound the wound, took his "doctored" sample and returned to bed.

By that time the orderly had just appeared at the door. "Watford?" he inquired.

"I'm Watford. You have my medication?"

The young man held up a small envelope with a half-dozen tablets. "Got it right here. Where's the attending physician?"

"Who?"

"The attending physician, Dr. Rashower. He called in for these."

"Oh, Rashower. He left about five minutes ago. Some kind of an emergency."

"He's gotta sign out for the pills, otherwise I can't release them."

Watford groaned and clutched his head. "You mean to tell me I can't have my medication? I'm in excruciating pain."

The orderly looked perplexed. "Sorry, that's regulation. We gotta have the AP's signature for all prescription drugs."

"You mean to say that just because the doctor happens to have forgotten that petty detail, you're going to deny me relief from pain? Rashower is going to hear about this. Believe me, heads will roll."

49

"I'm sorry. It's regulations. I can't. I just can't."

Watford groaned again. This time more volubly and with a deeper note of pathos.

"Okay, okay," the young orderly, none too fast on his feet, capitulated. "But you'd better tell your doctor to get that prescription down to the dispensary first thing in the morning."

Deep within his Demerol dreams, Watford dozed cozily before the TV. It had been on for hours but he was scarcely aware of anything he'd seen. The orderly had left him six pills, one to be taken every six hours and only in the event of extreme pain. Actually, he'd had no pain, but he'd had four Demerol anyway. That was the way with Demerol. He craved it always, particularly during times of stress. Besides, the proximity of pills, the fact that they were close at hand, invariably led to increased dosages.

Stuporous, he lay numb and far removed within a cool, totally silent chamber where the constant bickering of daily life could not impinge. While deadening his sense of unspecified dread, the Demerol had also the effect of enlarging his sense of perception. The scale of everything he looked at appeared greatly magnified. At the same time his response reaction to external stimuli was notably slowed.

He was distantly aware of nurses coming and going, the sound of spongy soles squeaking on waxed vinyl tile, and then the small sporadic movements of a barely conscious man in the bed beside him. In Watford's drugged state of heightened suggestibility, he noted that the aggravated breathing rhythms of his neighbor had imposed themselves on those of his own.

The technicolor figures of the eleven o'clock news drifted large and unanchored before Watford's unfocused eyes. Scenes of cataclysm swept across the screen—famine, earthquake, conflagration, a tidy, little tribal war comfortably distant in the African sub-Sahara, all liberally sprinkled, of course, with the daily catalog of carnage on the city streets—murders, assaults, defenestrations. He listened, scarcely hearing as the announcer described the puzzling death of a midtown pawnbroker from an object that had either fallen or been thrown from a rooftop somewhere in the Hell's Kitchen district the evening before.

Watford's head rolled drowsily on his chest and he fell asleep just as the police on the TV screen were scouring over a rooftop looking for evidence of foul play. Down below, the news cameras panned to a morgue van where several attendants were bundling a canvas-covered package onto a stretcher into the rear of the van.

A jowly, unshaven detective at the location was answering questions fired at him from a brash young female reporter.

Yes, he suspected foul play. Yes, there was some evidence that someone had been on the roof a short time before. Yes, someone, possibly injured, had been observed fleeing from the scene a short time later. And yes, this was indeed similar in pattern to five other such incidents over the past half-dozen years. Details were unclear. Witnesses were being sought. But, as of this moment, no one had yet come forth who might be able to supply descriptions of the fleeing figure. They were looking particularly for a man into whom the fleeing individual was said to have bumped. A telephone number, a hot line, was then flashed on the screen for the aid of those who had been in the vicinity at the time and might have seen something of significance.

A short time later, the plump, rosy nurse came in to check Watford. Finding him fast asleep, she tucked the blankets almost maternally about him. Sleeping, she noted, he seemed boyish and defenseless. There was something sad about him, she thought, then turned off the TV and moved across to the white-haired gentleman stirring intermittently in and out of anesthesia.

He murmured something and she knelt down the better to hear. "It's all right. All right, m'dear. I'm here now. You're doing fine. Just fine." The lovely Gaelic lilt of her voice made it sound like a lullaby.

She adjusted the flow of liquid nourishment gurgling down the long yellowish tubes leading from the suspended glassine bags into his nose. He was a proper gentleman, she noted. His white hair spread out like a halo on the pillow gave him the look of some transfigured saint.

The man's eyes fluttered open and he mumbled something. She tucked him under the chin playfully. "There now, How are we? You're looking better already. You did quite a job on yourself. The doctor had to put twenty stitches into your leg. But you're going to be just fine now. What's that, m'dear? What did you say?"

The man's parched lips moved feebly, struggling to shape sounds. "What's that, dear? I can't . . ."

Something deep within the man, far down, sounding like a croak or a hoarse dry rattle, issued from his throat.

"What's that, my dear?" she asked. "I'm sorry. I can't hear you."

11

"This guy, San Cristobal. Says he saw a man, directly after the drop, running east on Forty-ninth between Eighth and Ninth. Time approximately ten fifty-five."

"East? That puts him running toward the scene of the crime. Brilliant, Defasio. You show great promise. Next, we got here Weingarten, Sarah. Lives in the building next door. Returning home last night, approximately eleven-ten. Claims to have seen a suspicious-looking black guy lurking in the alleyway between two buildings."

"Just lurking? Not running?"

"Lurking is the word she used. Says so right here on the transcript of the call."

"Lots of black guys lurking around Forty-ninth Street that time of night."

"Right again, Defasio. And, besides, Weingarten has called in fourteen times before and always with some suspicious-looking black guy lurking. She's got lurking black guys up her ass. Next?"

In a back office just to the rear of the squad room of Manhattan South Precinct, Frank Mooney shuffled through a file of white index cards. In all, he had nearly a hundred such cards, each one representing a telephone response to the hot line number that had been flashed on TV screens the night before. He sat at a desk littered with police mug shots, paper cups, and half-eaten crullers on greasy wax paper.

Opposite him sat a dark, intense-looking young man with a smooth boyish face that would seem more fitting on a square somewhere in Tuscany than in a precinct squad room off Times Square. Except for a carefully coiffed wave of black hair at the nape of his neck, he was completely bald and his manner suggested that of a man nursing some chronic grievance. His name was Michael Defasio and he was Mooney's young partner.

". . . we got here now one Boorzoonian, Amadeo. Rug merchant, 316 West Forty-ninth. Says he was out walking his dog round eleven P.M. and a gang of Puerto Rican kids comin' up Eighth Avenue tried to swipe the dog."

"So?" Mooney fumed. "Are we investigatin' dognapping or skull bashing? What makes him think they had anything to do with a forty-pound cinder block dropping off a rooftop on Forty-ninth Street?"

"They were comin' from that direction, weren't they?"

"So were a million other people. Forget about Bosoomium. Next."

"Callahan, Mary . . ."

The stupefying drudgery of sifting through mostly moronic eye-witness telephone depositions droned on into the late night. Just past midnight the energies of the younger man began to flag noticeably. Not so Mooney, however, eyes closed and seated Buddhalike, coiled in curlicues of cigarette smoke, tirelessly absorbing information.

By 12:30 A.M. they had reduced all one hundred file cards into two distinct packs. The first, by far the larger, contained all of those depositions already dismissed as wildly improbable; the second, consisting of four or five cards, contained bits and shreds of information Mooney was eager to pursue.

One of the cards described having seen a man loitering in the vicinity of the building from which the lethal block had fallen. The witness claimed that she had never seen this man in the neighborhood before, but finally took notice after observing him in the same spot on four consecutive days, apparently watching the building. On her deposition she described the man as white, middle-aged, average height, basically nondescript. No special distinguishing characteristics. She could not be any more specific.

The next two cards described a youth, possibly eighteen, white, 180 pounds, six feet. He was fleeing the area at the time of the incident. While the physical descriptions on the two cards were nearly identical, one witness had the youth fleeing west on Forty-ninth Street, while the other had him fleeing east. However, since the physical descriptions of the fleeing youth tended to corroborate each other, as did the time at which he was observed fleeing, Mooney felt that the two cards were worth the time and effort of a follow-up.

A fourth card, and one of the most promising, was a deposition from a young Italian man, a construction worker, also resident of the building from which the block had fallen. He claimed to have had an assignation with a young woman on the site of the fatal drop. Occasionally, he said, they would meet on the roof, share a bottle of wine and make love.

That night he reached the roof earlier than his lady friend. While he waited for her there in a tangle of transoms, antennas and chimney pots, he thought he'd have a cigarette. As he struck his match he became aware out of the corner of his eye that he was not alone. About a hundred feet away at the ledge he spied a man, or what he assumed to be a man. It was a dark night, moonless, overcast, and what he saw in the distance was merely a shape, a silhouette.

At the moment in which his match burst into flame, casting its maximum illumination, the two men on the roof became acutely aware of each other. The man at the ledge started at once for the stairway door. But instead of continuing in that direction, he appeared to change his mind and veered sharply right, across the roof, then climbed over the side, down the fire escape.

For a moment the young construction worker stood frozen to the spot. A strapping big fellow, he admitted to a spasm of terror.

At last he summoned the courage to go over to the spot where the figure had disappeared. In that dim illumination he could see nothing but the spidery tangle of grillwork from the fire escapes nearest the upper stories. Below, however, he could hear the clatter of footsteps rattling down the iron rungs of the escape ladders. There was a moment of silence, followed shortly by a sharp grating thud, as of heels impacting on the cement of the alleyway below. A short groan ensued, followed by footsteps running, then silence.

In the next moment, the girl arrived. He told her what had happened. Instead of remaining on the roof, they concluded that it might be prudent to go downstairs. That's when they discovered from neighbors in the halls that a man lay dead on the sidewalk in front of the building, a forty-pound cinder block having cleft his skull.

The last card in Mooney's file was that of a retired postal worker, a widower, and resident of the same building, who'd been watching Johnny Carson and claimed to have glanced up just in time to see a fleeting shape on his fire escape. He happened to have the apartment on the first floor, and his fire escape, about twelve feet off the ground, fronted on the alleyway.

As he stood up to confront the intruder, the figure simply vanished over the side, making the drop between the last rung of the ladder and the alleyway below.

The old gentleman heard a groan, no doubt the same groan heard by the Italian construction worker, followed by the same running footsteps. He threw open his window and went out onto the fire escape to see what he could see. Whoever, or whatever had been there was clearly gone, but just below him, directly beneath the fire-escape ladder and in the light cast from his own windows, he could see a bright splash of red.

"Any word from the ME on those blood samples?" Mooney glanced up from the cards into the tired, petulant features before him. "Hey, Defasio," he snapped his fingers. "Do I bore you? Wake up."

"They're typing them now. We oughta have 'em first thing in the morning."

"And that patch of stuff they found on the ladder?"

"It's a piece of raincoat fabric. Probably from a pocket. They got it out now with a fiber expert. That's gonna be a lot of nothing."

"Oh?" Mooney snapped rubber bands round his packet of cards. "Get it for me."

"Sure—First thing in the morning."

"Right now."

"Come on, Mooney. Don't break my chops."

"I said, go get it for me."

"How special can raincoat fiber be? They'll tell you it's Egyptian cotton and rayon. So, big deal. What the hell's it gonna get you?"

"Get it for me now."

Defasio's expression appeared strained. "It's nearly eight o'clock. There's no one down there this hour. Gimme a break, for God's sake, will ya?"

"Now," Mooney snarled. "I don't go to bed. You don't go to bed."

Sergeant Defasio ground his teeth. There was a strong undercurrent of dislike between the two men. From a career point of view, to have been partnered with Mooney was tantamount to a demotion and the younger man knew it. "I told you, it's with an expert. Probably in some laboratory. I'll get it for you first thing in the morning. Lemme go, will ya, Mooney? I ain't seen my kids in three days. My wife's ready to run off with the circus."

"You'd both be better off. All right, go home. Get out of my face. Just be down here nine A.M. tomorrow. You hear me, nine A.M. Wear soft shoes. We got a lot of walkin' to do. Get me that swatch first thing. Then we're goin' over and see us some people at 310 West Forty-ninth."

Defasio rose and grabbed his jacket. "Aren't you goin'?"

Mooney was still shuffling through the cards, a distant, abstract look in his eye, shuffling as if he were a magician, conjuring the numbers.

"Hey, Mooney? Ain't you goin' home at all?"

"What the hell for?" Mooney's eyes swarmed upward. "It's almost time to come back. I'll hang around awhile."

The big, rumpled, slightly disreputable-looking detective pulled a stack of *Racing Forms* out of his desk top. "I'll catch up on some reading. Hey, since you're goin' home early, Defasio, whyn't you pick me up a few burgers and couple of Cokes before you leave?"

12

"You're a lucky man, I'll say that. A very lucky man."

Watford stretched luxuriously in bed, a tray of soiled breakfast dishes balanced on his covered knees. It was 9:00 A.M. and the soft May sunlight slanted through the rain-mottled plate windows of the room. Outside, the tips of spruce and newly bloomed dogwood spiked upward from the hospital courtyard just below.

Amiable and chatty, Watford rattled on at the gray, motionless figure supine in the bed beside him. "I'd judge you have an airtight case against the city. Imagine just going off like that and leaving a manhole uncovered. It's inexcusable. The height of irresponsibility. There were witnesses, I take it?"

Watford gazed across at his roommate who lay, eyes open, staring blankly at the ceiling. "There were witnesses to the accident, weren't there?"

"Yes, witnesses," the man replied in a manner that could have suggested affirmation or indifference. His eyes appeared to be transfixed on some indeterminate point across the room.

"You took their names, of course?" Watford persisted.

"Whose names?"

"The witnesses. The people on the site. You did get their names?"

The man shook his head dazedly.

A look of puzzlement crossed Watford's face and he shrugged.

"Well, I'm sure glad you made it here on time. The nurse told me they had you on the table for three and a half hours, sewing up your leg. Too bad about the witnesses though. You could've taken the city for a bundle. Say, aren't you going to eat your breakfast? With all that blood you lost, you need to get your strength back."

The man closed his eyes and merely nodded. Watford, however, was far from discouraged. He was feeling very fit that morning and the good spring weather had contributed mightily to a sense that he had licked the dark memories of the recent past. The sad indignity of banishment from his sister's home in Pittsburgh. The bleak embattled days of Inez. There was even a certain guarded optimism he felt about his prospects for the future. For the nonce, however, he was happy to be alive, secure and cozy in the hospital.

Watford grew curious about the sort of work the gentleman at his side might be engaged in. He was not so forward, however, as to ask the question directly.

"Say, what was your name again? 'Fraid I didn't quite catch it the first time."

"Boyd," the man murmured through lips taut with pain.

"What was that?"

"Boyd—Anthony Boyd."

"Boyd?" Watford pondered. "Don't think I know any Boyds. Has your family been notified? Your wife?"

"Abroad. Visiting relatives."

"Don't you think she should know?"

"No. No need. Only worry her."

"Is there anyone else? Any family to be notified?"

"No. No one else."

"What about your job? Shouldn't someone be told there?"

"Not necessary. Not necessary."

There was an awkward silence. Then Watford resumed. "Can't wait to get out of here and get back to work," he enthused brightly. "Been sick on and off for the past year or so. Air line work is my field, you know. Been a purser on most of your major lines. Pan Am, TWA, United, you name it. Been all over the world, too—Europe, the Far East, Russia. Love travel. Have ever since I was a kid. Joined up with the Air Force during Vietnam. Helicopter pilot, you know."

Watford waxed nostalgic. He appeared just then, with his wry boyish grin, to be a man fully enjoying his reveries. "Got myself shot down behind enemy lines," he continued. "Had to make my way back on foot through the jungle. Three days I walked, with a couple of 50mm slugs in my leg." He held his leg up for his roommate to see. "Still walk with a limp but they gave me a Purple Heart and a DFC." Watford smiled and glimpsed across at his neighbor. "That's how I got into airline work. Seemed the natural way to go. They wouldn't let me fly anymore because of my disability. So they made me a purser instead. I don't mind, though. I love it. The travel, the people, new experiences. Always something new. You see, with me it's always been a case of . . . Beg pardon?"

Watford had been chattering on so freely that he was unaware that the man had been muttering something to himself.

"Sorry," Watford leaned across the narrow space between the beds. "What was it you were saying?"

The man's head rolled sideward on his pillow. His eyes blazed open, fixing Watford angrily, then in the next moment closed.

"Are you all right?" Watford inquired uneasily.

Just at that moment, voices and a flurry of motion streamed through the doorway. A tall, brisk man in a white flowing coat breezed into the room. A flustered, somewhat breathless nurse tripped along behind at his heel.

"Good morning, Mr. Watford. I'm Dr. Rashower. Dr. Shavers' associate. How are you feeling this morning?"

Watford looked up into a pair of shrewd, assessing eyes. He had not been expecting this so soon and had to get himself into a proper frame of mind for what he was certain was to follow. Momentarily stunned, he had sufficient presence of mind to stall in order to suggest infirmity.

"I think I'm all right, Doctor." He spoke haltingly. The chirpy note of several moments before had become a kind of frail bleat.

The doctor glanced up and down his chart. "Still having pain, are you?"

"Yes. Across the lower back. Particularly at night. The pain is terrible at night."

"I see. Roll over, please. We'll have a look."

Dutifully, Watford rolled over on his stomach while the doctor untied the back of his smock and with strong, coolish fingers, palpated the area around his kidneys. Next he sounded the area with a stethoscope. Lastly, he slipped on a rubber glove, dipped one finger liberally in Vaseline, inserted it in Watford's rectum and routed about in there for a while.

"Okay. You can roll back over now," the doctor said, removing the glove and disposing of it neatly in a nearby wastebasket. "This is all a bit perplexing. You say that Dr. Shavers has been treating you for recurrent renal colic? But I find no sign of renal colic. There's nothing in your blood or your radiology to suggest renal colic. We have found some blood in your urine, but not in sufficient quantities to be alarming. The blood may simply be a sign of infection, but you're running no fever, nor do you have an elevated white blood cell count. I just checked your prostate and found it normal in size, possibly a trifle boggy. Nothing very significant. Frankly, I'm puzzled. Something else puzzles me, too."

Something in the man's voice and expression sent a red flag up for Watford's keen antennae.

"I've looked high and low through Dr. Shavers's records for your file and can find no trace of his ever having treated you."

"I can assure you he has," Watford retorted sharply. He could produce a fairly impressive moral indignation when the need was upon him, and the need was now definitely upon him. "Dr. Shavers has been my personal urologist for the past thirteen years. His records may be untidy. Go back and check them. I'm certain you'll find me there."

"And another thing, Mr. Watford," the imperturbable Rashower disregarded Watford's commands and instead bore down coolly, "the dispensary here has asked me to sign out three separate prescriptions for Demerol. I'm told I prescribed them for you."

"You prescribed them?"

"So I'm told, yet I have no recollection of phoning any such prescriptions into the dispensary. Have you received any Demerol here?"

"Why, yes. Of course."

"I never prescribed any Demerol for you. But apparently someone did, because you got it. Do you have any idea who might have called in the prescriptions?"

"Of course." Watford's heart thumped in his chest, but he was now determined to brazen it out. "Dr. Shavers called them in. He called here to ask how I felt. I told him I was in a good deal of pain and unable to get any medication stronger than aspirin. He wasn't about to let me suffer night after night in terrible pain, so he said he would call in a prescription at once. That idiot nurse would only give me aspirin."

Dr. Rashower stiffened and his voice grew clipped. "Let's understand each other, Mr. Watford—" With a snap of his head he indicated the nurse in question hovering behind him. "I will not tolerate disparagement of the nursing staff here. These people are tired and badly overworked. Mrs. Price in denying you medication was carrying out strict hospital policy. No medication until the attending physician has had an opportunity to examine the patient and prescribe medication and dosage himself. That's for your own protection. And number two—it is highly unlikely that Dr. Shavers called in any such prescription—"

"You're not suggesting that I'm lying?"

"I'm suggesting no such thing. All I'm suggesting is that I have no record that you are, in fact, a patient of Dr. Shavers. And in the absence of any records, I'm not going to treat you or prescribe anything. Not even aspirin."

"I see. Then you're prepared to let me lie here and suffer. Is that it?"

"Frankly, Mr. Watford, I can't find a blessed thing wrong with you. Except for a bit of blood in your urine you appear to be a perfectly hardy specimen. I've got a call into Shavers right now and I ought to be able to clear this whole matter up within the hour. In the meantime, please stay put right here in the room."

The doctor nodded to the nurse, still cowering off to the side. He then turned abruptly on his heel.

"You haven't heard the last of this." Watford's voice grew shrill. "Shavers will have your head for this. You've got one hell of a malpractice suit on your hands now."

It must have taken Watford all of five minutes to dress and throw his few shaving and toilet articles into a paper bag. He was no longer even barely aware of the white-haired gentleman with whom he'd been chatting so pleasantly only a few minutes before. Still lying flat on his back, eyes closed as though in sleep, the man appeared completely oblivious to the recent flurry of excitement. The steady respiratory rise and fall of the blanket across his chest was deep and tranquil. It occurred to Watford that the man was trying to tell him something. Anxious though he was to get away, he stepped across to the bed and stooped over, the better to hear the man. He appeared half-conscious and was mumbling to himself. "Killed a man—last night—dropped a block on his head. Killed him—killed him."

"What—what's that?" Watford gaped, then heard voices and footsteps approaching and forgetting the man, started up at once. Poking his head out the door of the room, the first thing he saw was a stern, hatchet-faced chief nurse glaring back at him from behind a reception counter at the center of the floor. She raised a cautionary finger as he started out. "Mr. Watford—"

He didn't stay around to hear the rest. He was off in a trice down the corridor with the chief nurse shouting his name, and a number of robed, shuffling inpatients turning to gaze after him in astonishment.

With the sound of a heavy tread bearing down fast, he had no intention of waiting round for an elevator. Instead, he ducked at once through a door with a red bulb glowing directly above it. It led to an emergency stairway down which he plunged, three steps at a time. At the top of the stair he could hear the nurse's voice booming into the empty stairwell, "Mr. Watford. Come back here. Mr. Watford—"

She started down the stairs. Then, instead, ran back to the desk and phoned for guards and husky orderlies to head Watford off at the exits.

By then Watford was three floors below, striding purposefully up a crowded corridor in the pediatric wing. No stranger to expedient departure, Watford was certain that a complete description of himself and his mode of attire had already been flashed to every guard in the building. Prudence strongly suggested that he remove himself temporarily from the scene.

Passing down a corridor of small individual offices, the partially open door of one, apparently vacant, seemed a welcome invitation. He ducked in and closed the door behind him.

It was a smart, compact space, lined floor to ceiling with books. A Danish teak desk sat in the center of the room on a small Oriental carpet, a large leather swivel chair behind it, and a pair of canvas slingback chairs before it. On the desk itself was a copy of the *PDR* (the *Physician's Desk Reference*), a manila file folder with a name typed across it, and a large meerschaum recently smoked and still warm, lying on its side in an ashtray. Beside that lay a tobacco pouch and matches.

From a walnut antique coat rack in the corner of the room, a long white physician's coat hung with a stethoscope poking out the side pocket. Watford, barely pausing to reflect, had donned it.

There was a light knock, and before Watford could respond the door swung open. Instantly, he snatched up the pipe, clapped it between his teeth and proceeded to scan the file before him. Looking up, he saw standing there, apparently as startled by Watford as he was by them, a somewhat apprehensive young couple. "Dr. Atwell?" inquired the husband.

Watford required no further prompting. "Yes. I'm Dr. Atwell."

"We're the Greeleys. We had an appointment."

A quick glance down at the folder he held quickly verified the name. Just outside and beyond the narrow shoulders of the husband, Watford saw two burly orderlies barrel past the open doorway. "Greeley. Oh, yes. Please come right in. Have a seat, won't you?"

Watford walked to the door, gently closed it behind them and returned to the desk with the air of a man who had occupied the space all of his life. He settled back in the chair, opposite the young couple, making a great show of bustling with the files on the desk top.

"You're here about—"

"Our baby, Alice. We were recommended to you by our pediatrician, Dr. Blaustein."

"Oh, yes, Blaustein. Excellent man." Watford tapped the ashes of the meerschaum into the tray, refilled it and with the most elaborate calm, relit the pipe. By that time he had fallen quite nicely into the role of the harried, much-in-demand Olympian, but nonetheless kindly, medical luminary. Despite all of the danger awaiting him just outside the door, he was rather relishing it. Not so much, however, that he'd lost all sense of self-preservation. He was keenly aware that the real Dr. Atwell, obviously on the premises, here precisely for this appointment, could, and probably would, reappear at any moment.

Like a parched desert wanderer coming upon water, Watford opened the Greeley file and drank in information from the reports and EKG spools lying there. He began to read aloud, quickly under his breath, mouthing all the technical verbiage perfectly as if he were completely familiar with the details and merely just refreshing his mind. "Aortal insufficiency. Valvular defect. Congenital, of course. Poor little tyke." In a swirl of pipe smoke, he glanced up at Mr. and Mrs. Greeley, who were gazing at him, both fear and adulation raging in their eyes.

Watford felt a surge of power. "You can never be certain with these valvular problems," he heard himself say suavely. "I've seen kids unable to catch their breath, already cyanotic, outgrow this sort of thing. One day they're blue, next day they're pink as peonies. Personally, I'm conservative. I'd prefer to watch her for six months more before I'd consider anything so drastic as surgical intervention. Quite frankly, from what I see here in Blaustein's records and the EKGs, I'm not at all certain it's warranted."

Gratitude and relief radiated from the youthful couple. Again, Watford heard footsteps pound past the outside door and he knew that time was pressing. He rose. "I'm afraid I rushed out without breakfast this morning. Look, why don't the two of you join me downstairs for a cup of coffee? There's a nice cafeteria down there and we can go over Alice's case more thoroughly."

By this time the Greeleys would have followed Watford out to the Jersey wetlands. Strolling and chatting in a most lively urbane fashion down the corridor to a bank of elevators, Watford in his flowing white coat gave a most convincing performance.

On the ground floor, he was immediately aware that a uniformed guard had been posted at every exit. In the cafeteria he guided the Greeleys to a table, sat them down, bustled up to a counter and brought them back steaming mugs of coffee. "Now, if you'll just wait one moment I'm going to get myself something a bit more substantial."

That was the last the Greeleys ever saw of Dr. Atwell or, for that matter, Charles Watford, for as they sipped their coffee and were thanking their lucky stars for the blessing of Dr. Atwell, Charles Watford had exited the cafeteria and was striding purposefully down the hall past the uniformed guard who held the large glass doors open for him as he passed out into the sunny, lilac-scented streets of May.

13

Watford did not go right home. The preternatural cunning of the professional fugitive advised strongly against that. Disposing of his physician's coat in a nearby trash can, but retaining the stethoscope for some future adventure, he hailed a cab. Since the day was mild and springlike, a Sunday as well, he thought he would go to the park. He had about thirty dollars in his pocket, certainly adequate for a pleasant day's outing.

His performance as a great pediatric surgeon, followed by his daredevil escape from the hospital, filled him with a kind of boyish glee. Several times during the ride uptown he laughed out loud, then finding the cabby's wary eyes on him in the rearview mirror, he launched into a wildly extended fiction about how he had just, inadvertently, been the prime figure in the apprehension of a dangerous drug addict at Beth Israel. The driver was enchanted. Shortly they were the best of friends, trading stories about crime and the dangers of the city. When they arrived at the Fifth Avenue entrance to the zoo, Watford rewarded the man with a handsome three-dollar tip.

In the zoo at last, amid a bustling, cheerful weekend crowd, Watford ceased to be a fugitive. Among the Sunday strollers he was just another man or, more accurately, another child. Carefree, giddy, he tossed peanuts to the elephants. At feeding time he stood amid crowds of laughing, squealing children as they watched fish being flung to the seals leaping and yawping in the pool. In the monkey house he watched in dazzled awe the vaulting acrobatics of the spider monkeys, the rhesus and the capuchins. Nearby, the polar bear paced restlessly the narrow confines of his caged den, and near the seal pool a street entertainer dressed in a yellow jerkin and green tights, a dunce cap, and pointed slippers, played a horn pipe and pantomimed fairy tales for the gathering crowds. The children laughed, but the overall effect on Watford had been a curious melancholy.

Later, eating a rubbery frankfurter beneath the orange umbrella of a park vendor, he watched the spastic promenade of bronze animals round the park clock above the North Gate, playing their bronze instruments and proclaiming the hour. He had a sudden flashing image of the clockworks within— *the hour wheel turns the minute wheel; the pin on the minute wheel raises the lever; the lever extends to the rear plate and has two arms attached to it; the lower arm contacts the pins on the driving wheel, and the upper arm contacts the pin on the arresting wheel. When the minute wheel turns, the heel of the lever falls off the pin of the minute wheel. At the same time the lower arm of the lever between the plates falls between the count pins on the driving wheel. The striking train is released, and the minute wheel starts the hour count. The striking is accomplished by the pins on the minute wheel lifting the arm which is attached to the hammer. When the last stroke is struck—*

Watford stood in a cold sweat, chewing numbly his frankfurter as the toylike animals swayed and lurched round the track, the chimes gonged, and a voice receded in his head. A moment later he flung the remains of his frankfurter into a nearby trash can, and fled the zoo, certain he was being followed by the police.

Reluctant to go home, he made his way across the park and wandered uptown in the direction of the Museum of Natural History. He recalled with great affection going there as a boy. Often he would go with his mother. His father professed a hatred of the place. Later, throughout adolescence, he would go by himself, particularly fond of it on cold wintry afternoons, with the snow falling silently outside in the park, festooning in a gauzy silver the sere, withered branches of the dogwood and cherry trees across the way.

The museum had those cozy associations for him, the sense of coming out of the cold into an absolutely secure environment; his favorite food at the cafeteria on the ground floor—a plate of homemade spicy baked beans and a mug of dark sweet hot cocoa, sometimes alternating with hot cider.

Then afterward, walking solitary and a little frightened down the hall of mammoths—great tuskers and stuffed mastodons who had trod the earth at the dawn of time. A turn to the right and into the hushed darkened corridors of dioramas—those small, illuminated boxes behind glass that would whisk him to an Amazonian rain forest, to the frozen Siberian tundra, to a pygmy village in Gabon, to a dark, snow-covered forest in the Himalayas where a Siberian tiger gnawed the bloody haunch of a fallen stag.

Watford wandered the museum that afternoon for nearly three hours, slightly dejected and unable to rekindle any sense of the wonder or delicious dread he had experienced there as a boy. The mystery was mostly gone now. The fearsome tuskers in the hall of mammoths looked innocuous and vaguely comic, like badly worn stuffed animals. The beans in the cafeteria were tasteless and canned and the cocoa was watery.

He left somewhere shortly after 5:00 P.M. Still unwilling to return home, he wandered down Eighth Avenue and into Times Square. Neon lights were just going on against the gray twilight sky. The streets were dirty and the stale air of daily lurid commerce hung like a sour pall above the place. Along with the pageantry of hawkers, greasers and pimps, were the three-card-monte dealers and the drab painted ladies.

At a loss for anything better to do, Watford wandered into a penny arcade. The air was charged with the numbing din of electrical games and canned acid rock booming over loudspeakers. A tired haze of kif floated uneasily through the place. Watford made his way through pinball, Skee-Ball, Pokerama, and a variety of electrical video-screen games that buzzed a great deal but amounted to no more than following the bouncing ball. When he ran out of single dollar bills, he left. Walking out once more into the electric glare of night, he found the whole thieves' carnival out in force.

Leaning against a corner stand he ate disconsolately a slice of pizza, and observed the spectacle. He wished somehow to be a part of it, but in the end he was repelled. He did not drink alcohol; the idea of casual sex, particularly sex for money, was repugnant; and that air of imminent violence pervading the place finally drove him off.

He walked several blocks east to the IND and took an F train home to Queens. He had no idea of what he would find when he got there, but in the quiet, elm-lined street of middle-class row homes where he lived, what he suspected he might find actually came to pass.

The police patrol car, its lights out, waited about 150 feet south of his front door on the opposite side of the street. He could see the glowing orange tips from the cigarettes of the two policemen inscribing arcs behind the windshield of the patrol car. The hospital had lost little time, indeed, notifying the police of the questionable activities of one of its patients, a Mr. Charles Watford, of 724 Hauser Street, Kew Gardens, New York.

The moment Watford spotted the car he ducked back into the doorway of a darkened tailor shop. In the window a headless dress form made of wires and white rubber foam glowed with a spectral radiance.

Watford's one advantage was that he had spotted them before they'd spotted him. Fear rushing back at him, senses acutely heightened, he reverted instantly to the psychology of the quarry. Waiting several minutes in the doorway of the tailor shop, he concluded the patrol car was not about to leave too quickly. He lingered a moment longer, then pulling his collar up about his neck, he stepped out of the doorway and strolled casually back up the street to a small cinema specializing in reruns of old foreign films. He purchased a ticket and went inside.

The film they featured that evening was an old British import called *Séance on a Wet Afternoon.* In it, Richard Attenborough played a drab nonentity of a man who gets caught up in his wife's schemes for extracting money as a hired medium from a couple trying to communicate with their dead child.

The playing time of the film was approximately eighty minutes. When Watford came out there were, inexplicably, tears in his eyes as he strolled warily back round the corner to Hauser Street.

Once again he positioned himself in the doorway of the tailor shop where the dress form in the window glowed more eerily than ever. From where he stood he could see that the patrol car had gone. The spot was now occupied by a late model Dodge panel van.

A congenital fugitive, the mere surface appearance of an "all clear" was not enough to convince him. Carefully, his eyes scanned both sides of the street to see if the patrol car had simply moved someplace else. He understood enough about the police to know that surveillance teams could also switch their tactic of waiting in one spot to that of cruising periodically round an area.

When he had satisfied himself on both scores, he surged back out into Hauser Street with an almost jaunty air to number 724, and whistling softly beneath his breath, let himself in the front door.

He lit no lights, but slipped out of his shoes and like a cat padded noiselessly up the stairs to his bedroom at the rear of the house.

In less than ten minutes, working deftly in the dark, he had packed a canvas suitcase with everything he might need for a somewhat protracted stay. He had no idea of his ultimate destination that night. When he had completed the packing, he inserted into the same suitcase his doctor's black leather bag, complete with an assortment of medical paraphernalia collected over the years—retinoscope, sphygmomanometer for blood pressure readings, his newly acquired stethoscope, a variety of hypodermics and needles, as well as a full range of prescription drugs, including an ample supply of meperidine—his beloved "Mother Demerol." He also packed a physician's prescription pad bearing the name and number of a Dr. Michael Breuer—to guarantee him sufficient refills of anything he wanted. As a final touch, he added his beloved *PDR*, and a *Merck Manual of Diagnosis and Therapy*, for him Holy Scripture to which he attributed dark powers, mysteries indited in a language so heady and seductive as to have an almost aphrodisiac effect upon him.

Transferring his toilet articles from his hospital kit to his suitcase, he then clapped the bag shut and buckled it. Still operating entirely in the dark, or rather just from whatever minimal light came from the streetlamps across the way, he then proceeded to dress.

His wardrobe that evening was the uniform of a Pan American flight purser. It bore wings over the left lapel and a black nameplate with the name WATFORD over the right.

The uniform was completely authentic in that it had once belonged to Watford when he had worked as a flight purser for Pan Am—a period of some eight months at the conclusion of which he had been cashiered by the airline for a number of undisclosed irregularities, or so his employment record stated. The same record attested to the fact that for the period of eight months in which he was employed, he phoned in sick approximately fifty percent of the time. His final task was to pack a lightweight gray tropical business suit into a Val-pac he could carry over his shoulder.

Before leaving the house that evening Watford attended to several tasks. First, he disconnected the phone from its trunk outlet; second, he unplugged the refrigerator, dumping all perishable foods into the trash can, which he would take down to the front stoop as he left. Next, he disconnected the furnace and finally, he emptied into his wallet his total cash savings of seven-hundred-some-odd dollars from a small steel box he kept in the attic.

There were no outstanding bills to pay. No mortgage on the house. He had been fortunate in that the house left to him by his mother he now owned scot-free. All that was due were the annual city taxes which, happily, were paid up till late in the fall. With a feeling of relief, almost exhilaration—the exhilaration he invariably felt at the prospect of flight—he carried his bag and Val-pac downstairs, then locked and double-bolted the door. In his impeccably pressed purser's uniform, white shirt and black tie, with the peaked hat and flight wings, he looked almost dashing as he stepped out from the doorway and into the street.

Gazing both right and left, and satisfied that the patrol car had not returned, he stepped down the three flagged steps onto the curbside, then made his way briskly to the corner where he hailed a cab and directed the driver to take him out to Kennedy.

14

"May I see the passenger manifold, please?"

"Yes, Purser. Which flight?"

"802."

"Dallas–San Francisco, 11:40 P.M. Still reporting on time. You posted for that?"

"So I'm told." Watford smiled at the pretty blond ticket agent behind the Pam Am desk and received a smile back. The girl who'd been behind the desk for nearly eight hours and was tired thought the purser was not uninteresting.

It was slightly past 10:00 P.M. Activity behind the desk was slow to virtually nonexistent, and the girl with the wheat-white hair and the flirtatious eyes made no secret she was pleased to see him. "So you're told?"

"Filling in for a buddy, that's all. Last-minute emergency. I just got in from Chicago about two hours ago. No sooner do I get home and get my shoes off than they call me and tell me to get right back down here again. This 802?"

She handed him the manifold. At a glance he had the information he wanted. Just as he suspected—for a flight at that hour, the big 747 was undersubscribed. Possibly just half-full. There were plenty of empty seats about so that a single, unclaimed one would scarcely be missed. Watford quickly noted that 11A, 13F, 16B and 22B were all unassigned. He committed the fact to memory.

"Where does she board?" Watford asked.

"Gate nine. You've got plenty of time. They won't start till ten forty-five or eleven. I don't think I've ever seen you around here before." She gazed up into his slightly reddened face, then glanced at his nameplate. "Watford, is it?"

"That's right. Charles. Charley, if you like." He smiled right back at her.

"I do. Charles is a bit stuffy for my taste."

He smiled crookedly and glanced at her tag. "You're Haines?"

"Millicent—Milly, if you like."

"My niece's name is Millicent. I prefer it to Milly. You're a perfect Millicent." He sensed he was making a conquest. "Can you check my bag through to Frisco? I'll keep the Val-pac with me."

She tagged the canvas bag and sent it wobbling off on a roller ramp. Together they watched it disappear through a port covered with strips of dangling leather.

With nothing left to do, and the girl smiling expectantly at him, Watford was momentarily at a loss. He gazed round the terminal uneasily. "Slow tonight, isn't it?"

"Typical week night. Very boring. The terminal pretty much empties after eleven. It's worse in the winter when the weather's cold."

A passenger presented himself at the desk. Watford watched her check his reservations on the computer and make his seat assignment. "Gate nine," she said cheerily.

"One of yours," she remarked after the man had gone.

Watford murmured something to himself, then said: "Guess I better get on down there now, too."

"You've still got plenty of time."

"I've got a lot of odds and ends to see to once I get on board."

She shrugged and gave him a wry little smile. "No one knows better than you. Good flight, Purser." She paused a moment, then corrected herself. "I mean, Charley."

"See you." He smiled, waved and started out toward gate 9. When he glanced back she was still there, head down at her empty counter, working over some papers. The immense hollow shadows of the nearly empty terminal, and the eerie cobalt light enveloping the Pan Am counter suddenly filled him with the most unaccountable sense of desolation.

It was yet far too early for any significant accumulation of passengers at the flight gate. The seat assignment desk was still empty, and there were no Pam Am personnel about. Even the destination placards had not yet been posted.

Beyond the desk, looming immense and unreal through the big panoramic glass that looked out onto the field, were the nose and fuselage of the big 747—Flight 802, Dallas, San Francisco. Striding easily back behind the desk, Watford moved in his purser's uniform as easily and naturally as he'd moved earlier that morning in the white coat of a pediatric surgeon.

It was a simple matter locating the concrete stairway leading down to the service area on the field. In another moment he was out on the tarmac. A blast of warm diesel-scented air pressed heavily against his cheek and suddenly he was in the midst of high-pitched engines warming, maintenance crews crawling over the wings, rubber fuel hoses coiling upward into the wing tanks, porters wrestling bags and boxes off the luggage carts and into the open bays of the big clipper ship.

None of the crew had yet appeared. But the doors were all open, including that of the flight cabin out of which a single orange night light glowed. Jaunty as ever, he mounted the aluminum ladder stair leading to the first-class section and boarded the plane as if it were his own.

He went forward and sat for a while in the pilot's seat in the dim illumination of the flight cabin. He had picked up a clipboard inside and by now he was checking dials and switches, making notations on his clipboard with the utmost care.

He was aware of passengers starting to gather at the gate, watching him from behind the big plate windows as if he were some uniquely privileged initiate of inner mysteries. The sensation of being observed in that fashion pleased him mightily.

Somewhere near 11:00 P.M., when he could see crowds and activity round the seat assignment desk, he finally thought it prudent to depart the cabin. With the plane still empty, he slung the Val-pac over his shoulder and made his way back to one of the lavatories in the rear. No sooner had he locked the door behind him, than he was slipping quickly out of the purser's uniform and into his light gray business suit.

Overhead in the lavatory canned music had been switched on through crackling loudspeakers. Watford completed his toilette to a Mantovani rendition of "Beyond the Blue Horizon," slipped his purser's uniform into the Val-pac, then sat down on the john and prepared to wait.

Outside, just beyond the door, he could hear the chatter of two flight attendants prepping their bar carts. Shortly, he heard the bang and clatter of passengers coming aboard, luggage being slammed up into the bays above the seats, outerwear going into the wardrobes, the rattle of glasses. There was a good deal of vibration when the engines were first switched on. A short time later he heard outside doors being sealed and the voice of a stewardess doing the flight-safety drill.

Sitting behind the steel door in the tiny cabinet, he had a sudden fleeting image of himself in the hospital that morning, lying half up in bed while the doctor wagged his finger and fulminated above him. Thinking of his masquerade as Dr. Atwell, the pediatric surgeon, he chuckled to himself and wondered half-regretfully about the nice young couple he had duped, then too, of the zoo and the museum and the sad movie with the sad little husband, and the police waiting outside his front door and the pretty Pan Am ticket agent. What a lot of ground he'd covered that day. "I killed a man," the phrase came drifting back at him and he was at first uncertain where he'd heard it. Then he recalled. Certainly that's what the man had said, the chap in the bed next to him at the hospital. But he couldn't have really said that, Watford reasoned. It was probably just the effects of the anesthesia wearing off. Partial hallucination. Bad dreams and the sudden excitement of that ass Rashower making accusations. "I killed a man," Watford strained for recall. ". . . Dropped something or other from the roof." Oh, he couldn't have . . . Probably just bad dreams—coming out of the anesthesia—

The next moment he felt a slight shudder and then the motion of the ship rolling backward, being pushed out onto the runways. All through the taxiing he remained in the lav, and even till after the takeoff when they had reached their cruising altitude of 30,000 feet.

Only then did he step out, then briskly and purposefully make his way to one of the preselected unclaimed seats he had committed to memory. It was at 22B where he finally settled, first, however, hanging his Val-pac, unnoticed by anyone, in one of the outerwear wardrobes.

Settling in with a *Time* magazine, and graciously accepting the ginger ale he had ordered from the flight attendant, he glanced out the window watching the glittering New York skyline recede behind him, and breathed a long sigh of relief.

15

"To me this is quintessential middle class. Genteel. Fastidious. Efficient. Murder by long distance. Nothing so coarse as the laying on of
hands. I'd say your man's over thirty. More probably into his forties."

"How can you tell?"

"By the fact that it's all so clean."

Mooney scoffed. "About as clean as a meat cleaver."

"Philosophically, yes. I grant you that. But, practically speaking,
as a form of homicide, it's all extremely neat. Look for black shoes
and button-down collars. A man in a gray suit."

"Not a kid?"

"My God, no." Dr. Kurt Baum, the police psychiatrist, flung his
arms outward expansively. He was a short, boxlike man with a back
slightly hunched, and wiry gray hair cropped close to the scalp.
"Your typical street kid would never be content tossing a cinder
block over the rooftop into the crowd below. A head is bashed.
Brains splattered over the pavement. But so what? You never get to
see it. Where's the kicks in that?" Baum scratched his chin reflectively. "The kid from the barrio wants the body contact. He loves
that part of it. Walking up to the designated victim. Skewering the
fellow's tripes with a switchblade. Seeing the blood spurt. Feeling
the victim squirm under his hand as he twists the blade. Looking into
the poor bugger's eyes, seeing the panic there as life oozes out. That's
the real kicker for the newly pubescent, Mooney. The confrontation.
The macho factor. Something to write home about. Standing up
there face-to-face with the victim. Experiencing it all with him. Your
fellow doesn't want that. He wouldn't touch it with a bargepole. He's
got the same psychotic rage inside him as the barrio kid but he

doesn't have the stomach to bring himself off quite the same way. No, your man's a secretive little rascal, Mooney. Furtive. Creeping. Outwardly inoffensive, law-abiding, but inwardly a ghoul."

The detective was skeptical. He had his own impressions. They didn't happen to coincide with Dr. Baum's. From the start, Mooney had always seen his "bombardier" as some crazed, disaffected youth—undoubtedly black or Puerto Rican. Up to his ears in coke; spouting vague, half-baked theory about the social injustices of the past. Nickel-a-dozen slogans and show-business high jinks for the six o'clock news. That's what Mooney had believed right from the start since it fit so comfortably with his own carefully cultivated theories of social history.

Now here was this police shrink attempting to explode all of that. What the hell did Baum know anyway—with his quaint laboratory criminology that bore no relation to the hard truths of the street? What kind of a shrink worth his salt would be working for the god-damned city anyway? A fucking civil servant sawbones.

"What about motives?" Mooney jeered. "Have you thought about motives?"

"What about them?"

"I mean the fact that there aren't any. Any old victim'll do in a pinch. To me that spells kid. K-I-D."

Baum appeared surprised at the detective's vehemence. He shook his head and sighed. "This is 1980, Mooney. Motives are passé. Even for the over-forty crowd, motives are Victorian. Really chic contemporary crime doesn't require anything as fusty and downright inhibiting as an excuse to murder. The really exciting thing is to play it as it lays. Let it just happen. Cool. Laid back. Someone stands in front of you on a subway platform. The train hurtles into the station. All you do is push. A man pulls up to a red light. You stroll over to the car as if to ask him a question. He rolls down his window. You put a .320-magnum to his head and POOF. Or you stand up on a rooftop under the stars with a forty-pound cinder block. Then just let it drop down, slip from your fingers into the crowd below. Roulette. Round and round it goes. Where it stops, nobody knows. No regrets. Baum's chubby little hands rummaged the litter of his desk for a tobacco pouch. "It's all part of the New Man construct," he continued enthusiastically. "Go to the movies. See a ball game. Bash someone's skull with a cinder block. It's all recreation. There are no motives because there are no real actions. It's just storybook. Purely imitative. Acting. Everyone is acting some cheap serial melodrama of bloodshed and retribution.

Baum glanced sharply at Mooney, then smirked. "You look a little puzzled, Francis. Why? What's troubling you? This is not exactly the way you see things, ay? You want it all neat and convenient with motives, the way it was a hundred years ago when you grew up. Well, it's not, my friend. All that's changed. I'm sorry to tell you that's not the way the game's played today."

Mooney sat for a time, eyes blinking, tongue sliding across his parched lips. He was unconvinced. At last he spoke. "I just don't buy this guy in the gray suit. Your model, God-fearing, tax-paying citizen, going back and forth to a job all year. Raising kids. Then, one night a year, going bonkers on a rooftop. That just don't wash. And like I told you—always in the same area and always the same time of the year."

"Repetition compulsion."

Mooney's eyes opened and he leaned forward. Baum hastened to clarify.

"Repetition compulsion. An overwhelming urge to replicate over and over again certain actions or activities, even if you recognize they are destructive to you. Like your eating, Mooney."

"Oh, Christ. Don't *you* start on that now."

"It's true. Think about it. It's not at all uncommon for people to have urges, associate certain actions and undefined emotions with a certain time of year. Why they do it, we can't say. You say it has something to do with the motion of heavenly bodies as they affect the human psyche. That's a kind of nice, kitschy little theory you've got there about the solstice and all. But it's voodoo and I just don't happen to buy it. Still, I grant you, your guy appears to grow active about the end of April, the beginning of May. But, more probably, the repetition of crime during that particular period is merely symbolic of some trauma that person may have suffered years ago during the same period. The person doesn't necessarily recall the events of the trauma. Undoubtedly, they were painful and he was forced to bury them deep somewhere in his mind. The subconscious, however, doesn't forget. Like a savings bank, it keeps all of your bad memories on deposit for you. And if you don't draw on those memories, I mean consciously, the interest builds and builds, compounding itself, until you've got quite a nice little bundle there. With your fellow it's all bottled up for twelve months. Then, on just one night a year, the whole thing is permitted to blow. That's when he goes up to the roof, beneath the stars, to reenact this perennial ritual."

Baum's arm snapped upward and he checked his wristwatch. "Gotta go. I have a session with a recidivist wife-beater." He laughed and started to gather his papers.

Mooney lumbered out of his chair. "Can we just review this thing before you go?"

Baum's eyes rose heavenward as though he were pleading for

mercy. "You asked for a silhouette, Mooney. I provided one but you've spurned it. For the record, however, I'll repeat. Fortyish. Middle class. Educated. Fastidious. Compulsive. A nitpicker. Highly civilized, but underneath a sump of guilt and self-loathing. In short, my friend," Baum shot the clasps on his battered briefcase and stuffed it beneath his arm, "look for a solid, upright, pious Christian, patriotic American. You should have no problem, Mooney. There are millions of them out there." Baum hooted, pounded the detective's back and bustled out.

16

"... and you say you were standing approximately here?"

"That's right."

"No moon?"

"No moon."

"So the light was poor. No illumination from any other place? Like across the way?"

"No, man. Like I told you. It was dark, dark, dark."

"You couldn't see his face?"

"Nothing."

"Features. Color. Build?"

"Nothing. Like I told you. The guy's a hundred feet on the other ..."

"Right. Okay. You told me. Let's check that." Mooney unwound a long steel tape from a spool. "Could you hold that for me just a minute?"

The young Italian construction worker, Enzo Vitali, grasped an end of the tape while the detective slowly walked the spool out over the tar roof.

It was noon, late May. Bright sunshine. Perfect kite-flying

weather. A day for the park, or possibly a ride up into northern Westchester or Connecticut. Eager to finish, Mooney moved along a bit more quickly, for he planned to make a dash out to the track that afternoon where they were racing yearlings.

Buffeting over the rooftops, the wind tended to barrel the big man along. His outsized powder blue trousers flapped and billowed in the twenty-mile-per-hour gusts.

"Now this is where you first saw him?" Mooney came to an abrupt halt at a point on the ledge.

"Yeah— Well, maybe a little more to the left."

Obediently, Mooney stepped sideways. "Like this?"

"Yeah. That's it."

The detective glanced downward at his tape. "It's 106 feet. And you say he was standing with his back to you? Elbows on the ledge? Gazing out, like this?"

Vitali studied the detective's pose reflectively. He was a lean, muscular man with dark restless eyes and wavy, meticulously coiffed hair. He was, Mooney judged, no more than twenty-five.

"That's right. Just lookin' out like that. Just like you're doin' now."

"When did you first see him?"

"I was standin' here. Leanin' against the chimney stack like I'm doin' now. See?" The young man had got himself into the spirit of the thing. "I'm just waitin' here for the girl, see? I got nothin' to do. So I light a cigarette, see? Like this?"

Vitali extracted a cigarette from his package and lit it. "The minute I light it, I see the guy. He must've heard my match 'cause he's turnin'."

"Like this?" Mooney swung round.

"Yeah. That's right. And then . . . then . . ."

"He sees you? Right?"

"Yeah. Right. He looks directly at me for a minute."

"A minute? That's a long time."

"Well, maybe less. A little less."

"Still you don't see his face?"

"No, man. How could I? Like I told you? It's too dark."

Mooney prodded him on. "Then?"

"Then he starts for me. He's a pretty good-sized guy. I mean I can see that all right. He starts comin' directly at me and I sense I'm gonna have trouble."

Mooney started walking toward the young man.

"He gets about halfway to me and already I'm lookin' round for somethin' I can bash the fucker with. A brick, a pipe, anything. But instead of comin' to me, he hangs a sharp right . . ."

"Like this?" Mooney veered sharply.

"That's right. Then heads off there. To the ledge. Where the fire escape is."

Mooney paced off the distances once again, his spool paying out the measures. "Here?"

"That's right. Right there."

Mooney recorded 191 feet in his note pad and glanced gingerly down over the ledge. No more than six feet below was the top-floor fire escape. At the point where he stood was a large chalk circle marked off by the detectives and the forensic unit that had gone over the area several days before for prints and any other possible telltale signs. They had found nothing.

But now, however, there were several witnesses who had actually claimed to have had a view of the alleged "Bombardier" as the newspapers had so fondly christened him. One was Vitali, the construction worker; the other was Mr. Rosenzweig, the widower and retired postal clerk who had seen a person on his fire escape the night of the fatal incident. He too, however, had not seen enough of the man to make any kind of a solid composite description. But just below his fire escape, ten feet or so to the pavement, was a sizable splash of dried blood. That too had a chalk circle marked round it. And a successful blood-typing had been taken from it.

At least Mooney knew now that his man was an AB positive. In the absence of prints, reliable witnesses with corroborating descriptions, or any other hard evidence, blood typing in and of itself was not going to be very helpful. AB positive is a relatively common blood type, far too common to make an ironclad case against a possible suspect. As a matter of fact, Mooney reflected, he himself was an AB positive. A pleasant irony, he thought. He and his quarry now shared a blood bond.

"Anything else?" Enzo Vitali called to Mooney across the roof.

Mooney looked up, suddenly recalling the young man.

"Can I go now?"

"Sure. Sure, go ahead. I'm goin' too." Mooney lumbered over the roof. A picture of strong, spirited yearlings lining up at the post flashed before his eye. "Just don't leave town without letting us know where we can reach you."

MARCH—MAY/'81

17

"A duplex watch beats eighteen thousand vibrations per hour."

There it was again, the voice strident, pedagogic, and hinting at impending chastisement. As usual, the voice was disembodied. It came from nowhere in particular. He was in a small bright room in the middle of the morning. He sat alone, a young boy at a kitchen table in a tiny room without doors. There were no curtains on the windows and the glare of the sun hurt his eyes. He was reading aloud from a voluminous text. He knew at once that text to be Saunier's *Treatise on Modern Horology.*

The room in which he sat was the old breakfast room off the kitchen before its refurbishment over a dozen years ago. No one but him appeared to be in the kitchen. Yet, as he read aloud in the high, tremulous voice of childhood, he had the inescapable conviction that his every move was being carefully monitored.

"The diameter of the impulse wheel is two-thirds that of the great wheel. It has thirteen teeth and beats 14,400 vibrations per hour. The balance moves slowly and is provided with a weaker balance spring that necessarily . . ."

Even in his half-sleep he felt a sense of growing agitation, and then brief, faintly erotic sensations. ". . . and therefore experience confirms that duplex escapements yielding as many as 21,600 vibrations per hour have been found to be accurate timekeepers. . . ."

The voice, his own, drifted off, while the feeling of agitation and excitement quickened. Quite suddenly the lineaments of the darkened room impinged upon his waking eye.

"What are you doing, Myrtle?" he whispered. He never once looked down at the figure huddled slightly below him. Instead he kept his eyes riveted on the shadow-mottled ceiling. "What are you up to?" His voice was quiet and infinitely patient, though he was overcome with disgust. A series of moaning grunts issued from the figure kneeling beside him. He touched the head gently, moving a finger through the kinked, wiry hair, and suffered with quiet forbearance the pawing of his genitals.

There was an uncomfortable sticky wetness now in the region of his unbuttoned pajama pants. Several times she raised her head and gasped for breath. For his part, it was a martyrdom. He suffered it all uncomplainingly, not wishing to interrupt her pleasure. All throughout it he stroked the coarse, oddly metallic hair so unpleasant to the touch.

When she was finished he rose without a word, went into the bathroom and washed himself. Returning to bed, he found her lying in the corner at the far side, her face to the wall, and weeping.

It was 4:10 A.M. now. He noted the fact from the red electric numerals on the integer clock beside the bed. How his father would have despised such a clock; charmless and unaesthetic; a clock stripped of all its inherent mystery, reduced to the vulgar functionalism of a common cash register.

She sat at the edge of the bed beside him, weeping. He reached across and stroked the knobby vertebrae beneath the cheap rayon gown.

"There, there."

"You must hate me, Charley."

"How could I possibly hate you, Myrtle?"

"I make you sick."

"You don't make me sick, Myrtle."

"Sure I do. I may be dumb, but I'm nobody's fool. You're so good—and me—I'm so—" Her voice sniveled at him out of the dark. "Why, you could have your pick of any of the girls down at the bank. What you see in me, I just don't . . ."

"I love you, Myrtle." It sounded hollow, even to him. But he was too weary, too disinterested, to simulate genuine ardor.

"You really mean that, Charley?" She turned round, and leaning on an elbow stared up at him. As she did so, a shaft of moonlight fell across her pinched, birdlike features.

"Of course I mean it."

She reached an arm round his head and roughly hugged him, pressing her nose into the warm crook of his neck. The odor of cigarette smoke rose out of her hair and mouth.

"Oh, Charley. Charley, darling. I'm so lucky. So lucky it's me you want. Me you need. Only I wish . . ." She started to whimper again.

"Now don't let's start that again, Myrtle."

"I know. I know." She swiped her teary eyes with the back of her hand. "It's just that I wish . . . I wish, just that you'd hold me more. And love me. It just ain't natural the way you keep yourself from me for so long. You know what I mean?"

He was quiet for a time, suffering her wet embrace and her nose boring into his neck. "I told you when we started this, Myrtle . . ."

"I know. I know, Charley."

"I said then I wasn't taking you in as a mistress or a lover."

"I know that, Charley. I know what you said. Still . . ."

"I told you then, Myrtle, I was not going to take advantage of your misfortune."

"I know, Charley. And you haven't. You've lived up to your word. And that's how come I have so much respect for you. Other guys I know . . . a girl without money, without a job, no friends or relations to help her out . . . other guys would have moved in on a situation like that."

"I told you, Myrtle, I respect you too much."

"I know, Charley. I know." She snuffled and wiped her eyes with a crumpled tissue. "Still, I wish you'd hold me more. And touch me. I'm a woman, Charley, and . . . and Christ, I need touching."

Watford lay on his back, hands cradled behind his head, and stared at the ceiling. He appeared to be pondering some careful, deeply considered point. Snuffling and daubing fitfully at her eyes, she watched him and waited. At last he spoke:

"When I saw you working in that bar that first night, Myrtle, and the way those fellows in there talked to you, and how the owners treated you, I just knew I had to somehow put a stop to that."

"I know it, Charley, and I bless you all my life for what you done. Ain't it been . . ." She laughed, catching herself up. "There I go again with the ain'ts. See what I mean when I say I'm just not good enough for you? She laughed again, somewhat self-consciously. *"Hasn't* it been great, though, is all I meant. These past five months. Just you and me together in this little place. You with your nice, steady job down at the bank. And me waiting here with supper when you get home. And you gettin' out of your uniform and all, and takin' off that awful pistol, and then us sittin' down and havin' a drink before dinner. Ain't that been nice, Charley?" Her face floated up at him out of the moonbeam, stupid and imploring. "Hasn't it, I mean, *been* nice?"

"Sure it's been nice, Myrtle." He patted her as if she were an old retriever. "I wouldn't change it, not any of it, for the world."

She sat up suddenly in bed and hugged her knees. "Well, then, why is it I can't make you happy?"

"You do make me happy, Myrtle."

"No, I don't. You're a million miles away. I want to do things for you. You're always doin' things for me. You give me money and presents. I want to give you things, too, Charley. But you don't seem to want nothin' back from me in return. That's not normal-like. Not like other relationshipslike. Other guys I've known have given me things too, but like they always wanted something back in return. That was the deal. They never had to say it. You just knew it. And you knew the deal would last just so long as they were happy with what they were gettin' back on their money. Not you, Charley. You always give. You don't ask for nothin' back. And I guess . . . I guess that's what makes me feel like"—her voice started to quaver—"like you don't care about me. Like either you just feel sorry for me, or maybe that I just plain old disgust you."

She buried her head in her knees, and in the next moment her entire body was convulsed with sobs.

"Now, now," he stroked her helplessly.

" 'Cause, let me tell you," she sobbed. "I don't need anyone's pity. And if I disgust you . . ."

"Oh, for God's sake, Myrtle." He hugged her hard to his chest. She was yielding and compliant, making happy little burbling sounds as he kissed and stroked her. "Don't ever . . . For pity's sake, don't you ever think such a crazy thing."

He could not bear the thought that his inattentiveness, his sexual complacency, had hurt her so deeply. Now he set out to disabuse her of such thoughts. Ardor at 4:00 A.M. was not easy to come by, but he was not going to let the hour stop him.

Myrtle Wells, for her part, was not about to be stopped either. Ambition and guile ran a little deeper and possibly darker there than Watford gave her credit for. Within the small compass of her drab, mean, thoroughly misbegotten life, Charles Watford loomed like the Prince of Wales. He was the best main chance. The daughter of a pipe welder at a naval yard in Puget Sound, the only kind of men Myrtle had been exposed to were those who used to regularly immobilize themselves on Saturday-night six-packs, and as a matter of principle, liked to cuff their women about a great deal. Charles Watford, for whatever his idiosyncrasies, was the closest she'd ever come to human tenderness and seeming economic security in a male. She was not about to let that go too easily.

"Charley, Charley," she swooned beneath him, biting his shoulder, smothering her moans in his armpit. "Oh, Charley, that's so good. Deeper—go deeper, Charley. More. More."

Her thighs coiled sinuously round his middle while he rocked above her in his cool, passionless way. "I love you, I love you," she kept gasping in his ear while the excitement in her voice mounted to sobs and little quivering shrieks.

Afterward, depleted and strangely sad, Watford slept. Myrtle Wells, however, lay awake on her pillow, still vibrating like a plucked string. Her skin tingled from the encounter and her chin was bruised from where his unshaven beard had abraded it. She minded none of that, but only folded her arms across her chest with a proud, defiant expression, as if embracing herself, and smiled enigmatically into the approaching dawn.

18

At the First National City Bank of Kansas City, Charles Watford was looked upon as very much a favorite son. In the six months he had served there as a security guard, he had won the affection of his colleagues and the admiration of his superiors. He had applied for the job on the basis of a record of service as a sergeant of the U.S. Military Police in Vietnam. He had never been any such thing, but he was buoyed by the unalterable conviction that having certified to that effect on his application, the odds were greatly in his favor that the deception would never be discovered.

He was right. Security checks in such matters are notoriously slipshod and, in Watford's case, only the most perfunctory check had been authorized. Consequently, Watford was hired and in no time at all had proved himself an invaluable asset to First National City as well as a fearless adversary of aspiring bank robbers. He may as well have been the very thing he attested to on his application, for with remarkable aplomb, he had foiled two attempted holdups. In addition, he had demonstrated that he was a man who conducted his affairs with such exemplary discretion as to make it highly unlikely that he would ever prove an embarrassment to the bank.

What's more, Watford looked the part perfectly. He was attractive, polite and unfailingly attentive to his duties. Given his strong predilection for masquerade, he naturally loved to don the smart gray flannel guard's uniform with the strip of navy piping running up the trousers. The crowning touch was the .45-caliber service revolver buckled smartly to his hip. At a time when he was still smarting from the indignity of banishment from his sister's home, and still imagining himself to be a four-starred item on the New York City Police Department's Ten Most Wanted list, his unremarkable job at the bank out in the boondocks of Kansas suited his needs perfectly. It afforded him an opportunity to keep a low profile as well as build his badly depleted financial reserves. How long he would stay, he could not say. In all his adult life he'd never been able to conceive of any job he held as anything more than merely transitory. For his part, he was always biding time and awaiting the propitious moment to bolt. And when it came to bolting, he had an unerring instinct for just the right moment. In much the same manner that epileptics describe the aura preceding the full attack, so, too, Watford's bolt was invariably preceded by a whole series of minute, but by now familiar, neuromuscular alarms. As of yet those alarms had not manifested themselves. But something in the uncanny, almost feral prescience of the man told him that shortly they would.

Watford's closest friend at the bank was T. Y. Bidwell, the second security guard and Watford's partner. A dozen years his senior, Bidwell was a gaunt, leathery individual with flinty, rakish features. He'd been married three times, and in the final instance to two ladies simultaneously. He was a Texan, or more precisely, a Texarkansan who preferred to pass himself off as pure Texan for whatever special cachet he thought attached to that. Lean, coppery, rawboned, he was the quintessential cowhand. A high liver, after hours he made directly for the more boisterous watering holes of Kansas City, where he could depend on an everready supply of bourbon and pretty women.

Temperamentally, Bidwell was poles apart from the instinctive monasticism of Watford. What drew them together in that improbable bond of friendship was a mystery to the two of them.

"Hey, Charley. What say we punch down a couple," Bidwell said one night at closing.

"I can't, T.Y. Myrtle's . . ."

"Oh, shit, Myrtle." Bidwell flapped his arms as if he were about to take wing. "Christ, Charley, I wish you'd get off that Myrtle thing. You got all this pussy over here just pantin' to drop their knickers for you—just itchin' to eatchaup alive, and you go skulkin' off to home—like some weaselly coonhound to Myrtle. Jeeesus."

Watford hung his uniform in one of the metal wardrobe lockers in the bank's basement.

"Christ, man. Ain't you ever got a good look at that woman? I don't mean to be unkind, Charley, but what's a good-lookin' dude like you wastin' your time with a bowwow like that?"

"I like Myrtle."

"Like. Like. Hell, what's sex got to do with liking? You feel sorry for her, that's all. You wanna take care of her, that's one thing. But Christ, that don't mean you have to go home and hold her hand every night. Even Myrtle don't expect you to be faithful. She knows she's plenty lucky. She ain't gonna deny you a little pleasure on the side. Jeeesus. What the hell's the matter with you, Watford? All that poontang out there packed up to the bar, them big tits just itchin' for your palms . . ."

Watford laughed good-naturedly. "Sorry, T.Y. But I'm going home and have a shower and some supper."

". . . watch *Hollywood Squares,* and then, my God, get into bed with Myrtle. Jeeesus, man, be careful. You may wind up marryin' her."

Watford pulled a basque shirt over his head, tucked its elasticized bottom into his trousers and belted up. "I wouldn't worry too much about that," he said and winked sagely.

Bidwell's expression of friendly concern turned slowly to a naughty smirk. "Just so long as it's understood tween the two of you, Charley. Christ . . . I'd hate to see you stuck with . . ."

"Not in the cards, old friend. Trust me." Watford slapped the big man across the shoulder. "Now don't go getting yourself a dose of something out there tonight."

Watford picked up the bag of groceries he'd purchased at lunchtime and started out.

"Hey, Charley," Bidwell called after him. Watford turned, "You thought any more about what I told you?"

"About what?"

" 'Bout what we discussed last week."

Impatience sparked in Watford's eye. "No, I haven't thought any more about it." He stared back at Bidwell.

"Piece of cake, Charley. Candy from a baby. No risk. No involvement. Clean and easy as you please. All we do is collect a nice big fat check at the end."

"Don't do it, T.Y. Don't get yourself messed up. It's not worth it. You don't know these people. You don't know anything about them."

"I don't have to." Bidwell's voice dropped, and he drew closer. Watford took a warm, sweet blast of bourbon from his breath. "All I got to do is say when certain things round here on the premises are gonna be moved off the premises. You get me? Then, just make sure I'm out on my coffee break when and if something happens." He winked at Watford. "That don't strike me as nothin' illegal."

"Nothin' illegal, T.Y. Just an accomplice to the crime. That's all. Just a matter of ten to fifteen years in the pen."

"Who's to say?"

"Not me. But that crowd you've been talkin' to. The first sign of trouble—push comes to shove, you won't see their heels for the dust."

"Oh, Christ, Charley. That ain't gonna happen. All we gotta do is . . ."

"I don't want to hear no more about it, T.Y." Watford waved it off like a puff of bad air. Hoisting his grocery bag in his arms, he started out. "I don't want to know a thing. I've already forgotten you ever spoke to me about it."

19

Nothing happened for several weeks. And by the time it did, Watford had completely forgotten his discussion with Bidwell. He was not at the bank that day, home sick with fever and chills. And that's what made things worse.

Whatever happened (Watford never had the whole story), it was a disaster. The two young thugs who had engineered the stickup were amateurs. It had been their simpleminded intention to interrupt a $300,000 transfer from the bank's vaults to a Wells Fargo truck outside and then divert it to an escape car waiting with a driver out front.

Evidently they'd had an agreement with Bidwell that he make himself scarce during the time planned for interception. Bidwell had done his part of the job—informed the thieves of the exact time of transfer, then intentionally withdrew himself to one of the vaults in the bank's basement where he could be safely out of the way.

The one thing the aspiring holdup men had not counted on was panic—not only that of the clients, but their own as well. The moment one lady started to scream, the younger of the two robbers started to shoot. People scattered in a dozen different directions. There was a blur of motion and a great deal of noise. One of the tellers managed to trip a direct signal to the Kansas City Police Department. At the same time an automatic Klaxon started whooping frantically, inside the bank and out on the street.

That was all the Wells Fargo drivers needed. They decamped at once, followed directly by the escape car, minus the two fledgling holdup men.

Though the two bank robbers sprayed a great deal of fire round the bank, miraculously they managed to hit no one. In three minutes the Kansas City police had the bank surrounded, and the two aspiring thieves in custody. They had given up without a struggle, and to add to the ignominy of it all, in the patrol car going down to the station, one of them burst into tears and immediately implicated Bidwell.

Within the next hour another patrol car was dispatched to the bank and Bidwell was taken into custody. An hour or so later, a plainclothes detective showed up at Watford's residence, informed him of what had happened and told him that Bidwell had been named as an accomplice and was now in custody. He then proceeded to question Watford very closely.

"How come you picked today to stay home?" the detective asked him.

"Because I got sick today." Watford coughed as if to legitimize the claim.

"Sick today, ay?" The detective rolled his eyes merrily. "That's a mighty big coincidence, isn't it, Watford?"

"What's a coincidence?" Watford's mind was racing a mile a minute.

"Why, your getting sick, just like that. On the very day the bank gets fingered. I hear you're something of a hero or something down at First National City. Like, I hear you nailed a couple of would-be James and Dalton brothers yourself. You're supposed to be quite a guy with a heater. Where'd you learn about guns, Watford?"

The more closely the detective interrogated him, the more frightened and confused Watford grew, casting even greater suspicion on himself.

By that time Watford grasped that he was in trouble. His personal assessment of the situation was that Bidwell had panicked and, desperate to save his own skin, had traded off the name of an additional accomplice in exchange for a more lenient sentence. The fact that the detective had not charged him formally, nor even taken him down to the station for further questioning was indication that they still hadn't enough of a case against him. Clearly, parts of Bidwell's story had not added up to the police.

"Okay, Watford. That's all for now." The detective rose and tipped his hat to Myrtle who'd been sitting in the corner pale with fright and close to tears. "I'll have to ask you not to leave town until the investigation is completed."

Something in the way he said it, pointedly, with an edge of sarcasm, suggested to Watford that they were at that very moment running a check with the New York City police and possibly the FBI. In both instances he did not expect that the information contained in his records would sit very well with the Kansas City police. Then, too, there was the touchy matter of his falsified military service in Vietnam.

The moment the detective left, Myrtle began to cry. Chivalrous, even under the worst of circumstances, Watford tried to pacify her. He stroked and patted her, held her like a small child and kissed her, all the while feeling the unmistakable foreshadowings of a deadly migraine.

The moment he felt she had gained sufficient control, he excused himself and went to his room. Once there, he took down from the shelf above the wardrobe closet his physician's bag out of which he quickly withdrew a hypodermic needle. He filled the syringe with a substantial dose of meperidine and unbuttoned his shirt-sleeve. Rolling it up, he clenched his fist several times and amid all the heavy needle tracking on his bare arm, he probed for a clean venipuncture site. When he found the small clean bulge he sought, he jabbed the needle into the heart of it, infused the clear liquid, then deftly withdrew it.

By this time his head felt as if hammers were pounding inside it, trying to break out the wall of the skull. In the little sitting room outside, Myrtle had turned on the TV, attempting to console herself with a daytime quiz show. In the next moment he turned off the light and lay down full length on the unmade bed. Shortly, he knew, Mother Demerol would wave her wand and commence her kindly work.

It started as it always had with the cool spot in the center of his forehead, this followed by a sense of gradual numbing within his skull. The pain was still there, but now mercifully muffled and growing distant.

Shortly after followed a period of muscular relaxation—the opening of clenched fists, the loosening of clamped jaws, the dreamy deconstriction of neck muscles, with the attendant warm rush of blood to the face. Then that sudden surge between his legs; the tautening and bloody engorgement of erectile tissue; that exquisite itch that only Mother Demerol could provide.

". . . escapements are commonly divided into three distinct . . ."

". . . recoil escapements in which the wheel moves backward or recoils, such as the verge escapement in wrist watches . . ."

". . . but I don't understand . . ."

"Dead beat escapements, characterized by the fact that except during the actual impulsion, the wheel remains stationary . . ."

"Lastly, detached escapements . . ."

Watford's head rolled sideways across the warm pillow. Even as the ominously quiet voice hectored him from the shadows beyond, he felt the enormous joy in his loins where hands stroked him lovingly.

"Come away, Charley," Mother said. "Come away with me." She untied her mesh reticule and withdrew from it a small cloisonné pillbox. "We don't have to tolerate this any longer," she said. He wondered at her haggard, fragile beauty. So thin she had become, so pale tissuey transparent that the blue tracery of delicate venation scrawled like calligraphy beneath her dry, taut flesh.

"If he can't appreciate us for what we are, Charley, darling, then let us go where we will be appreciated." She lay him down in the bed beside her, then folded his arms across his chest with an air of elaborate ceremony. "Now close your eyes and stick out your tongue." Her voice was a mischievous, girlish singsong. "Open wide," she giggled. "The way you used to take your cod liver and your vitamins."

He felt her finger press upon the back of his tongue, the involuntary audible gulp which followed, then the tiny bitter lozenge slowly dissolving at the back of his throat.

The detective, a man named Birge, returned the following day. And then again the day after. They went over the material they'd covered during the first interrogation, going exasperatingly round and round in circles.

The more Watford tried to clarify his position, the more, it seemed, he implicated himself with Bidwell and the two bank robbers. Incomprehensibly, he was trying to protect Bidwell, and as he did so, the more he entangled himself in a snare of truths and half-truths.

The detective had begun to smirk a great deal. He grew smug and almost gleefully sarcastic as he watched Watford churn and thrash about in pitfalls of his own creation.

"What do you want from me?" Watford at last threw his hands up in despair. "Am I a suspect?"

"Who said that?"

"Has Bidwell said anything?"

"You tell me."

"How can I tell you? You spoke to him. I didn't. But whatever he said about me, it's not true."

Once again the nasty, cunning wink. "Why would he say anything about you, Watford? You're an innocent man. We all know that."

"I am innocent. But he might have said something out of revenge."

The detective's eyes widened. "Revenge for what? He described you as his best buddy."

"We were friendly."

"Well, then, why would he be looking to screw his best buddy?" With the intonation of those final words, the detective fairly leered.

When at last the man left, Watford's head was pounding dangerously. Myrtle sat off in a corner, huddled in a chair, legs tucked up beneath her. Her pinched, avid features gazed blankly off into space and she appeared to be weighing something very carefully in her mind.

When Watford returned to the bank the following morning, peopled regarded him oddly. Gone was all the easy, joshing banter of former days. All of that "Hi, Charley," cheer was now supplanted by cool nods, uneasy grins and in some instances, naked contempt. Ogilvy, the president and chief operating officer of the bank, characteristically cordial on arrival each morning, was pointedly cold.

It stung him. It stung him badly, for Watford had prized greatly the wide circle of friends and acquaintances he had gained for himself during his short tenure at the bank. It pleased him that so many people were truly fond of him, and that he had their confidence. Now all of that was suddenly gone.

The most hurtful incident occurred that evening at closing. It had been Watford's job to lock up at night. He was therefore entrusted with a full set of keys to all exits and to the outer vault room as well. That night, however, Arbuthnot, the assistant treasurer, came down at closing and informed Watford that he himself would close up.

"I'll need your set of keys, Charley," he said and fixed Watford with a pair of beady, accusatory eyes.

"I can take care of it, Mr. Arbuthnot," Watford said.

"That's all right, Watford. I'll handle opening and closing for the time being. May I have the keys?"

Cheeks burning, eyes filling with shame, Watford dutifully handed over the keys, and though Arbuthnot had suggested that this was only a temporary situation, presumably until all the guilty parties had been arraigned, Watford knew in his heart that even if the cloud of suspicion were completely dispelled, he would never again enjoy the same unquestioning trust from his friends at the bank. The game was up for him at First National City of Kansas.

When he got home that night Myrtle was waiting for him. Still rattled by the events of the past few days, she had spent most of the afternoon drinking. Now she sought solace in Watford, but he was in scarcely any condition to provide it.

She'd gotten into her best dress and had applied, none too tastefully, a great deal of lipstick and mascara. Now she pressed close and stared up at him pleadingly. "Charley, I've had a lousy day. Let's go out and forget all this. Dinner and a few drinks. We'll both feel better. Come on." She tugged like a small child at his sleeve.

Watford stood there dazed, unspeaking. The pounding had resumed in his skull and he thought he was going to be sick. "Myrtle, I don't feel too well," he said in his quietly disarming manner, and left her whimpering in a corner.

The intensity of throbbing in his head had caused his vision to blur. He felt nauseous and dizzy. More alarmingly, when looking at objects he found them all encircled by glaring white halos. Slightly panicked, he started to rummage frantically about the bedroom for his medicine kit.

He took ergotamine in tablets, and the last of his Demerol in liquid form by means of a needle. Then, without bothering to undress, he lay down on the unmade bed in the dark. Myrtle followed shortly after and tried to talk with him.

"Charley, Charley, dear," she whimpered and lay down beside him. "I don't care what you done, darlin'. It don't matter to me. We'll get a lawyer. We can still make a life for ourselves. And I'm not too old yet for kids. You oughta be happy. You deserve to be. I just got the feelin' you ain't been for a long time. Why not just give me a chance? What d'ya say, honey?"

Watford concentrated hard on the mottled shadows shifting liquidly on the ceiling above him. In his shrieking head he could see Arbuthnot's lethal smile. "I'll need your set of keys, Charley." He did not know if it was his head or his heart that hurt him more.

In a vain effort to arouse him, Myrtle threw her arms about him, fastening her cold lips on his neck with the sucking intensity of a pilot fish. But Watford merely lay there, cold, impassive, unfeeling.

What was he doing here, he brooded, next to this haggard creature with the avid eyes and the sharp ferret features? She had told him when he met her that she was twenty-nine. But he knew she was closer to forty and had simply adjusted her age to something she perceived as more acceptable to his thirty-two years.

He had a sudden fleeting image of the pretty Pam Am ticket agent at Kennedy that wet April evening he had fled New York. The sparkling gray eyes, the pretty teeth, the soft cowl of wheat-white hair bathed in the cobalt blue of the terminal. He could have had her. He knew that, just as he knew he could have had so many—so pretty, so fair, so lovely to hold.

And yet, something drew him endlessly, fatally downward; always pairing him with the outcast and unseemly, bonding him in fatal unity with all the misbegotten freaks of nature. Like Myrtle Wells, he was part of the great universal freak show. Why? He used to tell himself that there was something chivalric about making his special cause the castouts and the undefended. Like some hapless Don Quixote, it was a lovely, self-serving fiction used to justify the whole catalog of his many and even self-fabricated personal failures. He saw at last that pity for others, of itself, practiced as a vocation, was more like self-pity, and had made a loveless shambles of his life. But he realized as well that knowledge and self-awareness, in his case at least, would not change a blessed thing.

Whimpering, clinging to him for dear life like a chastised child seeking forgiveness for its mischief, at last Myrtle fell asleep. Shortly her jaw fell open and she started to snore. Some scorched effluvia of malt Scotch and cigarettes rose from her mouth as if from some dank rotting place within her.

20

He left early the following morning while she was still asleep, packing his few belongings in his canvas duffle—shirts and underwear, toilet items, his two or three medical reference books and, of course, the physician's black bag. The Pan Am purser's uniform, freshly cleaned and pressed, as he always kept it, still encased in an envelope of cellophane, he would carry on a hanger over his shoulder.

Moments before departing he cracked the door of the bedroom

and looked in upon her. The room was dark and chill, and from the rumplement of the bed rose a faint distant snoring.

He had managed, in the time he had been there, to put together nearly a thousand dollars in savings. Now he peeled off seven hundred-dollar bills from his cache, clipped them together, and slipped them into a First National City of Kansas envelope. On the outside of the envelope he scrawled the date and the words "For Myrtle, Love, Charley." Then, propping the envelope against a glass cruet on the Formica breakfast table, he hoisted his bag, slung his purser's uniform over his shoulder and departed.

Although Detective Birge's passion for interrogation appeared to have flagged noticeably in the past week, as far as Watford knew, the police still considered him a prime suspect in the attempted holdup of First National City. The truth of the matter was that Birge's superiors had told him to forget about Watford. All of their attempts to get Bidwell to implicate his friend had, in fact, failed and Watford was no longer a suspect. Birge, of course, had not bothered to pass that information on to Watford.

Watford's situation, as he himself viewed it, seemed desperate. He had absolutely no idea where he was going, no destination, little money and, more importantly, he was out of Demerol and already experiencing the scary precursors of deprivation.

For all of its seeming desperation, there was something in the situation that he vaguely enjoyed. It had a kind of exciting chanciness. Like shooting craps in a casino, it carried with it the potential for either stunning victory or catastrophic loss. He didn't mind that. He rather liked the idea of starting in anew somewhere. All he asked was a fair crack at it.

By 7:00 A.M. he was out at a small suburban air terminal with perhaps a dozen other passengers. It was a gray, forlorn little operation set in a wide arid disk of prairie. There were perhaps two or three small buildings, a squat gray control tower, a couple of World War II–vintage Quonset huts, and a red wind-socket flapping disconsolately in the chill morning breeze. The runways, crisscrossing out on the field, looked untended and unkempt, with a tatty carpet of brownish grass growing up between them.

Watford checked the arrivals and departures on the flight board. The only thing going out at once was a Frontier Airlines twin-engine prop plane flying directly from Kansas City up to Denver. He had no wish to go to Denver, but just at that moment Watford spotted a KCPD patrol car drawn up outside the main building. He thought about Denver for a moment and quickly decided he was going there.

95

Marching up to the Frontier reservations desk, he inquired if anything was open on their 7:20 to Denver.

The ticket agent smiled wryly over the rims of his spectacles. "At this hour of the morning, everything's open."

Watford made a conspicuous display of his Pam Am purser's uniform which he carried slung across his shoulder. He explained that he had to get up to Denver to pick up a flight. He was a little short of cash, however. Did Frontier have a reciprocal exchange arrangement with Pan Am for their employees?

The agent had never heard of anything like an interairline ticket-exchange program for employees, but Pam Am was the big time and he wasn't anxious to show his ignorance. "You have any identification?" the agent asked.

Watford flashed his old Pan Am ID Card with his photograph and number boldly imprinted on the glossy plastic. The agent never noted the expiration date.

"Hold on," he said. "I'll see if I can't get you on."

The red Frontier twin-engine prop plane was sitting out on the runway. Watford could see it there through the big observation windows, being refueled, baggage being hoisted up through its cargo bays. Glancing over his shoulder, he noted that a policeman had gotten out of the patrol car and was staring into the terminal through the glass doors.

The Frontier agent had dialed directly out to the plane and in the next moment had the captain on the phone. He explained Watford's situation. They exchanged a few pleasantries, then the agent hung up.

"Captain says he'd be delighted to have your company up to Denver." He scribbled something on a ticket, stamped a boarding pass and handed it to Watford. "Leave your bag right there. I'll see to it that it gets on board."

Watford handed over his bag. "Hope I can return the favor someday."

"Hope you can, too," the agent laughed. "Good flight, Mr. Watford."

By that time the policeman was walking into the terminal. He appeared to be looking for someone. Without further adieus, Watford made for the large glass doors leading out to the field. He swung through them, descended a flight of steps and stepped out onto the cold tarmac of the service area. Still carrying his Pan Am purser's uniform slung across his shoulders, he ambled out across the weed-strewn field to the Douglas 340, just that moment beginning to spin its props in preparation for a takeoff.

The flight up to Denver was a little over an hour. It was a smooth, uneventful run, part of which Watford spent up in the cabin having coffee and crullers as special guest of the captain.

On arrival at Denver International, Watford thanked the captain and the crew of Frontier's flight 270 and disembarked. Once inside the terminal he made his way to a mezzanine lavatory before claiming his luggage. Standing at a sink he washed his face, carefully combed his hair and then dried himself thoroughly at one of those hot-air machines. Outside once again, looming dead ahead, he found himself confronted by a clear Lucite balustrade running the full length of the mezzanine. He walked slowly to it and looked down over the swarm of humanity flowing through the main lobby of the terminal below.

He stood there for several minutes, a dazed, dreamy expression on his face, the hint of an odd little smile playing about the corners of his mouth. He lifted his right leg over the balustrade, then his left, then stepped easily, almost unthinkingly out into space, dropping forty feet to the hard terrazzo floor below. During the descent the single thought that occupied his mind was the fervent hope that he would not fall upon and hurt anyone.

"All right, all right, coming through. Give us some room here. Give the guy some air. . . ."

A blur of color swarmed before his woozy vision. He lay flat on the floor, people crowding and pushing all about him, the wail of sirens coming at him over cold empty distances.

"Oh, Charley, Charley, what have you gone and done now?"

"Out of the way, for Chrissake. Let the stretcher through."

"Charley, Charley. What a fool thing to go and do. Rolling in poison ivy just so they'd have to put you in the infirmary. What's your father going to say? Sent home from camp like that. I swear, I just don't know what I can tell him this time."

Someone kneeling above him. Warm breath beside his ear. Strong, gentle, reassuring hands. He felt himself being lifted and rolled onto a canvas.

"Jesus, what the hell happened to him?"

"Guy over there says he just stepped off the mezzanine."

"He's okay. He's okay. Give the guy some air, for Chrissake."

"Okay. The show's over. Everyone go home now."

"Charley, how could you?"

"We're going to take you down to the hospital, Mr. Watford." The warm breath in his ear again. "Nothin' to worry about. Looks like you may have busted an ankle. Now when I say raise your hips and roll over, you do just that. Got it? Good. Now raise."

In the ambulance he passed out from the pain, but not before he'd managed to extract a dose of Demerol from the accompanying intern.

"Fracture of the right calcaneous," a voice came at him out of the dark. "Not serious but painful. We'll have to operate to pin the heel. You better plan on being with us a few weeks. Is there anyone you want us to notify? Family? Friends?"

"How long?" Watford asked dazedly.

"Two weeks, at least," the doctor replied.

Watford affected dejection; inwardly he was rejoicing. Safety, Reprieve. Quittance from all further worry and the chase.

"Need something for the pain, Doctor," he mumbled.

"Wasn't he given anything in the ambulance?"

"Demerol, Doctor," Watford heard a nervous nurse explain.

"Only two hundred milligrams," Watford, wincing, half-rose off the cot. "It's barely touched me."

"We'll take care of that right away. Nurse, have the dispensary send up . . ."

"Demerol," Watford gasped.

"Sure— You have any allergies?"

Watford's head rolled left and right.

"Nurse, let's start him on meperidine. Fifty milligrams. Tablets."

"Liquid. I prefer the liquid. Intravenous. Seven hundred milligrams."

The bed felt good, and after the shot there was no pain. Only the cool numb spot in the center of his forehead, and voices softly muted and distant. The cruel vise of anxiety had suddenly relaxed and he was at peace between the stiff medicinal-smelling sheets of the hospital bed. He had come home again.

21

May 13, 1981

Dear Commissioner Dowd:

I've tried to write this letter four times already . . . I . . .

Dear Commissioner Dowd:

In regard to the series of deaths from falling objects over the past five years, it has come to my . . .

Dear Commissioner:

I wish to dispute directly the findings of the 6th Homicide Detectives with special regard to . . .

Purple with exasperation, Mooney shredded the brown paper bag upon which he'd been scribbling, wadded it in his meaty fist and flung it aside. It hit the wall with a dull thud. The lank marmalade tabby dozing just below the point of impact raised its head, flicked an ear, yawned widely and dropped back to sleep.

It was 10:00 A.M. of a Sunday morning. Mooney sat at the kitchen table in his underwear. Coffee mug, a bag of greasy crullers, a half-dozen heavily notated *Racing Forms* strewn across the streaked plastic top. At that moment a kettle shrieking to a boil behind him and a battered thirties Philco portable tuned in to WCBS for the racing news were the total components of his universe.

Mooney snatched up the crumpled sheet of wax paper in which the crullers had been wrapped. Smoothing the edges of it carefully, he snatched the handicapping pencil from behind his ear and was ready once again to compose.

In addition to his morning costume of skivvy and boxer shorts, he wore black half-length socks gartered at his bulging calves and highly polished black oxfords reserved exclusively for Sundays and the track.

The *coup de maître* to the entire morning ensemble was a black shoulder holster containing a .45-Colt service revolver strapped like phylacteries across his capacious middle. Why Mooney felt the need for munitions in his underwear at that time of a Sabbath morning was not immediately apparent. It might have had something to do with the feeling of vulnerability that near nudity produced in him. Clothed, the man could be as brazen as a peacock; unclothed, he appeared suddenly embarrassed and defenseless.

Guns notwithstanding, there was something oddly touching about Mooney in his outsized underwear, scrawling figures through a track of confectioners' sugar on a sheet of greasy wax paper, lips moving as he strained for words that might achieve some semblance of literate expression.

Dear Mike:
I don't ask favors. Nor am I one to complain, and you will agree I make no waves. If I am pushed, however, I push back. I know just where I stand with the Force, and pretty much what I can expect from it. I don't like for the most part the men of Midtown South, and I sure don't expect them to like me.

I write now with regard to the five deaths over the past six years in the Hell's Kitchen area, and to protest the reluctance of the 6th Homicide Detectives to rule conclusively that death in each case was intentional, cold-blooded murder, due instead to accidental causes such as masonry falling naturally from buildings onto the street. Now I ask you, is that not ridiculous?

I myself in the past year have interrogated three people, all of whom claim to have seen a possible suspect. Two actually saw the suspect at the scene of the crime. A third saw a man fleeing from the scene of the crime.

True, one was a kid about eleven years old. The second and third, however, strike me as solid. One actually saw the possible suspect on the roof at the actual time of a fatal drop. The other observed a suspect on his fire escape moments after the drop.

How the 6th Homicide guys could ignore this, or wave it away like it didn't exist just for the sake of "what's easy" so as to classify this as accidental is beyond . . .

The old Philco crackled. Phil Kearney, the racing commentator, was going over the field at Aqueduct for that day. Mooney dropped his pencil, reached across to raise the volume and listened.

". . . Eighth race . . . 1 ⅛ miles (1:47), allowances purse, $11,000. Three-year-olds and upward." Mooney snatched up his pencil again and started to write, this time on the back of a nearby cleaning ticket. "Claiming or starter. Three-year-olds—119 pounds; older, 122 pounds. The announcer droned on in high nasalities. . . . "Value to winners, $6600; second, $2420; third, $1320; fourth, $660. Mutual Pool $240,079."

Mooney scribbled hectically, glanced at his watch, then once again snatched up his draft to the commissioner.

> . . . The real reason for my writing is that I believe beyond any reasonable doubt that these five deaths were in no way "accidental." I have studied the files on all five cases and I am pretty much convinced they are the work of some kind of nut case. Maybe a religious freak of some sort who performs something like a ritual sacrifice once a year or so.
>
> I have noted, and called the attention of my colleagues to this, the royal dunderheads of Manhattan South and the 6th Homicide, all to no avail. The fact that all these fatal drops occur without exception in the spring of the year, three having occurred in April and two in May, appear to make no impression on them.
>
> It is now, as of this writing, May 13th. So far April has been quiet, but I now have the strongest gut feeling that sometime this month our rooftop friend will strike again. I see no sense appealing to my buddies. They are mostly dim bulbs with nothing but suet between their ears. Now is the time for a full investigation. I have a plan. May I talk with you? This is urgent. Believe me, this nut case is going to strike again soon.
>
> I am willing to lay 6 to 2 odds it happens on or around the 16th. The offer is open to you and all comers.
>
> Respectfully,
> Francis X. Mooney

22

"Pardon me. Is this seat taken?"

"Which seat?"

"The seat right here. The one with your coat on it."

Mooney pretended not to notice the empty seat beside him, despite the fact that it was blatantly occupied by his neatly folded coat. He looked up from his *Racing Form*. The woman towering above him pointed to the coat.

"That is your coat, isn't it?"

"That coat?" Mooney made a vain effort to disassociate himself from the garment.

"That's right. That coat right there."

"Oh, sure. The seat," Mooney grumbled, then lugged his coat up and laid it down untidily across his knees. "Help yourself."

"You're very kind."

Mooney grumbled something and screwed his gaze to the *Form*, while the lady settled beside him. She was a tall, impressive figure, nearly six feet, not fat, by any means, but amply proportioned. Everything about her, in fact, was of noble scale—legs, torso, head, all crowned with a mane of startling red hair, the shade of which was absolutely natural.

Her features contained the same air of bold extravagance—the large, well-shaped nose, the fine expanse of eyes, a full, well-shaped mouth, all framed within large, well-sculpted bones. Tousled, slightly overpainted, she had the blousy, unbuttoned look of some latter-day Mistress Quickly. Mooney was instantly aware of something heavy and sweet wafting upward from beneath her outer clothing. Seated at last, she plucked a copy of the *Form* out of the

102

depths of a deep, reticulated bag. Propping onto the bridge of her nose, the tortoiseshell lorgnette dangling from a chain round her neck, she proceeded to scan the charts.

Mooney was peeved. It was not merely the awkward inconvenience of having to drape his coat across his lap. More pointedly, it was the strong sense of disapprobation he felt in the presence of women at the track. Particularly betting women. His own mother would never have dreamed of going to the track, no less betting there.

Several times he glanced up from his *Form* to gaze out at the drab monotony of the landscape sliding backward past the window—the cheek-by-jowl congestion of sprawling barrack-residences, row upon row of bogus colonial facades, followed shortly by the little saltbox houses farther out, and then the gaudy blur of billboard posters all along the tracks.

His wandering attention returned to his *Racing Form*, and he did some quick pencil work. Occasionally, out of the corner of his eye, he permitted himself a glimpse at the heavily notated *Form* of the lady seated beside him. Page after page was completely covered with a series of cryptic symbols and hieroglyphics—stars, pyramids, crosses, squares—all set down beside the names of horses, along with a great deal of fractional and algebraic computation.

Smirking at the notion of another "method" player, Mooney noted the choices she had circled for the first four races—Wild Joker, Fife and Drum, Daring Baby, Not Too Well. The latter was a turkey that had been running in $3000 company for most of the year, had recently been dropped to $1500, and in his last outing was trounced at 21 to 1. Mooney had to smother his amusement.

"What do you think?"

"Beg pardon?"

"I said, what do you think?"

Mooney was a little puzzled. "What do I think about what?"

"About my picks so far."

"How would I know your picks so far?"

"You've been studying them for the past quarter of an hour."

Mooney felt a rush of color to his face. "What the hell would I be studying your picks for?"

"Trying to cop a winner. I saw you clear as day, peeking under your hand there." Behind the glasses her large gray eyes fixed him with an expression of shrewd amusement.

"Listen. . . I can assure you . . ."

"Come on," she waved him off. "What do you think of Daring Baby in the third, and Not Too Well in the fourth? You can tell me. I don't mind."

"I don't mind either." Mooney reddened. "I don't care what horses you picked in the third and fourth." He snapped wide the pages of his *Form* and resumed his study.

"But you *were* spying on my *Form.*"

"Have it your way." Mooney spoke very softly, trying to control his mounting irritation. "Listen—I can pick my own horses very well, thank you, and I don't need any dumb-ass methods . . . oh . . ." Even as the words sputtered from his lips, he knew he'd been caught.

The lady beamed triumphantly.

Mooney turned a beet-red. Just as he was about to fling a choice epithet her way, he felt the rattling car decelerate, and one of the conductors came through bawling "Aqueduct."

After he'd got inside and secured his favorite seat in the first row of the First Tier, there was still time to go down to the stables, have a stroll round the paddocks, view the livestock and chat with the grooms and jockeys—one of the few subcultures of mankind with which Mooney felt a strong affinity.

Still smarting from his encounter with the redheaded lady on the Aqueduct Bullet, he sat down at a field stand and had several bourbon old-fashioneds just to take the edge off of things. Afterward, somewhat mellowed, he ambled onto the field for a look at the track. Knowing the Big A and the track bias like the lines of his own face, in warm dry weather such as they were enjoying that day, Mooney sought horses with early speed and inside post positions.

For the first race, a seven-furlong sprint, Mooney liked a three-year-old filly called Endgame. Her past performances showed she'd been unable to win on the main track for $5000, was tried out in an $8000 turf race and won by a length and a half. At a quick glance down in the paddocks, she looked a bit cheaper to Mooney than the rivals she was meeting today. But the filly she'd defeated March 14, Sagittarius, came back ten days later and won the $13,000 claiming race on the grass against males. Her victory suggested that Endgame was a legitimate $13,000 animal who was undervalued when she ran for an $8000 price tag, but was running at her proper level today. She couldn't have found an easier spot. All she had to do was beat one chronic loser as well as a generally weak field with animals of limited luster. Mooney wanted her.

Up at the betting windows he waited in line to bet $20 to win and $20 to place on Endgame. While he was collecting his change and stubs his attention was diverted by a commanding voice betting $50 to win and $50 to place on Wild Joker. There was no need for him to turn in order to see who was placing the bet. His neck retracted deeply into his collar. He took his stubs and was about to skulk off when the lady called out to him, "You still looking over my shoulder for a winner?"

Several people on line turned. Mooney made a sour face at her and started down to the First Tier. The bugle fanfare had already sounded at the post when Mooney settled into his seat. Through his binoculars he studied Endgame, taking satisfaction in her superbly favored inside post position of number 2. The filly was quiet and conveyed to him a sense of nicely controlled energy. She was clearly not champing or tossing about, squandering her energy before the race. Her ears were not pinned back as she strode up to the post. Instead, she carried them pricked and upright as if she were trying to hear something. To Mooney that suggested an *alert* creature without any indication of post-time flopsweat. Also her lively tail swish said she was feeling good, and she carried her head straight, not to the side and down, the way a horse in pain does. She wore no bandages on her front legs to suggest there was anything amiss with the tendons. When she put her hooves down, they grabbed the ground firmly, just the way a healthy pair of horse feet should. Mooney was pleased.

Several spots down he was delighted to see that Wild Joker was way off to the outside at position 8, bumping about inside her gate, thrashing and tossing her head and jolting her jockey about in his traces.

In the next moment there was a loud crack, the gates opened and a huge roar went up. At the same time that Mooney watched Endgame lunge out smartly into second position, he was aware of a slight disturbance just off to the side. He glanced up and saw the redheaded lady edging her way through the aisle with a lot of irritated people rising to let her through. Mooney's heart sank as he realized she was moving toward him, undoubtedly to the single empty seat to his right.

She'd seen him before he'd seen her, and as she approached there was the hint of some immensely satisfying private joke dancing about in her eye. In the next moment she was there, towering above him. "Is that your coat?"

Mooney glowered and once again went through the tiresome business of removing his coat from the empty seat to make room for her.

"I hope this doesn't inconvenience you," she said in that vaguely mocking manner as she settled in and watched the faded topcoat return to his lap.

"Not at all," Mooney growled, not looking at her. "My knees were cold anyway."

The field had just turned the half and Endgame was holding her own nicely. She was running no more than a neck behind the front-runner.

"Which is yours?" she asked.

"Endgame," he muttered, his eyes glued to the binoculars.

"She'll fade in the stretch. Probably finish fifth," the lady remarked unemotionally. "Where's Wild Joker?"

"Seventh. About twelve lengths out."

"She'll be fourth at the turn and cross second at the finish."

Mooney never once looked at her or took his eye from the binoculars. He knew Wild Joker for the next best thing to a sucker horse. She hadn't finished in the money her last four times out. Her running lines were those of a quitter after anything beyond four furlongs, and her bloodlines were unexceptional. Her best time had been a run on grass.

"Here she comes now," the lady remarked with infuriating self-assurance. It was about then that Endgame dropped back to third, and from there lapsed into her humiliating fade.

Wild Joker crossed the wire second just as the lady had predicted. She'd come on like a firecracker, gaining four lengths in the stretch. She paid $18.60 to place.

Amid a racket of cheers from the approving stands, the redhead rose, looking very pleased with herself. Mooney smoldered like old burning rags. He knew she had just won over $900 while he was out of pocket some $40 and that was unpardonable.

The second race was a repetition of the first. This time it was $600 she won on a horse that Mooney would not have touched with a bargepole—Fife and Drum—while he himself dropped $100 on a three-year-old called Seraphim that he'd been watching his last five times out and had looked upon as a solid blue chip.

Whenever the lady won she had the disconcerting habit of jabbing her elbow into Mooney's rib. When she hit the third race exacta she took down over $5000. By that time Mooney was out roughly $500 and the rib closest to the redhead was badly bruised. Despite that, over the past several races, he had begun cautiously, albeit begrudgingly, to look upon her with a new and somewhat heightened sense of regard.

A loss of $500 in the face of such clear-cut blatant success had shaken his self-confidence, so when she offered to buy him a drink at the break before the fourth race, he was somewhat astonished to find himself accepting.

They edged their way through the crowd down to the field bar and commandeered a small table. Her name was Mrs. Baumholz she told him right off. "Frances Baumholz. But my friends call me Fritzi."

"Fritzi?" Mooney made a face of delighted scorn.

"Kind of a nickname. My husband gave it to me years ago, and I guess it stuck. What might your name be?"

"Mooney."

She waited as though expecting more. "Mooney?"

"Francis. Like you. But my friends call me Frank."

She leaned back in her seat and gave him a long, unflinching stare. "You look like a cop."

"What was your first clue?"

Mrs. Baumholz pointed to his shoes. "The shoes. Those shiny oxfords. They're a dead giveaway."

"Remarkable," Mooney muttered sourly.

"How old are you?"

"Fifty-eight." He couldn't understand for the life of him why he lied.

"You're pretty worn round the ears for fifty-eight, aren't you, Mooney?" she went on.

"I've lived hard."

"And you're far too heavy for a man that age."

"And you've got lipstick smeared all over your incisors," he snapped right back.

Just then the waiter came and served them their bourbon old-fashioneds. She was a widow, she told him. Her husband had died several years ago and left her with a small but prosperous little pub called Fritzi's Balloon up on Lexington Avenue at Ninety-first. She lived around Yorkville. Her only real pleasure in life now was the horses. She and her husband used to go to the track all the time and they developed this system, you see.

Mooney stared disconsolately down at the limp fruit rinds at the bottom of his drink, listening with martyred patience as she proceeded to explain.

"I call it the N Gambit," she said. "Starting strong, fading back, then coming on in the finish. Gaining three, maybe four lengths in the stretch. Have you ever seen horses like that? It's beautiful. You can see it in the running lines if you look for that pattern. And if the horse finished out of the money his last one or two times out, that's a good sign. That means he's ready to go cash on you."

Mooney's stubby fingers drummed the tabletop, full of sticky rings left by innumerable other glasses. He was staring abstractedly out into the middle distance where a hoard of grounds keepers were sweeping the badly churned track. "You done pretty good so far by it today," he said. "So why the hell you tellin' me all this?"

The question appeared to surprise her. "I see no reason why I shouldn't share good fortune with friends. The track cashier has more than enough for the two of us." Her large merry eyes challenged his.

Mooney continued to study the orange rinds at the bottom of his glass as though he were reading auguries. "Want another?"

"Sure. There's time."

Mooney signaled the waiter for refills, then with chin cradled in his palm, he fretted vaguely. "So what does this system of yours pick for the fourth?" he asked with cool disinterest.

"Not Too Well."

Mooney shook his head despairingly. "What virtue can you possibly see in an animal that's lost each of his last eight races by a dozen lengths or more?"

"That's just it," Mrs. Baumholz accepted her second old-fashioned from the waiter and waxed enthusiastic. "Don't you see that the jockey and the trainer have just been holding him back till the price is right? Remember the N Gambit. Take it from me, Mooney, the odds are going to be at least twenty to one if not better. That horse is ready. Who are you betting?"

Mooney hesitated. It was unheard of for him to share information. "I kind of liked Doctor Dallas."

Her arms rose heavenward in a gesture of futility. "Pathetic."

"What's pathetic?"

"It's so obvious. So he's finished third seven times in his first nine starts. But he's never won. Either he can't or he's unwilling. He's got no guts."

"No guts? Come on. He earned $26,000 last year. You call that pathetic? That's plenty guts enough for me, sister. What the hell do you know anyway?"

Mrs. Baumholz opened her purse a crack, revealing wads of large-denomination bills crammed in up to the gunnels.

"So you got lucky," Mooney fumed. "That won't last."

She shrugged her shoulders and tossed off her drink. "Suit yourself, my friend."

Just then the warning buzzer flashed. Mooney reached for their tab, but Mrs. Baumholz insisted upon paying, and Mooney didn't protest too long. They rushed up to the windows to place their bets. Mrs. Baumholz bet a hundred on Not Too Well to win and another hundred to place.

Mooney standing behind her with his last $200 was going through a crisis of confidence. Stepping up to the window he peered hard into the face of the cashier behind the cage—a small, troll-like creature with a high voice and disapproving eyes.

"Yes?"

Mooney stood there, speechless, gaping at the man.

"Your horse, sir. Horse, please. There are people waiting."

Mooney stood there swelling visibly beneath his clothing, his mouth and jaws working uselessly. "Not Too Well," he blurted out at last. "A hundred to win, a hundred to show."

When he turned again, Mrs. Baumholz was waiting there, grinning

108

triumphantly. "Now that didn't hurt, did it?" She took his arm as they hurried back to their seats.

As the horses moved up to the post, Mooney had his first intimation of disaster. Not Too Well was in the extreme outside position. His ears were down. His coat was wet. His tail drooped and he was bucking slightly, giving his jockey a difficult time nosing him into the gate.

"Relax, Mooney." Mrs. Baumholz quickly caught in him the signs of premature regret. "That's high spirits. Nothing more."

He whimpered slightly to himself.

"Look at those odds." She jabbed him in the rib cage with her elbow, directing his gaze to the tote board. "Twenty-six to one. I told you. Didn't I tell you, Mooney? Remember the N."

"Right, right. Remember the N," Mooney muttered morosely. He tried to capture some of her self-assurance.

There was a loud crack. The gates went up. The field surged out in a cloud of dust and thundered up the track. All except Not Too Well who lumbered out, appeared to have regretted his decision and started back. He had the look of a person who discovers he's boarded the wrong train just as the doors are closing.

The jockey atop him, a tiny doll-like figure in red silks, flailed his arms wildly and kicked his heels into the animal. A high, falsetto burst of Puerto Rican obscenities wafted up at them from the track below as Not Too Well cantered into a side rail and caromed off. Next he proceeded to rotate.

Mooney glared incredibly down at the spectacle on the track. Roars of laughter rippled all about them in the stands. Mrs. Baumholz's characteristic animation had deserted her. Instead, she had grown very pensive. Staring dead ahead at the horse still spinning circles near the gate, the jockey lurching about on his back, Mooney watched his last $200 fly off into the sunset. When at last he spoke, his voice was civil and very quiet. "It looks like Not Too Well ain't too well, don't it?"

Mrs. Baumholz attempted to muster up some of her unfailing good cheer. "Well, can you beat that?"

"No, ma'm." Mooney shook his head in baffled wonderment. "I can't beat that. If I lived for the next thousand years, I don't believe I could beat that. It's very rare one is ever privileged to witness anything quite like that."

For the first time that day Fritzi Baumholz was speechless. The rest of the field was now going into the final stretch. From where they sat they couldn't see who was leading the pack, but Tribal Code was the name that kept crackling over the loudspeaker. "Tribal Code ... Tribal Code ... And it's Tribal Code ... followed by ..."

A loud roar went up as they tried to hear the second name. The tote board, however, was flashing a red light like an arterial pulse—number 9, Doctor Dallas, paying $9.40.

Mooney lumbered heavily to his feet and stood glowering down at Mrs. Baumholz. He swelled visibly, a balloon dangerously inflating. His brow was dark and fearsome.

There was nothing much Mrs. Baumholz could do but stare back and giggle a bit queasily. "Well, those things do happen."

Vile words racketed about in Mooney's head. They struggled to make their way past his lips, only to emerge in a series of breathy gasps.

When it became apparent that he was on the verge of suffocation, he snatched up his coat, cast a final withering glance at Mrs. Baumholz, then crashed heavily out the aisle, trampling anything unfortunate enough to be in his path.

"Mr. Mooney, Mr. Mooney," he heard her cry after him several times above the roar of the crowd. He would not deign to turn. He just kept moving ahead with the most disdainful bearing he could muster as he made his clumsy outraged way toward the exits.

23

It was nearly dusk when he reached the house. The street outside was gray and bleak. The branches of trees dark and full-leafed looked like thumb smears on the gray chalk sky.

He had come on the subway from the Port Authority Building. Walking from Queens Boulevard, then rounding the corner from Continental Avenue to Sutter Street, he experienced a sharp visceral spasm, like the cramps he used to feel as a child before school examinations. His tread slowed and his eyes squinted against the swiftly descending light. He was certain that the police patrol car that had been staked out there, awaiting him ten months earlier, would undoubtedly still be there now.

His heel aching from where it had been pinned, he limped down Hauser Street to number 724. The house was there, seemingly just as he'd left it, but with that forlorn and vaguely sinister air of vacancy. In his absence the little patch of front lawn had run amok. On the front door, stuck under the brass knocker, was an invoice for a recent oil delivery. A variety of circulars and throwaways were stuffed beneath the jamb. When he turned the key in the triple lock and opened the door, it stuck for having been shut so long. Only when he leaned a shoulder against it and heaved, did it yield with a harsh ripping sound. The door swung open and the momentum of his force propelled him inward, into the dank, musty gloom.

The house had been shut for nearly a year, and something in it smelled faintly of sewerage. Wavering on the threshold, slightly winded from his exertions, he stood peering upward at the rooms above, as if he half-expected some cheerful voice of greeting— "Charley dear, is that you?" The echo of his mother's voice trilled ghostly and musical through the vacant rooms. "How was school, darling?"

Something in him, something foreboding and wary, made him linger on the threshold. He was not afraid of the ghosts that dwelled there. On the contrary, he yearned for some kind of reunion with them. No, this was more a sinking feeling—some presentiment of failing fortune. The desolation he felt sprang from an awareness that for him there were no more places left to go. With a sigh of resignation, he flicked the hall light on and stepped inside.

There was not much to do once the water and heat were turned on. He heard the old furnace kick over in the basement, followed by the cozy rumble of the motor starting to heat water and fire up the boiler.

In the kitchen he discovered that one of the glass panes in the back door had been broken. Shards of glass lay shattered on the linoleum floor, beneath the door, and for a moment he imagined that the house had been burgled. The door itself remained locked, however, and so he concluded that the breakage had been due to wind or, possibly, a rock thrown by a child.

In the refrigerator he found an open jar of pickles that had gone soft and disintegrated in their brine. In addition, there was an opened jar of raspberry preserves, and a half pack of Tip Top bread mantled over with a lacy green furze. The freezer compartment was crystaled with ice run rampant. Several cartons of instant suppers lay about entombed in frost. Watford prized one out from behind the stalactites by means of a screwdriver, then left it on the sink top to defrost.

Even before he changed clothes and unpacked his few belongings, he went about the tiresome, but to him almost habitual, routine of

111

winding and setting the clocks—a routine that had been his job since boyhood when his father had assigned him the task of keeping all the clocks in his collection running. Why he still felt an obligation to do so, nearly twenty years after his father's death, was a mystery to him. At one time there had been nearly two hundred such clocks, but since the elder Watford's death the number had dwindled to possibly twenty-five of his very favorites, the others having been sold off from time to time as a means of raising money. Still, there were old French and English clocks, fine antique German and Italian timepieces, a venerable Yankee grandfather clock, hewn of polished oak and honeyed chestnut, that bonged its stately horary out of a noble brass throat. Other clocks were wrought of marble and porphyry, doré, jade and malachite.

His favorite by far bore a Phaeton driving the chariot of the sun across the sky. The bronze lariat of his reins rippled above the haunches of a pair of rearing stallions, and within the geat spoked wheel of the chariot, the polished porcelain clockface proclaimed the hours in fine black Roman numerals. Turning the windup key in its face, a bright clear bell chimed the hour of seven into the gloomy solitude of the house.

"First quarter-bell, G-sharp. Diameter, three feet nine and one-half inches. Weight one ton, one hundredweight.

"Second quarter-bell, F-sharp. Diameter, four feet zero inches. Weight one ton, six hundredweight."

"And now, Charley . . ."

"Dear God, please be with me now." Palms sweating. Stomach fluttering. "Third quarter-bell, E-natural. Diameter four feet six inches. Weight one ton, thirteen hundredweight."

"Good."

"Fourth quarter-bell. B-natural. Diameter, six feet zero inches. Weight . . ."

"Very good. Very good."

Exhilaration. Deliverance. The fist crushing his heart suddenly relaxed. The voice receded through the darkened upper rooms as he ascended the stairs.

In the upstairs bath adjoining his bedroom he found the cause of the broken kitchen window—a sparrow drowned in the nearly empty, rust-ringed bowl of the toilet. One of its wings was tucked close to its side; the other was fanned out, extended as if it had struggled to fly. Carefully he reached in and lifted it out, then held the small wet thing dripping above the sink. The head with its damp matted feathers lay cushioned on his palm, eyes closed beneath a thin yellow membrane. The yellow beak and the tiny jagged claws, thin as wire and dripping commode water, filled him with an incomprehensible sadness.

Unpacked, washed and changed, he limped back downstairs and prepared for himself a half-cooked and execrable frozen supper of beef Stroganoff that he had found in the freezer. As of then he had no plan, and very little in the way of resources to develop any prospects, assuming he had any. Of the money he'd earned in Kansas he had barely any left. Most of it had gone to Myrtle—and then into transportation home. The hospital where he had recuperated for nearly two weeks would shortly be after him, once they'd discovered that the medical insurance he presented them was fraudulent and out of date.

Once more he had come home, just as he always had—when his spirits were down, and adversity dogged him, and the world had given him another strapping. Retreat to the bosom of his mother's house. No money. No friends, No prospects.

He had been lonely before. But this was not just basic loneliness. He was not yearning for a friendly face or the reassuring pressure of a cordial hand. This was something larger and more disquieting. He glimpsed for a moment, or thought he did, an unfamiliar landscape. A terrain he'd never trod before. Icy, precipitous, inhospitable, unpeopled. A territory of boundless earth and sky untraversed by any other save himself.

He forked the last of the gluey, semigelid Stroganoff into his mouth and chewed disconsolately, like a weary old plow horse feeding in its yokes. Shortly he rose, carried the dishes to the sink and rinsed them under the coughing spigots.

24

It was at Forty-seventh and Seventh where he found the cinder block. It had been left in a pile of debris at a construction site where a new luxury office tower was going up. In one of those reticulated wire trash baskets, he found a paper bag and wrapped the block inside it. He carried the package against his chest. It gave him the appearance of a retired widower carrying home a bag of groceries.

At Eighth Avenue and Forty-third a wonderful calm had settled upon him. He was surrounded by lights and bustling humanity but within himself he had reached a zone of impenetrable quiet. Something had been reconciled and now it was no longer necessary to resist the tug of the leash. The tug was there, gentle but unrelenting, and now he could yield to it. He carried his package close to his heart, feeling it breathe next to him, a living, animate thing.

At the corner of Eighth and Forty-first he discovered where he was going. It was as if at a certain moment something whispered to him saying, "This is it. Here's the place." Warm welcoming arms reached out to draw him in. It was always like that, the spot never preselected, but simply just come upon. Part of his personal code dictated that. Nothing of the ceremony could be premeditated. In order that there be no taint of malice, everything must be fortuitous. Even the victim was entitled to a fair chance.

The lobby of the building when he entered it was empty, yet he could hear voices from behind closed doors and the muffled hollow drone of television sets. It was a dingy, rank-smelling place; crumbling plaster, the poorly lit hallways redolent of cabbage, fish and urine; lives lived on the shabby edge of respectability.

He stood there for a moment getting his bearings, accustoming his eyes to the dim light. In the next moment he heard the elevator purr. The cables creaked and whined as the steel cage dropped from somewhere up above. He stepped back into the darkness as a young Puerto Rican couple, laughing and chattering, exited the lobby and sallied out into the beckoning night.

He waited there in the dank shadows. Outside horns blared and a dog barked in the alleyway. It was nearly 10:00 P.M. Soon the theaters would be letting out and now he must ready himself. It was seven stories to the roof. He debated whether or not to take the elevator, decided against it, then started up the stairs. Ascending, he experienced a sensation of warmth, a wave of quiet, unutterable joy.

The cinder block in the bag pressed against his heart as he climbed from floor to floor. There was a slight smile on his face that could barely betray the exquisite sense of anticipation he felt. When he reached the top of the stairs, he opened the door, and stepped out onto the starlit rooftop. It was a perfect spring evening, the air mild and mostly still. Above the roof the sky glowed with a pale spectral orange. His heart pounded and there was a wild joyous drumming in his ears.

✿   ✿   ✿

Jeffrey Archer was not yet twenty-one, and he was in New York for the first time in his life. A whole new world was about to open before him. The recent graduate of a small Midwestern university, he'd come east to study dance with a major ballet troupe. His parents were not at all happy about that. His father, a chemist at a large pharmaceutical firm, wanted something more "sensible and safe" for his son. But in the end the boy's passion and commitment prevailed.

Now Jeffrey was in New York, by himself, still full of the shock and giddy excitement of transplantation. And for the first time in his life he had his own apartment, a one-room walk-up with a kitchenette, and a small parlor that converted at night into a bedroom. It was on the West Side near the river.

At the ballet school he had already made a few friends, but no one with whom he yet felt easy enough to spend a social evening. He was not concerned. An amiable young man, forthright, uncomplicated, consumed with his own interests, he was in no great rush. Soon enough, he knew, he would have all the companionship he desired.

He had been out every night since his arrival eight days before— concerts, cinemas, the theater, small, inexpensive restaurants with vaguely exotic menus. Sensations and tastes he had been starved for out West, so profligately abundant in New York.

That night he'd been to a production of *Uncle Vanya*. Almost in a trance he ambled west to his apartment, but in his mind he still lingered in that seedy, achingly beautiful Russian estate, eavesdropping on the jabbering, gossipy serfs, taking tea with the quarreling, feckless aristocrats, full of all their languour and ennui.

What made him look up the moment he did, he never knew. It was only that some small commotion off to the side of the crowded street had drawn his eye momentarily to the right, then inexplicably upward to the sky, still enflamed by the wattage of a million neon lights.

Framed within that orange glow he saw what he thought to be a black shape on the rooftop, leaning far out over the building parapet. He did not associate it with a human form until he saw the arms spread wide in a gesture of benevolence, resembling from that perspective below something quite like an angel ascending.

He recalled feeling no sense of danger or threat, but just being struck by the huge, transcendent grace of it. In the next instant he was aware of something like a mote, a tiny black speck glimpsed out of the corner of the eye, growing larger and larger. Then the impact of it, enormous, crushing, yet curiously devoid of pain. Just the shudder and then the legs suddenly waxen, no longer within his control. Watching all the light disappear like the taillight of an automobile racing ahead into the night, darkness filled his eyes. Then he heard from somewhere behind him the high, piercing scream. He never knew it was his own.

When at last he'd let the concrete drop, there were tears in his eyes. He'd waited there a moment before leaning over the edge, the lugging weight of it suspended between two slender fingers, as he challenged the force of his own will to reverse the act. But by that time the act had perversely achieved a life of its own, quite beyond his volition. He was merely some passive instrument through which the act must consummate itself.

Leaning over the coping, he waited a moment longer, feeling life within the concrete, beating between his fingers like a captive moth struggling to get free. Then suddenly it was free. The sudden absence of aching strain in his fingers told him so, even as his eyes watched the fragment, white and phantasmal, hurtle into the dark void above the teeming street blow. From his vantage point, it appeared to belly outward and inscribe a gentle curve as it descended.

Though there were tears in his eyes, he felt transfigured. Once again he knew what martyrs felt, and knew that he was smiling.

From somewhere below a cry shot upward. Leaning out over the roof's ledge, he could see crowds, small, impersonal dots, streaming toward a central focus of light. Something lay on the pavement below; something felled and huddled. The innumerable tiny dots swarmed round the huddled thing and shortly engulfed it. Then he could see no more.

In the next moment he turned and left. Quietly and unrushed, he walked between the transoms and chimney pots, negotiating the laundry lines and departing the roof the same way he'd come, through a door, down a dimly lit stair to the floor below where he took an elevator to the lobby. No one had seen him come or go.

Outside on the street he stood for a while and mingled with the crowds that typically gather round the daily morbid episodes of the city.

He asked a man what had happened. The fellow pointed to a fallen figure sprawled somewhere between the shuffling feet of the milling crowd. At first he had no clear vision of what it was that lay there. Then for a flash of a second, he caught a glimpse of a corner of the thing, the crook of an elbow, a neck bent at a sickening angle, a ribbon of scarlet unfurling on the pavement.

Shortly the police arrived—three patrol cars with their rotating dome lights and whooping sirens, the shrill sound of which made him physically ill. In no time the crowd had taken on a festive, rather giddy air.

The police began to push people back, cordoning off the scene.

116

For a moment, he had a full, uninterrupted view of the thing on the pavement.

It was a man, slight, youthful, in his twenties. At the side of his head a pink bulblike excrescence swelled outward. Feeling suddenly sick, he turned and walked quickly off.

25

"You got a nerve—"

"It's my right."

"Bullshit. You got no right sending a letter like this. Why the hell didn't you come to see me? I'm the man you're supposed to report to."

"I did come to you. Three times. Remember?"

"You came to me? Bullshit, you came to me."

"I did. Each time you shrugged it off. Leave it to the chief of detectives, you told me. Keep my goddamned nose out of it, you said."

"I never said no goddamned . . ."

"Don't shout at me, Mulvaney."

"I'll shout. I'm gonna shout plenty. No man serving under me is gonna bypass me. Stick his foot in the commissioner's door." Eyes bulging, Chief Larry Mulvaney flapped a letter defiantly in Mooney's face. "Don't you ever say my door isn't open to my people twenty-four hours a day, 365 days a year. Don't tell me I'm not accessible. Don't you ever pull a stunt like this again, Mooney."

"Like what?"

"Like going to the commissioner behind my back. And don't ever come in here with a dirty mouth again, sounding off at the top of your lungs." Mulvaney glared across the desk at the soiled, rumpled figure seated across from him. The spectacle of it appeared to revolt him. He covered his eyes with a hand and made a face of profound disgust. "Where the hell have you been anyway? Defasio's been calling your place the past sixteen hours. You look like you slept in a doorway."

"I've been on the far side of the moon. What's it to you? It's on my time."

"That means no doubt you blew a couple of hundred at the flats."

"If you're so smart, Mulvaney, how come you got posted to a flea-bag precinct like this?"

Once again Mulvaney snatched up the photocopy of Mooney's letter sent him by the commissioner. He proceeded to read aloud: "I wish to dispute directly the findings of the Sixth Homicide Detectives with special regard to . . . dunderheads . . ." Mulvaney looked up bitterly from the page. "Man, I'd like to circulate this among your colleagues."

"I hope you do. I wouldn't give a tub of pig shit for any of my colleagues' opinions." He pronounced the word "colleague" as if he had a bad taste in his mouth.

"You're a mean son of a bitch, you are, Mooney. A spoiler and a hard loser. You're a cop who struck out, and 'cause you never made it, now you've got it in for every one of your buddies."

"Buddies?" Mooney gave a short burst of contemptuous laughter.

"And so you go off and write the commissioner."

"I wrote the commissioner because I couldn't get no satisfaction out of my buddies."

"And I tell you we *did* check out every one of your leads. The little black kid two years ago. Last year the Italian construction guy. Whatsisname?"

"Vitali."

"Right, Vitali. And the old guy who saw someone on his fire escape, Rosenbaum."

"Rosenzweig."

"Whatever." Mulvaney flung his arm sideward. "Senile. A fruitcake. He sees people on fire escapes three times a day."

"What about the fresh puddle of blood below the scape? The scrap of fabric? The AB-pos sample? That's no mirage."

"Okay. Okay. But it's still only a puddle of blood. Blood—particularly in that neighborhood, means absolutely nothing. They got blood there up to their asses. It leads nowhere. We checked out hospitals, emergency rooms, morgues. We talked to every doctor in the area who might have treated an injured man that night."

Mooney rose and started marching up the room, brandishing an arm above his head. "Five. Count 'em. Five people dead over the past six years. All from junk dropped on their heads from a rooftop."

"Stuff drops from rooftops every day," Mulvaney's voice pleaded.

"You happen to live in a city where fifty percent of the buildings, particularly in ghetto areas, are falling apart."

"And that, too," Mooney whirled, leaping on his words. "How come it's always in the same area. The West Forties, anywhere west of Eighth to Tenth avenues. Ghettos. Slums. Derelict structures. And always the spring."

"So what? So it's always the spring."

"April or May. As we approach the summer solstice. Don't that say anything to you? Virgo and Aries in conjunction?"

"Oh, Jesus. If it ain't the fucking stars now."

"It's no accident, I'm telling you. Five deaths. All similar. All the same time of the year. Basically the same locale. It's no accident."

Mulvaney's eyes narrowed. "So that's how you come up with this?" Once again, he snatched the letter up and read. " 'I have the strongest gut feeling . . . our rooftop friend will strike again, etc.' And then this business. 'I am willing to lay six to two odds it happens on or around the sixteenth.' "

"And I was right, goddammit. Right on the money."

Mulvaney tilted his head and drew his tongue across his lower lip. The pugnacious thrust of his chin conveyed the sense of a reptile coiled to strike. "Come on, Mooney. You can level with me. Out of what hat did you pull this? Your letter is postdated the fourteenth of May. How did you know this thing was gonna happen on the sixteenth of May? And just like you said. With a forty-pound block dropped off a rooftop." Mulvaney flung the letter back at him with disgust. "The commissioner's been on the phone to me all day, reaming my ass. All because of this goddamned letter. How come I didn't know? he says. And how come Mooney knew? You really didn't predict this, Mooney. This is some kind of gimmick, isn't it? You had it rigged."

"Sure, sure. I had it rigged. I had advance information from the Bombardier himself. He sent me a postcard. Who's the guy got creamed, did you say? Is he dead?"

"He may as well be."

Mooney cocked a wary eye at the chief.

"Some say he's lucky," the chief continued. "I don't. This bag of concrete busted his spine. He'll never walk again. Poor bastard is some kind of a dancer."

The fog hovering above Mooney's bourbon-sodden mind was slowly lifting. "Where is he—this guy? Can I see him?"

"See him?" Mulvaney sat back in his chair and laughed ruefully at the ceiling. "Don't you understand? The commissioner says you're in charge of the whole investigation now. You can see anyone you fucking please. Take as many men as you need. The rest of this city can go to hell. But you get this Bombardier for me, Mooney, and you get him quick. I want Dowd off my back."

Mooney frowned and started out. "Thanks for your good wishes."

"Mooney," the chief cried after him. Mooney turned. "I don't suppppose it's any secret. It won't break my heart to see you go."

"Twenty-four months, Larry. That's all you have to wait." Mooney stared back at him gloomily. "All you assholes up here. Sit on your butts for thirty years. Hang your hat on a pension. All you do is count nickel-and-dime raises and argue with the PBA about sick days. You never wanna hear anything that's gonna make you get up off your duffs and work. 'Accidental,' 'Accidental.' Bullshit, accidental. The only thing you're browned off about now is the fact I wrote a letter and got the commissioner to put a blowtorch under your ass. Well, glory hallelujah. My compliments to the commissioner. It's about fucking time. So long, pal. See ya in the funnies."

Mooney doffed his battered fedora, winked spitefully and swaggered out.

"Hey, Mooney," Defasio called to him in the outer office.

Mooney glowered and kept right on going.

Defasio scurried out from behind the desk and started after him. "Hey. Where you going? I hear you're headin' up this thing. Burned Mulvaney good, didn't you?"

"That son of a bitch," Mooney smoldered, "I'll make his ass blister before this thing's over."

Defasio clapped his hands and hooted. "Hey, listen. Before you go. Someone was in here lookin' for you. Some dame."

Mooney stiffened. "A dame?"

"A lady."

"Who?"

"How the hell should I know? A big job. Red hair and a deep voice. Said her name was Baumholz or something."

At first the name failed to register. Then it dawned. "Oh, Jesus."

There was a look of playful mockery in Defasio's eyes. "A bit long in the tooth, as they say, but not a bad looker. Not at all bad."

Mooney glowered and started forward again. Defasio followed him out to the stair. "A little on the hefty side, but personally I like that sort of thing."

"Stuff it, Defasio."

"Sure." The younger man smirked. "Sure, Frank. I understand. Anyway, she left this for you."

A small white envelope came forward at the end of the younger man's arm. When Mooney's hand failed to accept it, he slowly crammed it into the detective's breast pocket. Still grinning, he turned and strolled back into the office.

Out on the landing, by himself, Mooney waited for a moment, gazing down at the envelope stuck half out of his pocket. Slowly, warily, he reached down, as if it were booby-trapped, then carefully plucked it out and opened it. Two crisp hundred-dollar bills lay tucked away inside. Along with that was a ticket for a reserved field seat at Aqueduct for the following Sunday.

26

Mooney was not good at hospitals. He did not like talking in whispers and deferring to doctors. He despised the smell of antiseptics, of Formalin, of Lysol and bedpans, of corridors reeking of urine. He did not like walking down hallways and seeing doors opening on beds curtained off. A glimpse of frightened eyes, a skull-like head limp upon a pillow. The prospect of death. In short, hospitals made him profoundly uneasy. Yet he knew he must see Jeffrey Archer.

"Only a few minutes," the nurse whispered. "He's under heavy sedation."

"Does he know what's happened to him?"

"He's perfectly lucid."

"But he doesn't know the extent of his injury?"

"I don't think the doctors have told him."

"About his spine?" Mooney inquired.

"I'm sorry. I'm not permitted . . ."

Mooney saw the girl's eyes flutter and shift to avoid his gaze. "That's all right," he whispered, hovering awkwardly outside the door. "I understand . . . A dancer, wasn't he?"

"He's lucky to be alive," the nurse said.

"You call that lucky?"

The girl frowned. "You can go in now. Follow me, please."

Several paces behind the nurse, he tiptoed into the gray cloistral shadows of the private room, queasy, as he'd always been, at the prospect of viewing catastrophic illness.

With a brisk single motion the girl swept aside white curtains that squealed round on a ceiling track, revealing a figure lying on a hospital bed. It took several moments for Mooney to decipher his impressions; first a head; then a face dominated by frightened eyes. Only then did Mooney grasp the fact that the long white tubular shape out of which the head emerged was a cast which encased the body from chin to foot.

The girl lit the table lamp beside the bed and leaned down to whisper. "How are you feeling, Mr. Archer?"

Mooney saw cracked dry lips move and overheard feeble mumbling.

"Would you like something to drink? A little juice or water?"

There was a glass of half-drunk orange juice on the table with a clear plastic angle straw inside it. The nurse held it while the head on the pillow sucked feebly. Mooney hovered awkwardly at the foot of the bed.

"Mr. Archer," the nurse went on. "This is Detective Mooney. He'd like to ask you a few questions. Do you think you're up to that?" The girl smiled cheerfully. Mooney watched the young man's eyelids flutter in response. "That's fine," she said, then turned to Mooney and whispered, "Only a few minutes. He's very weak."

Mooney lumbered forward to the head of the bed. He placed himself directly in the young man's line of vision for he could see that Archer could not move his neck. Looking down at the pale, haggard face, the detective saw a young man, barely in his twenties, fair, delicate, with gaunt, poetic features.

"Mr. Archer." Mooney stooped over, suddenly conscious that his voice was too loud. He lowered it and started over. "Mr. Archer, Detective Mooney here. Sorry to bother you at a time like this, but I got a few questions if you're up to it. It won't take but a minute." He laughed unconvincingly and swallowed. The effort of stooping over strained his back and made him slightly breathless. "Can you hear me?"

Mooney could see both comprehension and fright in the young man's eyes. He was no more than just a kid, in a strange city, drastically, irreversibly injured, and scared out of his wits. He still didn't know what had hit him.

Wanting to speak, the boy swallowed with great effort, causing the Adam's apple in his throat to bob up and down.

"You don't have to talk," Mooney smiled. "If you wanna nod or use your eyes, that's just as good."

Once again the parched lips moved. Mooney stooped a little lower to listen. "What? What's that? Oh, you *can* talk. Good. Sure. Either

122

way's okay with me. I'm easy." Mooney withdrew his note pad and pencil. He sighed and proceeded to write. "Can you give me some idea of how all this happened?"

The head on the pillow rolled heavily to the left, more the result of gravity than its own volition.

Mooney was a man who could confront unblinking the most grisly carnage in the city morgue, but Jeffrey Archer made him profoundly uneasy. "Let me try and help." He stood up and nearly tipped the juice over the night table. "You were comin' home Tuesday night. You'd been to the theater. Right?"

The eyes sparked momentarily.

"It was around eleven-fifteen. You were walkin' down Forty-third, just west of Eighth. You went past 243 West Forty-third and . . . now you tell me." Mooney looked down at young Archer and waited.

He had closed his eyes again and it appeared to Mooney that he had drifted back off. Unwilling to disturb him, yet reluctant to leave without the information he needed, the detective waited for what seemed an interminable time. Outside in the corridor, carts rolled past, rattling trays of medication and luncheon plates. Suddenly the air was full of the warm bland odor of mashed potatoes. Someone laughed in the room next door.

"Jeffrey," Mooney called softly, trying to rouse him. "Jeffrey? Can you hear me? This is Detective Mooney. I'm still here."

The eyes fluttered open with an expression of childish wonder. For a while they focused on the ceiling, then slowly rolled round and settled on the detective.

"This is Mooney. I'm still here. Can you tell me what happened?"

Jeffrey Archer's befogged mind appeared unable to grasp the question.

"Do you know what happened to you, Jeffrey?" Mooney persisted. "Did you see anyone? Anything? Is there anything you want to tell me?"

This time the pause was not quite so long. "Roof," he muttered. "Roof."

Mooney leaned forward. "Someone on the roof. You saw someone on the roof?"

Archer's nod was barely perceptible, but it was there.

"You saw him?"

The nod came once again.

"Could you describe him?"

There was a pause. Archer closed his eyes again. But this time it apeared to Mooney that he was summoning energy for some huge exertion of will. "Mr. Archer? . . . Jeffrey?" he whispered and restrained the impulse to prod him. "Jeffrey?"

The eyes struggled open again.

"Could you possibly describe him? The man who dropped . . . who did this?"

To Mooney's amazement, the young man smiled—a ruined, feeble little grin. The head stirred, or more possibly a breeze from somewhere had rustled faintly the wavy chestnut hair. Mooney heard him mutter something beneath his breath and bent down as if to scoop up the words. "What's that? I'm sorry . . . I can't . . . I'm afraid I don't . . . Angel?" Confused, the detective repeated the word several times, looking for signs of corroboration. "Was that 'angel' you said, Jeffrey?"

Again the smile—this time a little more crumpled and depleted.

"Angel," Mooney pondered and scribbled it into his pad. With a faint gasp he stood erect, closed his pad and tucked it away. "I see from your driver's license you're from Evansville, Indiana."

The head drooped and the frightened eyes closed.

"Has your family been notified? Do your people know?"

Once again the eyes opened. This time they were hard. Full of defiance and self-awareness.

"Okay, okay," Mooney said placatingly. "But sooner or later . . ."

"No."

The force behind that word astonished the detective. He waited there, helplessly. He had run out of ideas and now merely rolled his tongue over dry lips. "All right, Jeffrey. You're the boss."

Mooney planted his fedora hard on his head and stared gloomily down at Archer. The young man appeared to have finally dropped off. Mooney sighed and switched off the night lamp. For a while he stood quietly in the thickening shadows. A warm orange light glowed in the doorway from the corridor outside. Mooney's hand rose and stretched tentatively forward. It retracted, then inched forward again, touching at last with the back of his finger the young man's neck exposed above the lip of the full-length cast that encased him.

Even as Mooney departed the room, still walking on tiptoe so as not to violate the hushed sanctity of convalescence, his eye swept across the back of a squat, drab figure in a brown messenger's uniform. He stood at the counter of the reception area, stooping slightly toward the nurse seated there. He was in the process of handing her a tall plant wrapped in cellophane with a bright lavender bow tied gaily round its middle.

The image flitted swiftly across Mooney's visual field and was quickly gone, supplanted by a host of others swarming through the corridors before him and mingling with his own dark thoughts.

"Boyd," the messenger at the desk repeated the name to the nurse on duty there. "Mr. A. Boyd."

"Just that? No other message?"

"That's all I've been given. Just that. Best wishes, Mr. A. Boyd."

"He'll know who it's from then, I take it?"

"I guess so." The messenger shrugged and trundled off.

27

"You gotta be crazy."

"Not crazy. Just dumb to have overlooked something so obvious for so long."

"But it's over a year ago."

"So? They keep records."

"Not emergency ward activity. Only the regular inpatient, outpatient stuff. You got thousands of people stumbling in and out of emergency wards day and night in this city. Every wino and stumblebum who needs his nose bandaged. Where the hell am I supposed to start?"

"With the Yellow Pages, dummy. Under 'Hospitals, New York City.' Start with the night of April 30, 1979. What the hell are you asking me for? You're a big boy. You're supposed to know where to start. You wanna be a detective? So go be a detective."

Michael Defasio stood limp and depleted in his shirt-sleeves. Seated before him like some imperious zoo gorilla, Mooney lorded over a landscape strewn with the husks and rinds of assorted junk foods. With a slow, oddly fastidious motion, he swiped a smear of grease off his fleshy chin.

"You know how many hospitals there are in New York City?" Defasio spoke in a soft, faintly tremulous voice.

Mooney sat back in his seat and extracted a king-sized Hershey bar from the inside pocket of his jacket. "No. Tell me."

"Probably upward of two hundred. And what about doctors? Have you forgotten all the doctors' offices in the area of West Forty-ninth Street?"

"We'll check them after we check the emergency wards." Mooney stripped the candy bar wrapping with a sharp yank. "Look. I'll run this thing past you once more. When did the last fatality occur?"

Defasio moaned and palmed his forehead. "Oh, Jesus."

"When?"

"April 30, 1979."

"Where?"

"At 423 West Forty-ninth. Only six blocks from where Archer got creamed the other night."

"Marvelous." Mooney rammed the last half of the bar into his maw. "And the ME told you, only at least a dozen times, that the quantity of blood found at the bottom of the fire escape that night, and out in the alleyway, suggests a fairly serious injury. A possibly severed blood vessel, he said, didn't he?"

"Yeah? So?"

"So, if you were losing blood fast, where would you head first? The nearest hospital, right? Six'll get you ten that if it were an artery or something like that, you'd go for a hospital before a private physician's office. Okay?"

"Okay, okay," Defasio snapped.

"Easy, easy. Don't get your hot Latin blood up."

"So I start by looking for a hospital in the vicinity of 423 West Forty-ninth."

"Right. You start with the hospitals on the West Side, beginning with the closest to Forty-ninth, going as far north as Seventy-second Street, as far south as Eighth Street, and as far east as the river."

The younger man scowled.

"Now, another point," Mooney continued. He enjoyed greatly the role of pedagogic browbeater. "How did our Bombardier get to the hospital?"

"Not on foot, if he was that badly injured."

"Marvelous. But he wasn't waiting round for no bus either. With all the blood spurting out of him, he probably grabbed the first cab he could get. Not an easy thing to come by in that area, that time of night, with theaters letting out, and what not. But given the emergency, the quantity of blood all over him, he was probably able to commandeer something."

"So you want me to check the cab companies."

"Right again, Dick Tracy. Drivers and dispatchers."

"They keep records of injured fares like that?"

"Right, and moreover, drivers talk. They'd remember picking up a fare covered with blood and rushing him over to a hospital. Even if it was over a year ago."

Defasio shook his head despairingly. His shoulders bore the slump of defeat.

"One other thing before you go," Mooney said, pulling from his vest pocket a small ragged swatch of material. "Remember this?"

The young man stared at it blankly. "Sure. It's the stuff that was found stuck on the fire-escape ladder."

"Wonderful. And what did the police lab tell us about this 'stuff,' as you call it?"

"They said it tore off the guy's clothes when he jumped from the ladder to the ground. I think they said it was part linen, part . . ."

"The composition doesn't interest me," Mooney snapped. "Where did they say the piece probably came from?"

Momentarily bewildered, Defasio's jaw dropped open.

"I'll give you one hint. There were threads still clinging to it and part of a buttonhole."

"Okay," Defasio's face brightened. "I gotcha. They said it looked like it most probably ripped off from the back trouser pocket."

Mooney's eyes danced wickedly. "And what does that suggest to you about where our man most probably injured himself?"

"The leg. The thigh."

"What about the butt, my friend? This guy could have very well torn his ass open on that ladder. So when you tell the emergency wards to look in their files for the night of April 30, 1979, what will you tell them to be particularly on the lookout for?"

"Anyone who came in that night with injury to the extremities, especially the legs or butt. Like a deep cut that had to be sewn."

"I'm astonished by your keenness of mind, Defasio. You're a regular Nero Wolfe."

The young man stared back at him bitterly. "Am I glad they turned this investigation over to you, Mooney. What an opportunity to learn under a master. It gives a man something to look forward to every day."

"I, too, Defasio, am gratified," Mooney's eyes glinted wickedly. "It gives me a chance to kick your ass around a little more."

SEPTEMBER–DECEMBER / '81

28

"Who was Sevrenson?"

"The brother-in-law."

"Not the same one driving the car?"

"No. That was the brother. The one who was fencing the stuff out of the warehouse in Queens."

"Bauer?"

"No. For Chrissake. Don't you listen? Or am I talkin' to myself. Bauer is not related to these guys. Bauer's a small-time three-story man who's never done anything bigger than Class C felonies. Residences. Muggings. Auto theft. Peanut operations. He just happened to fall in with this Sevrenson crowd."

"And they needed a fall guy?"

"Right. Your classic klutz, if you know what I mean."

They were driving over the Queensboro Bridge from Queens where Mooney had just successfully closed a two-year investigation on a three-million-dollar-a-year fencing operation in Astoria.

It was slightly past 7:00 P.M., and the saw-toothed skyline of the city rose a luminous chalk-white against the indigo dusk of early fall. It was a Friday evening, the beginning of the weekend and just that hour when workers were spilling out onto the street from glass towers, homeward bound. Bars and restaurants had begun to fill. People were unwinding. So was Mooney, expansive, even kindly, in the flush of victory. "I knew I had that son of a bitch nailed the minute I got my hands on that pawn ticket. If he just hadn't tried to pawn that coat—"

"All the guy hadda do was hold it for a while."

"That's just it. They never do. They always need cash, and the minute they're tapped out, they panic. You got a twelve-grand mink sittin' round a warehouse collectin' dust. It's hot; you wanna unload it, right? So you try the first place you can, right? The fuckin' pawnshop down the block. Dumb. Just so fuckin' dumb."

"Lucky break for you, Mooney." Defasio drove the unmarked city car with characteristic Italian panache. It was as though he were conducting the Philharmonic. For every one required motion, he would execute four—cocky, swaggering, completely unnecessary. When they stopped at lights, he would eye the ladies in the cars alongside.

"Lucky?" Mooney's grin faded. "What d'ya mean lucky?"

"I mean the pawn ticket, and all. You just happened to be in the right place at the right time."

"What d'ya mean the right place at the right time? No one told me where that pawn ticket was. I hadda go find it. I hadda drag my can around to fifty different pawnshops in the Astoria, Corona section. I figured it hadda be somewhere in the vicinity, and I was right. No miracles. No luck, Defasio. Simple gumshoe, my friend. Hard work and experience. Right out of the Old School. Not like you, wise ass."

"Come on, Mooney. Don't start on me now. I done everything I could, didn't I?"

"Everything, and still you come up with nothing. Zero. Goose eggs. That can't be. That don't wash, my friend. You mean to tell me there's not a cab dispatcher in this city don't have a record the night of April 30, 1979, of one of his hacks pickin' up an injured fare, some guy bleedin' like a stuck pig all over his back seat?"

"Right." The younger man's voice grew shrill. "That's exactly what I mean. You know as well as I do most hacks won't file reports on injured passengers 'cause they know if they do they gotta go to court, or appear before insurance companies. Why the hell should they? It's a big hassle. Hangs 'em up a long time. Costs 'em money. And then their own companies get pissed off with them— 'Oh, you still hung up in court, Smith. That's tough shit. I'm gonna have to go get someone else to turn your trick! So that's why I got nothin' to show for talkin' three weeks to cab companies all over Queens and fuckin' Manhattan."

"And hospital emergency wards," Mooney fumed right back. "Nothin' to show for that, either?"

Defasio shook his head belligerently. "I didn't say that, now did I, Mooney? I didn't say I got *nothin'* to show."

"No. Instead you tell me for hospitals you got too much to show and you don't know where the fuck to start. Right?"

"Jesus, Mooney, can't I make you understand?" The car suddenly lurched and bounded through a series of potholes, jouncing the two of them in their seats.

The moment they were on smoother ground, Defasio resumed his explanations. "Emergency wards are busy places. In case you haven't heard. April 30, 1979, was relatively quiet. The New York City hospitals only admitted 84 people that night. You're lucky. They generally average more like 135 to 150. Now I gotta figure out some way of tracking down all these 84 . Some fun, ay? Half of them are not even local. They're from out of town. One guy was visiting from Algeria. Should I go check him out?"

Mooney slumped deeper into his seat. "You've always got some kind of goddamned excuse."

Defasio drove on grimly through the glittering dusk. "Don't bust my hump, Mooney. I'm too tired."

Suddenly Defasio braked hard in order to avoid a cab swinging out in front of him. "Motherfucker."

Mooney was hurled forward. "All right. That does it. Lemme out right here."

"I'm takin' you up to Eighty-first Street, I said."

"No way. It's worth my life. I'm gettin' out here."

"Hold your water, will you. I promised I'd get you up to the widow, Baumholz."

Mooney swelled dangerously. "I'm warnin' you, Defasio. You give me any more of that Widow Baumholz bullshit, and I'm gonna turn you inside out."

They were stopped in the middle of Third Avenue, glaring at each other. The light changed and horns shrieked. Mooney hoisted his great girth from the front seat, flung the door open and heaved out into the midst of the blaring, traffic-clogged night. Behind the car window Defasio muttered soundless and unrepeatable Sicilian epithets.

"Don't eat the potato salad, Mooney."

"Why'd you put it on my plate if you didn't want me to eat it?"

"In the first place, I didn't put it on your plate. Harold put it on your plate."

"Who told Harold to put it on my plate?" Mooney raised a forkful of the potato salad to his mouth. "He knows as well as you if you're gonna put potato salad on my plate, I'm gonna damned well eat it."

Frances Baumholz dipped into Mooney's plate with a large spoon and, in a single sweep, removed the offending potato salad. With an air of childish hurt Mooney watched it depart. He had the look of a famished dog having just been given his bowl, then seeing it whisked cruelly away.

They were seated in one of the spacious leather booths of Fritzi's Balloon. As pubs go, it was not much different from the other East side watering holes with a vaguely British theme—the same bare oak tables, the same booths, described grandly as ecclesiastical pews attributed to some quaint seventeenth-century abbey and allegedly shipped across from England at enormous expense.

The ceilings were stucco and timber. Coach lanterns hung on the bricked walls of three narrow sprawling rooms. In the larger main dining room was a stone hearth where a cozy fire licked and crackled behind a black cinder screen. A number of English riding prints hung from the walls, while directly above the hearth hung an antique pub sign depicting a huge red balloon soaring above the countryside. Its guy lines were attached to a small wicker basket in which a dapper Victorian gentleman in a plaid jacket and derby hat sipped champagne and gazed phlegmatically out over the tiny, toylike countryside below.

At dinner, trolleys of beef were wheeled round the floor from table to table while a stooping, bearlike creature in a *toque blanche* carved joints for famished diners. Another trolley, this one for desserts, featured trifle, berries, Stilton cheese and pastries.

In the adjoining room was an authentic London shilling bar. Dozens of pewter tankards hung above it, and on the bar itself at cocktail time great wheels of cheddar, wicker hampers crammed with fresh crudité and bowls of salty chips were constantly replenished to keep patrons waiting for tables happily drinking.

The final touch was a rude green parrot with clipped wings, who sat on a brass perch beside the hatcheck stand and insulted clients to their infinite delight. His name was Sanchez and he cursed in Castilian.

"Harold doesn't give a damn if you gain back thirty pounds," Fritzi went on earnestly.

"I already lost forty."

"And you feel much better. Right?"

"If you must know, I feel lousy. And what's more, I'm losing interest."

"But saving your life."

"Saving my life is a pain in the ass, if you must know. And for what? To live another two years? Screw it. I'm dying for a beer. That's a fate worse than death."

"No beer. That's the worst. You have a beer and you start to swell."

"Who cares if I swell? I like to swell. If I wanna swell that's my business—ain't it?"

Ignoring him, she rose majestically to greet more guests. Mooney was left alone to pick disconsolately at his peas and beef.

It was slightly past 8:00 P.M., Friday night, and the place was jammed to the gunnels, with sleek, stylish, upwardly mobile young

134

people just beginning to feel the release of week's end in New York. It was a payday, too, and the cash register at the bar jingled prosperously.

In the last half year Mooney had seen a great deal of Fritzi Baumholz. After the debacle of their first meeting at the track, she had lured him back, not with the two hundred dollars he'd lost following her tout, but with the good red beef and fine ale of Fritzi's Balloon.

Shortly, they were going out to the track weekends, and he was eating at the Balloon regularly. After a few evenings out, they spent several nights together and that's when she put him on a diet and told him to shape up. No bread, no butter, no starch, no sugar, no salt, no greasy, fried junk food, no sweet carbonated stuff, one drink a night and absolutely no beer. He told her he was not entirely sure it was worth giving all that up for a love life. Not at his age. And anyway he told her that he thought copulation was greatly overrated— mostly hype from the fashion mags, Seventh Avenue, cosmetics manufacturers, book publishers and film pornographers, in order to hawk their goods. He'd rather have ten hamburgers and a couple of quarts of beer at the track any day, then a roll in the sack with the most lusty wench imaginable.

"Suits me fine." Fritzi eyed him coldly. "I don't know who could stand the sight of you in the buff, anyway."

He lost some forty pounds not long after that and was working on another twenty. He started to feel better and thought vaguely of getting some new suits, or at the very least, having some of his old ones taken in. But the nature of his growing relationship with Mrs. Baumholz, their unfailing weekends at the track, the pajamas and the shaving kit he kept in her apartment near the pub, her proprietarial concern for his diet, the whole sense of a shared growing intimacy— all of that had begun to trouble him. He couldn't say precisely why, but he suspected that it frightened him. It alarmed him that he liked it so much and that it appeared to be taking him over like some insidiously seductive drug. More and more, after a day's work, he found himself looking forward to dashing up to the Balloon and seeing her. He liked the way he was treated there; more like family than clientele. When he walked in at night, Mitch, the bartender, had his Jack Daniel's standing right up there waiting for him, all beaded with chill, perfect, the way he loved it. It troubled him that he liked the whole cozy arrangement just a bit too much—like a neutered old cat coming home each night for its saucer and bowl.

Fritzi came back and slipped into the booth beside him. "What puts you in such a larky mood? Just the loss of some overmayonnaised potato salad? Harold," she waved for the waiter. "Bring Mr. Mooney potato salad. Heaps of potato salad. All he wants."

"I don't want no potato salad now." He waved the waiter off. "I'm in a dandy mood. Listen—what about an ale? A small one? Even a shot glass?"

"No ale. Harold"—she snapped at the baffled waiter—"bring Mr. Mooney a Tab. With a lot of ice and lemon, the way he likes it."

"No Tab, Harold. I wouldn't put it in my system. It's like something that's leaked out of a radiator."

"You *are* in a dreadful mood, Mooney. You ought to feel great. You broke this fencing operation. You bagged the big guy, plus a lot of the small fry. Everyone's proud of you. You're a terrific guy. They'll probably give you a medal and buck you back up to captain. And on top of that, you lost forty pounds."

"Forty-two pounds."

"I'm sure you put the two right back on with all that potato salad tonight. So what do we have going for us in the first tomorrow? Belvedere looks fine to me. A two-year-old, he's run second his last . . ."

"I'm not going to the track tomorrow."

He'd caught her off-guard and for a moment it was only sheer momentum kept her rattling cheerily on. Then the weight of his message sank in.

"I'm not going tomorrow," he said again. The waiter poured his Tab, and they didn't speak, waiting for the man to go.

"I knew something was wrong," she said. "What's up?"

A juke box was playing out in the bar and the din and smoke bothered him. She stared into his face as if he'd spoken, but he hadn't, only muttered several words beneath his breath.

"What's that, Frank? I'm sorry, I don't . . ."

"You can't depend on no one, I said." He spoke louder. "People just don't care anymore."

She watched him uneasily, expecting more to come. But it didn't; and what finally did, sounded a bit hollow and self-serving. She thought she was now in for one of those interminable tirades about the ills of civilization. Youth. Laziness. Lack of commitment. Undesirable ethnic types. Disrespect for authority. The decline of the Church. The full catalog of contemporary crimes. All of that delivered with a ringing self-righteousness, as if he were a deacon of the Church himself.

She'd heard it all before, but this time it was just a few sputters and feeble, halfhearted denunciations, then a kind of joyless resolve about doing his duty, whatever the hell that was.

"So I can't go out to the track with you tomorrow. I gotta stay right here in town and work."

"But why? It's Saturday. What's so important? They're running yearlings. Can't it wait?"

Head crooked to one side, he rested his cheek in the palm of a hand and swirled sugarless sweetener through his decaffeinated coffee. A fresh crowd surged in from the bar. The amplification of the jukebox had reduced whatever music there'd been to mere visceral thudding.

"What did you say, Frank? I'm sorry, I can't . . ." She strained toward him.

"Nothing." He gazed abstractly off at some point in the middle distance. "I didn't say anything."

Actually he had, but she'd caught only the tail end of it, and to her it made no sense. Something like "Equinox," is what she'd heard, or thought she'd heard. She shrugged and smiled. "Well, suit yourself."

He nodded, but he was still staring into emptiness.

"Are you going to be over on Sunday?" She waited for a reply, but he was a million miles away. The second time she called louder. "Frank."

"I hear you. I hear you."

"You think you'll go out to the track Sunday?"

"Maybe."

"Maybe?"

"Well, how the hell would I know, for Chrissake? If I get finished with everything tomorrow."

"Well, I've got to know. 'Cause if you are, I'll shop for dinner."

"Don't shop. We'll go out." He looked at her impatiently. "I'll try to make it for dinner. But I can't do the track."

Disappointment crept into her eyes. Several people stopped by to say good night. She started to show signs of irritability. When they were alone again she said, "Well, this is all just a bit too iffy for me. I'm going out to the track Saturday and Sunday. If you want to have dinner, you know where to find me. You've got the key."

29

"What about a gunshot wound, April 16?"

"Nope. I got no gunshot wound April 16. I got a reported coronary went to Mount Sinai, May 4, 1979. A DOA."

"Why would I want a DOA? And I told you, April 30. It's April 30, 1979."

"Okay. Okay. Don't blow your stack. I'm tryin' to help. You can see I'm up to my ass in work here. I got a sick dispatcher, and five drivers out with flu and the shits and Godknowswhatelse. I don't need all this aggravation."

The two men stood in the untidy rear office of the Fordham Cab Company on 138 Street, just off the Grand Concourse. Beyond the large glass window of the office was a gloomy, cavernous garage. The light emanating from within it was a kind of aquarium green through which the rapid flashes of cab yellow darted like tropical fish.

From beyond the glass, horns blared, drivers shouted, brakes squealed, taxis hovered, stranded in the air atop hydraulic lifts, while mechanics probed their innards from below. Tools whirred and ratcheted. The din was frightful and the air reeked from a palpable yellow smog of fumes.

The time was roughly 3:40 P.M. Mooney was tired. This was the ninth such garage he'd been to that day. His head whirled and he believed he was suffocating. "I keep telling you I'm looking for a guy who was bleeding heavily from an injury—probably in the area of the leg or thigh. This was on the night of April 30, 1979, around 11:00 P.M. in the vicinity of Forty-ninth Street and Ninth Avenue. The driver would have probably taken him to a doctor or a hospital in that area."

Mr. Melvin Wasserman, the owner and manager of the Fordham Cab Company, chewed fretfully on the saliva-sodden tip of a cheap, unlit cigar. He wore a pair of heavy, black-frame glasses, one broken arm of which was held in place by means of a thick rubber band.

"Didn't I go through all this once before with one of your people a couple of weeks ago?"

"That was probably my partner."

"What the hell am I doing it again for?"

" 'Cause he didn't find anything."

"Well, what can I tell you I didn't tell him already?"

"Just double-checking, that's all."

An enormous black man thrust his head in the door. "Hey, Melvin— Where's that distributor cap? Come on, man. I gotta move this stuff out."

"Hold your water. I'm comin'— Hey, look, Lieutenant—" Mr. Wasserman turned back to Mooney and appealed. "I'd really like to help you out, but like I told you"—he held up the slim, grease-streaked plastic folder of driver emergency reports as if for emphasis—"I got nothing here for the night of April 30, 1979. If you don't believe me, have a look for yourself."

"Is it true," Mooney asked, "that a lot of your drivers don't report emergencies even when they've been involved in one?"

Mr. Wasserman tilted his head to one side and shrugged. There was a tough, sagacious little smile about his lips. "What do I know? I only work here. But between you and me—and you gotta remember, I'm driving cabs for thirty years—for a hack to fill out one of those police emergency forms is pure hassle and heartburn. Now I ask you, Lieutenant, as an honest, patriotic, law-abiding citizen. What the hell would any man in his right mind wanna go and do a stupid thing like that for?"

Toward 5:00 P.M Mooney was over near the Yankee Stadium, finishing his final stop for the day. This time it was the Atlas Cab Company and the man in charge was a sallow, funereal apparition by the name of Bucarella.

"I tell you, Lieutenant . . ."

"I know, I know." Mooney wiped his damp forehead with a rumpled handkerchief. "Your drivers don't file emergency reports. Too much of a hassle, right?"

Mr. Bucarella smiled apologetically. "I didn't say that. But maybe it's true. Some of our boys do file reports though." He moistened a thumb with his tongue and continued flicking through an open file drawer. "I got reports here for May 4, May 7, May 16, May 22, but I don't see nothin' here for April 30."

Mooney sighed and hauled himself to his feet. "I didn't think you would."

Mr. Bucarella seemed genuinely sorry. "It's over a year and a half ago, and that's very hard."

"I understand. Thanks anyway," Mooney started out.

"You say there was a lotta blood?" Mr. Bucarella called out to him from behind the desk.

"That's right. We found a lot of it in an alley near the scene of the crime."

"So, you think there would have been a lot of blood in any cab that picked the guy up?"

"Hadda be."

"The reason I ask," Mr. Bucarella continued in his gentle, slightly self-deprecating manner, "is cause we had a cab in here awhile back got so messed up with blood from a fare that we hadda tear out the seats and replace them. It was an awful mess."

"Oh?" A vague flicker of interest flared momentarily in Mooney's eye. "When was that?"

Mr. Bucarella shrugged sadly. "I don't know. But I guess I could find out." He rose slowly and shuffled to a set of green metal files behind him. It was then that Mooney noted for the first time the clubfoot and the large, ungainly prosthetic shoe.

Shortly, Mr. Bucarella extracted a manila folder bound with a thick rubber band on which was scrawled the word REPAIRS. Starting from the front and moving backwards, he rifled through a stack of invoices, sometime reversing his field and going forward again. The process was slow and Mooney was impatient to get home, take his shoes off and put his feet up.

"Here's a whole new transmission job we hadda do. Brand-new Ford, right off the assembly line. Can you imagine that?"

"No, I can't," Mooney grumbled dispiritedly.

The process dragged on for another fifteen minutes. Mooney's face purpled with impatience.

"Jeez. It oughta be right here." Mr. Bucarella kept licking his thumb, flicking back and forth over the frayed, grease-streaked invoices that recorded a sorry history of deterioration and mechanical inefficiency.

"Ah," said Mr. Bucarella, faint triumph in his voice. "Repair rear seat. Replace rear floor carpet. Mitkin Brothers. Automotive Reupholstering. Six hundred eighty bucks. Highway robbery. That oughta be it. No wonder I couldn't find it. I was lookin' in the records for 1980."

"When was this?" Mooney stepped round the desk and peered down at the invoice.

"It was in 1979."

"When in seventy-nine?"

Mr. Bucarella studied the barely legible carbon scrawl on the pink slip. "May 7. But that's when it went to Mitkin. Coulda been sittin' around here a week, too. That close enough?"

"I'll buy that." Mooney 's reply was a dry whisper. He drew his breath in and held it until he felt a slight inflation of his stomach. "Can you tell me who was driving that cab?"

Mr. Bucarella moved his spectacles up and down the ridge of his nose, squinting at the pink invoice trembling in his hand. "Can you make out that number, Lieutenant?"

Mooney took the slip and held it up to the light. The numbers in the lower-left-hand corner were scribbled and the carbon itself was badly smeared.

"Looks like four digits," Mooney said.

"It is. It's the hack number. They're all four digits."

"The first looks like a five and the last a seven, but I can't make out the two digits in the middle."

Mr. Bucarella took the slip back and for a while the two of them tried to decipher the numbers. With the aid of a slab of glass used for magnification, they confirmed that 5 and 7 were the initial and terminal digits, but the two middle numbers would not yield to any interpretation.

"Wait a minute," Mr. Bucarella said. It was now slightly past 7:00 P.M. The lights from a small Spanish bodega twinkled in the gathering twilight beyond the window. Just let me check my registry for 1979."

"I'd appreciate that," Mooney said hopefully. "Can I use your phone a minute?"

"Help yourself. It's right over there in the corner."

He dialed Fritzi and to his surprise found her in. She'd been to the track and won several hundred dollars. She was excited. "I told you that Belvedere had guts. She came up six lengths in the stretch. You should have seen her, Frank. She was just beautiful. How'd it go with you?"

"I'm not sure yet. I might be on to something." They chatted awhile longer and gradually he felt less tired. "Hey, listen, can we still have supper?"

"I've got a sirloin in the freezer. I'll take it out."

"What about some fries, too?"

"No fries. Forget about fries. We'll have a salad, and I've got a nice cold melon in the fridge."

"Okay, okay," he grumbled. "Gimme about an hour."

When he hung up, Mr. Bucarella was awaiting him. The tentative little smile he wore gave his face a slightly crooked cast. Mr. Bucarella, it was clear, did not smile easily.

141

"It was 5107," he said, "because my registry reports 5107 was out of commission during the week of May 1 to May 7, 1979."

"Great," Mooney said, his spirits rising cautiously. "Who was the driver?"

"That's easy." Mr. Bucarella adjusted his glasses and once again ran his finger down the long white tally sheet of his hack registry.

"In seventy-nine, 5107 was checked out to Rudolph Uliano."

Mooney flicked out his small white pad and pencil. "Great—can you give me his address?"

"I can give you his address, but I'm afraid it won't help you very much."

Mooney looked up from his pad and felt his heart sink. He gazed into Mr. Bucarella's sad sweet smile.

"Rudy died eight months ago."

30

"Put your leg up over mine."

"The right one?"

"Right. Over my thigh."

"Like this?"

"Right. Now slide sidewards."

"Like this?"

"Right. Now just sort of ease forward."

"Where are you, for Chrissake? I can't find you."

"Never mind about me. I'll find you. Come forward a little and then left. Give me your hand. I'll guide you."

"Oh, Jesus."

Fritzi Baumholz rolled sidewards across the huge, naked shape beneath her. When she slid off Mooney's massive flank, the springs of the king-sized mattress wheezed beneath them, releasing a gasp of air under pressure, like a pair of huge bellows.

"Okay," Mooney persisted. "Let's try sideways."

She could see that his failure had mortified him.

Fritzi was a handsome woman, large but by no means fat, and splendidly proportioned. Every part of her was firm and muscular. She had the frame of an athlete, and in the nude, with her ruddy skin and her long tawny hair that came undone and tumbled on her shoulder, she was a pleasing sight.

That had made it all the harder for Mooney. If she had been somehow less attractive, he might have felt less pressured. In the darkened room there, with only the lights of the city shining in, he had a glimpse of his own unsightly girth. The outline of his paunch rose and fell like the white-parchment belly of some huge dying fish turned upward on its back.

He was grotesque, he thought. Fit not for the mutual exchange of tender gestures between normal man and woman, but only for the kind of beastly coupling he could find in the storefront cesspools of the West Side. There it was all easy, you never had to look at the girl and, more than likely, you would never see her again. When it was over, the exchange of moneys and sexual favors, one could leave, unburdened of any sense of having failed oneself.

"You've been eating again, Frank. You're bigger and fatter. You can't go on like this. Mind you, I'm not as concerned about the sex part as I am about your health."

"Oh, Jesus, don't start lecturing me now about cholesterol and blood pressure."

"If I do, it's because I'm fond of you. Under all that blubber there's a very attractive man."

Mooney folded his arms stolidly across his bare chest and stared at the dark ceiling. "I can't help it, I tell you, I'm doing my best."

"Your best is not good enough. We're going to reduce your calories by another three hundred. If necessary, we'll go to a straight liquid diet. Until you get down to about 180 pounds, you're not fit to share a bed with a decent woman."

"A hundred and eighty," Mooney whimpered. "Christ—that's another twenty pounds. As it is, I go around with my tongue hanging out all day. I'm sick of drinking water to fill the hole inside me."

She turned and looked up at him over her shoulder, then threw an arm across his chest. There was an arch little smirk on her face. "Just think how swell you'll look when we go to the beach this summer."

"Forget about that. I'm goin' to no beach."

"And we're going to take you downtown and get you all gussied up with a whole new wardrobe. You're looking awfully dowdy, Frank."

"That's just the way I like it. Dowdy Frank, that's me."

"And I want to get you some nice blazers for the tracks. And some spring plaids . . . and . . ."

"Drop it, for Chrissake. Just let me be."

Her finger dallied in the hairy nest of his chest, inscribing little circles. From somewhere deep within him a groan as ancient as time rose into the muffled darkness. A phrase, barely audible, trailed off in a sigh.

"What's that?"

"What's what?"

"Whatever you just said. What was it?"

"I said I don't have no business here."

"That's true. Not at two hundred pounds. At about one eighty you're in like Flynn."

"Leave me alone, Fritzi. Lemme go."

"Who's holding you? You can go any time you please. Back to Fritos and Devil Dogs."

"Knock off, I said. Lemme be. I'm tired fighting."

"Tired? You? You're a young boy."

"I'm sixty-one."

She sat up and squinted at him in the dark. "You told me you were fifty-eight."

"I was lying. I'm sixty-three."

"You just said sixty-one."

"I was still lying. Listen, I'm dead, I tell you. I'm a tired old fart. For all I know, I may be eighty."

She tossed him one of those gay, slightly mocking glances. "You're willing to settle for that?"

"Sure, I'm willing. More than willing. I got no records to break. No one to impress. Hey, what the hell are you doing?"

She suddenly rolled over and came up astride him.

"Fritzi—what the hell—"

"How does that feel?"

"Oh, jeez . . ."

"Shut up, Mooney and hold me. I've got lovely bosoms, don't I?"

An airless gasp broke from his lips. She turned and stretched full-length beside him. Warm lips sought his. "You *are* going to lose weight, Mooney. I swear it. I'm going to render you like a stuffed goose. You may hate me for it, but by the time I'm finished with you, you're going to be a goddamned sex symbol."

31

It had been months since he had thought about the boy, and then only at night, by himself. He didn't like to think about it. The waste, the pity, the total uselessness of it. A strong, vital young man, totally innocent of any wrongdoing, cut down like that in the prime of life. An aspiring dancer, now a quadraplegic consigned to the prison of a wheelchair for the rest of his life.

Plodding along the crowded street in that unseasonably raw evening, he raised his collar higher and retracted his neck deep within it. Then, for some unaccountable reason, he recalled having the temerity or the foolhardiness to have sent the plant around to the hospital by special messenger. A sharp detective might easily have made the connection. How many messenger services were there in the city anyway? Surely they kept records of deliveries to hospitals—but of course it was highly doubtful that they kept records of the contents of such deliveries.

Even so, it was a rash, stupid thing to have done. But he'd thought of it then as a kind of atonement. Putting himself at risk like that was a kind of self-purification. Surely the police would be monitoring all of young Archer's mail, and particularly gifts from perfect strangers. Wouldn't they be the first to be suspected, those who'd made offerings seeking expiation for their crimes? What could the police now make of the name A. Boyd given with no return address? Suddenly he viewed the whole exercise as cheap and theatrical—snickering up his sleeve at how close he could entice the law while still shrewdly evading it.

He thought if he walked vigorously, exhausting himself, he would forget about the boy. Whenever he had ghosts (and it was often), he

145

would banish them by means of strenuous physical activity. A hard, driving, self-punishing relentless walk until the heart banged and the calves ached. It had worked for him in the past. All the others: Catalonia, O'Meggins, Quigley, Soong, and Ransom. After violent exercise, the phantoms relented and would drift quietly off, as if flayed from his body. Not so Archer. The others had died, so it was easier to banish them. But Archer had survived. He lived in a hospice in Staten Island attended by Carmelite nuns who specialized in the care of quadraplegics.

He knew all about it. He'd kept abreast of young Archer by means of newsclips. Periodically, he'd even phone the rehabilitation center, identifyng himself as a relative in town very briefly and merely calling to inquire how the boy was getting on.

Respectfully, even eagerly, they'd answer all his questions. No one ever challenged the authenticity of the calls, and at the conclusion of each, invariably he'd add, "I'd rather Jeffrey didn't know I was asking about him. I wouldn't want him to think we were concerned."

The nuns always respected his wishes and never attempted to penetrate his privacy. Still, try as he might, he could not eradicate the memory of Jeffrey Archer from his mind.

After Archer he vowed it would never happen again. He had always thought of his rooftop escapades as being summary and final. He had never envisioned them as leading to permanent impairment. "No more," he proclaimed that anguished haunted day of self-loathing after the last drop when he sent the plant to Archer at the hospital. Afterward, he went to a small nearby church, fell on his knees and prayed. "This is the end of it," he had said over and over again to himself. "This is it. No more. I swear. This time it's really finished."

For several months after there were the bouts of remorse, the near-biblical grieving, all of which served to buttress his resolve to quit. He thought of going to the police but the possibility of jail horrified him. He could not bear the thought of being locked away, his freedom taken from him. Then came the months of quiescence. Blessed respite from the ghosts. The fog lifting. Entering another phase. Brighter. More hopeful. Thinking he'd licked it. The awful thing would never come again. Then, only yesterday—a small, unpleasant, totally unrelated incident and suddenly it had all come rushing back.

Up ahead the gaudy lights of the street twinkled in the mist-hung night and ran together like colored paints splashed by water.

"I won't," he said. "This is it. This is the end of it. No more. No more." He repeated the words in a kind of fierce litany. His face was wet, he thought, from rain. He didn't know that he was crying.

32

"After the war . . . after having been the sole survivor of a helicopter accident during a secret mission behind enemy lines . . . after coming home, I worked as a safety engineer for Trans World Airlines. . . ."

"And how long was that?"

"That was four years: 1970 through 1974. Then I became purser for Pan Am."

"Yes . . . And that lasted. . . ?"

"Two years. Then I worked as a free-lance writer."

"A writer?"

"That's right. For a salvage magazine. Sunken ships. Buried treasure. That sort of thing. And then I was an airplane mechanic, and then I was commissioned a commander in the Iranian navy. That was during the reign of the late shah, whom I knew quite well."

"I see." The eyes of the interviewer arched above the frames of heavy horn-rimmed glasses. She was a short, dark, intense woman with a light furze of hair above the upper lip. "Were you a mechanic and commander in the Iranian navy all at one time?"

The note of barely masked ridicule had not escaped Watford. "No. That was over a seven-year period."

"That puts us into 1983, Mr. Watford. This is still only 1981."

Watford shrugged and grinned wryly. "I guess I'm wrong, then."

If she thought his smile impertinent, she was no doubt right. He didn't like her any more than she liked him. The situation surrounding the interview was intolerable and he knew she hadn't believed a word he'd said. Since she had rejected him even before reading his résumé, he resolved to conduct himself as atrociously as possible. It took the sting out of the rejection and made him feel better.

147

This was the seventh agency he'd been to that day. He'd started eagerly at nine sharp that morning with reasonable hope, looking as he tried to explain to each interviewer, for a position with an airline. When it became apparent to him that most of the interviewers were not taking his application seriously, he became increasingly outrageous.

They were sitting now in a little three-walled glass cubicle furnished with a desk and two chairs in a one-flight-up employment agency directly off Fifth Avenue.

"I've been a magician, too," he went on quite earnestly.

"You don't say?"

"Yes, yes. You know, scarves, rope tricks, rabbits out of hats."

"I see."

"Do you?"

"Only too well. Thank you very much, Mr. Watford." She rose.

"I speak seven foreign languages, too."

"I'm sorry. I have nothing for a linguist today." She stood there stiffly, trying to leave, but not quite brazen enough to turn her back upon him and walk out. She was also a bit frightened.

He knew he had talked too much but by now he was no longer able to stop himself. "German, French, Arabic, Hebrew, Turkish, Croatian, Gaelic . . ."

"Thank you. I'm afraid we have nothing."

"And Russian, of course. I can start tomorrow, if you'd like."

He rose, nearly tipping his chair, watching her back out of the cubicle, her eyes suddenly filled with panic. In the next moment she turned and fled.

As he walked across the gray littered floor on his way out, he had a sudden ghastly prospect of aisles and rows of cubicles. They were all furnished in precisely the same rudimentary way as the one he'd just left. Even more disheartening was a glimpse he had of the occupants in each. Bathed blue under harsh fluorescent lights, applicant as well as interviewer, barely distinguishable, all uniformly shabby, mean and defeated; each hating the other; the barest pretense of civility between them.

Halfway across the floor he started to laugh. It had begun with a small, barely audible snicker, then mounted into gales of howling, scornful laughter.

People looked up. Several came out of the cubicles to see what was going on. But Watford kept right on walking, booming laughter into the stale, smoky air. For all of the hilarity, he was faintly sick. He had never before encountered so much rejection, and the thought that his money was fast running out, along with his Demerol and prescription pad, made his mouth dry and his throat constrict.

* * *

"Try to recall, Mrs. Uliano. I know it's tough."

"Aaah?"

"I say, I know it's tough."

"Aaah?"

"Difficult, difficult." Mooney was reduced to shouting into her ear, his problem compounded by the fact that not only did the wizened little Italian lady have a hearing deficit, but her English was virtually nonexistent.

"Rudy . . ."

"Sì, sì." Her eyes lit. "Rudy. Aaah?"

"Rudy. Cab. One night. Last year." He waved a finger in the air and gestured frantically as if he were playing charades. "Capeesh?"

"Sì. Sì. Rudy. Cab. Tax, aah? Sì, sì." She stood there before him, a hag mantled in mourning black, leaning on a stick. He suspected that she was not as old as she appeared. That impression arose from her black funereal clothing which he guessed she had not changed since the death of her husband nearly a year before. Mooney lowered his voice and tried to affect sorrow. He was certain she thought he was a lunatic.

"In Rudy's cab one night. Blood. Molto blood. Hombre. Mucho hurt. Remember?"

A stream of Italian spewed from her.

He gestured wildly and retreated next to a kind of lingua franca of the eyes and body.

"Ah," she said, a glint of seeming comprehension in her gaze. "Blood. Blood. Sì."

"Sì. Blood. Sì." His head nodded frantically at her while hers nodded back in the identical rhythm.

"Man hurt. Blood. Remember?"

She cocked her head sideways, like a small sparrow, and stared up at him. "Aaah?"

"Oh, shit."

"Aaah?"

"Nothing. Sorry."

He thought wistfully of Fritzi at the track and icy-minted bourbons, fresh March breezes buffeting out of the west, the roar of crowds and the good smell of leather and horseflesh. Afterward, lobsters, or maybe soft-shelled crabs somewhere out on the Island.

Mrs. Uliano's little parlor room with the linoleum floors was steeped in the odors of provolone cheese and decades of marinara sauce.

Just as he thought all of his linguistic ingenuity had been exhausted, he heard the click of a key in the outside door.

It swung open and a young man in jeans and Windbreaker stood there peering inward from the threshold.

"Dominick." The old lady waved her cane at him and rattled something in Italian.

Mooney watched the young man start falteringly forward. When he came within reach of the old lady, she snatched his sleeve and tugged him closer. "My boy. Dominick."

"Ah, your son." Mooney felt relief surge through him. He turned to the young man whom he judged to be about thirty. From his rough dress and dusty leather brogues, Mooney assumed that he was in some kind of construction work.

"You speak English, Dominick?"

"Sure."

"Aaah." Mrs. Uliano beamed satisfaction.

"My name is Mooney. I'm a detective." He flashed his badge and noted the frown that crossed the young man's face. Dominick Uliano fired off something in Italian. At once the old lady turned and vanished noiselessly into the gloom of a darkened kitchen beyond. She did not reappear.

"I don't know nothin' about that," Dominick Uliano said after Mooney had explained to him the reason for his visit. "My father never talked much about his work. When would this have been?"

"Two years ago."

"How do you know it was my father's cab?"

"I don't. All I know is your father probably had a badly injured guy in the backseat of his cab somewhere around the night of April 30, 1979." Mooney noted the look of distrust in the young man's eyes. "Your father's not accused of any wrongdoing, Dominick. It may just be that he holds the key to this whole series of so-called 'accidental deaths' around the theater district."

The young man continued to watch him warily. "You say this guy bled a lot in the backseat?"

"Like a stuck pig. Your father probably took him to a hospital and left him there. Did your father ever mention anything like that to you?"

Dominick Uliano's eyes bristled with that innate distrust of the lower classes for the police. "If he had, I would've remembered," he snapped.

"He didn't break no law, I want you to understand. Normally, cabdrivers are supposed to report any emergencies like that."

"You mean fill out a form?"

"Right." Mooney watched him uneasily. "But I want you to know, as far as we're concerned, your old man is clean. He did nothin' illegal."

"So?"

"So, I'm tryin' to find out where he might have taken that injured passenger."

150

"Oh."

Mooney could see the young man struggling to think quickly, but terrified of saying the wrong thing. "No. He never said nothin' like that to me."

"You didn't talk much with your old man?"

"Nope. Not too much."

"You know anyone who did?"

A faint flash glowed momentarily in the young man's eye, then sputtered and went out. "Nope."

"Sure you do, Dominick."

"No. I'm tellin' you, I don't."

"Come off it, Dominick. Don't be simpleminded. He must have had someone he spoke to."

"No. Now, I already told you. My old man spoke to no one. He was like . . . very private. See?"

"Not a friend? Not a close buddy? Not even your mother? Listen, if you knew you could save a life by recalling the name of a pal of his. Someone he drove with."

The notion appeared to spark something in the young man's imagination. "You sayin' this guy in the back of my old man's cab was some kind of killer?"

Mooney shrugged. He knew he'd hooked him. "More than likely."

The silence that followed was portentous. Mooney watched his quarry weaken.

"Well, there might've been some guy he drove with . . ."

"Yeah?"

"Nothin' you'd call a close pal, see."

"Sure—I understand."

The young man stretched his neck and gave it a sharp half-turn as if the collar were too tight. He rattled off some more Italian in the direction of the kitchen where Mooney could hear the old lady stir and start to shuffle about.

"There was a guy he used to drive with by the name of Harry Rothblatt."

"Rothblatt, Harry," Mooney scribbled the name into his pad.

"If there was a guy my father used to talk to a lot—real buddies sort of—it was him."

"I got you."

"Used to drive for Acme when my old man was there. Now I think he works with some outfit out in Queens."

"You wouldn't happen to know which one?"

"No, but if you're lookin' for him, just go to the Belmore Cafeteria on Twenty-eighth and Park Avenue South. If he's not there, they'll know where you can find him."

❖ ❖ ❖

151

Even as he drove down over the 138 Street Bridge, making his way west to Park Avenue South, he struggled to suppress a sense of gathering momentum. It was a bit like betting a horse who'd been out of the money his last six races, then suddenly makes an unexpectedly strong move coming out of the eighth pole.

Mooney knew the Belmore by reputation only. Occasionally, a garment manufacturer off his track might stumble in, but the ninety-year-old cafeteria was a landmark frequented by virtually every cabdriver in the city. Open seven days a week, twenty-four hours a day, it was a lighthouse to all those tired, angry men crisscrossing the city every day in yellow cabs, driving through the long reaches of the night, drawn there by the temptation of strong coffee and sweet pastries, hot meals at any hour. And, of course, always the raw, bitter, funny conversation—gossip from all the comrades of the road. There was about it more the raucous flavor of a clubhouse than that of a cafeteria located in the grimy, drably commercial section of Park Avenue South.

"Where would I find Harry Rothblatt?" Mooney asked a blowsy, overweight cashier, spilling out of the cramped little area behind the register. She ignored him pointedly and went about her pencil computation. He waited, until at last she looked up regarding him through rhinestone-framed sunglasses. For reply she nodded in the direction of a tall, bald counterman with his shirt open to the third button, proclaiming a hairy chest upon which the Hebrew letters for LIFE glittered in gold plate.

"Harry Rothblatt," Mooney inquired a moment later, and watched the man flip potato pancakes into a huge skillet of sizzling fat. The rancid smell of fried food wafted up about his face.

"Who wants him?"

Mooney flashed his badge over the glass counter. The man gave it a quick impassive glance and poured more pancake batter into his skillet. "He's not here right now."

"Does he come in regular?"

"Every day."

"When do you expect him?"

The counterman glanced at his watch. "Between six-fifteen and six-thirty. Just before he goes on. He drives at night."

Mooney glanced up at the cafeteria clock which read 6:10.

"Fifteen minutes or so," the counterman said. "You had your supper yet?"

Mooney gazed wistfully at the huge, pink corned beef and hams, the freshly made, still warm, brisket glistening with beads of brown burned fat. He had barely eaten all day. Now the warm, heady odors of roasts and frying food were merciless.

"Not yet," Mooney made a sheepish, pathetic face and started to back off.

"What can I offer you, my friend?"

He put his hands up as if he were warding off a blow. "Nothing, thanks. Not a thing . . ."

The counterman watched the detective's wistful gaze fall upon the crisp, lacy-fried potato pancakes. "What about a couple of these little beauties?"

"I can't, really. Thanks all the same." Mooney was weakening and the counterman saw it. He heaped a half-dozen pancakes on a plate, along with a dollop of sour cream and one of apple sauce. "How about a nice slice of brisket? Fresh out of the oven. To go with the pancakes?"

Mooney smiled queasily. The stern, disapproving gaze of Fritzi Baumholz flashed before his eyes. "I really shouldn't."

"Who says?"

"I'm supposed to be on a diet."

"Who's telling anyone? I didn't see a thing." The counterman winked and passed the plate along to Mooney, who took it with trembling hands. "Take a seat over there. Make yourself comfortable. I'll let you know when Harry comes in. Coffee's in the urn. Iced tea, if you prefer. Help yourself."

Mooney threaded his way across the floor, to an empty table beneath the cafeteria clock. In a little under six minutes he had jettisoned every rule of calorie conservation and was more ravenously hungry than ever. More than anything now he craved strawberry shortcake or an eclair, oozing custard and dark chocolate. The fact that he was so intimidated by the mere thought of Fritzi made him even more recklessly defiant.

Mooney was just about to rise and seek out sweets when he caught the eye of the counterman nodding at him, and then toward the door. As he turned he saw a gray, sixtyish, bearlike figure, with a dome of gauzy white hair shamble through the doors.

He sat back down in his chair and watched the man lumber across the floor waving to people, pausing occasionally at tables to chat with other drivers.

Once he reached the counter Mooney watched him lean quickly forward while the counterman whispered something in his ear and pointed to Mooney. The man turned and looked quickly at the detective, then turned back to the counterman who proceeded to serve him.

With his tray full, the man turned once more, and without looking at Mooney, made his way directly toward him.

"Hold on," he said, placing his tray at the same table opposite the detective. "Be with you in a minute. Just wanna get some tea."

The man turned and lumbered back to the big aluminum urns. He walked as if his feet hurt him. Mooney's jaded eye rambled over a tray full of salad, cottage cheese and stewed prunes.

"Ulcers," the big man remarked, returning to the table. He set his cup of tea down and took the seat opposite Mooney. He'd caught the look of repugnance on the detective's face. "Not exactly the food of the gods. Harry Rothblatt," he said. "I understand you're lookin' for me."

Rothblatt was a gloomy, talkative man. He'd lived in Flatbush all his life and driven a cab for forty years. His wife had died several years back and now he spoke ruefully of ungrateful children and rapacious relatives. But of course he had known Rudy Uliano. "Knew him for years. Sweetheart of a guy. We used to drive together for Washkowitz, that 'cheap, chiseling kike.' Then Rudy moved up to the Bronx and started driving for Acme. But how'd you find me?"

"It's a long story. Actually, I just went around to about forty garages. Finally hit one where the injury and date appeared to coincide. They gave me Uliano's name and that led to you."

Harry Rothblatt chewed lettuce with a weary air of obedience. "And you say this guy was injured in Rudy's cab?"

"Not in his cab. Outside. But he was probably spilling a lot of blood and flagged your pal. Bled all over the back of his cab."

Mr. Rothblatt nodded eagerly. "Oh, sure. Now I remember."

Mooney leaned forward in his chair. "You *do* remember?"

"How could I forget? Couple of years ago, wasn't it? What a night. Poor Rudy. Blood all over his shoes and trousers."

Outwardly calm, something like a locomotive roared full speed inside of Mooney's head. "Did Rudy tell you about it?"

"Sure. Well, you couldn't stop him. He come down here right afterward. I was sittin' over there at that table." Mr. Rothblatt pointed to a table across the cafeteria, presently occupied by a pair of voluble bag ladies who kept berating each other. "He was pretty shook up. I took him right into the men's room and we got him washed up. Then I brought him back out and gave him a cup of black coffee and he just started talking. Sure, I remember."

"Did he tell you how the guy happened to get the injury?"

Mr. Rothblatt closed his eyes and thought for a moment. Then he shook his head. "Nope. I don't think so. Least I don't recall nothin' about that."

"Did he happen to say where exactly the guy was injured?"

"You mean where he was injured on his body or where the accident occurred?"

"Both," Mooney snapped, unable to suppress his impatience.

"Lemme see." Mr. Rothblatt's spoon of sour cream paused midway between bowl and mouth. "It was somewhere over in the theater district. I think he said it was around Fortieth or Forty-first."

"Forty-first and where?"

"It strikes me it was pretty far west. Like Ninth Avenue."

Mooney's heart leaped. "You're sure?"

"Pretty sure. We talked about it for some time that night." Mr. Rothblatt spooned prunes into his mouth, chewed intently and let the pits slide back onto his spoon.

"And what about the injury," Mooney pressed on. "What about that? Like, where was it on the guy?"

Mr. Rothblatt pondered a moment, then shook his head. "I don't think he said."

"How d'ya suppose Rudy got all that blood on him?"

"Probably helping the guy in and out of the cab."

"Sure. Then if Rudy had blood on his trousers and shoes," Mooney reflected aloud, "it stands to reason this guy's injuries were below the belt rather than above."

"Could be." Mr. Rothblatt appeared unimpressed.

Mooney turned sharply back upon him. "Tell me. This is important. Did Rudy happen to say where he took the guy?"

"I think he said some hospital on the East Side."

"Yes?"

"But I can't remember the name. That's one of the things about getting older. You don't remember names so well anymore. Just places." The thought of that made him suddenly sad.

"Was it New York University Medical Center?"

"Nope. That wasn't it." Mr. Rothblatt drummed nervously on the table. "People get in my cab all the time. They ask me the names of places. I can never remember, but I know exactly how to get there."

"Was it Beth Israel Medical Center?"

Mr. Rothblatt thumped the table triumphantly. "That's it. That's the place. Beth Israel."

Mooney was at the edge of his chair. "You're sure now?"

"Course I'm sure. I remember because poor Rudy couldn't say it right. He kept calling it Bett Israel." The old driver laughed nostalgically. "He was one sweetheart of a guy, that Rudy. Give you the shirt off his back. But listen, ain't all this in the emergency report?"

"Should be, but Rudy never filed one." Mooney rose and took Harry Rothblatt's punch ticket off his tray. "This one's on the city."

33

Mooney's day had been a binge, a procession from one excess to the next. Having saturated himself at the Belmore Cafeteria, he wanted to go directly down to Beth Israel. It was only a matter of ten minutes by car. But it was Sunday night and, of course, the administrative offices would be closed. Tomorrow would be soon enough.

Still logy from gluttony, he could not bear the thought of facing Fritzi. Actually, the image of her silent reproach made him decidedly uneasy. One glance at him and she'd know all. On the way home he drove up Lexington Avenue past the gay Victorian gaslights outside the Balloon. Inside, the lights glowed—warm and festive. He felt more desolate than ever.

It was no doubt that feeling which drove Mooney up onto the roof of his apartment house that evening, seeking the solitude of the nighttime sky and the cold, nonjudgmental indifference of the stars. That, of course, plus the uneasy fact that the solstice was near at hand. No more than a week or ten days off, and from the point of view of his own theories, the calendar was rapidly approaching the most critical phase for the Bombardier.

34

"FILARIA." He rolled the word round several times on his tongue. "FILARIASIS—a diseased state due to the presence of nematode worms called FILARIAE within the body. BANCROFT's infection of the lymphatic system with the adult form of WUCHERERIA BANCROFTI."

He repeated the last two words, striving to achieve an easy fluency. He wanted the words to roll off his tongue as if he'd uttered them every day of his life. Then, too, Watford wished to give his intonation that special ring of the highly informed. After a period of constant repetition, the words took on a magic for him. They became incantatory. "Helminthic diseases. Nematodes. Insect vector, mosquitoes. Geographic range: Tropical Africa, North Africa, borders of Asia and Queensland, the West Indies and northern tier of South America.

"ETIOLOGY: caused by filarial worm. Lymphangitis with fibrosis. Insect vector, mosquitoes. Transfers to host. More than a year after infection microfilariae appear in the peripheral blood."

Watford reread the last sentence. He made some rapid computation in his mind, then scribbled the essence of it onto a pad. A point he carefully noted was that one of the loci of the disease were the borders of the Asian subcontinent.

"SYMPTOMATOLOGY: reactive hyperplasia seen in the lymph nodes along with small granulomas. Lymphatic obstruction becomes more extensive. Chronic edema develops in the infected areas affecting especially the lower limbs and scrotum. Eventually the giant limbs of elephantiasis are produced."

Watford had a sudden vision of himself, a boy fourteen years of age on a class excursion to Washington. The Smithsonian Institution. The

157

medical wing. Corridors of glass cases behind which resided in large transparent tubs of Formalin, three-headed fetuses and torsos from which multiple arms grew; sometimes merely hands with three or four fingers. Monstrosity following monstrosity. But for Watford, the most riveting and ghastly was an exhibition devoted to the effects of elephantiasis.

In a bath of Formalin the amputated grayish-yellow leg of an elephantiasis victim stood straight up, balanced on its foot. It was enormous, the calf matching the circumference of a fifty-year-old oak. Beside that was the photograph of a man sitting in a jungle clearing. His scrotum had swelled so from the disease that he was able to sit upon it as if it were a large ottoman. It was then that young Charles Watford grew sick and had to be whisked out of the hall by one of the teachers.

The night in the hotel where the group stayed, he dreamed of limbs—limbs of gargantuan size and genitals that were horrific.

"CLINICAL MANIFESTATIONS," he read further, devouring the ghastly symptoms enumerated on the page, unable to avert his eye from the color photographs.

When at last he lay the book down it was past 11:00 P.M. He would have to be up early tomorrow and out at the agencies. His funds were perilously low. He had incurred debts in the several weeks he'd been home and it was imperative that he make a connection soon.

In bed, lying weary yet sleepless, his mind twitched with visions of gross pathology, disfigurations, pernicious cellular infiltration of bacteria and viruses. He tried to lay out a plan of attack for the following day. First thing in the morning he would buy a *Times* and search the classified pages. He would go to every agency. Seek work. But what exactly was his line of work? He liked to think, of course, it was the airline industry. High mobility. Rapid transit. New faces. New places. The cheap, quickly fabricated glamour of flight. He enjoyed that sort of thing and, of course, one of its special dividends was that one was never obliged to stay any one place too long.

"FILARIASIS," he whispered the word into the gloomy shadows of his room, as if conjuring a god. "DIETHYLCARBAMAZINE. LYMPHANGITIS. QUANGDUC 1972. The rainy season. Monsoons. Slogging through the sodden, dripping, insect-ridden forest. The shriek of monkeys. Foot patrols. Sappers. Hostile forces. Sent back to base hospital. FILARIASIS. My head. My head hurts, Doctor."

35

There were couples strolling up and down West Forty-eighth Street. Children at play, running and shrieking in the gutters. Elderly folk sitting out on stoops before the huddled tenements. The din of traffic rumbling up Ninth Avenue. Gas fumes mingling with the sweetish fetor of uncollected trash set out in plastic bags before the buildings.

In front of 436 West Forty-eighth Street, a shabby derelict of a building, with most of its windows punched out, a group of Puerto Rican men drank beer and played dominoes on a wobbly bridge table. The tiles clicked rapidly over the tabletop, punctuated by hoots of laughter and the hiss of beer cans uncapping.

The women sat on the stoop, apart from the men, chattering among themselves. Above it all hovered the improbable scent of heliotrope growing rampantly outside in a window box.

At the corner, the lights of a little bodega twinkled like a Christmas tree. Squealing children rushed in and out of the shop with precious hoarded nickels and dimes, purchasing orangeade and colored frozen ice sticks. Despite the grimness of the surroundings there was an air of gaiety in the streets, a sense of the miraculous at having gotten through another day.

Across from 436, a man stood by himself in the shadows of the building opposite. About him was the indefinable air of something furtive, possibly even sinister. He appeared to be observing the dominoes players. From time to time his eyes ranged up and down the street, then swept upward over the facade of the building to the rooftops. In his right hand he carried a large paper bag, tied carefully with string.

The man watched the dominoes players. He enjoyed the sight of them sitting in shirt-sleeves in the glow from the bodega lights, gruff, hearty, boisterous, the reek of sweat in their soiled clothing, at their board games, laughing, gossiping, drinking wine and beer. They could carouse late into the night, shout and drink wine, tell ribald tales and rise the next morning to drag their bodies off to mean, futile jobs. They retained their toughness and their hope.

The man watched them. Their tough, weedy durability caused in him a kind of envy. In his mind at that moment he contemplated nothing. He had no specific plan, other than the bag he carried with the concrete cinder block inside, scavenged from one of the many construction sites round the city.

He had not the slightest idea of how he'd got there, and no recollection of having picked up the cinder block or carrying it to that place. The thought of it was appalling, but even more so was the total amnesia surrounding the incident.

Perversely, the thought persisted. Just walking in. Climbing up some narrow reeking stairway, several flights, dim corridors, defaced doorways, littered floors. Then, stepping out onto the rooftop . . . dangling the bag out over the ledge, directly above that point where the dominoes players laughed and drank below.

He tried to recall what thoughts had gone through his head on those other occasions. What feelings? Joy? Sorrow? Rage? Nothing. There had been nothing in any of the other incidents to distinguish one from the other. No clear, distinct reason to account for the awful compulsion. Why then would he choose to injure these men or their families? They were so decent. So obviously pleasant. Why? To what purpose? And that boy. That poor, poor boy. I promised you, Jeffrey. I swore. Never again. Not ever.

"Lookin' for someone?"

The man glanced up. He was staring into the pasty round face of an Irish policeman.

The patrolman looked at him curiously. His eye swept rapidly over him, taking in a multitude of detail.

"Anything I can help you with, Mac?"

"No, thank you," the man replied. "I've been waiting for someone, but I guess they're not coming."

"Yeah—that happens." The patrolman sounded sympathetic, but there was something distinctly wary in his eyes.

The dominoes players across the way had stopped to watch.

"I guess I'll be on my way," the man remarked.

The officer's eyes narrowed. "I guess you oughta. Ain't the best place to linger long."

36

"What did you say the name was?"

"Boyd. Mr. Anthony Boyd."

"That's O-Y-D?" Defasio mouth-lipped the word as he spelled it out in his pad in large capital letters.. "You're sure now?"

"Of course I'm sure. Am I not reading it right here before my eyes in the emergency patient intake for April 30, 1979? Mr. Anthony Boyd admitted 11:22 P.M. 4/30/79. Doesn't that sound like your man? Emergency surgery to close a severed femoral artery."

"Beg pardon?"

Ms. Sophie Solomon, administrative clerk of Beth Israel Hospital, squinted at Defasio through thick, pinkish lenses. She was a petulant spinster lady of sixty-seven who resented any form of intrusion into her daily routine, let alone her record books, which were sacrosanct. She guarded them like a gorgon, and was not intimidated by anyone, least of all the police.

Glaring up at Defasio, she put him in mind of a wasp about to sting. "That severed thing you mentioned," said Defasio.

"You mean, I take it, the femoral artery?"

The patronizing snarl in her voice made him more deferential. "Yeah. Right. The femoral artery."

"That's an artery in the leg."

"Where exactly in the leg?"

"In the thigh exactly. The whole length of the thigh, to be exact."

Defasio looked at her warily. She had her way of putting things and he wasn't certain if the solecisms were natural or merely a way of amusing herself at his expense. She went on enunciating through yellow dentures. "It says here on my card that he was in surgery for

161

little over one hour. It took twenty stitches and suturing to close the wound."

Defasio felt the wariness melting into cautious optimism. "Does it say anything there about how this Boyd fellow got the wound?"

Ms. Solomon's squinting gaze flowed up and down the wide, red-ruled ledgers of her intake book. "It says here the injury was incurred as a result of stumbling into an open manhole, and don't try and peer over my shoulder, sonny. I see what you're doing. That's privileged information on this page."

"Sorry." Defasio flushed and stepped quickly backwards. "Did anyone bother to verify the time and place of the injury?"

"That's not our job here," croaked Ms. Solomon. "We're not the police. We're a healing institution. The only thing we report are bullet wounds. A man comes in here having lost a couple of quarts of blood, we don't start interrogations. You understand, Officer?"

"Sure," Defasio nodded enthusiastically. "Sure . . . what about an address for this Mr. Boyd? You got some kind of an address?"

Once again Ms. Solomon's eyes swept over the ledger. Her lips mumbled as she went. "The only address I got here is A. Boyd, Import-Export, 3143 Crown Drive, Wilmette, Illinois."

"That's a business address. You got a residence?"

"I am telling you, Officer," Ms. Solomon's enunciation grew increasingly clipped, "the *only* address I have is the one I've already given you."

"Okay, okay. Don't get angry."

"Who's angry?" Ms. Solomon snarled. "I'm busy here. I'm way behind on my billing, but I am delighted to take valuable time out of my lunch hour and talk to you. It gives me genuine pleasure."

Defasio ground his teeth. "The only thing I'm saying, you understand, is that it does seem a little peculiar that an emergency patient should give his business address rather than his home address."

"Peculiar, but not unheard of. Particularly if the patient's major medical is taken out in his firm's name."

"Oh?" Once again she had him buffaloed. "How *was* the hospital bill paid?"

"By the insurance company, of course."

"Then they'd have Mr. Boyd's home address, wouldn't they?"

"I'd say you could more or less count on it, sonny."

Defasio made a valiant effort to ignore her. "What was the insurance company?"

Ms. Solomon tilted her ear in his direction. "What?"

He was certain she'd heard him.

"The insurance company? Which one was it?"

"The policy underwriter, I take it you mean?"

"That's it, the policy underwriter."

Ms. Solomon squinted down at her records. "That would be Hartford Trust and Traveler. Insurance number 683-914-2108."

A few minutes later Michael Defasio was outside in a reeking public phone booth the tattered walls of which had become a palimpsest of graffiti and ball-point pornography. He was shouting over a bad wire to the records chief of Hartford Trust and Traveler. Standing there for several minutes, he'd been tossing in additional coins while waiting for the records chief to come back on the line.

Finally he lost the connection, or he was cut off. In any event, he had to run round the corner to a small cigar store for change. There was a pay phone there. He ducked in at once and redialed Hartford.

"Where'd you go?" the records chief asked when he got him back on the line.

"We were cut off," Defasio explained breathlessly. "Did you find anything?"

"Well, if it's the address you're looking for, I've got it."

"Terrific."

"It's A. Boyd, Incorporated, Import-Export, 3143 Crown Drive . . ."

"Wilmette, Illinois."

"That's right. How come you knew that?"

"I'll tell you some other time." Defasio sounded tired. "Listen, that's a commercial address. Don't you have a residence?"

He could hear papers shuffle through the line. "Afraid not. This is a commercial health insurance policy. All the premiums were paid by the company. A. Boyd, Incorporated."

"Who's the guarantor of the policy?"

The proprietor—Mr. Anthony Boyd, I told you. If you wanna locate Mr. Boyd, what you've gotta do is call A. Boyd, Incorporated, in Wilmette."

"Okay," Defasio nodded. By then he was willing to try anything. "Do you happen to have the telephone number out there?"

"Sure. It's right here on the policy application. Area code 555-734-2664. But I should tell you one thing. This policy lapsed over two years ago."

In a sense, Defasio did not have to make the call to Wilmette. His good basic cop instincts told him that, just like the lapsed policy, the telephone at 3143 Crown Drive would be disconnected and Mr. A. Boyd, long gone. He knew, too, just as certainly, that when he'd finally located the landlord of the building in which A. Boyd, Inc. had operated, there would be no record of a forwarding address—just a trail that dropped off into nowhere—a trail that had started in a taxi garage in the Bronx and appeared to end at an office bulding in a suburb of Chicago.

He was no closer now to the badly injured mystery man in Rudy Uliano's cab than before when he'd started with the formidable Ms. Solomon. Who was Anthony Boyd and where could he be found? For starters, he might try the phone book. It was the most obvious approach and yet no one had done it.

A bank of local directories stood outside the booth. He started with Manhattan, in which five Anthony Boyds were listed; the Bronx yielded two; Brooklyn and Queens, three apiece. Staten Island had one Andrew Boyd, but no Anthony. Then, of course, there was Connecticut and New Jersey. And why did he so blithely assume that *his* Anthony Boyd had to reside in the tri-state area? Why not Montana or Utah or Texarkana? Or, why not Illinois, particularly when A. Boyd's import-export business was in Wilmette? Why then, not a check run of all Anthony Boyds or A. Boyds to be found through the central billing division of the Illinois Bell Company? Why then, not run the name through the FBI's central records office in Washington, D.C., as well as a fast check for military records at the Pentagon?

A great bone-weariness came over him as he contemplated the magnitude of the job. It would take weeks, months, perhaps, to cover all those check runs. Meanwhile, there was the problem of one Francis Mooney, the blowtorch scorching his backside. Over the past week Mooney had grown testier and more impatient than ever. He, too, had his own ax to grind with the captain and the commissioner. He was in no mood for the frustration of further delay. Also, Defasio had guessed that Mooney, in some curious, unspoken way, had taken the matter of the rooftop Bombardier to heart. Unlike his characteristically cynical approach to most investigative work, this case, Defasio noted, had taken on for Mooney the appearances of a personal cause. It had something to do with the man's fall from grace, and his quest for ultimate salvation.

Then, too, there was this incomprehensible cant he'd babble all day about the time of year, the stars, the solstice and the urgency of NOW, NOW NOW. Based on the vaguest information, gathered from a slightly forgetful cabdriver named Rothblatt, Mooney now genuinely believed that he had drawn close to the mystery man who'd commandeered Rudy Uliano's cab on the night of April 30, 1979. The same man who, bleeding and close to shock, had been driven from somewhere on Forty-first Street and Eighth Avenue to the emergency ward of Beth Israel Hospital. Now he would have to tell Mooney that he was unfortunately mistaken. He was no closer at all.

With sinking heart, Defasio dialed Headquarters to report to Mooney the results of his investigations.

37

"You checked the insurance company?"

"I already told you I did."

"I know what you told me. Tell me again. I'm stupid."

Defasio sighed and rolled his eyes heavenward. "The insurer was the Hartford Trust and Traveler. The policy number was 683 . . ."

"Never mind the number. Tell me about the premium payments."

"Paid by A. Boyd, Incorporated, Import-Export, 3143 Crown Drive, Wilmette."

"And that's a commercial address, not a residence, right?"

"Right."

"You checked that with the landlord?"

"I told you I did, for Chrissake. And Boyd, Incorporated, vacated the premises two years ago."

"Okay. I'm just getting it all straight in my head." Mooney spoke with a strange calm. Intermittently, he sipped from a mug of steaming consommé, wincing with revulsion each time he swallowed. "What about the landlord?"

"Quality Office Brokers, 14 Lake Drive, Chicago. I told you that too,"

"Right. Now tell me, Sherlock," Mooney's eyes narrowed to small gashes, "was rent on the office space paid directly to them?"

Defasio wore a look of immense personal delight. "I bet you think I didn't check that."

"Not for a moment," Mooney replied acidly. "But now that you mention it, did you?"

There was a weighty pause, followed by an abject sigh.

"Stupid fuck."

165

"I was gonna, Frank. So help me."

"But of course you forgot. I should've known. Stupid asshole. Get on that phone. Get hold of that landlord. Find out what bank those rent checks were drawn on. And out of whose account."

"It's gonna be A. Boyd, Inc. Don't you see, Frank? It's a dummy. Don't you know that by now?"

"Sure I do. Boyd's not the guy's name at all. It's an alias. And the dummy corporation is set up so he can write checks and not be traced. But why?" His voice trailed off in bafflement. "Still, I wanna hear it from the fucking landlord. Not from you. Then I'll start looking someplace else."

"Where, for Chrissake?" shouted Defasio. "The trail ends out there in Wilmette. Boyd's walked off into thin air."

"Not thin enough." Mooney gulped his consommé. "Not thin enough, my friend. Now you go find out about that goddamned dummy bank account."

In twenty minutes he was back. "Chicago First National City. Account number 437 109-680."

"And?"

"The account's in the name of A. Boyd, Incorporated."

"And who signs the checks?"

"A. Boyd."

"Is the account still active?"

"Closed out."

"When?"

"May 10, 1979."

"Just about the same time Mr. A. Boyd was released from Beth Israel, and let his health insurance lapse and vacated the premises at Crown Drive. This doesn't say anything to you, Defasio?"

The young detective pondered that a moment, then shrugged. "Maybe."

"Maybe?" Mooney's face purpled. "If I were you, Defasio, I'd think seriously about taking a TV repairman's course in night school. The odds are improving. Five'll get you eight that Mr. A. Boyd and our good friend, the Broadway Bombardier, are one and the same."

Mooney rose suddenly, the breeze of his huge motion scattering papers across the desk. "Come on."

"Where? I just got back. Where the hell are we going now?"

"Back down to Beth Israel." Mooney swayed massively through the door. "I wanna talk to your friend, Sophie Whatsherface again."

Charles Watford was just leaving the Premier Employment Agency where he'd been subjected to a particularly brutal interrogation at the hands of a brusque young personnel interviewer.

"None of these dates on your employment history tally, Mr. Watford. You can't possibly have been working for Pan Am and Braniff and TWA all at the same time."

"It's been so long. I guess I just got the dates confused. I'm sorry."

"Go back and fill out the application again, with the correct information, will you, please?"

The young man turned away, a curt, dismissive gesture, and pressed a buzzer on his desk.

Watford hovered there momentarily, red-faced and speechless, even as a tall black man in a gray suit was ushered in.

In the next moment Watford turned and left. He did not fill out another application. On the street in the midst of the noontime rush, he had the first inkling of an approaching migraine. Tentative and fleeting, it came as a sharp jab at his right temple and a momentary dimming of vision attended by some blurring. Long experience with such premonitory signals was enough to tell him that within an hour or two he'd be in agony.

Several capsules of Demerol remained in his pocket. Fairly weak prescriptions, they were certainly not enough to weather the full storm. He needed not only Demerol, but his ergotamine as well.

He had about thirty-eight dollars to his name and very grim prospects of getting any more within the foreseeable future. With full realization of that, he started to panic.

He started to walk very fast and with no particular destination in mind. The object was simply to move, and quickly, as if motion itself were the way to slough off the ominous symptoms.

But even as he walked he felt the throbbing commence at the back of his neck, then a distinct tightening like a band narrowing across his temples. Shortly his walk had changed to a half-stumbling trot, and he was craning his neck this way and that as though he were seeking something. He was somewhere on Fifth Avenue, just south of Thirty-fourth Street, when he recalled the Gramercy Park Medical Center, not far from where he was.

He veered sharply south and started down Fifth Avenue at a fairly brisk clip. In his gray plaid suit with shirt and tie, an expression of glazed desperation in his eye, he was a curious sight.

Ten minutes later he stood, as he had two years before, below the large black directory posted out front. There the physicians, along with their specialties, were listed like movie stars on a marquee. DR. GERALD NACHTIGAL—PROCTOLOGY. DR. SEYMOUR SCHNEIDERMAN—CARDIOLOGY, and so forth. There, too, was Dr. Rashower, the urologist whose name he'd borrowed in order to obtain a prescription of Demerol. He was not about to make the mistake of availing himself of that name again.

Watford's leaping eye caught the name of DR. JOSHUA SILBER-

FEIN—GASTROENTEROLOGY—and fixed there with a tenacity that suggested to him something of the providential. The name appeared to give off powerful vibrations of his own deliverance. Instantly, his mind summoned up a host of excruciatingly painful symptoms to accompany the attack of gastric colic he was about to invent.

Several minutes later, he was down the street at the Gramercy Pharmacy, inside the very booth he had used with such great success two years before. He dialed the number of the pharmacy and asked to be connected with the druggist. Though his head was already afflicted with a dull pounding, he experienced the same kind of erotic tickle when he heard the phone ringing behind the counter and watched the druggist reach for it. This time it was a different man from the one of two years before.

"Hello, this is Dr. Silberfein," his voice commenced, with a barely perceptible quaver, then evening out, assumed an impressive authority as he slipped easily into the role. A patient of his, he explained, a Mr. Bertram Mortimer, was in extreme pain from chronic intestinal colic. He was about to admit the man to New York University Hospital, but he would need some Demerol, about seven hundred milligrams, to tide him over until they could find him a bed. Mr. Mortimer was on his way over right now. He, Dr. Silberfein, was uptown on another emergency, but he would instruct his office to send a prescription over as soon as possible.

Watford watched the pharmacist, phone tucked between cheek and shoulder, nodding and scribbling onto a pad. Having set it all in motion, Watford could not help feeling a kind of wild excitement, like an artist under the spell of some great Promethean force. After he'd hung up, he waited in the booth approximately six minutes, then when the pharmacist was preoccupied with another customer, he made his way slowly across to the counter.

The pharmacist looked at him uneasily when he presented himself. Watford at once realized he might well look a fright after the sprint down from Thirty-fourth Street to Gramercy Park.

"Would you wait just a moment, Mr. Mortimer?" the man said. "I'm just making up your prescription now."

"Dr. Silberfein did phone it in?"

"Oh, yes. He did. Just one moment, please. I'll be right back."

Something in the way the man had said it, the stiffness of his voice, the visible tightening of his jaw and mostly the look of distrust in his eyes told Watford that something was up. Whatever might be said of the foolishness and wastefulness of Watford's life, one thing he had unmistakably in his favor was an uncanny acuity for self-protection. His powers of premonition were extraordinary.

He walked round the counter and peered into the back. Instantly

Watford surmised the whole situation—the pharmacist on the phone, leaning forward, whispering hastily into the speaker. Watford needed no additional information to verify that the man was at that moment checking the prescription with the doctor's office.

Suddenly, the pharmacist looked up and saw him. They gazed at each other like a pair of relatives who had not seen one another for years. Watford's face wore a pitiful expression, that of a man hurt and betrayed. He turned and bolted.

"Stop!" the pharmacist shouted and started out from behind. But Watford wasn't stopping for anyone. He barreled down an aisle lined with cosmetics and toiletries, careening off a wire basket full of soaps and sending it scattering. Several women screamed even as the pharmacist, in hot pursuit, kept shouting, "Stop him. Stop him."

A drab, smallish man grappled Watford by the lapel and made a heroic effort to detain him at the door. In vain, however; Watford thrust the man aside and bolted out onto the street. The pharmacist tore out after him, shouting at Watford over the heads of relentless waves of people bearing down upon him. Halfway down the block the pharmacist stopped short, watching the tail of Watford's gray plaid jacket disappear wraithlike round a corner. Puzzled, he paused a moment rethinking his situation, then turned, ran back to the pharmacy and immediately called the police.

38

It was nearly 6:00 P.M. and Sophie Solomon's dander was way up. You could tell that from the way her head shook and from the quick vertical up-down motion of the wen on her chin as she spoke.

Defasio's eye was fixed hypnotically on the small purple blemish with its solitary pole of hair thrusting up out of the center. Mortified that he was unable to avert his gaze, he watched transfixed as she read the riot act to Mooney.

"There's no way in the world I'm gonna go back and pull out record books now. Do you realize what time it is?"

Mooney hovered there, a look of martyrdom on his face, trying to slip a word in edgewise.

"I have a life too. I'm a human being with rights." She wagged a gnarled, arthritic finger under his nose. "Listen—I already went through this with your friend here this afternoon. Ask him." She shrieked at Defasio. "Didn't I already speak to you?"

"Yes, ma'am."

"Didn't I already tell you everything you wanted to know?"

"Unfortunately, Mrs. Solomon . . ."

"Ms."

"Ms.," Mooney pronounced the word with an odd buzz, "but unfortunately my colleague here neglected to . . ."

"Now, at six o'clock, you got the gall to come barging back in here with a whole new list of questions. I'm due at the airport in an hour to pick up my niece." She started to rise.

"I appreciate everything you've done for us already, Miss, Ms. Solomon." Mooney sounded his most reasonable.

"If you appreciated it you wouldn't be standing there asking me to go pull out records at closing time." Flustered and fuming, Ms. Solomon fumbled into a gray pillbox hat.

"One question is all I'm asking," Mooney persisted.

"One question comes to two questions. Two questions to four."

"Believe me, I don't want to take up any more of your time than I have to. This is critically important. Lives depend on our finding this man."

Ms. Solomon appeared unconvinced. "You say he's been missing over a year. He can wait another day." A second time she rose and started for the coat rack where her tan raincoat hung. Defasio reached for it in order to help, but she glowered at him through her pince-nez and snatched it herself. "I'll take that, thank you very much," she hissed coldly.

"Honest," Mooney implored, "this won't take more than five minutes."

"How would you know how long it'll take?" she demanded. "I know how long, Sergeant. You don't."

"Lieutenant," he corrected her and noticed that one of her legs was shorter than the other and that she walked with a pronounced limp, but briskly all the same. In a trice, he grasped her entire history. Spinsterhood. Small cramped apartment with kitchenette. Rolling beds that folded into walls. Cats for companionship. Suppers of canned soup. Evenings beside a small flickering TV or listening to radio concerts. Alone on holidays. By herself on packaged vacation tours. Not entirely unlike his own dismal regimen, although he never went on tours.

"Please, Ms. Solomon." He made one final impassioned appeal. The look in her eye was one of tired disgust.

"Okay." She flung her coat down. "You got just one question. Make it fast."

"The room Mr. Boyd was in that night—was it a private or a double?"

She looked at him, then past him as if she'd already forgotten the question. In the next moment she laughed despairingly to herself, a look of icy resignation on her face. Eyes fixed straight ahead, she limped past the two detectives into the small cubicle office where she kept her records.

They waited uneasily while she riffled through a long horizontal ledger bound in bogus black leather. The year 1979 was gold-stamped across the face of it. Neither man spoke. They barely breathed and never looked at one another for fear of distracting her or invoking her wrath.

At last they heard the pages stop flipping, followed by Sophie Solomon mumbling to herself. "Okay," she yelled at them through the open door. "I think I got what you want. Mr. Boyd was in room 382 that night. That happens to be a double."

"Wonderful." Mooney beamed gratefully. "That's wonderful, Ms. Solomon— Now don't—don't close that book yet." He rushed toward her even as she reared back, slightly alarmed. "May I see that page, please?"

For reply she whisked the ledger up and pressed it to her chest. "Private records. I don't reveal these. Even to the police. Not without a court order."

A wave of fatigue overtook him—almost despair.

"You're perfectly right, Ms. Solomon." The s's buzzed hard in his teeth. "I do need a court order to see your records. It'll take me seven to ten days to secure one. I'm trying very hard now to locate a man who may possibly kill someone within the very near future."

There was a look of contempt in her eyes. "You don't expect me to swallow that one, do you?"

"No," he replied, looking at her hopelessly. "But it happens to be the truth. I have a theory that this Mr. A. Boyd has already killed five people and crippled another for life. I'm trying to avert another tragedy. I have one last question . . . "

"Ah-ha." She glowed triumphantly and clacked her dentures. "Now already you got two questions."

"But this one is definitely the last. And I'm willing to lay seven to ten the answer is right there on that page you're already open to."

171

She watched him distrustfully through pinkish tinted glasses, her head nodding with a gentle palsy. "Didn't I say my niece was due at the airport? I should be there now."

"I appreciate that, Ms. Solomon."

"For one man you do a lot of appreciating." She folded her arms across the ledger and glared defiantly at the two detectives. "Okay— this is the last one. Definitely. Let's have it."

Mooney inhaled and held his breath a moment.

"Was anyone sharing the room with Boyd?"

Ms. Solomon's smile was edged with venom. "I knew you were going to ask me something smart like that."

"The answer's not on that page you're open to?"

Sophie Solomon started to laugh, a cheerless, bitter laugh, full of the painful wisdom of years. "No, it's not on that page." Her small, frail figure shook with laughter. "In the first place, we can't even be sure that anyone shared the room with Mr. Boyd. But in order to verify that I have to check the room numbers of every patient in residence at the hospital that night." Her smile deepened, became almost beatific. "Have you any idea just how many people we have hospitalized in Beth Israel on any given night?"

Mooney stared expectantly at her. "Nope. Tell me."

"What about you, young man?" she cooed at Defasio with all the cordiality of an ice pick.

"Two hundred," Defasio blustered, then gazed sheepishly at Mooney.

Ms. Solomon made a funny quacking sound, then turned back to Mooney. "How would you feel about four hundred?"

"I'd say it's a helluva lot of names to go through."

"You'd be right." Sophie Solomon's smile turned suddenly to a glare. "But as it turns out, it's closer to six hundred inpatients on a given night. Now you're asking me to check roughly six hundred names to see what other person might have shared room 382 with Mr. Boyd."

"I agree it seems unreasonable on the face of it."

"On the face of it?" Ms. Solomon's eyes narrowed to small gashes. Suddenly her mirthless cheer turned to frost. "I'm leaving now."

"Sophie . . ." Mooney started toward her.

Glaring at him above her glasses, she appeared to swell. "Forget it, my friend. There is no way that I'm going to spend the next four hours here, going through every name on the patient manifest for the evening of April 30, 1979. Call me tomorrow, then maybe we'll talk."

She hobbled to the coat rack and once again struggled into her tan raincoat. By that time her glasses were slightly askew. Then suddenly looking at the overweight, clearly exhausted detective, she hesitated.

"However, since I don't particularly care to have the guilt of unnecessary bloodshed on my head, I'm gonna walk out of here now and just forget to put my books away. If you should happen to look at them while I'm out, I can't help that. I'm off to meet my niece now." She turned and hobbled to the door. "Don't forget to turn the lights out when you leave."

Sophie Solomon had said that the job of checking six hundred names of patients against their room numbers would take four hours. As it worked out she was within ten minutes of her projected time.

The names were listed in the huge ledger in alphabetical order. The patient roll was made up each day, giving date, time of entry, a description of illness, room number and discharge date.

For the day of April 30, 1979, the hospital had logged 553 patients. Defasio groaned as they started with the A's and worked on through, checking each name and date against a room number. It was 10:35 P.M. when Mooney looked up bleary-eyed from the ledger and said, "Charles Watford, 724 Hauser Street, Kew Gardens, New York."

39

It was somewhere near 3:00 A.M. when he woke. His mouth was dry and something like a pulse throbbed inside his head. It wasn't the pain that woke him, however, but the hyperventilation—the gulping for air and getting nowhere near enough. The fear of suffocation caused him to sit bolt upright. When he did, his head swam and he nearly toppled over.

The Demerol bottle beside the bed was empty, and the pain was of an order that transcended mere mortal pain. It was so great and all-engulfing that it had the effect of transporting him into some other state. Woozy, half-conscious, hallucinatory, the sense of slipping one's moorings.

Then came those wracking paroxysms, the gasping for air, the awful terror that he might die (not the fear of death itself, but the idea of dying alone), his body undiscovered for weeks—mortification, decomposition, stench, all maggoty and obscene, discovered weeks later by strangers—some shapeless, reeking thing. The indignity, like fouling oneself in public.

When he threw a leg over the edge of the bed, his head shrieked and he sagged to the floor. The floor was uncarpeted and cold. He lay with his face flat down upon it, rolling his flamed cheeks against the cool wood as if to soothe himself.

He lay there for some time, vision unfocused and scintilla rocketing like comets across his visual field. Aware of a sound muffled and distant, like a moaning or whimpering that rose from the basement, he didn't realize that it was himself. He knew he had to get up off the floor, dress and seek medication. On the other hand, motion of any sort produced pain in him of an order that was transfiguring.

Assuming that he could move, where could he go at that hour? All pharmacies were closed and he had long ago worn out his welcome at every hospital in the immediate area. He was known at every emergency room in the borough of Queens.

He would never recall how he managed to dress that night; how he pulled shoes and pants on over pajamas, and threw a raincoat on top of that. Every time he moved he had the distinct impression that his skull would blow apart, shatter into smithereens. Going down the steps to the front door, his legs felt waxen and he thought he would faint. Spark showers continued to rocket madly inside his head.

Outside, the streets were damp and deserted. There had been recent rain. Misty halations encircled the streetlamps at every corner. Suddenly, he was striding purposefully out toward Austin Street, the heels of his shoes ringing on the damp cobbles.

On 74th Road he rounded the corner, walked beneath the black dripping trestle of the LIRR and emerged onto the ghostly vacancy of the boulevard before dawn. There was something phantasmagoric about it—the traffic lights, the dimly illuminated shop windows, shimmering in the rain-slicked streets. Out on the boulevard a solitary taxi bound for some unknown destination hurtled onward into the night. Within that mottled, woozy landscape, Watford knew exactly where he was going. Some internal gyroscope had guided him, and when at last he stood in the pale neon illumination of the Cardinal Pharmacy window with its phials and apothecary jars, its alarm clocks, heating pads, vitamins and trusses, it was to him as if everything had always been precisely that way—him standing there before the glass windows, looking in, knowing the end of it before the action had scarcely begun.

Leading round the back of the pharmacy into a cul-de-sac backing onto a synagogue was a small alleyway strewn with crates and boxes from an adjoining greengrocer. The brick wall behind was lined with aluminum trash cans exhaling into that narrow, huddled area, the sweetish breath of ripe spoilage.

Watford's throbbing head felt large and empty. Some mysterious defensive mechanism of the body had enabled him to transcend the normal thresholds of pain. It was not that pain was no longer present. It was, but it had become externalized. He was now merely witness to rather than victim of its decimating effects.

Threading his way now through the maze of litter, he experienced a peculiar sensation of buoyancy. Light-headed, light-footed, his feet seemed to skim airily above the alley concrete. The wood crate he upended below the frosted rear window of the Cardinal Pharmacy was stamped with an arc of vivid runny purple letters that read, MU-SACHIO RUTABAGAS—SACRAMENTO—CAL.

He went about his work directly. There was not a trace of stealth to his movements. Nor did he take any special pains to cover his actions with silence. Hefting a chunky stone he'd found at the rear of the alleyway, he took several noisy swipes at the frosted glass before it shattered. Instantly, the alarm tripped, ringing into the dark, mist-hung morning.

Unmindful of the racket, he reached through the gaping, punched-out glass and unlocked the window latch. Lifting the sash, he clambered over the frame with its jagged shards thrusting daggers up at him, then tumbled through into the drugstore.

Pitched into darkness, he groped his way along a wall, finding at last with his bleeding fingers a light switch. In the next moment he was bathed in the blue luminescence of overhead fluorescent lights. He was standing in the rear of the pharmacy amid shelves and racks of prescription drugs.

Despite the shrill, unceasing ring of the alarm he worked coolly, moving systematically up one aisle, then down the next until he found the big forty-six ounce jar brimming chockful with the pretty, pink-gray, candylike spansules of hundred-milligram meperidine.

As carelessly and conspicuously as he'd entered, so he departed. There was neither haste nor disarray. More disturbing, too, he was scarcely aware of having committed any crime. He merely walked out of the alley, raincoat open and flapping behind him, his striped pajama top clearly visible underneath, and the huge jar of Demerol carried under his arm as if it were a loaf of bread.

The alarm trilled insistently behind him, but the thought that he might be in danger from the imminently expected arrival of the police never entered his mind. As it happened, the police arrived six minutes later. By that time Watford was back home, just closing the door behind him.

40

"Is this 724 Hauser Street?"

"Huh?"

"I say, is this 724 Hauser Street?"

"That's right."

"And you're ..."

Watford's eyes wouldn't focus properly. He was looking directly into the sun and squinting. What he saw before him was more shadow than substance—more a blockage of light rather than any definable shape or form.

"Charles Watford?"

"Yes?"

Boring through his numbed senses a voice came, gruff and slightly impatient, followed by the grating noise of heels scuffing on the front step. His head pounded, though the Demerol he had taken during the night had at least muffled some of the jagged thrusting of the pain.

"Lieutenant Mooney, New York police. My partner, Detective Sergeant Defasio."

The shadow appeared to poke something at him momentarily, then withdraw it. Slowly the two blurred images came sharply together. All at once, he remembered and then something like a fist closed over his heart.

Mooney gazed critically at the rumpled, unshaven man in the tattered robe. "Got a few questions we'd like to ask you. May we come in?"

"Oh, God," Watford muttered.

"We'll just be a few minutes."

Watford's drugged mind whirled. Desperately he tried to recall where he'd left the stolen jeroboam of meperidine. He was already scrambling in his head for alibis.

"Sure." Watford stepped aside and hovered there in panicky confusion as the two men brushed past into the hallway.

"Looks like we woke you," Mooney remarked and stared at him with that vaguely disapproving look. At the same time he noted the gash of dried blood on the back of Watford's hand.

Staring blankly at them in the hallway, it suddenly occurred to Watford they were waiting to be led in. "Oh—sure. Of course. This way, please." He felt his body slowly waking and some of the fog in his head beginning to lift. Instantly, he began constructing an alibi for the night before.

"Afraid I'm a bit hung over."

"Party?" Mooney smiled frostily.

"No. Actually, I never met these folks before. Perfect strangers. Salesmen. From Cincinnati, I think. Met them in a bar. Nice fellows. They kept buying and I guess I just kept drinking." He moaned and held his head.

"Happens that way sometime," said the big detective.

"Sure does." Watford forced another laugh. "Have a seat." He'd noted that the other man—the swarthy younger fellow—had already settled into the little velvet puce settee his mother had so loved.

Watford chuckled uneasily. "These guys from Cincinnati . . ."

"Mr. Watford," interjected the big detective. "This won't take long. We've got just a few questions."

"Questions?" Watford feigned a look of surprise. All the while his mind sped. "Well, of course. What can I tell you?"

"I'm not sure yet," Mooney replied.

Watford caught the sharp, slightly bleary eyes fixed on the gash across the back of his hand. Slowly, and with a stiff nonchalance, he folded his arms, concealing the hand in an armpit.

"You see I was out all last night." Watford tried once more to emphasize the point. "I'm a bit hung over."

"We understand," Mooney nodded. "Am I right in saying that you were hospitalized for a short period two years ago?"

"What's that?"

"At Beth Israel. For a few days. End of April of seventy-nine, I believe. You were hospitalized. Is that right?"

Watford was thrown completely off-balance. That was not what he'd been expecting. "Beth Israel? Oh, sure." Then it suddenly all came rushing back to him. The forged prescription. Fleeing the hospital after impersonating the pediatric surgeon. The patrol car outside the house. Or was it possibly fleeing the Gramercy Park Pharmacy last week? Sure—that was it. Or was it a few days ago? No, it was yesterday. Or was it?

177

"You were at Beth Israel then?"

"That's right. I was there." Watford's heart pounded. "But I didn't do anything wrong."

"Who said you did?" There was a look of consternation on Mooney's red round face. "It *was* the end of April of seventy-nine, though?"

Watford was suddenly wary. He sat down on a small Victorian chair and rolled his head back against the lace antimacassar. "It may have been. I'm not sure."

"*We* are." Defasio spoke from the corner of the room. "We checked it with the hospital records."

"Oh?"

Mooney pulled up a chair next to Watford and sat. "Do you recall anything of your stay there?"

"Nothing in particular. I was in for a bladder infection."

"A bladder infection?"

"Right. You see, I'd been in the Air Force a couple of years before and I couldn't . . . "

Mooney rose and planted himself heavily before him. There was something immovable about the man. He appeared to swallow up all the light and air about him.

"Mr. Watford," the big detective went on. All the while Watford was aware of the other man staring around at all the clocks in the room. "While you were at Beth Israel you were in room 382."

"Was I? I don't really remember."

"I wouldn't expect you to. But you can take my word for it. While you were there you shared room 382 with another man."

"Another man?"

"A man in the bed beside you."

Completely baffled, Watford's eyes narrowed in an effort at recollection. He became even more guarded. "Well, there was a man . . ."

"You recall anything about him?"

The Demerol fog had almost completely lifted. Instead of the terrible gnawing anxiety he'd experienced moments before, there now came a rush of gratitude. They were not looking for him at all. It was the other man. The one in the bed beside him. He was suddenly eager to help.

"Like how he looked," Mooney rattled on. "What he was in for? His name? Anything?"

"He'd had some kind of surgery. His leg, I think."

The two detectives exchanged glances.

"What part of his leg?" Defasio asked.

"I don't know. He was under covers all the time."

"Did he say how he'd injured his leg?" Mooney asked.

178

Watford squinted, trying to recall. "Something about falling or tripping through an open manhole." He watched the two men exchange glances. "That's what he told me. I'm pretty sure."

"You had some conversation with him, then, I take it?" Mooney went on.

"Not very much. He was unconscious most of the time. Anesthesia, you know. He'd had surgery. They sewed up his leg, I think. They had to load him up with sedatives and pain-killers."

Seated on the sofa, Defasio scribbled quietly into his pad.

"You recall what he looked like?" Mooney pressed harder.

"Hard to say. He was lying down in bed all the time, under covers. White hair. Fifty. Sixtyish. Distinguished. Banker, broker sort of type. Possibly a diplomat. When he spoke . . . "

Watford had settled eagerly into the role of innocent bystander. For him, the heat was off. He'd caught their intent now, and the game rather pleased him.

It was quiet for a moment and the clocks ticked loudly. The big detective rose and began to tread heavily up and down the room. He was much too large for the cluttered little area and Watford held his breath, waiting for the man to collide with furniture or topple antique glass from tabletops.

"You don't happen to recall the guy's name, do you?"

"His name?" Watford gazed upward at the ceiling and chewed his lip. "Oh, golly, his name. Let me see now."

"Does the name Boyd mean anything to you? Anthony Boyd?"

"Boyd." Watford closed his eyes and rubbed his temples. "Boyd. Boyd. I don't know. I'm not sure. Maybe."

"That's the name he was registered under at the hospital." Defasio's voice rose from the corner.

"Boyd. Boyd. No, I don't . . . "

"Did you ever hear him addressed by any other name?" Mooney went on. "The nurses? The doctors? What did they call him?"

"I don't remember at all. It may very well have been Boyd. I just don't . . ."

"That's okay." Mooney caught his agitation and relented.

"There may have been some other name." Watford strained to recall. "As a matter of fact, he may have once told me. I'm sorry—I just don't remember. It wasn't Boyd though, I can tell you that."

"What was it? Try. Think back."

"Think."

Watford laughed helplessly. "Sorry, I can't. Listen, hey, that was over two years ago."

Mooney was suddenly very tired. He took his hat from where he'd left it on the chair. Defasio lumbered to his feet.

"Thanks very much. We may get back to you." Mooney held a

179

hand out to Watford. Together they walked back out to the front hall.

Watford opened the door. "I wish I could've been more helpful."

"You were helpful."

They stood there shaking hands while a gang of small boys squealed and played stoopball in the street.

"What did this fellow do, anyway?" Watford asked.

"I'll tell you about it some other time. We're in a bit of a hurry right now." Mooney scribbled something onto a pad. "Here's my number. If something should come to you—a brainstorm in the middle of the night—just gimme a ring. We'll be in touch."

The two men started down the front steps, Mooney in front, ponderous, huge, like some shuffling prehistoric biped, the dark, wiry man scurrying closely behind.

Suddenly, Watford cried out to them: "He said something to me once."

The two of them turned at the same moment.

Watford cried out once more, a furtive little smile upon his face. "He told me something once. Something strange."

Mooney and Defasio appeared to lean toward him. "Do you happen to recall what it was?" Mooney asked.

Watford closed his eyes, straining for recollection. When he opened them again he shrugged and smiled sheepishly. "I'm afraid not. I was feeling pretty strange those days myself."

APRIL–DECEMBER / '82

41

Mooney woke out of a fitful sleep. It was April 30 and as May approached he knew they were entering a critical period. At one o'clock the following day he had an appointment to see the commissioner. How would he begin to explain the embarrassment of the elusive Mr. A. Boyd, all of whose tracks led into an airy vapor? How to make comprehensible to a man of the commissioner's stolid, literal turn of mind a notion as whimsical as that of a homicidal maniac killing one night a year while dormant for all the rest? Even worse, how to make plausible the notion that the night of murder appeared to be keyed to a period between the vernal equinox and the summer solstice—as the sun's ecliptic moved toward a point farthest north of the equator? How to explain something as fanciful as that to an exceedingly pragmatic commissioner of police, and then persuade him to authorize the use of a helicopter, plus extremely costly night surveillance equipment to a man whose name had long been associated with trouble throughout the force.

Fritzi moaned lightly in her sleep. Lying beside her beneath a light comforter, Mooney watched her breathe. She rolled slightly sidewards and resumed her gentle breathing. Like him, she lay naked. Her body radiated a perfumed warmth along the flank of his own and he watched the calm, unhurried rise and fall of the quilt between her breasts.

Outside an ambulance wailed up Lexington Avenue. He moved closer to her, tucking the comforter up around her shoulders against the chill of the night wind rattling the blinds.

"The way I see it, we've got three days."
"Give me one good reason why I should believe you."

"Today's Thursday. I figure this guy for Saturday night."

"And on the basis of all this fancy stargazing I'm supposed to allocate twenty thousand dollars for three nights of skylarking about in a police helicopter, and also detach an additional fifteen plainclothesmen?"

"It's not fancy stargazing. It's the goods. I got the records to show. This Bombardier nut only gets busy the end of April to early May."

"Buy yourself a glass ball, Mooney, and a storefront on Eighth Avenue. You've had two years exclusive—all to yourself—on this thing. Extra men. Extra time. That's cost me, and what do I have to show for my money?"

"You owe it to me, Commissioner."

The tall gray man in the pale blue pinstripe stood with hands clasped behind his back, gazing thirty floors down onto Police Plaza below. "I told you, Mooney," the commissioner went on grimly, "the department owes you nothing."

"Just forty-two years of service. I call that something."

"Forty-two years of aggravation and intransigence . . ."

"With a couple of winners tossed in for good measure. Remember the Hardwell case, the Basilica gang, the Brooklyn warehouse murders . . ."

"Not enough of the winners, Mooney, and much too many of the other kind. On top of a record of chronic insubordination, you'll recall, as well, one or two episodes that cost the force heavily in terms of public embarrassment."

A smile, bitter yet tinged with melancholy, flickered in Mooney's eyes. "You don't let a guy forget, do you, Tom?"

The commissioner gazed through the big windows westward to the financial district dominated by the World Trade Center. Off to the east he had a splendid view of the docks and slips lining the East River, with the tugs and barges plying their way up and down the slick, choppy waters. He turned and wandered slowly back to his swivel chair behind the big walnut desk. "I don't dare. The moment I did you'd be off in a shot doing something stupid, then screaming how the department was victimizing you. We had a whole city out there screaming for your head once, Mooney. But this department stood behind you."

"Sure. They busted me from captain to lieutenant. That's how this department stood behind me."

The commissioner's large freckled fingers drummed nervous tattoos on his desk top. "You're lucky you didn't wind up in jail, you ungrateful bastard. You ought to get down and kiss the floor of the lobby out there, and all you've ever given in return is grousing, poormouthing and peaching on your colleagues whenever it suited you. . . ."

184

Mooney scowled. "Fair is fair. There were plenty of them poor-mouthing me when I was in the soup. Mulvaney knew I was next in line for chief, Manhattan South."

The commissioner laughed ruefully. "Mooney, I don't know whether to laugh or pity you. Maybe you're just plain dumb. What makes you think you were ever seriously considered for that spot?"

"I was next in line. Ahead of Mulvaney."

"Mulvaney didn't have a questionable murder rap decorating his record."

"There were no questions about that."

"There are always questions. Particularly when the victim is black and a minor."

"No questions, Tom." Mooney's lip trembled. The great mass of him hunched forward in his chair. "The court exonerated me. The department gave me a clean bill."

"And knocked you down to lieutenant. That's how clean a bill. And furthermore, my friend, even if there hadn't been the other business, you would never have been appointed chief of a precinct like Manhattan South. Not once have you ever demonstrated an iota of administrative tact. You have always been a thorn and a burr in the ass of the force, and you know as well as I do, Frank, that the only reason you're still here is that you happen to still have a few good friends in high places at City Hall. Okay?" The commissioner rapped the desk top with a glass paperweight in which a blizzard slowly descended through water onto a tiny Alpine village.

"No—I'm sorry, Mooney. The department owes you nothing, and why, in Christ's good name, you should think I'd be idiot enough to authorize an expenditure of another twenty thousand dollars on more men and fancy equipment on the basis of some astrological argle-bargle is beyond me."

"You did two years ago," Mooney spoke softly with a stiff reserve.

"That's right. I did. I thought then that despite your many liabilities you had the makings of a first-class investigator. This case, I figured, had all of the right ingredients for you. A big challenge. A real toughie. No leads. No motives. No hard evidence. Had you scored, the rewards would have been considerable. And, personally, I would've loved to see it happen. It would have vindicated my trust in you when everyone else advised me to fire your ass. But after two years and the addition of thousands of dollars' worth of expenses to a badly strained budget, all I've got to show are a couple of dead ends in Wilmette, Illinois, and a hospital in New York, plus the wrath and scorn of the mayor's office, not to mention the public's outrage."

"There's always that, isn't there? You can always count on the public's outrage."

The commissioner sighed, leaned back in his chair and gently patted his stomach as if to pacify some gnawing ulcerous pain there. "A lot of people have been after me about this, Frank. Not just your good friend, Mulvaney, either. Civic groups. Theater owners. Restaurateurs. I simply can't justify these additional expenditures without something a helluva lot more concrete."

"So that's that," Mooney replied abruptly. He clapped his knees and made a funny wry smile.

The commissioner sat silently with his arms folded, his brow lowering. He watched the big, rumpled man seated opposite him and noted with surprise the rather handsome features that had recently resurfaced as a result of dramatic weight loss.

"I really feel I'm close to this guy now," Mooney continued with disconcerting calm.

"Boyd?"

"If that's really his name. I can't actually say why, but over the past few months I've sensed a lot of things all starting to fall into some kind of logical pattern. I can't express it in words, but I've got it all down in my notes." Mooney tapped the place above his chest where the two small pads resided in his vest pocket.

"You were a great detective, Tom. You know yourself the feeling that comes over you after you've been on something a long time. First, it's all confusion. Odds and ends. Little bits of things. Disconnected. Nothing adding up. You live with it daily. You wake up in the middle of the night and you're thinking about it. You're thinking about it even when you're not thinking about it."

The commissioner struck a match and put it to his pipe. He puffed deeply and nodded with his eyes closed.

"Then suddenly"—Mooney's face flared momentarily—"shape and direction. I'm at that point now so I want to make a deal."

Dowd's eyes opened, instantly alert. Even as Mooney had lulled him into the cozy affability of old friendship, the commissioner had been waiting, slightly tense. Now here it was. At last the kicker. "What kind of a deal?"

"Don't get antsy, Tom. I think you'll like what I have to propose. I know my buddies at Manhattan South will like it."

Elbows on desk, Dowd leaned slightly forward, inching his way like a man approaching a live bomb. Mooney's boyish smile seemed more lethal than ever. Dowd waited, his voice barely above a whisper. "Well?"

"Since I'm such a burr in the ass of the department," Mooney said, repeating bitterly those rankling words, "for the use of one helicopter, plus night surveillance, infrared equipment and a detachment of fifteen additional men, for limited duty over the next three nights, I, Francis Mooney, will take early retirement."

The commissioner's eyes blinked behind a veil of pipe smoke.

"If I fail to make my man," Mooney's voice rose, "if the operation's a bust, I will serve my walking papers Monday morning next."

A mixture of both hope and disbelief leapt into the commissioner's eyes. "You will?"

Mooney thumped the desk top. "I wish to cause no further embarrassment to my esteemed colleagues."

The few moments of vulnerability were over, Dowd observed. More likely, they'd never begun. Mooney was his own sweet self again—all craftiness and self-promotion. Playing the angles.

"For a man who has wanted all of his professional life to walk out of here age sixty-five, covered with honors and a full pension, you sound pretty cocksure."

"Pretty cocksure," Mooney beamed.

42

It was going on 4:00 P.M. Charles Watford was in his pajamas and robe. It was not that he'd gotten into pajamas early for the night but rather, that he'd not yet gotten out of them from the day before.

He'd gone to bed the evening before fully intending to rise early and get back out on the street, canvassing agencies in his search for work. But he'd had an extremely restless night, fraught with anxiety and sleeplessness which finally yielded to a double dose of Demerol. So thoroughly had the good little "Mother" done her work that Watford failed to rise the next morning, sleeping through till noon and missing, as a result, whatever appointments he'd so carefully managed to arrange for the day.

He laid the blame for it on Mooney, whose visit, it seemed, had scared the wits out of him. It hadn't been bad, he recalled, while Mooney and the other man were there. As a matter of fact, he'd started to enjoy being the focal point of their attention. It was only when they'd left that the doubts and misgivings began.

"Who do they think they're kidding?" he fumed. "They must take me for some kind of sap. All of that hokum about a man in the bed next to me in the hospital two years ago. Just a pretense to come in here, nose and poke around looking for bottles and pills. I'm a suspect. They're on to me."

It started like that, gradually. But then he began to work it up into a mild frenzy. Winding the clocks for the evening, his agitation escalated into a huge, self-inflicted panic. "It's me that big cop was looking for. Not anybody in the hospital. They've got something on me. Either I left fingerprints at the pharmacy, or I dropped something."

Struggling to reconstruct his every move at the Cardinal Pharmacy, he started to make his way through the clock collection, winding and resetting them distractedly. Forcing windup keys into clocks, at one point he very nearly upended a rare French Napoleonic clock of doré and marble. All the time he kept muttering, working himself into a frenzy about the big cop and who the devil was he to come into someone's home like that, snooping around on a cheap pretense about some man in a hospital bed next to him? So obvious a lie it was, unless . . . unless it wasn't the Cardinal Pharmacy at all. It was Myrtle. That was it. She'd notified the New York police, who'd finally tracked him down. My God. Oh, my God, it's Myrtle.

It was just about then that he'd had the first intimations of a rapidly onrushing migraine. He'd not wanted to take the Demerol. Some deep vestige of self-preservation had cautioned him over the past several months to curtail his intake. He had actually made some conscientious effort to cut back. But if Myrtle had the New York police track him here . . . this was clearly not the time to start denying himself.

"But maybe it's not that at all," he reasoned. "Maybe it's the prescription yesterday. All those fake prescriptions. My God, and that doctor, the gastroenterologist I impersonated. Jesus. Oh, Jesus."

A thousand chimeras whirled through his head. Phantoms of past crimes, actual and imagined. Forgeries. Impersonations. Thefts, petty and grand. Breaking and entering. In his mind he recalled dozens more. The Cardinal Pharmacy was but one of a string of many. Vividly, with almost preternatural acuity, he relived the crime over and over again. The shattered glass. The high, persistent shriek of the alarm. Lurching up and down the aisles of canisters and phials.

It was then that he'd bolted down the second Demerol, forgetting completely that he'd taken one only minutes before. A cold sweat erupted on his forehead, and though it was close to eighty degrees outside, he started to shiver. He climbed into bed that night fully ex-

188

pecting never to awaken. A dull throb had commenced at the back of his neck. Lying there anticipating the arrival of pain was more ghastly than the pain itself. That slow, insidious creep upward from the back of the skull into the right ear, radiating spokes of agony outward into the right hemisphere of the head as far as the right eye.

Outside in the harsh, fast dusk, he could hear the squeal of children playing stoopball in the street below. Lying spread-eagled atop the cover, he continued to wrack his brain for some hint of past guilt. What stupid blunder had he made? How had they found him? Where did they get his name?

Still awake at 2:00 A.M., lathered in a sweat of irrational dread, he got out of bed, intending to call his sister Renee in Pittsburgh. He meant to dash out there immediately and seek refuge until the whole affair blew over. But no sooner had he started to dial than he had an image of his brother-in-law, Edgar, remorseless and unforgiving, followed by a humiliating picture of himself begging sanctuary of Edgar. He could see the brow lowering, the eyes glinting with scorn.

Slowly he replaced the phone and slumped into a chair. He would have bolted right then, but he was convinced that the police were just outside the door, waiting in a darkened, unmarked car for precisely such an action. In their eyes, flight at that moment would seal his guilt forever.

"Who was that man in the bed next to me?" He ransacked his memory for a name. It seemed to him that if he could come up with one his salvation was assured. "It certainly wasn't Boyd. That wasn't the name he told me. Or was it? He did give me a name. And there was something else—something strange he told me."

He could recall the face, as if he were seeing it just then—haggard, pale, drowsy with sedation. Generally he had a good memory for faces. But this impression was somewhat less vivid because he had only seen the man on his back, recumbent beneath sheets and with plastic tubes dangling from his nose.

"What is it?" He stood suddenly, peering into the upper reaches of the house. "What is it?" he called once more. "Filariasis," he murmured as if answering himself. "Chronic lymphadenopathy. Retrograde lymph . . . Epidemiology Coastal borders Asia, Queensland." He recited the words, the symptoms over and over again with the hypnotic force of incantation, invoking the old gods he knew had the power to deliver him.

In his tatty robe and floppy slippers he walked round and round the damp, unlit regions of the house. The dull throb in his head had intensified to sharp, ripping detonations. Waves of sickening pain that came and went. In the bathroom, concealed behind a radiator cover, he found the precious jeroboam of meperidine. Forgetting the dosage he had taken before, he took two additional pills. When he awoke the next day it was 1:00 P.M. and he was lying on the bathroom floor. He had no memory of anything other than a fleeting impression of a bad dream, like a foul taste in one's mouth.

The room came gradually into sharper focus. Staring into the mirror above the sink, he noted a drawn, scruffy visage staring disdainfully back at him. Something in those bland, familiar features was different, however. Something askew. But he couldn't tell exactly what. Then, on the sink top he spied his shaving kit—a mug of shaving lather, a beaver brush still wet with dried soap caked to the bristles as if recently used, and a single-edged barber's razor his father had given him at age sixteen. He had no recollection of having either taken them out or shaved. But suddenly he knew why his features had taken on that slightly crooked, off-kilter cast. The brow above his right eye had been completely shaved off.

43

"Without even knowing it the guy did you a tremendous favor."

"Like what? Telling me I hadn't a friend in the world?"

"I'm your friend."

"Or sweet things like telling me I'm a thorn in the ass of the department. And quite frankly, the son of a bitch says, the department can't wait for my retirement."

Fritzi set a plate of cold sliced cucumbers and tomatoes in front of Mooney. "You got your helicopter, didn't you? You got your ten men."

"I asked for fifteen."

"And your snooperscopes."

"Sniperscopes."

"Whatever. You got all that, didn't you? And will you kindly remove that article from your person. At my dinner table we do not wear guns."

She came round behind him, encircled his chest with her arms and deftly unbuckled the pistol harness. Obediently, almost childlike, he raised his arms and submitted as she unstrapped him.

"Pissed me off how quickly he agreed. Pissed me plenty. They must want me out real bad."

"Their loss." Fritzi sat down at the small kitchen table opposite him and proceeded to slice their steak. "He did you the biggest favor of your life. Thank him tomorrow for me. Medium or rare?"

Mooney fumed and clapped a cucumber between his great jaws. "Pink. Not purple like the other night. Jesus, can't we ever get a potato here? Or a slice of bread? What I'd give for a slice of . . ."

"You're down fifty pounds. What're you complaining about? You look almost human. I can actually see the bones in your face, and it's no longer that sick beet-red. Why blow it all now with bread and potatoes?"

Mooney frowned and held his plate up while she carefully placed an austere portion of lean steak there.

"And you know something else," Fritzi went on breathlessly in her gay, chirpy fashion, "personally, I hope the whole thing is a bust so you do have to retire."

"Thanks a lot." He gulped a small gobbet of steak. "I needed that."

"Well, it's the truth. I'm sorry. They don't deserve you—the lousy way they've treated you all these years. You know what Rudy Baumholz used to say?"

"No," Mooney grumbled. "Tell me."

"He used to say, 'Fritzi. Any man who gives his whole life working for some organization deserves everything he gets. In the end, they screw you.' That's what Rudy used to say."

"Three cheers for Rudy. How about another slice of steak?"

"Stop wolfing your food. Take small bites. Chew."

He held his plate out, a martyred expression on his face.

"And you know what else is going to happen when you retire from this dumb, thankless job?"

"Is there any coffee?"

"You're going to go to work."

"Oh, yeah?" Mooney gulped water with his eyes raised to the ceiling. "Not on a bet. Once I'm done, I'm done." He went on chewing his steak irritably, as if it were a task.

"How does manager of Fritzi's Balloon strike you?"

The chewing ceased momentarily and he looked up. "A head-waiter?"

She could see the contempt in his eyes. "Maître d'. Major domo."

"A bouncer?"

"No bouncer. Manager, I told you."

"A mortician in a tuxedo. A freak in a starched dickey."

"No dickeys. No tuxedos. All smart stuff. Sport jackets. Brooks and Paul Stuart."

Mooney made an unpleasant sound. "You don't by any chance happen to have some pie?"

"And you know what else?" Fritzi chattered on irrepressibly. "All the free time you want. Whenever you want to go to the track, bang, you got it. No permission required. And maybe if you want to knock off for a couple of months and go, like maybe, to Spain, bang, we go."

"On what?" Mooney smoldered. "My miserable pension plus my miserable Social Security?" A short, bitter laugh rippled from his throat.

"On your wages from the Balloon." Fritzi spooned out heaping portions of fresh raspberries. "Fritzi pays good wages. Fritzi pays top dollar to the right guy."

She had meant to cheer him, but instead, what she saw was regret sinking into despair. Second thoughts on the wisdom of his brash wager with the commissioner stood out all over his face.

She leaned across the table and with her large, rough palm covered the back of his hand. "You've always been a good handicapper, Mooney. Careful. Shrewd. You called these odds. Now live with them."

"More likely die with them."

"Now let's have none of that." She'd grown curt and testy. "You're feeling sorry for yourself. You know what Rudy would say?"

"No. And don't tell me."

"You're a smart fellow. I don't think you're impulsive. The odds had to be there for you to make this bet with the commissioner."

"They are. In spades."

She thought he looked like some incorrigible child, pleading innocence, seeking vindication. Her eyes suddenly sparked. "What odds do you pay he makes a drop in the next five days?"

"Make it a week and I'll give you three to one."

"You got it. What about quinellas?"

"Pick any two consecutive nights between now and next Thursday."

"What odds?"

"Eight to one if you hit the night. Three to one if you hit on a date either side of the drop night."

"I got a hundred that says it's this Friday."

"The twenty-ninth," Mooney said, his spirits noticeably rising. "I hate to take your money, Fritz, but you're on."

She poured coffee. "When's the first surveillance?"

"Tomorrow night. We go out from the heliport on South Street."

They rose and carried their coffee into the little sitting room that looked out over Seventy-third Street toward the East River. "Now," she said, sitting down beside him, "tell me all about this funny little guy you met today."

Mooney was momentarily baffled. "What funny little guy?"

"The guy you saw this morning. The one out in Queens."

"Oh, Watford." He leaned back and put his feet up on the hassock. "Strange fellow. Nervous. Jumpy. He kept acting like he was expecting us to beat the hell out of him any minute."

"It's not every day that two of New York's Finest pay you a house call."

"I'd ask him one thing and he'd look at me kind of funny, and answer some other question. Go off completely on another tangent. Middle of the day, and he's still there in his pajamas. The place was an unholy mess. Stunk from cats, although I didn't see any around. Just clocks. All these clocks . . ."

Dusk had fallen over Seventy-third Street, and they had drawn close in the comfort of the gathering shadows, the odor of fresh coffee lingering on the quiet air. Like figures in a frieze, they appeared as if they'd been sitting just that way, chatting and sipping coffee, for the past thousand years, and would probably do so for the next.

"But he didn't know anything about this other man?" Fritzi asked.

"The Bombardier?" Mooney stared pensively at the rose-streaked twilight sky above the river. "The guy's a nut case. He doesn't know anything about anything."

They were silent for a time, sipping their coffee. Then suddenly he turned to her. "Listen, I been meaning to ask you . . ."

"What?"

His hands rose outward into the shadows of the unlit apartment. "Us together like this. I mean, I take up a lot of your time."

"I'll let you know when it gets to be a sacrifice."

The fact that she was amused annoyed him. "I mean"—he persisted awkwardly, trying to articulate what had been gnawing at him for days—"I mean, don't get me wrong. I'm enjoying myself. You're good for me. Maybe too good. I just want to go on record as saying I'm not . . . Well . . . you know me. I'm pretty set in my ways."

"So am I."

"I wouldn't want you to get any dumb ideas."

"You know me, Mooney. I don't have too many dumb ideas."

"Well, I mean all this stuff about my managing the Balloon and our going off to Spain together. I don't like that, see. Makes me uneasy. Like jumping to conclusions."

"I don't jump to conclusions," she said. Something shrewd and tough leaped in her eyes. He saw now a side of her she had seldom shown him—the side that had made her the proprietor of a highly successful East Side tavern and a woman of not inconsiderable means. "For me it's strictly business," she went on. "Like an investment. Like horseflesh. I see a creature I like, I bet him. If I lose, I lose. No hard feelings."

"Fair enough," he said. "Just so we understand each other." He appeared momentarily placated. She knew, however, the subject would come up again.

"We understand each other perfectly." She smiled, and there was the wisdom of the ages in that smile. "But you know me, Mooney. When I bet, I seldom lose."

44

"The escapement is the Grimthorpe Double Three-Legged Gravity."

"Excellent, Charles. Now recite the table of error for the clock signals."

Charles Watford spoke earnestly into the shadows of the little sitting room. The sudden chiming of nearly fifty clocks jarred him from his reverie even as the voice of his father receded into the upper reaches of the house.

"Can you recall anything at all about the man?"

"No."

"His name? What was his name?"

"No. I told you. I don't recall."

"Think. Think."

Watford stared blankly at the worn little settee with the antimacassars and pillows crushed and askew, where the policeman had sat the day before.

"Was it Boyd?"

"No. I don't think . . ."

"Think. Think."

Still in his robe and slippers, unkempt and unshaven, he had not ventured out for several days. Much of the brow he had shaved off had started to grow back in. Across the way he could see lights flickering in the upper stories of the house abutting his yard. Within it people walked about like robot figures—mechanical, impersonal, inhuman.

When he looked again, the man on the settee was gone. He was alone, bathed in sweat, his heart thumping wildly. "I'm guilty," he whispered. "Guilty." Of what, he could not say.

Upstairs in his bedroom, in the rickety pine bureau that had been his since childhood, he found at the back of a bottom drawer, secured within a small leather case, his needle and hypodermic syringe. He rinsed them off under the sink tap in the bathroom and padded slowly back down the stairs into the kitchen.

"Oh, Charles. Look what you've gone and done now."

"If anything should come to mind you can always reach me at this number."

"Pardon my saying so. You really missed an opportunity not notifying your insurance company at once. It's not as if you're stealing, or anything like that. You've paid for it. You're entitled to it. First thing I would've done was to get the name of the contractor."

When he looked up he was standing in front of the refrigerator, peering at the bright, harsh glare from within. There was nothing much there in the way of food. An open jar of jelly and some overripe vegetables sat about forlornly on the bare shelves. A sweet, slightly disagreeable odor wafted outward on the smoky waves of condensation.

"I don't have to take this harassment, Sergeant. I had nothing to do with any bank robbery in Kansas. I know no Myrtle Wells. I want to speak to my lawyers."

"Charles, your father will be getting home shortly."

At the rear of the top shelf he found precisely what he was looking for.

"For your own good and mine, I don't think it would be good if he found you here, still in your pajamas."

A quarter of a container of cream that had been sitting there nearly a month had curdled and a green furze had settled like a lacy mantle over it.

" . . . Wait till he hears you've been sent home from camp."

Prizing open the collapsible crush-top lid, he raised the container to his nose and sniffed gingerly. Strong, rank fumes came up at him in waves. The nauseous odor of putrefaction was almost voluptuous. He closed the refrigerator and took a small saucer down from the cupboard above. Even as he decanted a portion of the green curdled substance into the saucer, the voices continued to racket about his whirling thoughts.

The voice of a man sounded from across the way. It was loud and blustery. It conveyed to him a suggestion of anger and impending violence. *"You've got a bad temper. You must learn to control . . ."*

Slowly, fastidiously, Watford inserted his needle into the reeking green substance, drawing it upward into the syringe. With almost hypnotic intensity, he watched the fluid creep past the red calibration lines until the shaft of the column was at last full.

In the next instant he turned and started back up the stairs.

"I'm coming, Mother. I'll be right there."

"That's a good boy, Charles. That's my good boy."

Once in his room he lay down and extended his body the full length of the bed. Then, closing his eyes and still holding the needle poised above him, he inhaled deeply several times, like a man about to dive deep into cold water.

He waited for his breathing to slow, along with the agitated pulsations in his chest. Without further hesitation, he jerked the elastic band of his pajama pant down below his thigh and with faintly tremulous fingers, he sought an ideal location (for him, a point not easily detected) for venipuncture.

His fingers wandered down over his bare, flat stomach to a spot high up on the inner thigh. He sought a point near the scrotal area, on the inner wall of the thigh. Pinching the flesh there hard between his fingers, and without any hesitation at all, he drove the needle far in.

There was a momentary prick and a short muscular spasm, followed by the sensation of fluid infused into the vein. With his eyes closed, he gnawed the inside of his cheek and waited until the syringe was empty.

When at last it was, he rose, rinsed off the needle and replaced it in the drawer. In the medicine cabinet of the bathroom he found several packages of a fairly common laxative he knew to contain phenolphthalein. From his readings he knew the substance to be a pyrogen, having the effect upon ingestion of raising body temperature. While normal dosage was one to two tablets at most, he had unhesitatingly swallowed the contents of nearly two full packages.

Afterward, he went directly to bed, lay down in the dark and waited.

45

Like a huge silvery moth, the helicopter rose and fell, its engines drumming, blades battering the hot air that rose in wind drafts all about it. Each rotation hurled down a shower of dull concussive blows into the steamy streets below.

They veered north, bucketing up the West Side Drive. Ahead of them the long, graceful span of the George Washington Bridge loomed lacy and luminescent above the river. Somewhere at Seventieth Street the copter's engines whined as the craft curved right and headed eastward toward the park. Turning through a wide arc, the centrifugal force tilted Mooney sidewards, sending his stomach upward into his chest. Defasio seated directly to his left appeared to sag rightward and across him.

The chopping of the blades and the heat of the cabin were taking their toll. With each rise and descent of the craft, Mooney had grown queasier. At the last turn over the park, he'd tasted the sour chyme of his partially digested supper. At the same moment a grayish pallor spread across the characteristically pink flush of his cheeks.

Hovering above the West Side of New York, bucketing low over the rooftops with nothing but a thin aluminum skin between himself and the concrete pavements several hundred feet below, Mooney felt himself the butt of some cosmic amusement. Once again the plaything of the gods—particularly with the door of the craft open only a few feet to the right of him.

Out that door a police officer by the name of Ramirez peered straight downward into the green-orange neon sheen. He was scanning the rooftops through powerful infrared night surveillance equipment. To his left a stolid, young black man by the name of Youngblood piloted the copter impassively.

197

Youngblood seldom spoke. Ramirez chattered incessantly, mostly into the helmet microphones linked up to the radio patrol cars and the rooftop stakeout teams working below. At the moment it was 10:16 P.M., and the helicopter was coasting low over the rooftops between Eighth and Ninth in the Fifties.

"I got what looks like a pair of suspects on a roof on Fifty-third, just east of Ninth. Lemme see now." He checked the street map spread out on his lap. "Looks like 366 West Fifty-third. Would you give us a check on that and call back?"

Ramirez clicked off his radio and shot a toothy grin back at Mooney. "Probably nothin', but we gotta check it out. Right, Lieutenant?"

"Right," Mooney gasped. Waves of hot, fumey air wafted through the open door, battering his face and making a tuft of dark hair dance crazily upon his skull.

"There's the Felt Forum," Defasio shrieked wildly. He'd been going on in that fashion ever since they'd started two hours ago, like a tour guide, pointing out landmarks.

"Wonderful," Mooney muttered. He'd begun to regret that he'd insisted upon coming. Surely Defasio could have handled this part of the operation himself, while he might just as well, and far more profitably, have stayed below with one of the radio reconnaissance cars.

He could well imagine the barrage of scornful jibes he'd incur at the hands of his colleagues at Manhattan South had he taken such a course. Even more troubling, Mooney was suddenly paralyzed with doubt. The cabin radio began to buzz and crackle. Ramirez flicked it on. At once the small space filled with the scratchy static of voices from one of the radio cars below. "On your query, 366 West Fifty-third—your party on the roof was just a guy and a dame ballin'. We chased 'em off and sent 'em home."

Ramirez flicked off the radio, glanced back at Mooney and smiled. "That's life, ay, Lieutenant? You lose one, you lose one." Ramirez thought that was immensely funny. Mooney scowled as the copter momentarily lurched, suddenly tilted ponderously forward like a harbor buoy rising on a swell.

"Lotta ballin' on the rooftops," Defasio said.

"That makes five tonight alone."

"It's the season," Mooney muttered. "Warm weather gets their blood up."

Ramirez nodded in agreement. "In my time we used to screw in the basement. Never the roof."

"There's the UN," Defasio wheeled and gazed back.

"Little too public for me." Ramirez popped a wad of gum into his mouth and proceeded to chew. "Too exposed like, you know? I'd never drop my drawers on a rooftop. Ain't that right, Youngblood?" The pilot muttered some barely audible reply.

Mooney's stomach rumbled as the pall settled more oppressively upon him.

"Well," Ramirez went on with unflagging good cheer, "so far we got us a man training a pigeon, a man with binoculars watching ladies undress, another guy barbecuing chicken illegally, and five separate couples screwing, one of which was a pair of queens. How much longer you wanna keep this up, Lieutenant?"

Mooney was none too anxious to prolong the agony. "Another half hour. Till all the theaters are out and the streets get a bit emptier."

Ramirez flashed his toothy grin. "You're the boss, Lieutenant." Once again he poked his telescopic night-scanner outside the door. "What d'ya say we hit the Forties, Youngblood? Start between Tenth and Eleventh and work east."

The copter yawed. Mooney glared down at the shimmering grid of streets and avenues as the earth whirled past below him.

46

"I see no sign of filariasis."

"You're certain?"

"Positively. Where'd you ever get such an idea? Bancroftian filariasis is virtually unknown in North America."

"I picked it up in Asia. In the army."

" 'Nam?"

"Thailand and then Vietnam."

The doctor who had just examined Watford shot him a quick, inquisitive smile. "Me too. What years?"

"Seventy-two and seventy-three."

"What outfit?"

"Eleventh Armored Cav."

"You're kidding. Me too. I was in Medivac." The doctor, whose name was Ramsay, was a dapper little man with a pelt of shiny black hair that lay flat and slick as a wet otter's across his bullet-shaped head. The smile still wavered in his eyes, followed by something like puzzlement. "But that couldn't have been seventy-two to seventy-three. The Eleventh Cav only got there in seventy-four."

Watford had been lying on his back on an examination table. Attired in a dingy white examination gown, he gazed up at the doctor with a glow of gratitude upon his face. "You're right. I came with the Third Armored in seventy-two and seventy-three. I was transferred later to the Eleventh Cav."

"What unit?"

"The 345th Helicopter Reconnaissance."

"Helicopter?" Dr. Ramsay's puzzlement appeared to deepen. "Eleventh Cav had no helicopter detachments."

"That's right." Watford lay there unflapped and smiling. "That's how I was transferred from the Third Armored to the Eleventh Cav."

"Oh. But then you had to be there after seventy-three."

"Well, I guess I was there also in seventy-four. The early part."

The physician folded his arms inside his capacious white coat and peered down at the patient. Watford had been admitted on an emergency basis that evening, with acute pelvic pain and running a high fever. The doctor was smiling but he appeared troubled. His small onyx eyes ranged up and down the length of his patient, observing, registering, collating, diagnosing.

"Where was your filariasis diagnosed? Here or there?"

"There. Base hospital."

"Army medics?"

"That's right."

Ramsay swiped the side of his nose and sniffled. "Offhand, I'd say they were crazy. Aside from some high fever and headache, I see nothing here consistent with such a diagnosis. No sign of lymphatic obstruction. There is some swelling around the pelvis, and possibly a small varicose nodule in the vicinity of the groin. But nothing at all consistent with the scrotal lymphedema we find in filariasis. Take it from me, Mr. Watford, you don't have any filariasis."

"But the doctor . . ."

"Forget it. Soon as you put most army doctors into a tropical setting, they start talking exotic pathology, about which most of them know nothing. We did have a couple of men in 'Nam walk in out of the jungle with classic Bancroftian filariasis. A handful at most. We'd knock most of it out with antibiotics in fourteen days. You've got no filariasis, Mr. Watford. You've got something, but I'm not sure what."

The doctor scratched the back of his head and swiped his nose again. All the while the restless beady eyes swept up and down the length of Watford's gowned figure. "I don't know," he said at last. "You're running a helluva fever. Forty-one degrees centigrade. There's a tachycardia. Not at all unusual with that kind of fever. I find a subcutaneous abscess with some splenomegaly."

"What's that?" Watford's head rose slightly from the table.

"Enlargement of the spleen. I can't say I like that. This swelling in your pelvis . . ." The doctor's finger pressed down gently in the area of Watford's groin, causing him to wince. Some kind of bacteremia. You haven't eaten anything that's made you sick recently? Something spoiled? Shellfish, possibly?"

Watford shook his head negatively in response to all queries.

"You haven't swallowed anything nonorganic? Metal or anything like that?"

"Why would I do a thing like that?" Watford beamed. There was something arch about him, an impish child harboring some delicious secret.

"It's almost as if"—the doctor went on, pondering aloud to himself—"as if some foreign agent had been inadvertently introduced to the system."

"Why would I do that?"

"Who said you did it?" Ramsay grew peevish. "Let's have another look at that swelling."

Watford's gown was hiked above his flaccid, milky thighs while the doctor probed carefully in the region of the pelvis. "Spread your legs, please."

Docile as a child, Watford obeyed, and the doctor continued his probing in the tender swollen area between thigh and scrotum. At the point of greatest tenderness, the small, darting eyes of the physician detected a tiny circle of inflammation. While Watford held his breath, Ramsay peered down and examined the area closely. "There appears to be a little puncture here," he said with an air of slightly heightened curiosity. Something slightly chary had entered his voice and the beady eyes fixed Watford sharply. "You know anything about that?"

"How would I know anything about it?" Watford's heart had begun to accelerate in his chest.

Ramsay shrugged. "Probably just some kind of insect bite."

"I don't remember any bite in that region. Wouldn't I remember being bitten there?"

"Sometimes it happens while you're sleeping. If the toxins are virulent enough, the bites go into abscess. Sometimes they burst. I've seen bites go into peritonitis."

"Are you sure?"

"I'm not sure of anything," Ramsay remarked. He appeared preoccupied with some other matter. "I guess we ought to keep you here a couple of days and watch you. At least till that fever comes down. In any event, just to rule out forever the filariasis nonsense, I'd like to do some blood workups on you. Your eyes . . . " He leaned forward and rolled the lower lid of Watford's eye down, noting instantly the pale, milky white of the inner lining of the lid. "Whatever else is bothering you, I'll wager you're anemic, too."

Ramsay rose and scribbled something onto Watford's chart. "Bacteremia we can handle," he said. "That goes also for anemia, subcutaneous abscess, and even filariasis, if it does turn out you've got yourself a dose of that. What does trouble me, Mr. Watford, are all those needle tracks on your arms and legs."

47

Hot blasts of exhaust. Nauseous waves of fumes. Mooney sick and green, huddled in the rear of the cabin, trying not to hear Defasio pointing out sights, and the chatter of Ramirez buzzing back and forth with the surveillance teams below. For Youngblood's almost metaphysical silence, the detective was eternally grateful.

It was Mooney's second night in the helicopter. They'd been skimming rooftops up and down the West Side for nearly two hours. He vowed he would not go up for the third night. Unsentimental. Remorselessly realistic, like any good handicapper, he knew the odds were off and he'd bet the wrong pony. Let Dowd and Mulvaney have their victory. He would slip gladly off with neither fuss nor fanfare. No need to endure the charade for yet another night.

"Want half a hero?"

Mooney looked up to see a hand flapping a sausage and pepper wedge beneath his nose. Defasio was attached to the other end of it, a thin gash of marinara sauce streaking his chin. "I can't eat all this. Shame to let it go to waste."

The smell of oil, garlic and Parmesan hit Mooney like a fist. Something approaching a belch rose in his throat, bringing with it a jet of sour lava he was barely able to suppress. "Will you take that goddamned thing out of my face?"

Defasio appeared hurt. The pencil line of sauce on his chin made him look silly and oddly tragic, like a clown. "Don't you want any supper?"

"No, goddamn it. I'm on a diet. And even if I wasn't, I'd eat a mile of the Jersey Turnpike before I'd put that thing in my mouth. Now for Chrissake stop waving it at me."

Gloomily, Defasio wrapped the hero sandwich in its oily papers, rebagged it and stuck it beneath his seat.

"Go wipe your face off," Mooney added cruelly, then tapped Ramirez on the shoulder. "Anything going on down there?"

"They got some junkie shootin' up at 424 West Fifty-first Street. Wanna see him?"

"How old is he?" asked Mooney.

Ramirez chattered into the radio, then leaned back. "Fifteen."

"He got anything up there with him? Stones? Blocks? Stuff like that?"

Again Ramirez chattered into the radio. When he turned back to Mooney his expression told all. "Just the hash, Lieutenant."

"Tell 'em to take him down to Juvenile Court and book him for the night."

The engines droned on. The air, as well as the mood in the cabin, grew worse. When Ramirez was not chattering on the radio, he crooned Puerto Rican love songs. Mooney smoldered to himself while Defasio, slumped listlessly in his seat, sat staring out at the evening sky.

When the helicopter turned at Sixty-third Street and started back downtown, Mooney closed his eyes and tried to forget his anger and disappointment. For a while he concentrated on Fritzi. He had a vision of her and himself seated at a quiet table, eating prime beef and drinking imported ale.

In the next moment, the scene shifted to a paddock, painted a fresh bright white and spanking clean. Mares ran with their new foals. The air was clear, the grass green and there was the sharp resinous scent of pine and fir.

Mooney could not say why the scene moved him to such anger. Had it something to do with the landscape? Too idyllic? Too pristine? Too fraudulent? Unpeopled and untrafficked? An illustration for a child's book. More probably, it was the horses themselves. Their nobility and unselfconscious grace; magnificent power tempered with godlike gentleness. And the colts, sportive and frolicking, banging into the paddock rails, stumbling and starting up; unpracticed grace; the seed of champions—striving beyond all else for perfection. Nothing else was like that in life.

"What d'ya say we go down?" Defasio's voice intruded upon his reverie. Mooney reopened his bleary eyes and the paddock and horses were suddenly gone. In its place was the square back of Youngblood's head and Ramirez's amused stare. Mooney could see they thought he'd been sleeping.

"What time is it?" he asked.

"A little past eleven," Defasio replied.

"Where are we?"

"Right over the Fifty-third Street heliport," Ramirez said, looking hopeful. For a moment Mooney entertained the idea of one more pass over the sight. But by that time he had little heart for it. He leaned forward and tapped the pilot on the shoulder. "You can take her down now," he said.

On the ground again at Fifty-third Street and the East River, a Manhattan South patrol car picked them up and ran them over to the precinct house where the night's catch awaited them.

"What d'ya got for us, Corelli?" Defasio asked the desk sergeant when they limped in shortly after midnight.

"It's all lined up and waitin' in the back. How d'ya want 'em, Mooney? Separately or en masse?"

"Together—line 'em up. Let's get this over with fast."

There was a total of eight in the lineup room when they got there. It took Mooney approximately forty minutes to chat briefly with each and finally discharge them all as harmless. The peeping Tom with his powerful Japanese binoculars they knew for years and viewed with affection as almost an old friend. The three winos, each plucked from a different site, had all sought rooftops as refuge from the harshness of the streets below. If you had to be unconscious from alcohol for a number of hours, it was safer to be so on a rooftop than undefended in an alley or a park somewhere.

A fifth was a bag lady by the name of Seraphina. She'd set up housekeeping on a tar roof nine stories above the city. The sixth was an amiable Neapolitan gentleman with handlebar mustaches. He'd been apprehended on a rooftop trapping and barbecuing pigeons for his supper.

The last two were a couple—one, the black superintendent of a West Side cold-water, walk-up, and his companion, a white lady. A slatternly creature with bleached hair and pasty skin, she was mortified at having been caught in flagrante delicto. She pleaded with Mooney to release her without further delay. Her husband, she explained, was a musician. He worked at night, but he would be home shortly. It would not go well for her if she was not there when he arrived.

It was all harmless and curiously depressing—this catalog of little sins and shabby, unheroic transgressions. When Mooney dismissed them with a disgusted wave of his hand, he thought he spied Corelli smirking.

"Will you be wantin' the helicopter again tomorrow evenin', Lieutenant?" the beefy man asked. His voice reeked with sarcasm.

It had been Mooney's intention to call it quits that night. But the smirk on the desk sergeant's gaze was a bit more than Mooney could choke down. He looked across at Defasio, who was watching him intently, as though he'd never seen him before. Then he looked back at Corelli. "You bet your ass I do. Have it ready for me by eight P.M."

48

"How's that fever tonight, Mr. Watford?" Dr. Ramsay breezed across the room, the tails of his surgical gown flaring slightly behind him. He picked up the clipboard at the foot of the bed and briefly scanned it. A nurse stood just behind him.

"Forty degrees centigrade. We're still high." He slipped two fingers over Watford's inside wrist and took his pulse. "How's the headache?"

"Awful."

"Pulse is fast too. Enjoying your stay so far?" With a sweeping motion, he drew the privacy curtain round the bed to screen them from the patient in the adjoining bed. While the doctor probed and palpated, Watford launched into a series of complaints and indignities he'd suffered during the course of the day. "I can't say I find the staff here very responsive."

Ramsay took the stethoscope down from his ears and clipped them round his neck. "How so?"

"My needs," Watford fretted. "My needs, Doctor, I am not accustomed . . ."

"By your needs," Ramsay resumed his tapping and palpating, "I take it you mean the nurses get a bit sticky when you call the dispensary, impersonate me, and order Demerol for yourself."

That took a bit of the wind out of Watford's sails. He slumped back breathless, and sullen, while the doctor's fingers probed up under his armpits. "That hurt?"

"Somewhat."

"Tender, isn't it?"

"Yes." Chastened now, Watford's voice was unnaturally low. He watched Ramsay warily.

"How long have you been addicted to Demerol?"

Watford was about to protest, but the physician was far too acute for him. "You have a hypodermic concealed around here. I suggest you turn it over to the nurse right now."

Watford felt his face redden.

"I noticed the needle mark on your inner thigh last night," Ramsay went on. "I know your game, Watford. What did you inject yourself with? Spoiled food? Feces?"

"Hey—wait a minute . . ."

"What you're doing is dumb. Very dumb. How much Ex-Lax did you have to punch down to get your fever up so high?"

Watford squirmed quietly beneath the sheets.

"Your blood samples were loaded with phenolphthalein." Ramsay's fierce beady eyes were merciless. "Who do you think you're kidding? How long have you been going on like this?"

For reply, Watford turned his head to the wall and remained silent.

But Ramsay was not yet finished. "Now listen to me, my friend. If it's Demerol you want, I'll get it for you. But in reasonable quantities. Without your having to commit fraud and impersonate a physician. Both of which, incidentally, are felony crimes, punishable by imprisonment. Before I do that, however, you'll have to agree to get yourself onto a good detoxification program. I can arrange that for you too. We have a very good outpatient drug-rehab clinic right here."

Watford turned and stared pitifully up at him. "But I don't . . ."

"Let me finish, please. Before you start to deny all this, I think you should first hear what I have to tell you. I'm sure you'll find it to be of considerable importance."

As he spoke he lay his cool, hard palm across the back of Watford's hand. "In the first place, I have no intention of reporting this matter to the police."

Watford's eyes narrowed and he could feel his body stiffen as the doctor spoke.

"In the second place, I can assure you that, just as I suspected, there is not the slightest trace of filarial infection in either your urine or blood samples. Quite honestly," Ramsay went on rather less harshly, "I wish there were."

Watford watched the doctor blankly, incomprehension in his eyes.

Ramsay went on, seeming to feel his way through something unpleasant. "You see, filariasis I can treat. A regimen of Banocide or Hetrazan—and I can pretty well knock it out in a week." The doctor's awl-bit eyes suddenly skewered his patient. "Your blood smears came back today with a leukocyte count of 42,000/mm^3, and I'm afraid that far from having anything remotely to do with filariasis, a white blood cell count of that magnitude, along with the enlarged lymphatic glands I feel in your armpits and scrotum, and the pronounced splenomegaly I picked up in your stomach yesterday, is all quite consistent with . . . "

"Leukemia," Watford murmured and closed his eyes. When he opened them once more, he was smiling.

Ramsay found the smile disconcerting. "You knew that?"

"No. But as you spoke it became increasingly apparent."

Ramsay sighed and leaned back in his chair. It occurred to him that the man whom he'd examined so meticulously over the past two days, the man whose serology he was now so intimately familiar with, he knew nothing about. It was the opacity of that smile that ultimately chilled him. "Watford. You do understand what I'm saying? You're not confused, are you?"

"I understand what you're saying, Doctor."

"With a leukocytic count elevated to the range of yours, life expectancy is not long."

"How long?"

"Three to six months, if untreated."

The smile never faltered and that's when it occurred to Ramsay that the man was quite out of touch.

"And if treated?" Watford inquired. He showed no sign of fright. His voice was gentle, as if he wished to spare the doctor any unpleasantness.

"With new drugs, chemotherapy, I've seen remissions that last . . ."

"A year or two," Watford completed the doctor's sentence for him.

If moments before Ramsay had assumed that Watford was out of touch, he now had the distinct impression that the fellow was now disconcertingly right on target.

"Sometimes longer," he said. "But 42,000/mm^3 is quite advanced and you must get on therapy immediately."

"I have no money, I have no insurance. I have no prospects." It was a sad litany, recited straight out with neither rancor nor self-pity. It was one of those rare moments of candor in the life of a pathological liar.

"Don't worry about any of that." Ramsay rose stiffly to his feet. "There's all kinds of federal money available for this sort of thing. I'll get you on a program. But the Demerol and the funny stuff with syringes has got to stop. Also the phone calls to the dispensary. Every nurse on the floor has been alerted now, as well as the dispensary personnel. If you get so strung out that you must have Demerol, I'll see to it that you get it. We're going to put you on tetracycline now for the bacteremia and I've ordered bone marrow scans for tomorrow—" Momentarily out of breath, Ramsay paused and regarded the man oddly. "You're sure you understand all of this, Watford? You seem so goddamned remote."

Shortly after the doctor left, a nurse came in with an enormous shot of tetracycline. Before she left she gave him sedatives and a glass of milk with cookies.

"Now, Mr. Watford," she said with her breezy, bustling efficiency. "We understand each other perfectly, don't we? There'll be no further problems, will there?" She pushed the tousled forelock off his brow and laughed warmly. It made him feel good, this gentle chastisement.

The man in the bed beside him had fallen asleep. A thin Plasticine hose dangling from his nose gurgled softly into the shadows. Watford lay listening to the bubbling sound and the familiar hospital noises from the corridor outside, and contemplated his future.

The doctor had told him that the odds were that he would die within six months. The doctor had described him as remote. To him it seemed more like indifferent with a most curious twist. The news that treatment for acute chronic myelogenous leukemia was lengthy, complicated and involved long periods of hospitalization, with only a bare hope of cure, filled him with an odd glow of pleasure. His future, however brief, for the time being was at least secure. He knew where he would be. His bed at the hospital was guaranteed. He had finally caught up with a fate he had so doggedly pursued for all these many years.

49

He thought that it was going to be traumatic. He thought that after he'd tendered his resignation he would have to go out and get drunk. He looked grimly toward weeks of despondency followed by the numb listlessness of after-shock.

Nothing of the sort occurred. It had all been so simple. No bitterness. No regrets. Not even a fleeting melancholy for the more than forty years of service. What he felt instead was a sense of relief, along with a startling sense of affection for his former colleagues.

That third and final night Mooney hovered aloft for five hours above the rooftops. He no longer had any real expectation of success. Even the gnawing, relentless need for vindication was gone. Setting down near midnight on terra firma, and knowing he'd never have to go aloft in that hellish instrument again, was satisfaction enough.

Then coming back to the precinct house, the cursory interrogation of a handful of human plankton, litter scooped from rooftops and hustled unceremoniously into a lineup, he knew the game was up.

Dismissing them all, he went directly to his office, closed the door behind him and proceeded to draft his resignation.

"Dear Captain Mulvaney," he began, but in the next instant changed it to "Dear Larry."

> I have had my fling. Forty years on the job is enough for any man. Particularly a tired, overweight detective whose last hunches have all fizzled.
>
> So far as strict police procedure goes, I realize that I have been known over the years as one to cut corners. For that I'm sorry, too. I have always had a sort of arrogance, God help me,

and so far as my work goes, no one could convince me that I couldn't tell right from wrong. I'm willing to concede that on this particular score I may have been wrong.

So far as the Bombardier goes, I do not concede a thing. I know his method now and I thought I knew his timing. I guess I was wrong on that score. Whether or not my surveillance of rooftops from the air over the past three nights was successful is not the point. The point to remember is that the Bombardier strikes only one night a year and so far this year, he has yet to be heard from. I would be particularly vigilant over the next two weeks.

As per my agreement with the commissioner, may this note serve as my resignation and request for retirement. In view of the kind of feelings I inspire down at Manhattan South among my brethren, I can't say I'm sorry to be going.

Will you kindly send me all necessary forms to file for retirement and pension?

A copy of this letter goes to the commissioner and to the president of the PBA. Many thanks for all past favors.

Francis (Frank) Mooney

When he'd completed the letter, he licked the envelope flap, sealed it and took it out to Corelli, the desk sergeant.

"Would you give that to Mulvaney in the morning?"

Corelli took it gingerly, a look of embarrassment on his face. He knew very well what it contained.

Mooney did not go home that evening. Instead, he called Fritzi at the Balloon and told her he would meet her at the apartment in fifteen minutes.

She greeted him at the door with a kiss and a glass of champagne. Smiling, full of chatter, as if he'd come fresh from victory rather than defeat, she led him to the big leather chesterfield, took his shoes off and had him put his feet up. She had her own plans, she said, and proceeded to lay out a timetable for the next five years. It involved travel, a good deal of time at the track and a place out on the South Shore. It also involved Mooney, but at no time did she ever mention marriage.

Tomorrow, they would celebrate the start of his new freedom with a drive up to Saratoga for the annual yearling auctions. There was a glint in her eye. "Yes," she said with a charming air of fomenting mischief, that was another surprise she'd been planning. She wanted to get into breeding and racing her own horses.

He closed his eyes and lay his head back against the soft tufted leather of the backrest. He was no longer thinking about Dowd,

Mulvaney or the Manhattan South. Nor, for that matter, did he think about the shadowy figure who made his way once each year to the rooftops above the teeming city, toting with him forty pounds of lethal cinder block.

Fritzi noted how well he looked. Fully fifty pounds lighter. More youthful, and yes, attractive. Even attractive.

She made him a light snack and, as a treat, offered him a second glass of champagne which he characterized as "putrid." He drank it, then asked for a cold beer which she reluctantly gave him.

When they went to bed that evening, it occurred to him that for the first time, for as long as he could recall, for that matter, he was content. He slept like an infant.

They were on the road by 8:00 A.M. the next day, breezing up the thruway at a brisk clip. By eight o'clock they had turned onto the Taconic Parkway at Hawthorne, and several hours later, they were nosing west on the Massachusetts Turnpike, heading for the Northway.

All the way up Fritzi kept talking about what a shrewd investment a horse was—a hedge against inflation, a hefty tax shelter, security for the future and a pure ego trip.

Some four hours after they'd set out, they hit the track at Saratoga and dove directly into a beer tent. Having each wolfed down a frankfurter and a diet soda, they proceeded at once to the auction hall. The auditorium was small, but what it lacked in size it more than made up for in tone. Several hundred conspicuously wealthy people all pursuing tax shelters sat about in red-plush fanned seats, encircling a raised platform covered in green astro-turf, roped off with a thick velvet cord. Atop the platform two auctioneers sat behind a semicircular desk, gaveling bids while some of the most extraordinary horseflesh Mooney had ever seen was paraded on and off the platform.

Mooney resisted the inclination to be impressed. Instead, he affected his old standby, scorn. With her typically shrewd amusement, Fritzi noted that most of the time he was at the edge of his seat. Even she was cowed a bit by the big numbers and the august surroundings.

Two hundred and thirty-three yearlings were to be auctioned off that day, averaging $111,159 per head, bringing in a total of $25.9 million dollars. Fritzi and Mooney watched twenty-one horses go by before they even dared to stir. The twenty-second horse to come out was a small, well-proportioned roan yearling, Capricorn out of Courtesan. Born in Kentucky at Saybrook Farms, his catalogue number 76 shot up on the big electric tote board at the rear of the auditorium.

Fritzi leaned over and whispered, "What do you think?"

211

"What are you gonna do with him?"

"Race him, what d'ya think?"

"You're crazy."

The auctioneer opened the bid at $15,000. The tote board flashed the figure immediately, only to bounce up to $20,000 at the next bid.

"Look at those swell legs and his head, Mooney. Come on—What do you think?"

Fritzi's whisper grew slightly more shrill. The attendant led the animal smartly round the little roped-off ring.

"Twenty-five thousand," the auctioneer remarked almost inaudibly and the board lights flashed at the rear.

"It's your money," Mooney mumbled.

"I know whose money it is, for Chrissake. What d'ya think of him?"

"You must be nuts," Mooney whispered, but he was sweating heavily.

"Thirty thousand," the auctioneer announced.

"Come on, Mooney," Fritzi shot him an exasperated glance. "What do you make of this animal?"

Mooney's mind was whirling. His eyes swarmed over the horse's major points—feet ears, legs, tail, head, chest. He was slightly smaller than average on height, Mooney noted, but exceedingly graceful and marked by a reserve that was unusual in yearlings. He liked the way the ears stood erect, and the attitude of the tail. He liked also the manageability of the animal, the way it turned within the confinement of that narrow space. It was not docility or lack of spirit either, but rather an instinctive comprehension of what was expected of him.

"What about the chest?" Fritzi whispered.

"Narrow."

"I think so, too."

Thirty-five thousand was the figure now flashing on the board.

"Come on, Mooney," Fritzi fairly hissed. "This is costing me money. What d'ya say?"

"What d'ya need it for? It's a lot of work."

"Don't worry about the work. Do you like the horse?"

"Forty thousand," the auctioneer murmured softly.

"It's a lot of money," Mooney whispered.

"Forget about the money. What about the horse?"

He cast one last rueful gaze at the animal. "Okay," he said finally and closed his eyes. "I'll take half the action."

"Forty-five thousand," Fritzi bounded up instantly, then winced at the volume of her voice. There was an interminable pause while they looked about waiting for someone to top their bid.

Then came the dull clap of a gavel. "Sold to the lady. Third row, aisle three. Forty-five thousand."

Fritzi appeared a bit awed by the magnitude of what she'd just committed. It all seemed so rash now, and irrevocable.

"You didn't mean what you said?" she asked, as they moved toward the rear to fill out papers and proffer checks.

"About what?"

"About half the action."

"I certainly did. I want fifty percent of that animal."

"Don't be silly, Mooney. Where are you going to get twenty-two thousand, five hundred bucks?"

"I'm retired now, don't forget. I can take a loan out on my pension."

"That's dumb. I won't let you."

"Who the hell are you to tell me?"

She glanced sharply into his eyes, gauging the depth of his determination. "In that case, you're in for ten percent."

"Fifteen."

"Okay, fifteen. Not a penny more. Don't argue. Come on." She took his arm. "The officials are waiting for us." Suddenly she was overcome with excitement. "We'll have to arrange transportation. He'll need a groom and stable. A trainer. Oh, Mooney, did you see that little guy prancing around up there? He's ours. Isn't he nifty?"

"Nifty," Mooney muttered, already overcome with misgivings. Her face was flushed, he noted, and her eyes fairly beaming.

50

They breezed back into the city at about 9:00 P.M., their minds whirling from the numerous contracts and checks they had signed that day. Fritzi insisted on stopping by the pub to pick up some papers before going back to the apartment.

When they walked through the big swinging doors that opened onto the dark teak shilling bar, something struck Mooney as odd. Possibly it was the silence and, unaccountably, the sense of all motion suddenly frozen. Then a bright light flashed. There was a burst of applause and the old 49er saloon piano in the corner burst forth into a tinny version of "He's a Jolly Good Fellow."

At first he thought it was for some other person; they had inadvertently stumbled in on someone else's party. He glanced over his shoulder to see if someone had come in behind them. Then he turned back and saw them all behind the bar in funny hats and the big banner dangling above them with bright green letters: FREE AT LAST. FREE AT LAST. THANK GOD ALMIGHTY, FREE AT LAST.

There was a rush of heat to his face and the taut beginnings of a frown. When he turned to Fritzi, about to growl his displeasure, she was absolutely radiant. Amid the loud rattles and cracks of party noisemakers, she tugged at his sleeve.

There must have been at least a hundred people pumping his hand and slapping his back. Most of them were Fritzi's friends, staunch habitués of the Balloon. But, amazingly, she'd managed to round up two or three of his old buddies from the force. Carpenter, Hewitt, Delgado—good, longtime friends of Mooney's who'd stood by him during the dark days of the past. Big, red-faced, good old boys, retired pensioners, they encircled him, grinning awkwardly in shiny blue suits. How she'd learned about them, or where she'd dug them up on such short notice, he never knew. But what he'd come to understand that day was that as a woman, Fritzi Baumholz was formidable. When she set out to get something, she seldom if ever failed.

They ate and drank late into the night. Fritzi sat beside him, and at the end of dinner, she helped him to slice a large chocolate cake log, baked expressly for the occasion in the shape of a policeman's night stick. Across the top of it, in a thin wobbly line of vanilla frosting, was a horse surmounted by a jockey just crossing the finish line. Just beneath that in large, wavering birthday-cake script were the words, GUMSHOE—THE WINNER. Somehow the name for the new yearling stuck. They never would have called him Capricorn anyway, and while the name Gumshoe was hardly flattering, it was affectionate.

Fritzi sliced the cake, serving everyone graciously. When it came time for Mooney to get his piece, the chef sent out a thin, sugarless wafer with a solitary, badly mashed strawberry cresting it.

Roars and applause went up. Mooney laughed, but at a certain point in the lull of festivities, he turned to Fritzi as if seeing her for the very first time. He had scarcely been aware of the deep bond forged between them, so gradual and subtle a process it was. He hadn't known her quite a year yet, but that day, in some inexplicable fashion, the joint acquisition of a slightly undersized roan yearling called Gumshoe, had suddenly given their ambiguous relationship an astonishing solidity.

Somewhere along about midnight, while they were having coffee and brandies, and while good Havana cigars were passed round, Mitch, the bartender, came over to the table and whispered uneasily that there were a couple of "fellows" out front looking for him.

Mooney looked up inquiringly, then excused himself, and followed the bartender back out. Defasio and another detective, Wilkinson, were waiting there, looking sheepish and uneasy in the festive gaiety and litter of that place.

"Sorry to bother you, Frank." Defasio's fingers threaded nervously along the pockets of his jacket. "Mulvaney would like you to come right down."

"I'm out of it now," he snapped. "Haven't you heard?"

"The Bombardier was out tonight. He creamed someone real good over on Forty-seventh Street."

51

"When did they bring him in?"

" 'Bout twelve-thirty."

"They say when it happened?"

"An hour before."

"Eleven-thirty."

"Somewhere's around there."

Mooney hovered over the morgue attendant. They stood at the foot of a large refrigerator drawer. The object of their discussion was a corpse, now stripped of its clothing, and lying partially covered beneath a canvas tarpaulin.

Two hours ago the body beneath the tarpaulin had been that of a hale and hearty man of thirty years. The attendant had pulled the tarpaulin down around the ankles of the man in order to display the remains more effectively for Mooney.

There was nothing remarkable about the body save for the unusual sense of power conveyed by its perfect proportion and muscularity. The head, or rather what remained of it, had the look of something crumpled. Shattered crockery, perhaps. The eyes beneath that awful devastation remained open and wore a strangely calm expression, as if the final image imprinted on the retinas had not been at all unpleasant.

"Splat," the attendant muttered. He was a small, chatty fellow with frightened eyes and large yellow incisors that drooped above his lower lip. At the conclusion of each sentence he would produce a disconcerting little giggle while his face remained a perfect blank.

"Splat," Mooney nodded slowly. A fan droned overhead, pushing waves of Formalin and the sweetish rotten smell of mortification all about them. Deep within his pockets his fists clenched tight and he forced himself to look.

It was now slightly past 1:30 A.M. Not more than an hour ago, Mooney recalled ruefully, he was the guest of honor at his own retirement party. People toasted him and sang songs in praise of his good fortune. Twenty minutes after Defasio's arrival at the Balloon, however, he was right back in the stale, unventilated air of the precinct house on Forty-third Street, being briefed by Mulvaney. There was the same old knot in his stomach and it was as though nothing at all had changed.

"So I'm asking you to reconsider." Mulvaney scanned the resignation Mooney had tendered the night before. Watching Mulvaney squirm, he experienced a twinge of pleasure.

Still full of his first full day of freedom, Mooney was not prepared to be charitable. "Why," he asked. "Why should I reconsider?"

Red blotches erupted on Mulvaney's pitted cheeks. "Because the commissioner was on the phone to me ten minutes after we scraped this mess off of Forty-seventh Street. Because the mayor's office has been on the phone to him. Because restaurant owners, theater producers, even the goddamned massage parlor operators have all been tearing my ear off on the phone since eleven-thirty. Some civic-minded organization calling themselves Concerned Citizens for a Safer New York just cabled, inviting me to resign. That's why, my friend. And since I don't know where to start with this rooftop freak, since I have no idea whether this is a man or a gorilla running around up there, and since you're the only one in the precinct with any background on this, I must decline to accept your resignation." Eyes flashing, wattles trembling, Mulvaney wadded the sheet of paper in his fist and flung it into his desk drawer, slamming it shut with a thunderous clap. "I trust now I've answered all your questions, Mooney?"

Mooney appeared blissfully unfazed. "It's not as if I didn't warn you."

"Okay—I grant you that."

"Also, I did tell you when this was going to happen."

"Approximately."

"Don't weasel, Larry. I missed by one night."

Mulvaney nodded stiffly. "I grant you that, too. This is a one-night-a-year man."

"Thank your lucky stars for that."

"And he does appear to be active around the start of warm weather."

"The solstice, Captain. You can say it."

"Sure," Mulvaney spluttered. His face had turned a dangerous purple. "Sure, sure—the solstice." Up until that moment he'd been merely livid. Now he boiled over. "This is not my idea, goddammit."

"Oh, so it was Dowd who put you up to this. Well, kindly give my regards to the commissioner and tell him I'm no longer a member of the force. I'm no longer at his beck and call. My resignation took effect as of yesterday and as a burr in the ass of this department and a blight on its public relations image, my decision stands."

"You want me to beg? You want me to get down on my knees?"

"No, just get someone else."

"There is no one else around here knows beans about this case."

"There's Defasio. He knows all about it."

"Defasio's a basket case. Anyway, that's all academic. Dowd wants you."

"And just because the commissioner speaks, you think all you've got to do is snap your fingers?"

By the time Mooney had left the precinct house that evening he had recovered his captaincy, unconditionally, with a full rank of detective, first grade. When he'd left for the morgue, Mulvaney was still sitting there behind the desk, looking rumpled and very contrite.

"You got the block upstairs?" Mooney asked the morgue attendant.

"They got it up in Forensic right now. Trying to lift prints."

"They won't find any. Was it cinder?"

"Forty pounds. Taken right off some construction site. Must've hit like a pile driver."

"Who was he?" Mooney took out his pad and prepared to write.

The attendant leaned over and read something from a tag clipped to the tarpaulin. "Name of Krauss, Willie. German citizen. Tourist. Thirty years old. Here on a honeymoon with his bride."

"She with him when it happened?"

"Yeah. They were coming out of the theater. Just seen a show."

Mooney shook his head, and took one final glance at the shattered wreckage in the drawer. "Quite a wedding present."

52

The papers were full of it the next day. And not only the papers. The TV and radio shrieked with accounts down to the most grisly detail. Editorials throughout the media excoriated the police.

The precinct house was swamped with calls from outraged citizenry. Groups of merchants in the Broadway area posted a $10,000 reward for hard information. Another group of concerned citizens adorned themselves with U.S. Army surplus steel helmets and picketed with placards up and down West Forty-eighth and Forty-ninth streets. The Bombardier made the editorial pages and in one instance became the subject of a famous political cartoonist.

Then, of course, came the nut calls—hundreds of them from individuals claiming to know the identity of the Bombardier; some even proudly proclaimed themselves to be him. The clairvoyants and soothsayers, and ultimately a dowser with a divining rod were the final touches in that parade of the angry, the self-righteous and the bizarre.

The mayor's office, under heavy fire, gazed desperately about for someone to blame. Their gaze fell at once on Commissioner Dowd, who was summoned to City Hall late one night to explain himself.

The next morning *The New York Times*, chronically temperate and evenhanded, amazed everyone by calling for Dowd's resignation in fourteen-point banner headlines on their editorial pages. The article, signed by the editors, was entitled "Enough Is Enough."

The *New York Post* featured ghastly cover photographs of the victim sprawled on the pavement.

After that came the evening news shows with camera crews and smartly coutured young women reporters scurrying breathlessly about.

Mooney, now the official "chief" of the investigation, declined to speak with anyone. "Show business," he muttered to himself and drove off fuming in a patrol car. By 7:00 A.M. the next morning, he was out pacing up and down, taking measurements at the crime site. He no longer suffered a shortage of manpower and now found himself directing the movements of dozens of men. Those who were so unfortunate as to still address him as Lieutenant were quickly and sharply corrected. In a short time scores of police and plainclothesmen were pouring over Forty-seventh Street—clattering through alleyways, cellars, rooftops, up and down vacant stairwells, interrogating superintendents, elevator operators, stagehands, actors, shopkeepers, local denizens and the dregs of the earth.

"The guy flies, I'm tellin' you."
"He flies?"
"That's right. The guy flies. I seen it myself."
"You seen it?"
"That's right."

Michael Defasio peered into the bleared, unfocused eyes of a diminutive Eighth Avenue local type. He had one of those badly inflamed noses and large saucerlike ears inflected forward like a bat. The overall impression was that of a circus clown. An Emmett Kelly of the netherworld.

They were sitting in a small Cuban bar on Forty-sixth Street, just west of Eighth Avenue. Smoke and machine-gun Spanish filled the air. The throb of cowbells, timbales and salsa rhythms blared out of a jukebox at a decibel level that could more easily be experienced by the viscera than the ear. Hovering above them in a thick, almost palpable haze, was a concert of odors for the most part completely alien to Sergeant Defasio. From simple peppers and onions they deepened and grew more bewilderingly complex with goat stew, black cigars and ganja.

"How does he do it?" Defasio inquired, his curiosity now piqued.
"Fly?"
"Yeah."

"Climbs up on the ledge and whirls around three times."

"Whirls three times?"

"Yeah. Then he starts moving his arms up and down. Real slow, see? Flailin' himself about like. Then gradually faster and faster until the son of a bitch's arms are vibratin' so fast he just rises. Whatsa matter? You got a funny look on your face."

"Who, me?"

"The son of a bitch flies, I tell you. The guy's a Filipino. He learned it over there from the witch doctors."

"The witch doctors?"

"Yeah, they taught him how to do it. It's religiouslike. Can I have another rum?"

Defasio looked at the man skeptically. He'd already been around to seven bars in the theater district—dropping drinks and buying gossip. So far that evening he had listened to stories even more garish and bizarre than the Flying Filipino, and he knew that the present line of inquiry was all but fruitless.

Attired as a construction worker in overalls, sweat shirt, and yellow gum-soled boots, with a red hard hat rather too prominently displayed on the bar beside him, Defasio had a distinct premonition of impending failure. He was not particularly good at impersonation, and he was honest enough at self-appraisal to know he wasn't fooling anyone, except possibly the demented little fellow he was chatting with at the moment.

The prospect of a long night of such work ahead did not make him particularly happy. The only consolation was knowledge that a half-dozen of his buddies from Manhattan South were out right then going through the same mind-numbing motions—dragging, probing, scrounging for whatever crumbs of information might be dredged up out of the sprawling demimonde of little bars and saloons proliferating about the theater district west of Eighth Avenue.

"Another rum for my friend." Defasio rattled his empty beer bottle on the bar. "And another Budweiser for me." He rose gingerly. "I'll be right back. Just gotta drain the tanks."

"Sure. Go ahead." The little fellow sniggered cheerlessly. "I'll keep your beer cold."

When Defasio returned a short time later, the man was still there, huddled avidly above his rum, rapacious eyes shifting round like a hungry dog guarding its bone.

"So like I was saying," the little fellow resumed precisely where he'd left off. "This guy's up on the roof all the time. Practicin'. Wants to try out for the circus. Be an acrobat, you know?"

"Sure. There's good money in being an acrobat," Defasio remarked without much enthusiasm. He was wondering where he'd go next. It was only ten-thirty and he was on duty another four hours.

The little man's rum glass was once again depleted and he could see that his benefactor's interest was flagging. "I know another guy who hangs out up on the roofs a lot," he offered hopefully.

Defasio turned back to him, a spark of interest flaring in his eye. "Oh?"

"He bowls up there."

"Oh, come on now."

"No. I'm tellin' you. He's in the West Side Bowlin' Association and his wife won't let him practice in the apartment. So he takes his ball and . . ."

53

"Nice of you to come."

"I was in the neighborhood."

"How'd you find me?"

"Easy. I just went back to the hospital. Your records showed that you'd been sent from there up to a rehabilitation center in White Plains."

"That's right. Burke."

"They told me you'd been transferred here to Thornwood." Mooney gazed round the spacious white room with its lofty ceilings. "Nice."

"It's okay. The Sisters are kind." Jeffrey Archer smiled stiffly as though it hurt him to do so. If it is possible for a twenty-year-old to age drastically in one year, Jeffrey Archer had accomplished that feat.

"Carmelites," Mooney reflected quietly. "They make the best nurses."

"So they tell me." Archer conceded the point listlessly, as though it really didn't matter. It didn't to Mooney, either. It was merely conversation.

"What can I do for you?" Archer asked abruptly.

"I just wanted to say hello. It's been over a year."

"Didn't we speak before, when I was in the hospital?"

"Very little. You were barely conscious when I came. The second time you were in a lot of pain. You look a hundred percent better today."

Archer gave him a sharp, rather cynical grin. "Do I?"

"You couldn't possibly know."

The young man looked down at himself strapped into the wheelchair. A neck brace supported his head to prevent it from falling to one side and he was wired to several electrical contraptions that enabled him to lift forks and spoons and turn book pages. His self-examination followed by a long silence conveyed a state of unimaginable loss. "They ever get the guy?"

"Not yet. He hit again the other night. Only this time I'm afraid the guy wasn't as lucky as you were."

"Lucky?" The word made Archer smirk. This time Mooney noted the crooked, somewhat off-kilter cast of his features. It was then he realized that only one-half of Archer's face was capable of smiling. The other was paralyzed.

"Could've been worse," Mooney remarked.

"You mean death? That would've been better." He stared at Mooney, challenging him to open his eyes and take in the full horror of the picture.

"I'm not pretending you didn't get a lousy break."

"Okay, then," Archer snapped. He'd won his point. He didn't want pep talks and bromides about how much was still left in life that he could do. Even now in his head he dreamed of leaps and turns and grand batements—the exquisite freedom of soaring. "You think you'll ever get this guy?"

"We're giving it our best shot." Mooney appeared slightly defensive, as if he could read in the young man's eyes a judgment on his own professional performance. "That's why . . . you see . . . I came. I just thought we might run through the whole thing once more. That is, if . . ."

"It's a long time ago."

"As best as you can recall. That's all I'm asking."

"I'm not sure I recall anything."

"The last time we talked you were coked to the gills with sedatives and pain-killers." Mooney flipped hastily through his pad. "You mentioned something then about suddenly looking up."

"And seeing a figure on the rooftop."

"That's right." Mooney found the page in his pad and read with

222

his lips, "Arms outspread like an angel. Any more about that? I mean, any sharper detail?"

Archer reflected a moment. He made a gesture as if he'd wanted to shrug, but his neck brace restrained him. "No. Nothing. Only that I keep thinking over and over again in my head how everything was the moment before. Who I was the moment before. How happy I was. And then . . . after. The moment after. And how things might have been now had I just stepped an inch or two to the right or left. Or walked slower or faster . . ."

Mooney watched him silently, nodding his head, fathoming something of Archer's unreconcilable bitterness. The capriciousness of fate. The unjust, irrevocable nature of its sentence.

One of the Carmelite sisters entered, her starched white robes whispering over the cool tiled floors. A bland waxen face smiled at Mooney from beneath the enormous brim of a white-winged bonnet, then turned its quiet gaze to her charge. She carried a small two-gram dosage glass of pale green liquid directly over to Archer and held it to his lips. He drank with his eyes closed. When he opened them again he smiled up at her like a child who'd been vouchsafed a special treat. "More," he pleaded appealingly.

"Not so much as a drop, Archer," the sister scolded with her gentle severity. "I'm here to medicate you—not launch you into the cosmos." She turned to Mooney. "Not much longer, now. He needs his rest."

After she'd gone they sat together, quietly chatting about nothing in particular. At one point Archer confided to him that his parents had come only once to see him. It had been a lacerating experience. All the time they were there they'd blamed him for what had happened. Had he but listened to them, had he never come to New York to pursue his frivolous dream, he'd be fine today. Married, possibly, with children. A good job at his father's factory, and all that.

"It hasn't been entirely rotten, though." The ruined boyish smile broke once again across his crippled face. "I've made a lot of friends since then."

"Friends?"

"People. They write. They tell me they've read about me in the papers or heard about me on TV. Mostly, it's a lot of rubbish about faith and God. Praying and keeping up hope. That sort of thing. I've had a couple of hundred of those. I answer them all."

"That's good," Mooney said, suddenly anxious to leave.

"Some even send gifts. Sweaters, ties, socks they've knit themselves. I got about a dozen paperweights, letter-openers, wallets, souvenirs. Here," he indicated with a movement of his eyes a shelf above his shoulders, "look at some of those."

Mooney rose and lumbered halfheartedly to the shelves. There, in-

deed, was a multitude of gift offerings, bric-a-brac and various odd-
ments sent to Archer by strangers who had read about his plight.

There were curios, knickknacks, small toys, vases, ashtrays, puzzles, numerous small inexpensive objects intended to amuse—to
make more tolerable the hours of the invalid consigned for the rest of
his days to the bondage of a wheelchair. Each bore upon it a message
of courage and faith from a well-wisher:

Dear Mr. Archer:

I heard about you on the news. Have Faith. Christ heals.
> Mrs. Viryl T. Crider
> 2523 Avenue C
> Dayton, Ohio

Dear Mr. Archer:

I have been paralyzed since age 12. I have just celebrated my
73rd birthday. Life is beautiful.
> Olive Denby
> 41 Congress Street
> Bethlehem, New Hamp-
> shire

Dear Jeffrey:

God has not forgotten you.
> Millard F. Cowley
> RFD
> Turnbull, Utah

Mooney moved without enthusiasm from one specimen to the
next, reading their scant messages of hope with a sense of odd distaste. "You keep all their letters?" he asked over his shoulder.

"I have to. I write them all back. Someday I'll make a scrapbook."

Mooney's peregrinations led him to a tall, dangling green plant
with long spatulate leaves that shot off in a dozen directions. Very
near the top was a small card tied securely round an upper branch.
Slowly, with his lips he read the simple message inscribed there:
"Best wishes, A. Boyd."

Mooney stood staring up at it, skewered amid the tanglement of
tall, rubbery branches. His eyes watered slightly. Before anything
had actually registered in his mind, some deep buried part of himself
recognized and identified the tiny card with its brief message indited
in a small, immaculate hand.

"Best wishes," he repeated the words half aloud to himself. "A. Boyd."

His throat was dry as he carefully untied the card from the branch and took it down as though it were a damaged bird unable to fly. His blood quickening, he carried it back to the young man in the wheelchair. Holding the card up before him, he said, "Where'd you get this?"

Archer shaped the words softly with his lips. "Best wishes, A. Boyd." The name appeared to mean nothing to him.

"It was tied up on that big plant over there," Mooney said.

"The big cactus, you mean?"

Mooney cocked an ear at him. "How did you get it?"

Archer appeared perplexed.

"How did it come to you? Messenger? Special delivery?"

"I don't know."

"Oh come on. You must." Mooney was suddenly aware of the gruffness in his voice. Instantly his tone softened. "I mean, when did you get it?"

"When I was in the hospital. Right after the accident."

"But you don't know who brought it? How it arrived?"

"By messenger, I guess. I was still pretty much out of it most of the time. When I awoke, it was just there. On the night table. It was much smaller then. It's grown like wild in just a year."

"Is that all you can remember?"

Something in Mooney's voice alarmed the young man.

"That's all. I never heard from the guy again. Why? What is it?"

"Nothing," Mooney muttered numbly. "I don't know what it is." He continued to stare down hard at the card in his hand.

"Sister Avila knows all about that plant. Soon as she saw it she knew what it was. It's some kind of cactus. They have the biggest blossoms you've ever seen. And you know something strange about them—they bloom just one night a year."

"One night a year," Mooney mumbled.

"That's right. Cereus, I think she calls it, nightblooming cereus."

Mooney turned and gazed at the boy. There was a crooked little smile on his face.

54

"Don't you ever pull that stuff again."

"I didn't do it. I swear."

"You hear me, Watford? Once more, just once more and you're out. Now that comes straight from Ramsay. And believe me, Ramsay is not one for idle chatter."

"I don't care what Ramsay says. I didn't . . ."

"You lie, Watford. You lie like other people breathe. The truth of it is that you lie so much you don't even know when you're lying anymore."

"I don't have to take this."

"No, you don't. You can get up and leave anytime. I'll be delighted to see you go. You're not worth the time and the money it costs to keep you here. Imagine the gall. . . . Needles lying right out next to the bed, along with that phial. Believe me, Watford, they're gonna find out who's supplying you, and when they do . . ."

"I haven't had Demerol in weeks."

"You low-down suffering . . ."

"Someone put those things there." Watford glared down at the hypodermic and the empty phial beside his bed. "Someone's trying to frame me."

"Now who'd care enough about you to want to frame you? The only one framing you is you. Don't you ever call that dispensary again and make out you're Doctor this or Doctor that. You hear me?"

"But I'm telling you, I didn't."

"Now you listen up, Watford. The next time is IT. You pull that stunt once more and you're back out on the street faster than you can say DEMEROL."

"I told you I haven't had any stuff for weeks."

"You lie. For shame. You suffering skunk."

"Stop shouting at me."

Watford's last words were uttered through a long, piteous wail. The sound of it was eerie and slightly unearthly, like that of muezzins summoning the faithful to worship. Whatever its tonal qualities, the device worked. It had the effect of derailing the nurse momentarily.

Nurse Emmy Blysworth was a tiny, leathery West Indian of indeterminate age, and framed out of sinew and tendon. She was a mere five-foot-two, but when she rose to one of her fine moral dudgeons, as she was wont on occasion to do, she conveyed the impression of one much taller.

"Stop shouting?" she mouthed his words incredulously as a knot of nerves throbbed in her cheek. "Stop shouting? If you think this is shouting, my man, you're in need of some real shoutin' lessons. I've seen five of my sister nurses here—good decent ladies all—driven off this ward because of you. Five nurses in two weeks, Mr. Watford, whose only sins was they tried to serve you too well."

Glaring down at him, a glint of demonic merriment flashed in her eye. "Now, you hear me, Watford. You may not know this yet, so I'm gonna tell you. No matter what thieving, skunking, lying dirty tricks you pull, I'm here to stay. You can leave all the needles and phials around you like. That don't embarrass me at all 'cause you're in a fight now. And when it's over, I can promise you, just as I'm standin' here before you, only one of us still gonna be around."

Before Watford could reply, a pert pink face thrust its head through the door. "Visitor for Watford."

Watford sat halfway up in bed. "It's my sister. I wrote her last week." His eyes sparkled with relief.

The Irish nurse hovering in the doorway frowned. "This don't look like any sister to me, Watford. Can he have his guest, Blysworth?"

Nurse Blysworth scowled. "I can't see what for anyone'd care to call on him, but show 'em in. I'm just on my way out." Muttering, she moved off. Then at the door the peppery little black lady turned and glared back at him. "Now you mind, Watford. Hear?"

Even as she was departing, another was arriving.

The shadows of late afternoon had begun to slant across the hospital room and the figure that hovered momentarily in the doorframe loomed large within the mote-filled sunlight. Coming at Watford, its motion seemed implacable and the face, though at once familiar, he could not immediately place.

"Mr. Watford." Mooney thrust a beefy paw at him. "Sorry to bother you like this."

Watford's innards turned and then he recalled. *Oh, my God*, he said to himself. *Oh, my God.* The words sounded over and over again in his head as he struggled to smile. "Nice to see you." *Oh, my God—Myrtle—Jesus—Oh, dear God, what the hell now—*

"Haven't seen you for a while," the detective went on affably. "Just thought I'd drop over—say hello. Your next-door neighbor, Mrs. Stein, said you were here."

"Oh, Mrs. Stein, was it? Nice lady." Watford smiled desperately.

"Happened kind of suddenly, didn't it?"

"Yes. Very. Some trouble I had in the army. Relapse, you know." Trying hard to smile, he felt his face out of control, as if his expression was all wrong, stamped with guilt. Looking at Mooney, he was certain the detective knew everything.

His mind whirled. *It's that pharmacy. They got my fingerprints. They searched the house while I was here and found the Demerol. Oh, Jesus, Jesus.*

"I'm afraid I've had some bad luck." Watford spoke feebly, making a shameless pitch for leniency. "Very sick, I'm afraid."

"Oh?"

"I've had news from the doctor. I've just been told I have leukemia."

Mooney stared down at the floor, casting about for something to say.

"Only a matter of time."

"I'm sorry."

"You mind passing me those pills there?"

Mooney handed him a small box of tablets.

"Asparaginase. Extract of asparagus, as you may have guessed." Watford's laugh was high and thin. "Specific in the treatment of chronic myelogenous leukemia." He pronounced it with a touch of braggadocio, as if he were enormously proud of his accomplishment. Like an overly precocious child, he rattled off a great deal of information about his long-range prognosis. He'd been reading up on it in books in the hospital library, he said.

From the way he spoke, the prognosis was decidedly gloomy. Yet, as Mooney listened, it occurred to him that horrendous as the story was, the man either didn't grasp its full implication or else he didn't seem to care. Further, he had the dim but growing suspicion that all of Watford's talking, his compulsive spewing of words, hopping illogically from one subject to the next, was a stall to prevent him from getting down to the business for which he'd come.

"Mr. Watford?"

"They say we'll have thunder showers tonight. We need it. Might break this awful humidity. You know, when I was a child my father—"

"Mr. Watford. I have a couple of questions I'd like to ask—"

"Questions?" His heart banged in his chest. *Oh, Christ. Oh, God.* "Look, I don't know anything. Honest."

Mystified, Mooney gazed at him. The man's pallor was alarming. He'd gone white, the color of parchment, and his lips trembled.

He rattled on disjointedly. "I'm really not well. If you don't believe me, ask Dr. Ramsay. He says I've only got a few months left, and now, now"—his eyes started to water unashamedly—"Now, they say I've been stealing medication. Stealing. Me. Can you imagine?

"Look," he said, clearing his throat, "I just wanted to ask a few more questions about that man who shared the room with you at Beth Israel two years ago."

"What man?" Watford was momentarily bewildered. "Oh, him."

"Yes. Remember, I already questioned you about him."

"Oh, sure, that's okay. Sure. Go ahead." Watford giggled nervously.

Mooney pulled out his pad of scribbled notes. "Two weeks ago you said this Mr. Boyd—"

"Boyd?"

"That's his name."

"The man in the bed next to me? In the hospital?"

"That's right. Only you said you didn't recall that name."

"Yes," Watford said and his eyes glowed. Then, just as quickly his expression drooped. "I still don't. He was sort of a strange fellow."

"Strange? In what way?"

Having revealed the fact that the man was strange, Watford was at a loss to elucidate the precise quality of that strangeness. Mooney attempted to help him. "Did he look strange? His appearance, I mean?"

"No. It wasn't that. He was sort of nice-looking. Pleasant, actually."

"Pleasant?" Mooney scribbled, recalling Baum's theory of the murderous God-fearing chap in the gray flannels. "How old, would you say?"

"Fifty. Sixty. I don't know."

Mooney repeated the words beneath his breath as he scribbled onto the page. Dr. Kurt Baum's silhouette came more sharply into focus.

"Was there anything special about him? Distinctive?"

Watford thought a moment. By that time he wanted genuinely to help. "No. I don't believe so. There was nothing especially distinctive. Hey, what do you want this guy for, anyway? What did he do?"

"He's killed a few people."

"Oh." Watford nodded. His response to the information was one of almost astonishing indifference. He reflected a moment longer. "Gosh, he seemed awfully nice to me. How do you know?"

"I don't. I've got a pretty good hunch though. I'm trying to locate the guy. That's why I came to see you."

Watford smiled dreamily.

To Mooney the man's smile appeared to reflect a harmless idiocy, yet he was clearly the key to everything. "Can you give me a physical description of the man? Was he tall or short?"

"Tall. At least he appeared to be. He was lying down all the time. Under sheets. Didn't I give you all this already?"

"Yeah, but what the hell—give it to me again. How tall would you say? Six feet?"

"Sure—he could've been six feet."

"Could've been?" Mooney wore a face of despair.

"That's right. And thin. He looked thin. Actually a little sickly, but he'd lost a lot of blood. And, like I said, pleasant-looking. A teacher or a musician or something. He didn't look like any killer, if you know what I mean."

Mooney scribbled. "If you saw the guy in a lineup or a photograph, you think you could identify him?"

"Sure," Watford nodded excitedly. "Sure I could."

"You told me before that the guy said he'd had some kind of accident. An open manhole or something?"

"That's right. He'd been walking in the street, he said, and the utility people had quit work for the night and gone off and left the manhole cover off. I told the guy I would have sued for a million."

"And the guy fell through the hole, you say?" Mooney pressed harder. "Did you ever think the guy was lying? That maybe he got injured some other way?"

Watford stared blankly back at him. "Nope."

"Where was his injury? Do you recall?"

"I think I told you the first time you came to see me. It was his leg. Took thirty-two stitches to close him up."

His string of questions run out, Mooney experienced a small rush of desperation. "Was he discharged before or after you?"

Watford had a ghastly recollection of himself in physician's gown, lunging down a corridor, the thud of footsteps in pursuit, hoarse angry shouts bellowing from behind. The last question had reignited his terrifying suspicion. Suddenly he was antagonistic. "How come you need to know all this?"

Mooney reared back slightly, a light whistling noise issuing from his nose. "I'd just like to know if anyone came while you were there. Did he have visitors?"

"No. There were no visitors."

"You're certain?"

"Of course I'm certain. I was there, wasn't I?"

"Okay, okay. Don't go getting all hot and bothered. I'm just trying to get some additional facts."

"I'm sick," Watford whined at the detective as if he were responsible for the condition. But in the next instant, he was apologetic and a little frightened. "I'm sick, you see. I don't know what's going to happen to me. I've got filariasis. Bancroftian filariasis. Picked it up in the army. In 'Nam."

Mooney's head tilted sideways. "I thought you said you had leukemia."

"That's what they tell me. But I don't believe them. They're all liars. I'm sure this is a relapse of my filariasis."

Something in the man's eyes at that moment caused the detective to set his pencil down. "Why would they lie to you?"

"They do that in hospitals," Watford confided in a whisper. "They're trained to lie. Particularly if you're a veteran. The government doesn't want to pay the benefits, you see."

"Yeah, I see." Mooney's spirit sagged. He was just about ready to rip out all the pages of Watford's deposition and tear them in shreds. They were the ramblings of a madman. "Well, I guess that's all the questions I've got. In case your memory sparks, you know where to find me."

"You gave me your number the last time we spoke."

Mooney scribbled his office and home numbers onto the pad, then tore out the page. He lay it down on the night table beside Watford. "Just in case something comes to mind."

"Sure," Watford cried eagerly. "Sure. I'll call. I'd love to see you get this guy. He sure didn't look like any killer to me."

Mooney had a final impression of the man lying in bed in his gown. With his wide, staring, childlike face, he seemed pathetic and unbearably alone. "I hope you feel better soon." He took the cool, smooth palm in his hand.

For a terrible moment Watford clung to the hand and wouldn't let it go. "Listen," he said, "I didn't do anything wrong. Honest."

55

The light in the room was bright but Watford's vision was dim and hazy. He'd had his eggs and toast and juice and the nurses, following Dr. Ramsay's directions, had given him his morning allotment of Demerol.

Now, as was always the case after taking the drug, he was drowsy and wanted to sleep. Several nurses moved about the room on gummed soles that squeaked over the vinyl tile floors. They were straightening up, changing sheets on the bed beside Watford's, where a man just operated on for bleeding ulcers lay with a plastic hose inserted into his vein. From time to time a bubble of glucose slid audibly down the tube into his arm.

Knowing that Watford liked to drift off watching TV, the nurse had put the set on softly so he might watch the morning talk shows without disturbing his neighbor.

Through drowsy, heavy-lidded eyes, Watford watched the blue-green cathode phantoms floating eerily above him, their voices coming at him over long, cold distances. On the screen he watched an ambulance and police cars and then several men lugging a heavy canvas bag between them to a waiting van.

The television reporter, a pert, all-American girl, stood in the foreground with morning breezes lashing wisps of hair about her face. In breathy, portentous whispers, she explained what had occurred there. It appeared that someone had broken into an art gallery somewhere uptown. Burglar alarms had gone off. Thieves or a single thief, she couldn't be certain (Watford's eyes were nearly closed now and he listened with only one ear), had been interrupted by the police during the act. When asked to surrender, they, or he (they couldn't say if there were more than one), refused, trying instead to escape. One was subsequently killed.

"Quintius," the pert young thing murmured breathlessly. "Mr. Peter Quintius ... owner of ... father of ... internationally renowned collector ... dealer. When notified at his Long Island estate last night ..."

Watford turned drowsily on his pillow and gazed blankly at the screen. Between the moist cage of his lashes he saw for a moment a face. It was strikingly handsome in a haggard way. Full of some ageless dignifying sorrow.

The face hovered unsteadily on the screen before Watford's woozy vision. A voice, hoarse, broken with grief, replied numbly to questions. Then, like some troubled wraith, was gone.

Watford's eyes had opened fully by then, still focused upon an afterimage that persisted, even as the bright, perky mask of the reporter had reoccupied the screen, signing herself off and transferring the show back to the studio.

Watford had a slightly baffled feeling, like a man jarred rudely out of deep sleep. He had no idea why he continued to watch the screen expectantly. In the next moment he shrugged, rolled over and fell soundly asleep.

Late the next afternoon one of the nurses brought him a newspaper. It was her own copy of the *Daily News* which she delivered to him unfailingly each day. Watford loved the *Daily News*. It embodied for him some vestige of his childhood when, as a small boy, he looked forward each Sunday to the comic strips—Dick Tracy, Popeye, Gasoline Alley—although most of the old strips were gone now and what remained lacked the color and engaging good spirits of the old favorites.

He read slowly from one page to the next, his mouth lipping words as he read, stories about small, unheroic wars in distant places, labor strife, sordid little page 4 stories reeking of treachery and deceit—a paternity suit involving a cinema star; the body of a numbers runner found pulped and bloody in the trunk of a car in Staten Island; a Long Island heiress who drove an ice pick into the heart of her philandering husband. Watford devoured everything on the page. As always he experienced a sharp twinge of affinity for the victims and losers. Next was a story about a young man shot to death attempting to break into a prominent uptown gallery. " ... the victim identified as 26-year-old William Quintius, paradoxically the son of the ..."

"Peter Quintius," Watford uttered the name aloud without reaction. Inset was a photograph of Mr. Quintius himself at the crime site being questioned by the police.

"Peter Quintius." He murmured the words once more under his breath, then vaguely, he recalled the television news early that morning, the pretty young reporter standing before the gallery, interviewing the tall, dignified gentleman, caught that moment full-face by the camera. A stricken, disheveled figure beleaguered by reporters.

"Peter Quintius," he said once more, and in his mind's eye he saw a face. It lay propped on a pillow in three-quarter view surmounted by a crown of thick, white hair, partially eclipsed in shadow.

"What's your name?" he heard himself ask. The face turned laboriously toward him on the pillow. The large eyes fluttered open.

"Boyd," came the hoarse reply. "My name is Anthony Boyd." Not Quintius. It was Boyd. Just as the police had said. "My name is Anthony Boyd." Unable to believe, yet unable to discount, he repeated the name over and over, like a man trying to shake something sticky and unpleasant from his hand.

My God. How strange. Watford reread the story, pity welling up within him for the man he'd known only briefly in a hospital room two years before. The son killed like that, breaking into his own father's place of business. And the father having to come down. Making the identification and all that. Imagine the shame. The pity of it. His own son. My God. It's him, all right. That's him. A. Boyd. A. Boyd. Not P. Quintius. A. Boyd.

He laughed to himself, then suddenly broke off, recalling the detective who had come to him. Just two days ago. How strange. How come I couldn't recall then? It was the face. Seeing the face like that. How strange. My God. I've got to call. I've got to get in touch with that policeman, what's his name? He snatched at the strip of paper. His eyes swam over the letters. "Mooney." That's it. Captain Mooney. My God, I've got to call.

He sat up quickly, nearly dislodging a tumbler of juice, then lunged for the phone beside the bed. Dialing, his brain spun and his fingers trembled over the digit holes. Then suddenly he put the receiver back on the hook and replaced the phone on the table beside him. He took a deep breath.

"My God." His heart thumped. I must be mad. As it is he already suspects me of the Cardinal Pharmacy. And then there's Myrtle and the bank robbery in Kansas City. Now all I need is this. If I tell this Mooney about Quintius, or Boyd, or whatever, he'll think I'm mad. Possibly even an accomplice of some kind to the son. Of course. That's it. They suspect me of being involved with the son in the burglary and—Oh, but that's mad.

His voice trailed off as he caught the note of wild irrationality in it. Beside his bed on the night table was a pill and a tepid glass of milk.

Cramming the pill into his mouth, he gulped it down, then fell back heavily onto the pillows and clamped his eyes shut.

Soon, he knew, the pain would start. That thin wire noose of constriction banding his head from temple to temple, gradually radiating outward to the ears, rising upward round the parietal and occipital areas, reaching down finally like steel fingers and seizing him by the scruff of the neck. He cringed in anticipation of it. The nurse going past in the hall heard the infantile pathetic whimper.

56

Having restored Mooney to full captaincy, Chief Mulvaney felt certain that the mystery of the phantom Bombardier was now safely out of his hair. It was Mooney's problem now and let him take the heat for it. The Bombardier was still at large, the furor went on unabated, and Chief Mulvaney could not resist a twinge of spiteful delight. Mooney had failed before and he would fail again. Mooney was a sham. He knew no more about the phantom Bombardier than anyone else. How he had managed to euchre the commissioner and the whole force into believing that he had the inside track on the case, and had himself anointed God's foremost expert in the matter was all part of the man's colossal malarkey.

Mulvaney was right, of course. After five years of special investigations, tens of thousands of dollars in overtime and special requisitions, the department was no closer to an arrest now than they were the night the first cinder block dropped from the sky.

In terms of hard, objective data, Mooney had little to show. A pseudonym, a canceled insurance policy with a dummy address, a two-year-old hospital record, and now incomprehensibly, a link between the pseudonymous A. Boyd and a large, ungainly cactus that cast off huge fragrant blooms one night a year.

It was early June in New York City. For Fritzi there was now the lively, spirited yearling Gumshoe, who occupied her waking thoughts and lured her almost daily to the track to watch the morning workouts, talk with the trainer, consult with the vet. There were supplies to order, expenditures and decisions to make. Increasingly, she sought Mooney's guidance in these matters. On the one hand, he loved every bit of it. But, increasingly, he found the demands of the investigation on his time greater than he could fulfill. More disturbing, he sensed the department's mocking cynicism and that made him crave vindication as never before.

The truth was Mooney was stalemated. Of course, he could not admit that to anyone, least of all himself. The investigation, after much hoopla, had ground to a sputtering halt. Now Mooney and his team of special investigators were reduced to the indignity of backtracking and treading water. Hours were spent scouring through years of dusty police files. There were the computers, too, and the FBI master file in Washington, D.C., with its list of over a million offenders.

Instinctively, Mooney knew all this to be futile—the hum and buzz of expensive new technology to mask the fact that, in the absence of any truly significant new evidence, the investigation was bankrupt.

Up on the rooftop overlooking 161 Street, sipping at a beer he had sneaked, Mooney gazed across at the molten glow of floodlights in the sky above the stadium where the Yankees were playing Baltimore. From over the Grand Concourse the steady roar of traffic wafted upward from below and occasionally he could hear the sharp crack of a bat impacting on a ball and the roar of a weekend crowd like a cataract of rushing water.

Leo, Virgo, Cepheus and the Lynx wheeled overhead. Boötes, like a bright kite, scudded low above the rooftops. Even the stars failed to console him. They filled him, instead, with a sense of desolation and reminded him that he was sixty-two. Implausibly, too, they reminded him of Fritzi and the rancorous thought that it had taken him a long time to find her and, having found her, she was almost too much too late. It was just another one of those wildly promising but heartbreakingly unplayable hands that life had always delighted in dealing him.

About to leave, he turned sharply, his foot colliding with something on the rooftop. He reached down, groping along the tar until his fingers found a smallish plank of 2" by 4", undoubtedly left there by workmen repairing the roof.

He stood for a time hefting it in his hand. The wood was light, wide-grained, probably pine. He appeared to be pondering something. In the next moment, slowly, almost dreamily, he walked back over to the edge, then inexplicably flung the plank far out into the inky void. A second or two later a sharp clatter wafted up from below, followed at once by a long muted roar from the stadium.

He hovered there a moment at the ledge, perplexed, peering hard down into the blackened alleyway below. He had the look of a man trying to recover something he had lost.

Ultimately, his thoughts returned to the Bombardier, a shadowy figure of diabolic patience who knew how to wait, a man who knew how to hang back and let his trail cool. The stars looked down on that man now, whoever he was, surely as they looked down on Mooney. Even as Mooney pondered that, his eye fastened on the bright glow of Arcturus in the tail of Boötes, and in his mind's eye, he triangulated the points between himself, the great star, and the Bombardier, thus mystically linking all three together.

57

"As of yet, the commissioner is harnessed to an exceedingly hot seat. Between the mayor's office and the cries of public outrage, the department finds itself, as never before, beleaguered by proliferating crime and meaningless violence, the most recent example of which is perhaps the most heinous. Mr. Willie Krauss and his young bride of several days, honeymooning here from . . ."

"Quintius," Watford murmured and thrust his newspaper aside. Surely it couldn't be the same man, he thought. Not that quiet fellow in the bed beside me at the hospital. Surely the police are wrong. I just can't believe . . . And why in heaven's name . . . So cruel, so stupid.

For several days now, the name had racketed about in his head. . . .

"Quintius." He rolled the word around in his mouth as if he were tasting it. He thought next of the detective, the big, rugged Irish face, the eyes regarding him shrewdly. "Maybe I should . . . This way, if I don't, I'm an accessory. Concealing evidence, I mean. No. I mean—I just can't afford to get involved now. What if the hospital or Ramsay got wind that the police were talking to me? What then? I'd be out on the street before I could bat an eye."

He didn't want to leave the hospital, he thought. "Not ever again. No sir— Not ever. . . ."

"Hello, Charles."

Watford looked up into the gaunt, tired smile of Dr. Ramsay, who slipped down into the chair beside Watford's bed. "You getting enough exercise? Walking round the esplanade outside, like I told you?"

"Sometimes," Watford replied evasively.

"I can see that you don't. Just from the way your eyes are avoiding mine. You should, you know, Charles."

Lately the doctor had taken to calling him Charles, or sometimes in less guarded moments, Charley. Watford disapproved of that sort of informality, particularly since he'd never invited the doctor to call him by his first name.

"What you need is exercise, Charles. And fresh air." The physician's gaze lingered on him for a strangely protracted moment. The eyes were probing, yet uncertain, as if he weighed the wisdom of pursuing their talk on any deeper level. "Don't you have any family?" he asked suddenly.

"My mother and father are dead."

"Any sisters or brothers? You never seem to have visitors."

"I have a sister and a brother-in-law and a niece in Pittsburgh."

"Do they know about you?"

Watford appeared troubled. "Me?"

"Your health, I mean. Your condition. The fact that you've been hospitalized."

"I wrote my sister several weeks ago and told her."

"Have you heard from her yet?"

"The other day. She called."

"And she's coming up to see you, I s'pose?"

Watford's eyes focused on some distant part of the city skyline. "She's very busy now. Her husband runs a big plumbing supply business. This time of the year, the spring and all, happens to be the height of the construction season." He broke off suddenly.

"I see," Ramsay replied softly. "Well, that's all right. It doesn't really matter. I just wondered . . ."

"I know you did." Watford's gaze wandered to that point on the

238

skyline. There, tiny antlike dots of men inched up and down a gigantic crane surmounting a building under construction.

"... if a friend might be ..."

"Friends? I have a lot of friends, plenty of friends," Watford broke in belligerently. "I just don't care to see them. That's all."

The physician tapped nervously at his knee. "I've got your new blood workups from the lab."

"How are they?"

There was a pause as Ramsay regarded him keenly. "Not as encouraging as I would have hoped." His voice grew brusque and professional.

Watford took a deep breath. "What does that mean?"

"It means you're not responding to the radiation or the chemotherapy."

"The drugs make me sick. They make me vomit. I hate them."

"Nobody expects you to love them, Charles. I'm perfectly aware of the side effects. But I'll take unpleasant side effects any day if I can reduce the leukocyte count."

"Have they reduced mine?"

Ramsay's mouth opened, then closed as though he were about to speak but changed his mind. "No," he said after another moment. "As a matter of fact, your white blood count appears to have increased."

He watched Watford warily as though he expected some sign of panic. There was none. Watford's face remained blank and impassive, his eyes still transfixed on the huge crane.

"What's more, your spleen is quite enlarged, the lymph nodes appear to be involved, and I see indications now of liver involvement." He addressed him in a strangely harsh whisper. "You understand? You know what I'm saying?"

Watford nodded.

"You must forgive me for being sharp, Charles, but I don't think you do."

"You're saying that I'm dying," Watford replied flatly, without emotion.

"I'm saying that you're not responding to treatment."

"That's not my fault, is it?"

"No, of course not," Ramsay was quick to clarify. The question, direct as it was, struck him as pitiful. As if Watford had perceived his inability to respond to the best that medicine had to offer as just one more failure in his long, unbroken string of failures.

"Of course it's not your fault," the physician went on apologetically. "It's more my fault. I haven't been able to come up with the right combination of drugs—the right balance between your radiation and chemotherapy. It's not your fault at all. I'll try harder. There are some new compounds just out on the market. Purely a hunch, mind you, but the literature on them is encouraging. Certainly worth a try. Are you sure you wouldn't like me to call your sister? I could, you know. No problem at all."

Watford pondered that a moment. "I don't think so. They're really very busy now and I'd prefer not to bother them."

After Ramsay left he sat there for some time, thinking. He had understood perfectly the physician's meaning but, in some perfectly natural and self-protective stance, he couldn't really believe that the deadly prognosis just described pertained in any way to him. It was someone else the doctor had been discussing, as if they were two old friends chatting about an unfortunate acquaintance they both hadn't seen in years.

Watford picked up his newspaper again and resumed reading the editorial. "The plain unpleasant truth is," the editorialist of *The Times* continued, "that nothing lies between the innocent citizen and wanton violence but a constabularly, undermanned, underfinanced, riddled with inefficiency at the highest levels and badly demoralized by loss of confidence in their capacity to cope. The era of creative violence—that is, violence as an art form, where the act of imagination is every bit as important as the consequence of the act itself— appears to have entered its golden age."

58

Watford spent a restless evening. He waited out the long reaches of the night on his back, gazing at the ceiling. He thought about himself and Quintius. Or was it Boyd? Sometimes he called him Quintius and sometimes Boyd. In his mind he saw the young honeymoon couple amid crowds surging out of a brightly lit theater into the glare and festive tumult of the street. There were restaurants and bars and horse-mounted police urging traffic through the narrow clogged byways. Crowds laughed and pushed through the gaudy night. Suddenly there was a shattering sound. Something from up above had plummeted into the street. A gasp and screams, people shouting. Then a slowly widening aperture with something lying at the bottom of it, huddled and broken at its center.

Toward dawn it finally occurred to Watford that he was going to die. He had always known that people died. Hadn't his mother and father and a slew of uncles and cousins all done so? He understood that, but like most people never seriously entertained the notion of its happening to him.

Ramsay, he knew now, had been urging him to prepare himself. Doubtless that was the reason for all those questions about his family. And then there were the legal matters regarding insurance and next of kin that the hospital would have to contend with afterward.

Watford had never been a particularly religious person. His father, when questioned on the matter, described himself in typically airy fashion as something called a Universalist. Pressed for a definition, the elder Watford would fall back on vague, lofty generalities such as brotherhood, mutual respect, behaving with civility and common decency to one's fellowman.

Mrs. Watford had no strong opinions on the matter, either. Whatever Cyril said, she would sweetly concur. What she might have felt privately, however, she kept to herself. So Charles Watford, at the age of thirty-six, never having to confront the sticky business of tidying up one's mortal affairs, had at last to face the dismal prospect of his final days.

Somewhere in the still gray hours before dawn, Watford tried to pray. He clasped his hands as he'd seen others do and recited the well-known nursery invocation his mother had tried halfheartedly to teach him as a child. "Now I lay me down to sleep . . ." He knew no other way of approaching his Maker—if indeed there were such a thing. The gist of his prayer was that he be saved. He knew that he had sinned, committed crimes, told lies. But if he were saved just this one time, he vowed he would change his ways. Defeat his addiction. Work steadily at a job. Marry. Possibly even have children.

Failing that, he prayed that if indeed he must die, there be no fear. He feared fear even more than he feared extinction.

As he prayed he tried to imagine the God to whom he was appealing. The Being that he imagined was not anthropomorphic, but more one of those fanciful creatures comprised of the parts of various creatures drawn from an ancient bestiary. Watford's deity had a great deal of bear and reptile in it, with several other ambiguous appendages thrown in for good measure. In that feeble, fumbling and ill-conceived image, he had created something he could accept, something having powers greater than his own. Thus, he could appeal to it for both strength as well as mercy.

As the sun rose that morning above the great stirring engine of the city, Watford at last drifted off to sleep. The obelisk he had imagined in his prayer recurred throughout his fitful dreams. It appeared as a large statuesque creature seemingly carved of stone implanted in a vast arid disk of plain stretching outward to an azure infinity. It stared toward the distant horizon as if in a state of impenetrable meditation and from somewhere deep within it a low unvarying hum pulsated outward for miles and miles.

There was no content or narrative to Watford's dream. Nor was he any part of it. He was merely a spectator outside of the frame of reference. It was as if he were watching a slide show that consisted of a single view, unchanging, hour after hour. But, most oddly, throughout the duration of the dream, he continued to hear the voice of his mother.

"Charles, Charles," it said in that chiding, faintly sniveling way that was nonetheless so replete with endearment. "You mustn't go on like this. You know how your father counts on your getting ahead in school, getting a proper education so you can come into the business with him someday. But that will never happen if you go on like this. Your father hates a slacker. And worse even than a slacker, he loathes a liar. Make us proud, Charles. Do the right thing by us and everything will come right for you in the end."

Late in the morning, when at last he awoke, he had scarcely any recollection of his dream. Seemingly unfazed, he took his breakfast, read his paper, watched the morning news in the hospital day room with a number of convalescents.

Later the nurses came and took him downstairs for his radiation treatment. Like a small child, eager to please, he submitted uncomplainingly to the medication and procedure he knew would shortly make him deathly ill.

The nurses and doctors attending him noted no significant change in their patient. Nor was Watford himself aware of the subtle sea-change that had begun to stir within him. He was rather startled himself later that afternoon when he picked up the phone, dialed Francis Mooney's office and left a message asking him to stop by the next day. He had something he wanted to tell him.

59

"You see, I did live with her. And I did sort of say I would marry her. Well, I mean, I didn't actually say it. . . . I just sort of suggested that it could happen. But I was never involved in that bank robbery. I swear. You can check that out with T.Y. yourself."

Mooney blinked doubtfully at the man sitting on the edge of the bed before him. "T.Y.?"

"Bidwell. T. Y. Bidwell—the guy who actually was involved in the . . . You don't believe me," Watford moaned bitterly. "I can tell you don't."

"I believe you. I'm just trying to follow all this as you relate it. Now you're telling me that you ran out on some lady named Myrtle, and at the same time there was a bank robbery in Kansas City. Have I got you right so far?"

"Right. That's it."

"And your closest buddy was involved in the robbery and he tried to incriminate you. But you weren't involved."

"That's right. I wasn't."

"But the Kansas City police are after you. Right?"

"Right. I mean, at least, I think so."

Mooney's eyes narrowed. Inside, he was berating himself for being idiot enough to have come. "Why are you telling me all this?"

"You're the police, aren't you?"

Mooney sighed and sank back into the armchair beside the bed. "This is why you called me?"

"Well, sure. Like I told you. What the doctor said and all that. I mean, about my white blood cell count and my chances and all that. I just wanted to square the books."

243

"I see." Mooney fumed quietly. He'd rushed up directly from the station the moment he'd been informed of Watford's call. He'd been chasing up a homicide all day. I should've known better, he thought, eyeing the pallid figure sitting upright before him. "Well," he said, starting to rise, "I'll be glad to make some inquiries of the Kansas City police, if you'd like me to."

Watford appeared uncertain. "If you're sure it's okay."

"Sure, it's okay." Mooney set his hat back on his head. "Thanks for calling. I always like to hear from old clients."

"Where are you going?" Watford's voice bore a note of alarm.

"I'm going back to the station."

"You don't have to leave just yet, do you?"

Mooney's bewilderment deepened. "I've got a lot of paperwork waiting for me, Mr. Watford. I promise to get back to you as soon as I've spoken to Kansas City." He made a move toward the door.

"I also broke into a pharmacy in Kew Gardens the other night." Watford shouted it defiantly at the detective's back. Mooney turned and stared at the man sitting rigid and erect at the edge of the bed.

"I've got this addiction to Demerol."

"Demerol?"

"When I need it, I really need it. That's how come the pharmacy. I told you what the doctor said about my health and all, didn't I?"

"A couple of times now."

"They don't give you the full sentence if you're . . . like dying, do they? I mean, the judge can show leniency in cases like that. Right?"

"Sure. Sure. Now what's all this about a pharmacy?"

"I broke into one. Two weeks ago Thursday. I needed a prescription. It was late. Everything was closed. I couldn't help myself. I fully intend to pay them back."

"What pharmacy was this?"

"The Cardinal Pharmacy. Round the corner from me on Austin Street. Didn't you hear about it?"

"No," Mooney growled. He'd begun to show signs of irritation. "I missed that one."

"Well, I did it," Watford announced with almost touching pride. "It was me. I confess. But I didn't take anything but my medication, I swear it."

"Medication?" Mooney ears pricked.

"Demerol. I told you I have this addiction, didn't I?"

"Did you notify the police?"

"You're the police, aren't you? I'm notifying you."

Mooney crossed back to the bed and sat down gloomily in the chair. He was suddenly very tired. "Queens is not my jurisdiction, but if you'd like I'd be glad to check on it for you with your local precinct."

Mooney's temper had been growing gradually shorter. It had the effect of making Watford contrite. "You see . . . I called you because . . ."

"You're dying and you wanted to square the books. I know, you told me."

"You don't believe me, do you? You don't believe a word I've said."

"I wouldn't say that. I just wish you could have picked a more convenient time for all these confessions. Well, if that's it . . . " Once again Mooney lumbered to his feet and extended his hand.

Watford took it and held on tight. "You don't have to go now, do you? We could play some cards. I just got a new deck."

"I'd like to but I can't. I really have a lot of work." Mooney had to pry his hand loose, leaving Watford looking spurned and a bit bereft.

"Don't go," he called out again. "Stay a bit longer. Just talk is all."

By that time Mooney had reached the door and was crossing the threshold.

"His name was Peter Quintius," Watford suddenly cried out.

It was the sound of it more than the name that brought Mooney around.

Watford seemed suddenly frightened, as if he regretted the words just uttered and wanted to take them back.

"What did you say?" Mooney took a step forward, then paused again.

"Peter Quintius. His name was Peter Quintius."

"Whose name?"

"The man. The man you're looking for. The one in the bed next to me at the hospital," Watford rattled on with large frightened eyes. "You called him Boyd, but his real name was—"

"I'm sorry. I don't quite . . . "

"Quintius," Watford nearly shouted. "Peter Quintius was his name."

There was no sound in the room save for the detective's high, wheezing breath. On his face was that look of impatient disbelief. "How come you remembered today and couldn't remember two days ago?"

"Because of the TV."

"The TV?"

"It was on TV. The other night. Didn't you see it? On the news. The guy who broke into his father's shop or gallery or something like that. You mean, you haven't heard about that either?"

As a matter of fact, Mooney had heard something. But only remotely. A snatch of conversation overheard in the locker rooms above the din and horseplay of fellow officers. Besides, it was an uptown job. Distinctly off his beat.

"Let me get this straight, now," said Mooney, more perplexed than ever. "You're telling me that you saw something on the TV news the other night . . ."

"That's right. The guy. The one you called Boyd . . . Quintius. Here . . . I wrote it down for you with the address."

Mooney slouched forward, took the slip of paper and read with his lips. "Peter Quintius & Sons, Galleries, Sixty-seventh Street and Madison Avenue. He looked up. "And this guy? Quintius? He's the guy you say was in the bed next to you at Beth Israel?"

"That's right. That's what I said."

"It was two years ago. How can you be sure, just seeing the guy for a second or two on TV."

"I'm sure, alright. I lived next to him for nearly a whole week, didn't I?"

Mooney broke into a scornful laugh. "You mean to tell me you saw this guy Quintius on TV, just out of the blue like that, and lo and behold, you decide he's the guy?"

"It's him. It's him, I'm telling you," Watford began to shout. "Why don't you believe me? What the hell's the matter with you? Gosh—I thought if I told you that, I could, like, turn state's evidence. Trade it for leniency from the judge."

"Leniency from the judge? You haven't been convicted of anything."

"But I will be. I will be," Watford groaned. "I know that."

Mooney shook his head incredulously. "Forgive me, Mr. Watford. This all sounds just a bit farfetched."

Watford looked as if he'd been struck. "Okay, it's farfetched. Forget what I told you. I take it all back. It was a lie. I was lying, see?"

Long after Mooney had left, Watford lay in bed fuming with anger and trying to figure out exactly what he'd done.

"Now why'd I tell him that?" he asked himself. "It's his fault. That damned cop put it all in my head in the first place. Coming around all the time and pumping me about this character Boyd. That Quintius fellow on the TV. He's not the same man who was in the bed next to me at the hospital." He made a funny, bewildered face. "Was he? No. Certainly not. It's all that cop putting ideas in my head. It's his damned fault. I've never seen that Quintius character before. Have I?"

He uttered the question aloud into the darkened hospital room, and waited there as though expecting an answer.

When none came he felt more muddled and lost than ever.

60

"He's been getting mile workouts every other day. They alternate that with sprints on the off days. José thinks he'd like to enter him in the first mile's stakes race that comes up. Maybe the Roses."

"Too soon. It's too soon."

"José wouldn't enter him in a race where he doesn't belong. Obviously he feels the horse belongs in stakes company right now. Why be so cautious? We enter him at a mile. Nothing farther. He's been testing well at that distance regularly. If José didn't like what he saw he could've damned well looked elsewhere for six-furlongs stakes. But he didn't. He thinks the animal is up to the Roses right now. He's a trainer. That's what you pay him for, right? He swears the Baby'll win by a length and a half at maybe five to one. What's wrong with that?" Fritzi had taken to referring to the horse as "the Baby."

"Wonderful. Fantastic." Mooney rolled over and burrowed his nose into the pillows.

She folded her arms and shook her head. "What the hell's the matter with you, anyway? You've been grousing and snapping ever since you got here."

Mooney closed his eyes and fumed in silence. Oh, Christ, he thought. Now we're gonna have a blow.

Still smarting, Fritzi went on sharply. "I just thought you'd be interested in the progress of your investment. You've got about seven thou into this, as I recall."

It was going on toward midnight and they lay together stiffly, embattled in the king-size bed. It was June now and they'd been together for over a year.

"I recall only too well," Mooney groaned.

247

"Nobody bent your arm, my friend."

"Who said anyone did?"

"I detect a note of regret in your voice."

"I regret nothing."

"I'll be more than happy to return your money anytime you wish."

"Forget it. Let's quit this talk. I'm sick of the goddamned horse anyway."

She tossed the covers off and started out of bed. "In that case, I'm writing you a check now."

"I don't want it, I told you."

"Well, Christ almighty, what's bothering you?"

"Nothing's bothering me."

"Tell me. I can't sleep with you in this state of mind."

"Would you like me to leave?" Mooney snarled. "I can go now."

"I'm sorry this Bomber business . . ."

"Bombardier," he corrected her. "Bombardier."

"Whatever. I'm sorry it's all going so lousy for you."

"Who said it was going lousy?"

"You didn't have to. I can tell. It's this man you saw today, isn't it? This—what's his name?"

"Watford."

"Right. Watford," she sang out triumphantly. "He must've really knocked your socks off this time. You're on a prize bummer."

"Look. Maybe I should leave now."

"What did this Watford character say to you, anyway?"

"As a matter of fact, he told me the name and address of the guy on the roof."

She'd already barged ahead before the weight of what he'd said registered. "The Bombardier?"

"His very self."

Head tilted back, she regarded him warily. "I don't believe you."

"The man's name is Quintius. Peter Quintius."

"He's the Bombardier?"

"That's what Watford says. The guy in the bed next to him at the hospital."

The ghost of a smile flickered in her eyes, then trailed off. "Well, what's wrong with that, for God's sake?"

"Nothing," Mooney sat up in bed scratching his scalp. "Except for the fact the guy's bananas."

"How do you know?"

"You don't have to be no shrink from Vienna to figure it out." Mooney belched sourly. "Excuse me. Listen, how about a glass of milk?"

"Tell me about this guy first. What's his name?"

248

"Watford." Mooney got up and put on his robe. "I'll tell you in the kitchen."

She padded out behind him into the cool darkness of the apartment. "How do you know Watford's bananas?" she asked, after pouring him a glass of milk.

Mooney drank deeply with an almost greedy, audible sucking. "Because," he said, swiping the mustache of milk from his upper lip, "before he told me about the Bombardier, he confessed to robbing a bank in Kansas City and breaking into a pharmacy in Kew Gardens."

She pondered that a moment. "Maybe he did."

"I knew you'd say that."

"Well, why couldn't he be telling the truth?"

"If you knew anything about the guy, you wouldn't even bother asking. He's a screwball. A nut case. Anyway, I thought I'd give him the benefit of the doubt. I checked. I called Kansas City. They never heard of him. He's a suspect for nothing."

"And the pharmacy?"

"Kew Gardens?" Mooney yawned deeply. "I checked that, too. There was a pharmacy broken into out there. Roughly the same time as he said he made his break-in. Only the cops out there already picked up a couple of kids who confessed to the job, along with busting into a dozen other pharmacies out there over the past year."

"Oh." Fritzi sat back and stared up at the ceiling. "Sorry."

"So am I." Mooney rose and carried his glass over to the sink.

"What was that name he gave you again?" she asked suddenly.

"Quintius. Let's go to bed." He flicked out the kitchen light and they started back through the darkened apartment to the bedroom. "He told me he saw the guy on the late TV news. Some cockamamie story about an attempted robbery of a gallery uptown. Claims he recognized the guy immediately. Same guy in the bed next to him. Only he was using the name Boyd then."

"Maybe it's the truth."

Mooney gazed across at her hopelessly. "Come on, Fritzi. Don't knock me out."

She slipped back into bed. "Did you bother to check it out?"

He turned out the light and crawled into bed beside her. "Life's too short."

"Come on, Mooney. What'd you find out?"

He rolled over on his side and dug his head into the pillow. "There is a gallery up on Madison and Sixty-seventh with that name."

"But he probably got that off the TV news show."

"Right. And there is a Peter Quintius, too. I checked him out. Guy's from a prominent Long Island family. Place has been in business up on Madison Avenue about a hundred years. All the swells buy fancy art off him. Philanthropist. Humanitarian. Pillar of society. And all that crap. Clean as a whistle."

"But why couldn't this Watford be telling the truth?" she persisted with strange urgency.

Mooney stared into the darkness, almost too tired to speak. "Because he's incapable of the truth," he growled and turned away. "He's a pathological liar. Add to that, he's a junkie. Up to his ears in Demerol."

"Demerol? That's some kind of painkiller, isn't it?"

"Yeah."

"Too bad."

"Yeah. Too bad," he echoed the words, staring ruefully into the dark.

"I wish you'd retire again," she mumbled before she fell asleep. "You were more fun then."

Fritzi fell off quickly, but Mooney lay awake, going over, replaying obsessively every bit of dialogue exchanged between himself and Watford that afternoon. He had very little doubt regarding Watford's state of mind. If he had any nagging reservations about the gallery story, he could march right up to Sixty-seventh Street and question Quintius himself. But God help him if Watford were wrong. People like Quintius fairly bristled with expensive lawyers. He could be charged with defamation of character. Harassment. The city could be sued for millions.

Mooney pushed it all out of his mind. Still, one tiny item gnawed implacably at him. Nearly a month before when he'd gone to see Watford, he asked him if he'd ever heard the name A. Boyd. He hadn't he claimed, but at the conclusion of that visit Watford appeared to know, or hint at, something unusual regarding his erstwhile roommate at Beth Israel. "He told me something strange," he'd remarked. Yet at that time he was either unwilling or unable to share any information with the detective.

"Get the hell out of here, all of you. And don't come back until you get me something solid. Something I can build on. Now go on, for Chrissake. Get the hell out."

Twelve badly shaken plainclothesmen from Mooney's special Bombardier Task Force skulked from the squad room of Manhattan South and out to their designated beats.

After they'd left, Mooney sat at his desk sifting through the torrent of reports that had poured in over the wire in the wake of Willie Krauss's death—tips from individuals claiming to know the identity of the Bombardier, others claiming to have sighted him. A spurt of activity generated by the city's offer of a $10,000 reward for information had the phones going twenty-four hours a day. Everything had to be checked, and when it was, all tips, it was discovered, invariably led to the same dead end.

At the bottom of the pile of reports was a handful of newspaper clippings that Mooney had pulled from the morgue of the *Daily News*.

"Quintius." Even as he read the name aloud, it rang in his head. But it was Watford's high, faintly querulous voice that he heard speaking. "That's him, I tell you. It's him."

He read the story again. It was pretty much as Watford had first reported it—a young man shot to death by police as he tried to break into a wall safe in his father's gallery after working hours. The *Daily News* printed a picture of the son, William Quintius, whom they described as a dapper young man about town; a fast liver and a high roller known at all the tracks and nearby casinos. The youth, Mooney noted, appeared attractive and intelligent, but with that soft, pampered look that suggested some underlying corruption.

The photograph of the father, Peter Quintius, told a different story. It was an arresting portrait, the eyes haunted with a mixture of arrogance and grief. It was the kind of face Mooney instinctively disliked, conveying an air of privilege and class, of automatically assumed prerogatives. Moreover, Mooney could not associate this face with that of a man who would drop a forty-pound cinder block from a rooftop into an unsuspecting crowd below. This man would not be caught dead on a rooftop, let alone a pissy, reeking ghetto rooftop somewhere over in Hell's Kitchen.

It was past 9:00 A.M. Outside in the assembly room they were mustering for the day ahead. The roll call was being taken, the duty roster recited. Mooney could hear the bang of lockers opening and closing as the night men changed to go home.

The detective pushed aside the clippings. Why he'd bothered to dig them out, he couldn't say. He gave no credence to Watford's story. It was wildly farfetched. "I was just watching the eleven o'clock news and I see this face come on the screen. So I ..." Mooney laughed ruefully. He had seen Watford's kind before—innocuous, inoffensive little freaks fading into the wallpaper; confessing to every crime on the police blotter. A pathetic, tortured, self-lacerating nut case who thought that by blanket confessions he could buy leniency for all of those ghastly crimes he imagined he'd committed.

Mooney shook his head despairingly and rose.

Throughout the rest of the day he was busy. Not with the Bombardier but with a flurry of new emergencies. The murder of a bag lady on the West Side; the mutilation murder of a prostitute in a midtown hotel; a street knifing in the Times Square area—all fell to him that day. Several times his movements had him crisscrossing the city. At one point he was as far down as the Battery and then as far north as Seventy-fifth Street to interview several witnesses to the knifing.

Gratefully, he had not thought once about the Bombardier. He had pushed it all out of his mind. But at 5:00 P.M., as dusk slowly purpled the streets, the shadowy phantom of the rooftops muscled its way back in upon him. He called his office from a small cigar store to get an up-date. Defasio took the call and assured him in a slightly tremulous voice that there was nothing new.

It was twenty past five when he stepped back out onto the street. It occurred to him that it was just about quitting time and that he might take a slow walk up to the Balloon and have a drink with Fritzi.

The Balloon was at Ninety-first and Lexington. He was at Sixty-fourth and Madison and so he started to walk north. At Sixty-seventh Street he happened to glance up and found himself passing directly in front of the Quintius Gallery. His sudden presence there was not fortuitous, he knew.

The lights were lit and there were people inside. On the street, crowds buffeted past him, people streaming from out of office buildings and department stores, dashing for subways and buses. Mooney lingered before the big plate-glass windows, gazing up at the smart marble tablet graven with a large Q outside the door.

Through the windows he could see paintings on the walls and tall potted trees set all about. A slight, officious figure glided airily round the floor. He was followed by a tall, smartly turned out matron. The whole setting reeked of money and privilege.

Curiosity piqued the detective. He maneuvered through the crowd to the window, seething at his own gullibility. The fact that he had even taken the time to go there suddenly infuriated him. He was vaguely conscious of trying to slip into the disguise of a potential customer.

For a time he busied himself staring at a cluster of medieval miniatures. There were martyrs, aspostles, angels, hermits and saints—triptychs framed in gilt and antique reredos. It all filled him with a rush of anger and distaste.

When he looked up, the man and the woman had moved to a point a mere several feet from where Mooney stood on the opposite side of the glass.

Suddenly a third figure appeared within his purview. Spied first within a flurry of motion on the periphery of his vision, the figure approached, striding fast, looming large, then coming to a halt before the two people. Mooney watched the woman turn and smile. She leaned forward to accept a kiss on the cheek from the man who'd just arrived. Their lips moved soundlessly behind the glass, while the third figure, the short, officious fellow remained silent, a disturbingly ambiguous smile flickering at the corners of his lips.

But it was the tall man from whom Mooney could not avert his gaze. Undoubtedly, this was Quintius, the same individual who'd figured so prominently in Watford's wildly improbable story.

Standing at the window peering in, squinting against the reflection of lights from nearby shops, Mooney could not recall precisely the chain of events that had led him to this point, only that at that moment, he experienced a strange, incomprehensible agitation at being there. A part of him wondered at this feeling, but another part was simply confounded by it. Try as he did, he was unable to shake it off.

The three people behind the glass turned and walked toward the back of the gallery. Mooney watched them disappear into a lighted office at the rear. For several moments he watched figures move back and forth in the plane of light cast across the partially opened door.

Suddenly he started to laugh. Several people standing nearby, looking in the windows, stared at him. Still laughing, he stared back hard and in the next moment he turned and strode quickly off.

61

"You discharged him?"

"On an outpatient basis. There was nothing much left we could do here."

"He told me he had some kind of fatal disease. Is that true?"

"I'm afraid so. We'll continue to treat him, of course, but as an outpatient only. He wanted to stay. He begged us not to release him."

"Why toss a guy out if he's dying?" Mooney fumed.

"Because it's likely to take him six months to accomplish the task. Quite frankly we needed the bed."

Ramsay reached across the litter of his desk for a cigarette. "Why did you want to see him?" he asked, puffing smoke from the corner of his mouth.

"It'd be hard to explain."

"Has he done anything wrong?"

"Not that I know of, but that doesn't stop him from confessing to crimes with which he's never been involved."

"I'm not surprised." Ramsay reflected a moment. "Any man who can inflict as much disease on himself as Watford would have no trouble confessing to crimes he hasn't committed."

"I'm not sure I follow."

"He's addicted to Demerol, you know."

"He told me— He also told me he broke into a pharmacy out in Queens."

"He very well might have. If he ran out of Demerol and got flaky enough." Ramsay shrugged. In his white gown with the blue name tag, he looked small and oddly like a ventriloquist's doll. "Who knows? Devilishly clever, our Watford."

"A nut case, if you ask me."

"Borderline psychotic, to put it more clinically." Ramsay paused, then went on confidentially.

"I shouldn't tell you this, but while he was here we ran a Wechsler Adult Intelligence Scale on him. He's a 142 IQ. That's well above average. Forget about the impression he gives, Captain. This is a bright man. A very bright man. Lied to me every day for about three months. I was fascinated." Ramsay continued, caught up in the force of his own narrative. "We also did a Minnesota Multiphasic."

Mooney made an odd face.

"Personality profile."

"What'd you find?"

"The obvious things, of course. Brief psychotic episodes. Unstable interpersonal relations. Inadequate social functioning. The list goes on and on. Here's a man who's brimming over with guilt and rage, most of it associated with feelings he's suppressed about his parents for years. Father was something of a bully, I gather. The mother was addicted to drugs. It was she who gave him his first blast of Demerol."

Mooney nodded, his mind flashing back to Quintius on Sixty-seventh Street, even as the doctor spoke.

"Essentially, what you've got here is a man in tremendous psychological distress."

"I knew he was lying to me most of the time," Mooney said. "I can't say I got the feeling of psychological distress. You don't think he's dangerous?" Mooney asked.

"He could be. There's a great deal of anger in poor Watford. But since he's not the sort to externalize it, he turns it inward against himself. That manifests itself in all these crippling migraines he suffers and in self-punishment, such as infecting his own bloodstream with dirty needles, and inducing sickness. In medicine we call that Munchausen's Syndrome."

"Beg pardon?"

"Munchausen," Ramsay smiled in spite of himself. "After Baron Munchausen, the infamous eighteenth-century liar. Watford's a classic study of Munchausen's Syndrome."

"You say these people pretend to be sick?"

"Not pretend. They are sick. They induce real symptoms in themselves."

"Just to get into a hospital."

"More or less."

Mooney smiled oddly. "Ain't that a kick? A hospital? Why, in God's name?"

"Simply because they feel more secure being cared for on the inside than having to cope on the outside. Hospitals are great surrogate mothers for some." Ramsay's pencil scratched randomly on the pad beside him. "I got very interested in Watford's odyssey. Once he told me all about his wartime experiences, so I got hold of his VA records."

"He was in the service?"

"He was, but it was not the way he tells it." Ramsay grinned at the detective's growing bewilderment. "To hear him tell it, he was a helicopter pilot in Vietnam. Actually, he never left the States. The truth is he was in the Coast Guard. Served as a medic on an isolated lighthouse off the coast of Washington. Pity, because there's a fellow who'd have probably been happier in a theater of war. In the lighthouse he was just bored and depressed. Then one day, to escape the tedium, he faked an attack of acute appendicitis. Just got up one morning and started to complain of sharp pains in the side and feelings of nausea. As a medic he had access to the drug locker. He started taking ipecac to induce vomiting. Then, with a stolen hypodermic, he injected small amounts of saliva subcutaneously in the popliteal area."

"Come again?" Mooney cocked an ear toward the doctor.

"Popliteal—the area behind the knee. Wonderful spot for the spread of infection. Within a day he developed an abscess and became febrile. Also, his white blood cell count shot up. A local physi-

255

cian was called in and Watford was savvy enough to be able to fake rebound tenderness in the correct anatomical location. The physician put him right into the hospital for an appendectomy."

Ramsay took a certain pleasure in recounting the tale. "When he was telling me all this, he roared with delight, particularly at the part where the surgeon, postoperatively, described to him his 'badly inflamed appendix.' He thought that was a hoot."

Just then the phone rang. Ramsay signaled the detective to stay put while he murmured dosage directions into the phone. When he'd finished he looked up. "Where was I?"

"At an inflamed appendix."

"Right. Well, that was all fine for Watford. While he was hospitalized he had a grand time. He loves being fussed over. But the moment he got better the Coast Guard sent him right back out to the lighthouse. Once again he was in the middle of Puget Sound, stuck there with the long hours and the boredom and depression. That's where he learned to fight depression with Demerol. There again, his access to the medicine locker served him in good stead. Eventually, the CO of the lighthouse noticed that larger and larger reorders of Demerol were being requisitioned. He also noticed that they were being used up at a disturbing rate. The source of the reorders and their disappearance were eventually traced to Watford and he was discharged."

"For misappropriation of drugs?" Mooney asked.

"No. It was actually for enuresis. Bed-wetting. The drug thefts they could handle," Ramsay rattled on. "It was the bed-wetting that actually sprang him."

Mooney looked away, surprised at his own embarrassment.

"The Armed Services have plenty of experience with guys looking for medical discharges. For reasons that should be obvious, bed-wetters, once they're spotted, are quickly mustered out."

"And Watford was that?"

"Possibly. But knowing as much about him now as I do, I doubt it. Actually, I think he was just clever enough to know how to fake a good case of it. He wanted to get off that rock in Puget Sound so he kept pissing in his bed until, after eight months, they just got tired and let him go with a medical discharge.

"After the Coast Guard he must have thought that living in civilian life was going to be a piece of cake. It didn't turn out that way. He got a few jobs with airlines but he couldn't hack that. The regimentation, the regular hours, the performance reports. Before he knew it, he was stealing flight tickets and travel documents issued only to top executives. And he got caught there, too. He was fired by Pan Am but they never pressed charges. They just let him go. But, with something like that on his employment record, another airline wouldn't touch him with a bargepole. As a matter of fact, he couldn't get any work at all. That's when it occurred to him that prison might be his salvation. Almost as good as the hospital."

"That's one helluva salvation."

Ramsay's brow shot up. "Better, isn't it, then the hassle of life on the outside. The daily scrounge for shelter and fodder. So he contrived to get himself arrested."

Mooney sighed and pushed the brim of his hat back on his head. By that time he'd given up being amazed.

"He started passing bad checks. Seven thousand dollars' worth. It's all in the VA report. For that he was rewarded with two years on Rikers Island."

"This is all in the VA record?" Mooney asked.

"Pretty much. The rest is easy enough to put together."

"Pathetic."

"Pathetic," Ramsay nodded in agreement, then continued. "And he enjoyed prison. Lots of leisure time and no responsibilities. He spent most of his days studying medical and law books in the prison library. *Merck Manual*. Torts and civil law. That sort of thing. Eventually, he became adept in the terminology of both fields. But for a clever, enterprising fellow like our Charles, this was simply not enough. He was very shortly bored out of his mind and started looking for new kinds of trouble to get into. So one day he swallowed a spoon in order to escape to the soft environment of the prison hospital."

"Good Christ. A spoon? How the hell—"

"Don't ask me. The prison doctor couldn't figure it out either. Anyway, they got it out, but he was right back there the next week. This time he'd incised the skin of the abdominal wall with a sharp tool. Claimed he'd accidentally become impaled on it while in the prison workshop. Just to give zest to the diagnostic picture, he pulled the old saliva-behind-the-knee stunt again. Fever and leukocytosis induced by the unnoticed abscess and his expertly feigned signs of peritoneal inflammation got him a laparotomy which revealed no disease but resulted in the secondary gain of a secure hospital environment for several weeks. There he was able to get all the Demerol he wanted. He learned to counterfeit hematuria by introducing a few drops of blood into his urine sample. This was always good for a few days in the infirmary. After that you couldn't stop him." Ramsay was beaming with wicked delight. "You have to give it to the man. He has imagination and flair, our Charles."

Mooney shook his head in wonderment. "Beats me how he could con everyone like that."

"Doctors can be incredibly gullible. His VA records show admissions to hospitals all over the country—Chicago, San Diego, Denver, Madison, Wilkes-Barre, Kansas City, New York. You name it. He's been there. The VA estimates he's been hospitalized a total of nearly four hundred times over the past dozen years. But the strangest, most ironic twist of the story is the marriage."

Mooney sat back in his chair. "I didn't realize he was married."

"Well, he's not any longer, But he was at the ripe old age of seventeen. He entered a common-law marriage with a woman of twenty-five. He told me he didn't love her at all. Actually, she revolted him, but he married her just to rescue her from a dismal home situation. Within a few months after their marriage, while pregnant, she died of acute leukemia."

Mooney made a slight startled sound. "Which he claims to have now."

"And he does," Ramsay said emphatically. "There's no faking that, although in his mind he's faking this just like all the other times. But this time it's for real. I don't think he quite grasps it yet, but he is truly dying."

Ramsay, his head tilted to one side, caught the detective's dismay. "May I ask why you wanted to see him, Captain?"

"He gave me some information the other day."

"About what?"

"About a man he shared a hospital room with two years ago—a man who may just be the key to several murders in the city."

"And, now, of course, you're concerned about the reliability of his information?"

Mooney turned his frank, questioning gaze on the doctor. "Wouldn't you be?"

Ramsay shrugged and rose to indicate the conclusion of their talk. "Probably. It's like the little boy crying wolf, isn't it? Who knows? Maybe this time the wolf's really there."

62

It was several days before Mooney thought again of the Watford lead. Ironically, while the detective now believed none of Watford's revelations, he was strangely unable to put them aside. And then too, Peter Quintius was disturbingly, uncannily close to the profile Baum, the police psychiatrist, had given him months back.

Four days later Mooney was in an unmarked police car, driving out over the Queensboro Bridge. The Manhattan skyline dropped away behind him; the dark, grim jungle gym of elevated IND tracks loomed up ahead, raining down the thunderous clatter of subway cars, racketing their way through the cobbled, motley landscape of Queens. Once more he was on his way to Kew Gardens. He took no driver with him. Nor had he asked Defasio to come along. His skepticism was such that he was unwilling to risk the possibility of having any of the special task force see him make a jackass of himself.

Then, at last, Watford was there standing at the door of the brick row house on the quiet, tree-lined street with the leaves falling noiselessly all about in the first chill of autumn. This time he was not in his bathrobe and pajamas, but in overalls and wearing gloves, a look of momentary startlement upon his face, followed by something amused, and half-shrewd, as if he'd known all along the detective would be back.

"Been working out in the garden," Watford apologized for his appearance and led him back into the musty little sitting room where all the clocks ticked with their sharp implacable assertion of the pre-eminence of time.

Would he care to go into town with him? the detective asked. Now, right then and there. To the gallery. Up to Sixty-seventh Street to see this Quintius fellow for himself. He had not intended it, but it had come out in the form of a challenge.

"Sure," Watford replied with disconcerting calm. Mooney would have preferred a response somewhat more guarded.

In a matter of moments Watford had changed and they were back in the car, tooling west down Queens Boulevard and back over the bridge. All the way there Watford chatted easily about his plans for the future. My God, Mooney thought, the fool is dying and at the same time keeps making plans for the future.

Slightly past noon they stood outside the gallery in precisely the same spot Mooney had stood a week before. This time the gallery appeared to be empty except for a tall, stocky man in plaids who sat behind a desk.

Mooney had simply taken it for granted that Mr. Quintius would, of course, be there, walking freely about, on display as it were, for their special convenience. They would simply stand outside the window and Watford would either confirm or rescind his identification.

They waited twenty minutes but nothing of the sort occurred. The gentleman in the plaids continued to sit at the desk in the rear, riffling through papers, pausing from time to time to study some more attentively than others.

Watford grew restless. "When is he going to come?"

"Any minute. Just wait."

They waited another ten minutes. The man at the desk appeared to be blithely unaware of the fact that two men had been standing outside the window, peering in, for at least a half hour.

"I don't think he's here," Watford frowned.

"He's here all right. Just hold your horses."

"Why can't we just go in and ask for him?"

The idea, direct, uncomplicated, would never have occurred to Mooney. He stood there ransacking his mind for reasons why it would be imprudent to take Watford's suggestion. Unorthodox police procedure, to say the least. But then again, wasn't the whole situation unorthodox? "Okay," he conceded finally, "why not? If you're game, I am. All they can do is throw us out and charge me with harassment. Maybe if I'm lucky, I'll get fired."

Walking in, Watford trailing at his heel, Mooney felt slightly foolish. He fairly glided across the parqueted floors. The cushioned prosthetic shoes he wore felt spongy going over the thick pile Kirman area carpets. The air about him smelled faintly of turpentine, pipe smoke and the moist, fecund smell unique to large commercial greenhouses.

"May I help you, gentlemen?" The man at the desk rose as they approached him. Mooney took command at once.

"We'd like to see Mr. Quintius."

"Which Mr. Quintius? There are two."

Mooney noted the cautious skepticism in the man's eyes as he sized them up.

"Mr. Peter Quintius," Mooney replied.

"Ah." There was a pause while the gentleman seated at the desk continued to take their measure. "I'm Frederick Quintius, his son. Who shall I say is calling?"

"Captain Mooney," the detective replied and opened his shield for identification. He didn't bother to introduce Watford. The younger Quintius merely assumed he was another policeman.

"Is this in connection with my late brother?"

Mooney noted the man's eyes shifting and the mind behind them whirling quickly. "In a manner of speaking. Is Mr. Quintius here?"

"In the back. One moment, please. I'll see if he's available."

They waited out front beside the desk, shifting awkwardly on their feet. Mooney could hear muted voices conversing through the open door. A few moments later Frederick Quintius reappeared. He was followed by the towering presence Mooney recognized at once as Peter Quintius.

At this point Mooney had already strayed dangerously far from standard police procedure. Even as the two men approached, it occurred to him that he had absolutely no idea where to start. His heart leaped, his mind went blank and he experienced panic.

Providentially, however, Watford did not. The moment he saw Quintius his face lit up with boyish warmth. Before Mooney could stop him, he moved forward, smiling, his hand outstretched to meet Quintius.

"Hello, Mr. Quintius. Remember me? Charles Watford. We shared a hospital room two years ago."

There was a pause and evident confusion. Mooney saw the man frown and take an involuntary step backward as Watford grasped his hand and pumped it enthusiastically. Fully a whole head taller than Watford, Quintius gazed down speechless at the affectionate puppy tugging at his hand. "I beg your pardon."

Watford beamed. He appeared breathless and overjoyed, as though he were waiting to be embraced. "It's me, Charles Watford. You remember. Beth Israel. In the bed beside you. You'd injured your leg. Fell through an open manhole or something."

Something flashed in Quintius's eye. Mooney couldn't call it fear. It was more a flash of sudden guardedness; the woodchuck scurrying into its hole. In the next instant it was gone and another mask had replaced it.

"I saw you on television the other night," Watford rattled on cheerfully. "I was sorry to hear about your son. It was horrible. Tragic."

Quintius's brow lowered, his face darkened. Watford appeared not to notice. He went on, offering condolences and paying his respects. Quintius's withering stare impeded him not in the least. At that moment Watford took on, in Mooney's jaded eyes, a new, and unexpected stature.

"There's some mistake," Quintius said.

"There's no mistake at all," Watford cordially persisted.

Quintius stiffened. "I don't know you."

"Of course you do. It's Charles Watford. Charley. I used to sit by your bed and chat with you. You were having a lot of pain and . . . "

Clearly agitated, Quintius's voice rose. "I don't know you. I've never seen you before."

"Look here," Frederick Quintius blustered forward. "You said you were here to talk about my brother."

"I don't recall saying any such thing," Mooney replied.

Not the sort to take control of a situation gracefully, the younger Quintius stiffened and grew red. "I'm afraid you'll have to leave."

Mooney turned from him. He hadn't heard a word he'd said. Instead his eyes were riveted on Quintius.

Watford continued to badger the man with smiles. His irrepressible goodwill put Mr. Quintius off-balance, but still he did not appear guilty. This was not the face of a murderer tracked to his lair, Mooney thought. This was not cinder blocks dropped from rooftops into the midst of unsuspecting crowds. This was not sleazy or craven or loutish or malicious. This was the face of civilization at its summit—refined, sensitive, urbane, the apex of the evolutionary process.

"Look for gray flannel," Dr. Baum had said.

"You'll have to go now," Frederick Quintius persisted, "or I'll have to call the police."

With his bulky frame he started to crowd them toward the door. Watford was nearly trampled underfoot, but Mooney, who had yielded several feet, suddenly stiffened and thrust the young man back at arm's length.

"That's all right," he spoke between clenched teeth. "We're going now."

But Watford was not yet finished. He started back. "You know me, Mr. Quintius. Tell the truth. Tell the inspector. Don't be frightened. You do know me."

As Mooney went out the door, the last glimpse he had of Peter Quintius, his face was ashen.

63

In the end, Mooney had to physically remove Watford from the gallery, hauling him out and cramming him into the front seat of the car. All the way out to Queens he sat scrunched into a corner as if he were trying to shrink inside himself. Not once did he speak.

"That *is* the man. I'm not lying," Watford said when they'd drawn up to his front door.

"Who said you were lying?"

"You don't have to. I can see what you think."

"Don't be ridiculous."

"Well, then, what do you think?"

Mooney was momentarily stumped. "I'm not sure I know."

"There. See? I told you. You do think I'm lying." Watford smiled suddenly with a kind of wistful triumph.

"Well, for Christ's sake." Mooney slammed the wheel with his hand. "How could anyone be expected to make a foolproof identification of a perfect stranger he happened to share a hospital room with two years before?" Mooney blustered. He couldn't meet Watford's eyes. "And, let's be perfectly frank with each other," Mooney hurtled onward, "when it comes to telling the truth you've got something less than a sparkling record."

News of his deficiency appeared to leave Watford crestfallen. "Okay," he muttered. "I won't argue that. But this time it happens to be different. I'm telling the truth. I swear it. Oh, God," his fingers fluttered at his temples. "That did it. I'm working up to an awful bummer."

When Mooney reached across his lap to open the door, he noted that Watford's eyes were watery. "Go on in, why don't you, and lie down."

Watford sat there huddled and unmoving.

O dear God, Mooney thought. Please don't let him start to blubber now.

"I must be pretty worthless," Watford mumbled, "if no one can believe a word I say."

Mooney switched on the ignition. Looking more defeated than ever, Watford fumbled, opened the door, and started out.

"One question," Mooney called after him. "Do you know what this man is suspected of?"

Watford, standing outside the car, tilted his head as if he were contemplating a point. "He once told me something. One morning, half-drugged, just coming out of the anesthesia."

"Oh, yeah," Mooney snapped his head toward him. "What was that?"

"I don't remember—I was in kind of a rush then. But it was pretty strange."

As soon as he got back to the station, Mooney wrote it all down in his notes. He wouldn't tell Dowd, or even Defasio. Most of it, he thought in retrospect, was improbable. But a part of it, a very small part to be sure, still felt real enough to have left him twitching from the experience. And once again Watford had repeated that business which he still could not recall about Quintius telling him something "strange."

It was shortly after six. He called Fritzi at home but got no answer and finally caught up with her at the Balloon. He asked her to meet him at a Chinese restaurant in the East Fifties. He was tired of steak and salad and wanted to saturate himself in fried batter and monosodium glutamate.

Forty minutes later they were seated together in a booth, spooning egg drop soup and fried wonton out of deep bowls. After that came a course of hot hors d'oeuvres—more pork fat sizzling round the blue flames of a Sterno can.

He drank several beers and gorged on duck and lobster, then more pork. Having not indulged himself like that for nearly a year (at least not when Fritzi was looking), she could see that it was his way of making a point. She knew him well enough not to interfere. She spent most of the meal watching him devour lethal quantities of fat and salt. She spoke little and hoped that her face betrayed no disapproval.

"Enough?" she asked when he'd spoon-scraped a thick coating of lobster and mandarin sauce from his plate.

He looked up, suddenly recalling she was there. "Aren't you eating?"

"I've had enough, thank you. What's the problem?"

"What problem? There's no problem. I just couldn't face another steak. Waiter." He snapped a finger at a passing waiter. "Another beer, please. Something for you, Fritz? Brandy? Dessert?"

Fritzi gazed up at the ceiling, permitting her eyes to linger there. She could see that he was unusually agitated. "I'll bet you had a grand day."

Hot towels were brought and Mooney wiped his mouth vigorously. "Nothing wrong with today. Chrissake, goddamn wonderful day. How's the pony?"

"I didn't think you cared."

"I've got almost seven grand in him, don't I? Course I care."

It was like a blood transfusion. Suddenly she was animated, talking rapidly. "He did six furlongs at 1:11 this morning."

"What about the fractions?"

"He did 22 3/5 at the quarter; 46 3/5 at the half. José still says he should go for the Roses."

"And I say what's the rush?"

"José says he's ready."

"José has hot pants. All Latins have hot pants."

The waiter cleared the table and poured tea. He asked if they would have dessert. Fritzi declined. Mooney ordered ice cream with almond cookies.

"You're killing yourself with kindness, my friend." Even as she said it she knew she'd made a mistake. It was the opening salvo of the campaign he had so carefully staged. As he spoke now, there was a spiteful glee upon his face.

"It's the first satisfying meal I've had in months."

"I'm glad you enjoyed it." She looked away, pretending disinterest. "Why did you call me down here, anyway? So I could watch you kill yourself?"

"I wanted to make you hate me."

"You've succeeded."

"So I could say good-bye. This is wrong. All wrong."

"It wasn't great. But I didn't think it was all that wrong."

"You're not wrong." He appeared to relent for a moment. "I'm wrong. It's me. I'm the one."

She continued to look away, this time at an elderly couple drinking tea. "For this you had to drag me out to a lousy meal?"

"I can't go on with this," he spoke, shaking his head. "It's me. All me. And I won't change. Not now at sixty-two."

She didn't speak for a long while, afraid she would cry. Yet outwardly she appeared composed. Not teary, not weak, even a little scornful. "What would you like me to do about the horse?"

"What about him?"

"Your share. You get fifteen percent of him."

"Keep it. It's yours."

She rose. "I'll send you a check in the morning."

He reached for her hand, but she snatched it back. "I'm sorry. I should've known better by this time."

She stared down at him a long moment, then turned and walked out.

That evening he reverted to his old haunts on the Stroll. Unsatiated, like a sailor on a shore binge, Mooney went from the restaurant to a small private club called Cipango. He entered a dark mirrored room with a lot of small tables around which young women sat in various stages of undress.

When he entered, one or two eyed him suggestively, assumed a variety of poses and invited him to sit. Several men sat about at the table with hostesses who were young and not unattractive. They drank tall, sticky Polynesian drinks, surmounted by chunks of pineapple and tiny paper umbrellas.

Several of the girls gestured and hissed at him. He felt foolish in his business suit, his paunch swollen with lobster and pork.

The girl he chose was a tall black girl with marvelous breasts and legs, and hair cropped close to the skull. Even tarted up as she was she had the noble bearing of an Ethiopian princess.

He chose her because she didn't whistle and hiss and roll her eyes. She sat with her legs crossed and an air of quiet self-possession. "You want to drink first?" she asked with a light West Indian lilt. "Take your time. There's plenty time."

They had a drink together and he slipped a hand between her thighs under the table.

"You want to go to the room now?" she asked. Her eyes showed no pleasure, but at least there was no contempt.

She watched him steadily, something profound and imperturbable within her gaze. "No rush. Take your time. You look tired."

"I'm fine." He rose. "Fine. Let's go."

"You sure you're okay?"

"Sure. Sure I'm okay."

She led him into the rear of the building through a labyrinth of damp, rank corridors into a warren of little rooms, past closed doors from behind which a variety of gasps and moans issued. The place reeked of sex and sour bedding.

A number of elderly black lady attendants in white nurses' uniforms moved in and out of the rooms with fresh supplies of sheets and towels, not unlike a hospital.

The girl's name was Georgette, she told him. She came from Barbados to study ballet. There were not many places in New York to study ballet, and fewer jobs once you completed your studies. She fell in with the wrong crowd and soon she was here.

She led him to a small mirrored room with a narrow double bed upon which the sheets had the rumpled, faintly grayish cast of recent use. In an effort to suggest sybaritic opulence, a small sunken tub with tile coping had been installed in a corner of the room. A tarnished brass faucet in the shape of a griffin spat tired jets of pine-scented water onto the tepid bubbly surface.

She asked him if he wanted to bathe first. Actually, he would have enjoyed that. He was hot and uncomfortable from a surfeit of food and alcohol. A bath, he felt, would be renewing, but the water, like the bed, had a used oily look, and so he declined.

She appeared to read the reticence in his eyes and nodded understandingly. "Where you want to start?" she asked.

He mumbled something and permitted her to push him backward on the bed. Flat on his back and staring at the ceiling, he lay docile and slightly damp as she drew his shorts down. Then, with the firm, unembarrassed hands of a thorough professional, she began to massage him.

Eyes closed, he lay back and succumbed to the deep tidal pull of blood and nerves. His heart slugged in his chest. "Fritzi," he muttered, half-aloud.

"What, dahling?" the girl asked. "You say something?"

"Nothing."

"You comfortable now? You easy? I make it better for you."

Her tongue ranged over his pelvis, went up his body, and darted into his ear. "You ready to come into me now?" she whispered.

The sense of dampness he'd felt earlier had turned into a sweat. Not a sweat of passion but rather one that left him spent and cold.

"You all right, dahling?"

"I'm fine."

"You want to come into me now?" Whispering into his ear again, there was now a slight edge of impatience to her tone.

"Sure."

"You like me on the bottom or the top?" She patted his great belly and grinned as if to remind him of that huge impediment.

He took the gesture as a slight. "Don't worry about me, Sheba." He started up as if to grab her and took instantly what was the first of several hard jolts. Coming so close, one on the heels of the other, they might have been mistaken for a single smashing blow. It had the effect of knocking him backward, as if he'd been struck in the chest. Pain followed, viselike, crushing, steadily intensifying. Watching the naked light bulb overhead grow dim, he could feel the breath slowly being squeezed out of him.

"What the hell . . . " The girl scurried off the bed. "What's the matter with you? Dotrice. Dotrice," she cried out.

There was a sharp rap on the door. Someone jiggled the knob outside and the door burst open. Several people streamed into the room.

His shorts drawn down about his ankles, Mooney flailed and gasped on the bed. He had the look of a hooked fish whomping out the final moments of its life on the deck of a boat. Though barely conscious, he was still aware of voices and movement all about him. He perceived it all as shadows rushing past. There was an annoying buzz in his ears and a sharp pain shooting up the length of his right arm.

The girl cowered in the corner, gaping at him, her eyes wide and rolling with fright.

"Get an ambulance," someone hissed. "The son of a bitch is croaking."

"Get him the fuck out of here."

"Quintius," he cried, as a candle wick guttered and died in his head.

64

He awoke and she was there, sitting by the bed, light streaming in from the window behind her. Through slitted eyes he watched her, all the while pretending to be asleep. At that moment he had not yet realized that he was in a hospital, hooked to tubes in his nostrils and veins. At the foot of the bed an oscilloscope projected an image of his pulse at regular time intervals.

He stirred and she glanced up from her newspaper, peering at him over the frames of her glasses. He shut his eyes tighter, unwilling to meet hers.

What had happened he couldn't say, unaware as he was of specific details. Nevertheless, he knew it entailed something unpleasant. He was conscious of discomfort. His buttocks, beneath the gown which had ridden up beneath him, were raw from the steady abrasion of overly starched sheets. He tried to move. She was up at once and moving toward the bed.

"Mooney?"

She leaned over, enveloping him in the kind, familiar scent of soap and cologne.

"Mooney? Are you awake?"

He rolled his head sidewards on the pillow. "What happened?"

"No one knows for sure. You blacked out. Rest now."

When he opened his eyes he found her hand resting lightly on his. Cool, and slightly coarse, he found it comforting. "What happened to me?"

She made an effort to be flip and gay. "Nothing much. You might have had a heart attack. They won't say for sure until they've done some tests."

He mumbled something, then opened his eyes wide for the first time.

"What do you want?" She tried to push him back, then saw his need at once. "Hold on. I'll get it for you."

He started to protest. He wanted a nurse, but he was too feeble to make much of a case for that. She was back in a moment with a glittering steel pot, helping to raise his thighs above it, then afterward, carrying the thing away when he'd done with it.

In his shame and awful desolation he heard her flush the waste off in the toilet and rinse the pot out in the sink.

By then it had all come back to him. He knew the whole squalid thing and, no doubt, she did, too.

It had taken two whole weeks for Mooney to get his legs back before he could be discharged from the hospital. But not until he'd had a few sobering words from a resident cardiologist plus a trunkful of pills from a lady internist who made it clear she disapproved of him.

It had not been a heart attack. It had been a spasm, a dysrhythmia. Fortunately, there had been no damage, but the warning had been loud and clear. The cardiologist had characterized his body as a museum of self-inflicted abuses.

"Lose weight. Fifteen pounds, at least," the man fulminated and thumped his desk top. "Give up fats and salt. Absolutely no alcohol. Your blood pressure and cholesterol levels are screaming stroke."

In the light of all the bitterness that had transpired between them, Mooney was mystified by Fritzi's insistence that he come home with her. Three times he refused. He wanted to go back to 161 Street, he said, where he belonged. The fourth time, and out of pure exhaustion, he capitulated and went back with her, instead, in a cab to Seventy-third Street.

For three weeks she fed him thin unsalted consommé and dry salad. All he drank was water and, occasionally, tea. He'd lost five pounds in the hospital. He lost another ten pounds over the three-week period he spent with her.

In the morning she gave him his medication and breakfast—a half grapefruit, a slice of unbuttered toast, a cup of unsugared tea, along with an eighty-milligram indiral, followed by a diuril. Then she'd go off to work, leaving him with the *Daily News, TV Guide* and the *Racing Form.* To the refrigerator she would tack a luncheon menu, generally consisting of a half-cup of cottage cheese with either vegetables or sliced fruit.

At the end of three weeks he was down an additional eighteen pounds. None of his clothing fit. When Fritzi took him back to the cardiologist after four weeks for a checkup, the man beamed with pleasure and declared that some kind of miracle had taken place.

In all of that time Mooney spoke to Manhattan South only four times, three times to Mulvaney and once to Defasio. He was on sick leave with full pay, Mulvaney assured him, and urged him not to worry about the investigation. Everything was proceeding apace. The captain sounded pleased over the phone. "Take your time, Mooney. Don't rush back till you're one hundred percent better."

Those calls rankled. Each time Mooney hung up, he did so convinced that Mulvaney was delighted to have him out of the way. More than anything, that spurred him on to full recovery.

While Fritzi was off at the Balloon, Mooney watched TV, sat in the park and read endless 87th Precinct mysteries. Strangely enough, he did not think of Watford or even Peter Quintius. He had put them both aside as if he perceived in them the root of all his misfortune.

On weekends Fritzi would bundle him into the car and off they'd go to the track to see the yearling and watch the trainer put him through his paces. Invariably, Fritzi came away exhilarated. The Roses was three weeks off and, studying Gumshoe's daily workout chart and fractions, she computed his chances.

Going back in the car Mooney would sit glum and unspeaking. He was brooding over the unsatisfactory past and the uncertain future. While Fritzi chatted happily about handicapping odds and sprint fractions, Mooney toted up his scorecard and computed his own odds for winning. None of the figures, however, had anything to do with racing.

During the period of Mooney's recuperation, they were both civil, even overly solicitous to each other. Nonetheless, a stiffness and reserve hobbled each daily encounter. On one occasion they spoke of what they called their "Last Supper" brawl the night of Mooney's attack. But neither of them had broached the subject of the attack itself and the rather indelicate circumstances under which it had occurred.

It was going on five weeks that Mooney had stayed out of work. With each day he grew increasingly restless. It was brilliant October weather. There was a snap in the air. All the trees in the park had gone a vivid wine red, shot through with threads of russet and yellow. Squirrels scampered over the footpaths, trundling off precious cargoes of acorns down winter holes.

Coming in late one afternoon from the park and waiting for Fritzi to get home, he put on the 6:00 P.M. news and was nearly knocked off his seat by a report that the police had had their first major break in the seven-year-old Broadway Bombardier case.

A thirty-year-old itinerant by the name of Gary Holmes from Seattle had been picked up by one of the Special Task Forces men on a West Forty-ninth Street rooftop.

Holmes had a police record. There was a long string of arrests. Ever since his fifteenth birthday he had been in trouble with the police and in and out of various correctional institutions. His crimes had been mostly of a minor order, but more recently, his operations had escalated into armed robbery.

Holmes admitted that he had lived for years on various rooftops round the city. Asked why he chose rooftops he maintained that (1) they were easily accessible, and (2) they were safer than basements or abandoned buildings, both of which frightened him.

Apprehended by two plainclothesmen on a roof in the theater district, Holmes admitted to raining objects down on the crowds below. They were good-sized rocks, however, nothing of the forty-pound cinder-block class. When questioned specifically regarding the cinder-block incidents over the past years, he proudly proclaimed himself to be the Broadway Bombardier but he had no clear recollection of specific events. In addition, he conceded that he suffered from a severe drinking problem, had lapses of memory and couldn't remember much of what he'd been up to over the past five years. Taken into custody that day, he was now at Bellevue undergoing psychiatric evaluation.

They then showed some footage of rooftops where Holmes had been active. Two or three people were interviewed on the street. They smiled and said they could now breathe a bit more easily, knowing that this "maniac" was in custody.

Next, pictures were shown of Holmes being booked at the station

271

house. He was a lank, scruffy individual with furtive eyes and a huge mop of uncombed hair. All the while he was being booked, there was an idiotic grin on his face—a look of satisfaction as if after a life devoid of any significant accomplishment, he had finally hit the big time.

Mooney watched it all with a sense of mounting anger. Surely a good part of that stemmed from the fact that it had taken place without him. He perceived something unjust in that—even conspiratorial, as if his good friends at Manhattan South had meanly and deliberately stolen his show.

When Dowd came on the screen, expatiating on the ardors of the investigation, which he personally had moved forward, despite one heartbreaking setback after the next, Mooney was nearly purple with rage.

The next day Mooney went back to the cardiologist. An EKG and a series of blood tests were done. He was weighed, then clapped on the back by the doctor and pronounced fit enough to return to work. On the following day, dressed in blue serge, but still a bit wobbly on his legs, he strode purposefully through the heavy swinging front doors of Manhattan South.

65

Holmes did not look at all like the man Mooney had seen on TV. This was a tall, bony man, all sinew and knots who gave the impression of great physical strength. The first thing Mooney noted were the hands clasped lightly together, as if in prayer, then the face, phlegmatic and dull, staring out at him from behind the wire mesh. The dark, beetled brow and the prognathous jaw created a vaguely simian expression. His large hands moved incessantly, as he spoke nonstop to Mooney, who all the while scribbled into his pad.

"It wasn't that I disliked any of them," Gary Holmes's voice was unexpectedly wispy. "It wasn't as if I cared one way or the other which one of them or who I got. Just so's I got me one."

"Did you plan any of those things?" Mooney asked.

Holmes's eyes flared with indignation. "Hell. Sure I planned them. I sat down and planned 'em all. Right down to the last detail. I hadda do it that way. It was that important to me."

"Important? How?"

"How?" Holmes gaped at him as if he pitied the man's stupidity. "I wanted to get it right. I was makin' my statement."

"Your statement?"

"Sure. Like I told you. About injustice, like, and bigotry and folks beatin' up on each other. Kids starvin' like, you know?" Pathetic bravado made him appear to swell behind the mesh screen, and his head nodded as if in passionate agreement with himself.

"What does creaming a crowd with a forty-pound cinder block have to do with starving kids?"

"Can't you see that?" Holmes snapped. "All them folks comin' out of theaters. Goin' to fancy restaurants with their credit cards and all. Feedin' their faces, like, while little kids starve."

"What little kids?"

The question appeared to baffle Holmes. He shrugged. "Hell, I don't know. They're all around."

They were sitting in a small visitors area of the Creedmore Psychiatric Hospital. The room was small, institutional green, with low ceilings and a wire partition dividing the patients' area from that of the visitors'. On either side of the partition were long green metal tables with hard wood chairs set at intervals down its entire length.

At that moment no one else was in the room, only Mooney and Gary Holmes, the man who had proclaimed himself the Broadway Bombardier. Mooney had been granted a half hour to speak with him and he'd had to fight with Mulvaney for every minute of that time.

"Who was it you confessed to, Gary?"

Holmes's brows arched as if the question had made him suddenly wary. "How would I know their names?"

Mooney sighed. "When making an arrest, police officers often identify themselves. I was just curious." Mooney watched him gauging the effect of his words. "Did they?"

"No. They didn't do nothin' like that."

"Never mind. I can find out who they were. How come you let them catch you?"

"I didn't let them catch me. I was just up on the roof tossin' rocks . . ."

"And you tossed a couple and just waited around for someone to come up and get you. Right?"

The intent of the detective's question appeared to elude him. Mooney attempted to clarify it. "When you toss rocks down on crowds of people, do you generally wait around for the cops to come up and . . . Never mind. What kind of rocks were these you tossed? How big?"

Holmes's face flooded with childish animation. "Big as footballs." He demonstrated the size by spreading his thumb and forefinger. "That big."

Mooney didn't have to ask the question. He knew very well the size of the missiles, having examined shattered fragments of them closely at the police laboratory. The rocks recovered from the area where Holmes had hurled them down into the theater crowds weighed one or two pounds apiece, certainly nothing of the order of a football. As missiles designed to be dropped from a height, they might have done damage, but it was doubtful they would have killed.

By this time Mooney had learned quite a bit about Gary Holmes—an itinerant, a bit of plankton that had washed up in the city. As criminal records go, Holmes's was decidedly small beer. What he did have going for him was a hefty psychiatric dossier. In and out of mental institutions all of his life, he'd been examined on several occasions by state psychiatrists—a number of times for petty theft, and once for having exposed himself to lady passengers on a subway platform.

"What were you doing up on the roof that night, Gary?"

"I told you, man. I was makin' my statement."

"Oh, you mean the starving kids?"

Holmes looked hurt. "That's right. The starvin' kids. And you're part of that same stinkin' system that takes the food out of their mouths and gives it all to the rich."

"Okay," Mooney conceded. "I'm part of that system. Still, if you've gotta cream people to make your statement, you could just as well do it on the street. Anyplace. Why does it have to be the roof?"

" 'Cause I like roofs, man. Like I told you. When I first come to the city I used to live up on the roof. I can breathe up there. I'm free."

"How long did you live on the roofs?"

Once again Holmes's eyes narrowed with distrust. "How long? Like ever since I come to New York."

"When was that?"

"In 1975."

"When in seventy-five?"

"Hell, I don't know. The spring sometime."

"And you got yourself a roof as soon as you arrived?"

"No. Not then." The questions had started to come a bit too rapidly for Holmes. "When I first come, I lived in the Village."

"The Village?"

"On Barrow Street. Then after that I lived up in Harlem awhile. It was a lot cheaper but I couldn't stand the jigs. They'd rip you off for anything up there. For a nickel."

"So that's when you took to the rooftops?"

"Sure. Much safer. Safer than bein' on the goddamn ground."

"When'd you cream your first victim?"

"In 1977."

"Who was that? Do you know?"

"Sure. That was Carrera."

Mooney shook his head. "You mean Catalonia? That was seventy-five."

Holmes frowned. "Oh, seventy-five? Oh, that's right. Catalonia was seventy-five."

"When did you do the second?"

"The second? That was 1976. May thirty-first. That was O'Meggins."

Mooney's eyes fluttered. "I gotta hand it to you, Holmes. You know your stuff."

It was pure ridicule, but Gary Holmes took it as a compliment. He grinned with good-natured idiocy. "I make it my business to know."

"When'd you first go to Wilmette, Gary?"

"Where?"

"Wilmette. Wilmette, Illinois."

"Illinois? Never been there." Holmes leered smugly as if he'd felt he'd just successfully parried a clever investigative thrust.

"When'd you start using the Boyd alias?"

"Who?"

"Boyd. Boyd." Mooney's rising bark momentarily stunned him. "When you called yourself Anthony Boyd and were in the import-export business at 3143 Crown Drive, Wilmette."

Holmes's confusion deepened. "I never . . . Say, what the hell is this, anyway?"

"That's what I'm asking you, Gary. What the hell is this? What the hell are you trying to pull here?"

Holmes half rose, then sat, then rose again. "I don't . . ."

"Have you ever been hospitalized in New York?" Mooney snapped at him through the cage.

"Hospitalized?"

"Have you ever been treated for injuries of any sort at Beth Israel Hospital?"

For the first time, Holmes seemed frightened.

"Beth Israel," Mooney shouted the words at him.

"What the hell's that?"

Mooney stood. "Never mind. You're a phony, Holmes. You're nothing."

"Who the fuck you callin' nothin'?" The heavy boned face came up close against the wire mesh, sending a blast of warm sour breath against Mooney's cheek.

"You're a lot of bullshit," Mooney snarled. "You did nothing."

Holmes lunged at the divider, flinging his chair backward against the concrete wall as he did so. Mooney watched the chair shatter. The wire mesh swelled outward toward him, along with Holmes spread-eagled athwart it. His stubby fingers squirmed toward Mooney like serpents through the reticulations.

Mooney stepped back, watching the mesh sag toward him, bearing with it the bulk of Holmes's big frame splayed wide against it.

"I wasted them fuckers," Holmes bellowed, "all seven of them. The honeymoon couple last spring. And the guy that's crippled for life. I suppose you didn't read about that? I did him, too. That was me."

Mooney watched three guards slip unseen into the inmates' pen behind him.

"You call that nothin'? Hah! I suppose you didn't see me on TV. I suppose . . ."

Mooney watched transfixed as the three guards pounced on the big, flailing figure, wrestling him to the ground. The noise was sickening. Holmes's bellowing had the sound of a stricken animal being slaughtered.

After, when they'd subdued him and led him off, Mooney slumped back down into a chair. His damp forehead propped in the palm of his hand, he tried to compose himself.

Outside in the hospital parking lot, Michael Defasio watched him climb back into the car, then switched the ignition on. He peered across at the big detective through the gathering dusk. "You look like you seen a ghost."

They started to roll out down the wide gravel drive, wet and steaming from the recent rain. Out on the Van Wyck Expressway the tires began to whine over the wet macadam. Mooney, who'd been silent, suddenly started to speak. "Don't tell me you swallowed that bullshit in there? How'd you get this confession? Come on. Out with it. Did Mulvaney put you up to it? How'd they get this phony confession? Come on. Tell me."

"Phony? Hey, wait a minute . . ."

"Don't tell me you didn't steamroll this poor apehead."

276

"No one steamrolled anyone." Defasio's knuckles whitened on the steering wheel. Rain streamed down the windshield, and the wipers, carving clear arcs in the glass, made a high, squeaking sound.

"For one thing, the guy's a nutso. He'd confess to anything, including snatching the Lindbergh kid. Don't you see what you've done, dummy? You got the wrong fucking guy."

66

"I don't care what you tell him, or how. Just so long as you tell him."

"Why don't you tell him?"

"If I have to tell him, Mulvaney, you might just as well turn in your shield. You're of no use to me. I still can't believe you authorized that visit to Creedmore."

"I couldn't very well deny it, could I? As of that moment he was still in charge of the investigation. So far as I knew, right?"

"Well, now you know differently. As of now it's official," Commissioner Dowd bellowed into the phone. On the other end Mulvaney winced and yanked the receiver away from his ear. "He's off the investigation. Now you go tell him."

The voice continued to rail, but distantly now, into the roiled dusty air of the ancient precinct house.

"I take it you'll be issuing a directive then, Commissioner?"

"The moment I hang up this phone. And you keep him away from Holmes now. Away from anything that has to do with this case. I don't care what you tell him. Just keep him out of everyone's hair. Give him something else to do."

"Like what, for instance?"

"I don't care, I told you. That's your job, Mulvaney. You just keep him off this. As far as we're concerned the case is closed. Holmes is our man. The investigation is closed. Everything's peaceful. Every-one's happy."

Dowd slammed down the phone. Mulvaney winced again on the other end, but he was smiling. It was a smug little smile, full of tri-umph and self-vindication. What he'd been telling them all along had finally come to pass. Mooney was a fraud, and now everyone knew that.

Why he continued to insist without qualification that this Mr. A. Boyd, the man in the hospital, and the Phantom Bombardier were one and the same was beyond comprehension. Mulvaney took it to be just one further proof of the stupid, mulish, irrationality that had doomed Frank Mooney's career from the start.

The Bombardier had done them the singular good turn of surren-dering himself and getting everyone off the hook. Mooney, of course, could never be content with that. It had all happened while he was away. Gary Holmes had not even the simple decency to time his sur-render so that Mooney could have been there to make the arrest.

Now Mooney was going about discrediting the suspect's story and, at the same time, the DA's case. Mooney had to be silenced before he blew the case against Holmes out of the water, causing not only pro-found embarrassment to the department, but to Mulvaney himself. There was no question of firing Mooney as a means of silencing him. Such actions, Mulvaney knew only too well, would have Mooney out broadcasting his story to every newspaper and network within shouting distance. And there were plenty, with axes to grind, who would be more than happy to tell the story of how the police railroaded a demented itinerant into confessing that he was the Bombardier. It was not that Mulvaney didn't believe that Holmes was the real Bombardier. He did, but he also understood that there were enough holes in his story to demonstrate effectively that he wasn't the Bombardier, even if he did toss a few rocks off a rooftop.

The most effective way to silence Mooney, Mulvaney reasoned, was by rewarding him with some new investigation. Even if it was somewhat less than a plum, it had to be all gussied up to look like one. It had to be perceived by one and all as a bonus for superb in-vestigative work on the Bombardier case and not the chastisement and banishment it really was.

Mulvaney lit his cold cigar and buzzed the intercom on his desk. In the next moment a tall, black female police sergeant, who served as Mulvaney's administrative assistant, poked her head in the door.

"Priscilla—is Mooney still out there?"

The sergeant checked her wristwatch. "He should be. He doesn't go off duty for another twenty minutes."

"Send him in, will you please?"

67

The investigation Mooney was reassigned to had been given a Class I priority. A molester of small children rampaging through a low-income West Side housing project was sensational enough for it to have brought out the media in droves. Pressure from parent and school groups had been persistent enough to have earned the investigation its priority rating.

Mooney had been told that his assignment to the case was a reward for the splendid job he'd done on the Bombardier investigation.

He tried hard to believe that but the tough realist in him told him otherwise. His work on the Bombardier case, he knew, was perceived by his colleagues and superiors as a total failure. Now he'd been given a jackal to hunt while the lions had gone to all the others. The molester, he knew, was a nickel-and-dime operation. The spoor he left behind each of his predations was about as subtle as a rhino track. The man they were looking for begged to be caught and shortly, Mooney knew, he would oblige him.

Meanwhile, there were the outraged parents, the concerned deputations of educators, church groups, all deploring the demise of solid, middle-class neighborhoods. Politicians up for reelection mounted lecterns to suddenly rediscover long-forgotten pieties. Inevitably, there were the windy denunciations of the police in newspaper editorials and the promises by the mayor to restore calm and guarantee that more police would be out in force in the affected area.

It was a bitter Christmas for Mooney. On the one hand, there was a part of his life that had never been better. The Fritzi Baumholz part. He had lost nearly seventy pounds (down from 245 when they'd first met). He was, for Francis Mooney, lean, vigorous and, in some

279

oddly indefinable way, even attractive. For one thing, his face had recovered its once youthful bone structure. For another, his stride was more erect and he seemed taller. His relationship with the proprietress of Fritzi's Balloon was also better than ever. To be sure, they still quarreled on any subject and on almost a daily basis. But there was always the tacit assurance that by dusk there would be truce. It had taken him over six decades to unlock the mystery of living with another person. Knowing that he had undoubtedly forfeited significant freedoms under the new arrangement, he would have now conceded that it also brought to him certain undeniable advantages.

The sense of warmth and cheer at finally belonging to something other than himself stirred deep within him. He could not say why, but it had roused some barely suspected part of himself that had long been dormant. And yet, coming to him almost daily, creeping up on him, soundless, furtive, the lion stirred in the bush behind so close, so tantalizingly near, that it seemed to Mooney he could feel the hot, meaty fetor of its breath upon his cheek.

One late winter afternoon, with time to kill, Mooney strolled up Madison to Sixty-seventh Street, past the windows of Quintius Gallery. In keeping with the season the gallery was decorated with a Byzantine crèche. He didn't stop but, instead, peered in while striding by, as if trying to discern through the gray reflective surface of the glass the vague, shadowy figures that moved behind there.

On Christmas Eve he thought of Watford and was surprised that he had. An image flashed in his eye of the forlorn, forgotten man in the seedy flannel robe, in the musty parlor with the clocks and the old-lady furniture—the chintz and brocades, the bead lampshades, and the antimacassars still bearing the imprint of oily heads no longer present. He thought about their two or three encounters and wondered what the season of the Prince of Peace had brought for Watford.

On New Year's Eve the Pleiades hung low in the bright clear sky. The little cluster of five stars glittered like a rabbit's paw above the jagged East Side skyline near the river. In the gray dawn of the New Year the constellation rose higher, like some blessed augury of renewal.

68

It had been three months since Watford had seen Francis Mooney. That had been on the stormy occasion of their visit to Quintius & Sons.

The episode had stayed very much in Watford's mind. In the interim since that visit he had been unable to find work. Finally, though the idea of it filled him with repugnance, he sought and gained public assistance.

As eccentric as his life-style was, living on the fringes of criminal life as he did, he nonetheless clung to a strict code of ethics. The "code," as contradictory and inconsistent as it was, contained proscriptions against the peddling of drugs, promiscuous sex, the use of alcohol on all but special occasions and finally and most emphatically, sponging on the public dole.

Public assistance was a special category for Watford. There was no room there for easy casuistry. It was simply repugnant to him. He didn't despise people who accepted it; he merely pitied them. The sense of loathing he felt for any public charity went beyond reason and, undoubtedly, was an offshoot of his father's own fiercely independent and mostly misguided notions regarding pride and manliness.

That Christmas season found Watford demoralized. More so than ever before. Whatever might have been said of him, he had always been a sanguine and resilient creature. He was willing to take the daily drubbings that life administered because he subscribed wholeheartedly to the notion of a better day. Recognition now, however dim, of the chronic, possibly fatal nature of his illness, along with the daily rejection he'd encountered in his search for work, had just about throttled whatever final vestiges of hope he could muster. Above all holiday seasons, Christmas without hope is undoubtedly the most hopeless—the zero point of despair.

With characteristic fashion of trying to make the best of things, he rose early the day before Christmas and prepared a small bird for Christmas Eve. Following that, he went out and purchased yams and salad greens at a local greengrocer, plus a bottle of inexpensive claret and a mince pie. As an afterthought he asked a neighbor, a recently widowed lachrymose lady as solitary as himself, to join him for dinner.

The meal was pleasant enough, but the two of them there by themselves in the musty little house, eating off his mother's Spode with nothing but the most desultory talk between them, served only to heighten his sense of isolation and bereavement.

Much to his relief, the lady departed shortly after dinner, leaving him to himself—to the parlor and the ticking of numerous clocks and the crackling fire expiring on the hearth. His sense of gloom deepened. For no particular reason, he thought of Quintius, his meeting with him at the gallery and the man's refusal to acknowledge their acquaintance. That, for Watford, was unpardonable, even more so than the alleged crimes of which he was suspected. In the next instant the red of rage enflamed his features.

Granted a wide social gulf lay between them, but did that mean that Quintius had been so mortified to have shared a hospital room with him that he had to disavow the incident entirely? During that vague, scarcely remembered period of convalescence, Watford felt he had given Quintius not only companionship but the will to recover. Surely he deserved better than the kind of scorn that Quintius had heaped upon him.

By the time he had gotten into bed that night he'd worked himself into a fine fettle. So great was his sense of personal affront that he was unable to sleep. He tossed and turned while anger churned inside him. Perhaps a deep intuition that his days now grew short made him all the more determined to square his books.

He rose early the next morning, Christmas Day, and dressed. He drank a cup of coffee at a neighborhood stall and took a subway to Pennsylvania Station, where he bought a ticket and boarded a train for Huntington, Long Island. He had found Quintius's Long Island number and address in the Manhattan directory where it appeared directly beneath the entry for Quintius Gallery, Madison Avenue.

When he reached Huntington he took a cab from the station to Cold Spring Harbor, instructing the driver to take him out to the Quintius place.

From the depot they reached the Quintius residence in a little under twenty minutes. The driver was about to turn into the long, winding gravel drive, but Watford asked to be let off at the entrance instead.

"It's a long way in." The driver stared at him through the rearview mirror.

"That's okay. I prefer to walk."

"Suit yourself."

The driver handed him change and accepted his tip without looking back. Watford got out and started through the two big stone stanchions. Momentarily wavering, he paused and glanced back over his shoulder. The driver was still there, staring queerly at him. Watford could see the man shrug, then tear off with a shriek of tires.

Watford trudged up the drive, his collar up and his ungloved hands balled into fists deep inside his overcoat pockets. For no immediately apparent reason, he had dressed in his best Sunday finery. The fact that it was Christmas Day may have had something to do with it.

Moving up a gentle acclivity, rounding a wide curve in the drive, looming up ahead through a stand of bare birch, Watford saw stone chimneys surmounting a slate mansard roof. A small, late-model Porsche stood drawn up at the head of a circular drive that swept round to the front of the house.

Watford veered off the drive and stood shivering for a while in a thick screen of evergreens encroaching upon the house. There were gardens all about, mulched and covered over with plastic sheets for the winter. Cold frames were set out all round, and innumerable plantings of rhododendron and azalea stood wrapped in burlap. To the left of the house and just beyond a gentle rise, Watford could see an immense slab of Sound, gray-green and tumbling shoreward, whitecaps churned by icy blasts of wind coming out of the north. Other than the smart little Porsche, there was no sign of anyone about the house.

He wore a heavy overcoat and beneath that a suit. But even at that, the icy blasts sweeping through the trees took his breath away. With each gust his trousers buffeted about his legs and his feet grew tingly numb inside his shoes. Nevertheless, he drew his collar up more tightly round his throat and waited.

He must have waited there for upward of twenty minutes, growing colder and more desolate by the minute. Wavering between irresolution and his need to set things aright, he had begun to question the wisdom of his being there at all, and wondering whether he should not slink off at once before he was discovered.

In the next moment the choice was taken completely out of his hands. The front door swung open and someone, a man, stood framed in the doorway, his back facing Watford. Given the height and noble proportion of the figure in the doorway, Watford knew at once the man to be Peter Quintius. He stood talking with someone just inside the door. Craning his neck and leaning forward, Watford caught a glimpse of pale rose, then a flash of movement. It was a woman's robe.

The figure of the man appeared to turn slowly, and in the next instant Watford had a clear view of profile, followed shortly by a full prospect of the woman just beyond. The man was indeed Quintius, and the woman, he presumed, was his wife.

Quintius turned another ninety degrees and started briskly down the front steps. Even as the massive oak door closed behind him, Watford could hear the squeal of ancient brass fastenings rend the frozen air.

Quintius moved down the steps and round to the side of his car. At that moment Watford stepped out from the concealment of the woods and started toward him. The distance between them was possibly fifty yards. Without actually running, Watford moved with remarkable swiftness, seeming to accelerate as he drew closer. With the first definitive crunch of his foot on the gravel drive, Quintius whirled and stared at him. Something in the man's eyes had the effect of stopping Watford dead in his tracks.

"Mr. Quintius?"

"Yes?"

"It's me. Charles Watford. Remember?"

The expression on Quintius's face registered no recognition. Quite the contrary, it was more that of a bemused curiosity as he watched the slight, stooped figure scrambling toward him.

Watford's hand shot out before him and he was smiling. "You do remember? Beth Israel? The bed next to you? I came up to see you a few months ago. At your gallery? Remember?"

Something wary leapt at once into Quintius's eye. "I don't know you. I have never . . ."

"But you do. You shared a room with me. At the hospital."

"You have no business on this property. Get out of here. "

Watford felt himself cringe but stood his ground. When at last he did speak, it was softly, with the most poignant affability. "I will. Just as soon as you admit you know me."

Quintius stood uncertainly while Watford confronted him. Staring up at him, he gave the appearance of a small hound who's treed a bear.

"Mr. Quintius," Watford resumed—politely, reasonably, arguing with quiet force. "I'm certain you know me."

"Isobel." Quintius shouted over his shoulder. "Isobel."

"I'll be happy to leave the moment you . . ."

The door squealed open and Isobel Quintius stood framed there in a pink robe, staring at the two of them. "Peter? What in God's—"

"Isobel," Quintius snapped at her, his eyes riveted on Watford as though he were a deadly serpent about to strike. "Call the police."

"Mrs. Quintius . . ." Watford's hand rose in appeal. "I'm sorry to . . ."

"Call the police, Isobel. For God's sake."

At once the door slammed shut and she was gone.

Watford seemed puzzled and hurt. "There's no need for police. I'm not a criminal."

"You're trespassing here. You have no right here."

"You *do* remember me from Beth Israel. I see it in your eyes. Why do you deny it?"

"I deny nothing. I don't know you. I've never been to Beth Israel."

Quintius glowered down at him, then spun round and started back up the steps. Just as he reached the door he turned and started back down as if something had just occurred to him. "Except for that time you came into my gallery, I've never seen you before. Now will you stop annoying me and my family? The police will be here any minute. If you're not off this property by then I'll press charges. I will prosecute to the fullest extent of the law."

Quintius was right. A local police patrol car was there within the next several minutes and two Huntington policemen got out and stared back and forth from Quintius to Watford while the two men shouted at each other. Mrs. Quintius looked on helplessly.

"Who is he?" one of the policemen asked.

Quintius shook his head. "I don't have the slightest idea."

"Yes, he does. He knows me all right." Watford appealed to one of the policemen. "We shared a hospital room together."

"He lies. I've never seen the man."

"Get him out of here," Mrs. Quintius called from the safety of the door.

"I just want him to admit he knows me."

Quintius glared down at Watford from the upper step. "The man's insane."

Whatever Quintius had denied before, whatever slur or indignities he had heaped on Watford were all as nothing compared to those last three words. The charge of insanity, of mental instability, was absolutely intolerable.

Like a small fierce terrier, Watford hurled himself on Quintius. Mrs. Quintius screamed and the big man staggered backward even as the two policemen pounced on Watford, dragging him, kicking and struggling, to the car.

"You lie." Watford spat and kicked. "You lie. You know me. You know you know me."

The patrol car doors were flung open and while one of the policemen encircled Watford from behind with his arms, struggling to hoist him off the ground, the other tried to force his head down so that it would clear the door frame.

"You know me all right. You know I was in that hospital room with you."

Quintius stood aghast on the top step; Isobel cowered beyond the door, watching in horror while the police struggled to subdue the shrieking, flailing figure.

At one point they heard a grunt and Watford's head banged with a queasy thud against the top of the car. His face was bleeding and his glasses were askew. As hard as the police tried to cram his head down below the doorframe of the patrol car, the more it came bouncing right up. Arms flailing all the while, Watford spat obscenities at Quintius. "You son of a bitch. You know me. I helped you when you were in pain. Why don't you admit it? You bastard. Aren't I good enough?"

There was a grunt and a shudder. Watford's head cleared the top of the doorframe and he was propelled sprawling headlong into the backseat of the patrol car. The doors were slammed, and as the car lurched off down the drive, the Quintiuses, badly shaken, could see one of the policemen in the backseat still thrashing about trying to subdue Watford.

For some time after the car had disappeared behind a rise, the Quintiuses stood staring at the troubled vacancy left in its wake. An icy wind soughed in off the Sound and the bare birches clicked fretfully against each other in the near-zero air. Mrs. Quintius turned and looked at her husband. A frightened, inquisitive look haunted her eyes. "What was that man talking about, Peter? What was all this about a hospital? What in God's name was he trying to say?"

286

69

It was Christmas Day. No one was about. Not the chief of police. Not the town magistrate. Not even a local justice of the peace. Everyone was on holiday and the two police who'd taken Watford into custody had not the faintest notion of what to do with him. Until that could be determined, they decided to detain their prisoner in one of the small temporary holding cells in the basement of the Cold Spring Harbor Town Hall.

They kept Watford there for nearly eight hours unable to decide what to do next. Shortly after jailing him they called Quintius and asked if he wished to prefer charges. For reasons best known to Quintius alone, he declined. This was fine for Watford, but it created a problem for the police.

Both of the patrolmen were scheduled to go off duty shortly. In the absence of the regular clerk-typist, who was at home having Christmas dinner, neither man had the time nor the inclination to fill out in quadruplicate the forms necessary to detain a prisoner in the county jail overnight.

In the eight or nine hours that Watford had been in their custody, he had regained his composure. At the small washstand in the cell he had sponged clean the coagulated scratches on his face, combed his hair and straightened his tie.

The policemen gave him medication for the scratches, ice for the bump on his head and then coffee and doughnuts in the late afternoon. They had asked him a number of questions about himself and what he had been doing out on the Quintius property. He told them that he'd only wanted to say hello to Quintius whom he'd met in the hospital several years before. He'd liked Quintius and had read about the tragedy he'd recently suffered with his son. He'd only wanted to say hello and wish him the very best for the New Year.

He was asked if he wished to contact his attorney. He said he had no attorney and even if he had, there'd be no reason to do so. He had no wish to cause trouble, for Quintius, or himself.

They took identification from his Social Security card and driver's license. It was getting on to 5:00 P.M. and they were both anxious to get home to their families and their own Christmas dinners. One of them, however, would have to stay if Watford was to remain in custody.

Looking at him there in the cell, in his white shirt and tie, his nicely turned out flannel suit, he looked no more threatening than, say, a sort of affable crackpot. As it drew closer to 5:00 P.M., Watford appeared to them increasingly harmless—even slightly put upon. In the absence of any charges, there appeared to be no compelling reason to detain him further. With each passing minute, the temptation grew greater to release him.

Somewhere just after five, they put Watford back in the patrol car and drove him down to Huntington Depot with a one-way ticket to Pennsylvania Station. They patted him on the back, wished him a Merry Christmas and extracted from him a promise that he would never try anything so foolhardy again. At least not in their jurisdiction.

Once on the train, chugging down the track west out of Huntington, Watford's mask of affability quickly faded. A man seated opposite him noted at once the glower, and could not help but overhear the incessant muttering comprised principally of obscenities. The fact that it had all come leaching out like raw sewerage from such a pleasant-looking fellow made it all the more disquieting. At the next stop the man got up and changed his seat for one in a different car.

All the way into New York, Watford smoldered like burning rags. The idea that he'd spent most of Christmas Day in a fetid little jail cell was infuriating enough. However, the fact that he'd been consigned there by Quintius was absolutely insupportable. Once again Quintius had disavowed him, this time treating him like a common criminal.

By the time the train had reached Penn Station not only had Watford worked himself into a fresh pique of rage, but now all the old familiar flags of massive migraine were flying.

Leaving the station and walking out between the great marble pillars fronting Seventh Avenue and Thirty-third Street, Watford weaved his way dizzily through crowds of holiday travelers. As the dreaded vise of pain gripped the back of his neck, creeping insidiously forward like an iron claw round his temple, all the light, color and motion of the gaudy night took on the impression of a great blur, shapes dimly discerned through a pane of rain-streaked glass.

Walking through the clogged, whirling streets, he moved unsteadily, giving the impression of mild intoxication. He noted with an almost clinically scientific detachment that he was unable to walk a straight line. Instead, he had to thread his way very deliberately, with an uncontrollable obliqueness for which he had constantly to correct, like a sailboat on a very broad tack.

What he sought now was a cab. He needed to get home before the attack struck full force. Home to bed and blessed Mother Demerol. Out on Seventh Avenue he wandered, dazed by the full roar of noise and light. The nature of his condition tended to amplify the jarring effect of the streets, increasing his state of confusion. He tried unsuccessfully to orient himself. At one point, holding his throbbing head between his hands, he started walking south when he'd intended to go north.

At the corner of Thirty-second and Seventh he waited for a red light to turn green. Intending to flag a cab, he stepped, or rather lurched, headlong off the curb, misjudging its height completely. He stumbled, waving at an onrushing cab, but his timing was off. The cabdriver had seen him even though he'd waved late. In an effort to reach him, the driver veered sharply left from the middle of Seventh Avenue. Watford, grasping the driver's predicament, wobbled forward out into the street. Another car, just to the left of the cab, loomed suddenly out of nowhere, impaling Watford on the converging spikes of its blinding headlights.

There was time to step back, but he didn't. Instead, he did something very curious. He raised his arms, stretching them out wide, then turned and faced the juggernaut directly.

Afterward, after the ambulance had driven off, the driver, badly shaken as he tried to answer the traffic policeman's questions, insisted, as improbable as it sounded, that Watford had walked directly into the path of his car. Caught in the headlights, the figure, the man swore, coming at him arms outstretched, was smiling.

70

"How long has he been here?"

"About a week. As a matter of fact, one week ago Thursday night. He asked to be brought here expressly. Favors the accommodations. Requested his old room. It just happened to be available."

The two of them smiled, Mooney and Dr. Ramsay, a pair of improbable conspirators drawn together through the bond of shared secrets.

The detective shook his head with an air of weary sagacity. "So you thought you got rid of him?"

"You don't get rid of Watford that easily."

"You should never have bothered trying to discharge him. What's he in for this time?"

"Bilateral fractured tibias and fibulas. We had to take his spleen out."

"What's all that supposed to mean?"

"It means he's pretty sick. Police report says he walked deliberately in front of a car."

Mooney lifted his battered fedora and whistled softly.

Ramsay nodded. "I guess he just can't bear to leave us. How come you're back?"

"He called me. Sent me this first." Mooney pulled a Christmas card out of his inside pocket. It bore a view of three Magi on camels following a star above the desert. "Followed this up with a phone call. Told me he had to see me."

Ramsay waved an arm expansively. "By all means. Be my guest. He's holding court right down the hall."

"You have any idea what's on his mind?"

290

"Not the foggiest."

The two men stared at each other as if trying to divine each other's thoughts. Mooney started to speak, slapped his knee instead, then rose with a groan. "Well, I guess I'll amble over now. What room?"

"Same as before: 1501."

"How's his overall condition?"

"The leukemia's spread all through him. According to his white blood cell count, he ought to be dead."

Mooney stared hard at the floor for a moment, then turned abruptly and left.

Room 1501 was a double, about thirty feet from Ramsay's office. When Mooney walked in, Watford was sitting up, having his dinner and watching the evening news. He appeared comfortable, relaxed, perfectly at home. Forking small portions of meat fastidiously into his mouth, seasoning his salad with Plasticine envelopes of dressing, he gave the impression of one who completely dominated his own small space.

As Mooney entered, he looked up at once and smiled. There was something sly in his expression, as if he were enjoying some private joke.

Mooney frowned, on the verge of saying something unpleasant, but Watford waved him to silence. In the next instant the smile was gone and his mood was at once disturbingly sober.

"That bastard Quintius." He shook a finger at the detective. "I finally remembered what he told me in the hospital. He said he killed someone. That's what he told me. Now I recall. The son of a bitch said he dropped a block on someone's head off a rooftop."

71

It was icy cold that night and flurries of wet snow pelted slowly down as Mooney left the hospital. He drove at a brisk clip all the way out to Cold Spring Harbor.

Once past Forest Hills, the expressway was dismal and empty. The flurries had escalated into a fast hail that hissed and rattled on the Buick's rooftop. Whooshing away, the wipers cut wide arcs in the frosty windshield. Outside, the big calcium highway lights, ringed with halations, cast a stark white glare on the slick roadway unraveling before him.

Mooney watched the phantom of a red taillight up ahead receding into vapory distance and wondered what mad demons sent him speeding over icy slick roads this night.

It was uncanny the way Watford had suddenly uttered those careless words spoken to him by a man waking from the stupor of anesthesia over two years ago. "Son of a bitch dropped a block on someone's head off a rooftop."

The words rang out like pealing bells in Mooney's ear. Evidence of guilt. How else could Watford have known that? No way, unless he'd been told. Mooney hadn't told him. He'd only said that the man was quite possibly a murderer. The fellow's method of operation had been left unsaid. If only he could now forge the seemingly incontrovertible link between A. Boyd and P. Quintius. He almost thought he could.

Still, maddeningly, beneath the giddy sense that he was within a hairbreadth of vindication was that taunting undercurrent of doubt—a doubt that sprang from the knowledge that whatever evidence he boasted had as its questionable source Charles Watford.

Mooney's foot pressed down harder on the accelerator. The studded snow tires of the Buick clattered over the lightly powdered macadam. He had not bothered to call the Quintius home to announce that he was coming. If he had, he felt certain that an audience would have been denied. Had he then been so foolish as to insist, he would have undoubtedly been referred to a lawyer. And also, he had no authority there. The case was officially closed, Gary Holmes committed for life to a psychiatric institute upstate.

Arriving at Cold Spring Harbor, he got directions to the house at a filling station. In another ten minutes he was there. As the car turned between the two big stanchions and rolled in second gear up the gravel drive, he had a picture of Dowd and Mulvaney trying to explain themselves to the press. He laughed softly to himself.

A diminutive, apple-cheeked German lady in a starched white uniform answered the front door.

"Mr. Quintius, please."

"He is expecting you?"

"I'm afraid not."

She eyed the detective warily. "Whom shall I say is calling, please?"

"Captain Mooney. New York City police." He flashed his badge.

She leaned forward and read it with her lips, then stared up at him standing in a cone of light cast from the big coach lanterns just outside the door. His hat dangled at his thigh and a light, white powder mantled the shoulders of his coat.

The woman studied him a moment longer, then signaled him to come in out of the snow, standing to one side as he entered.

"One moment, please. You would wait right here?"

She disappeared noiselessly down a long hall and through a divider made from a pair of large Coromandel screens. From just beyond that point voices, muffled and tentative, drifted back at him. They came from an area defined by a soft diffusion of orange light. In the next moment he could hear two pair of footsteps treading back up the passage.

The woman confronting him now was tall and striking. She wore a blue silk peignoir and satin slippers. Her feet seemed disproportionately small for her height. The little apple-cheeked German lady hovered just behind her, smiling hospitably.

"I'm Isobel Quintius. Can I help you?"

Mooney showed his badge again. "Captain Mooney. New York City police. Sorry to barge in like this."

She eyed him with distrust. "You wanted to see my husband?"

"If that's okay."

"In connection with what, may I ask?"

293

"If it's all the same to you, I'd prefer to speak directly to him."

Her tone grew noticeably sharper. "In connection with my son, William Quintius?"

"No, ma'am."

Her perturbation deepened. "Then it must have something to do with that awful little man who showed up here last week."

Mooney made a wry face. "What awful little man?" But he knew the answer even as he asked the question. "You mean Charles Watford?"

"Yes. That's the man." She caught her breath. "My husband has not been well. We've been through a great deal over the past several months."

"I understand."

"My son, William . . ."

"Yes. I know."

"So far as that other unfortunate incident," she hurried on in a whisper, "I'm certain that my husband would prefer to drop the whole matter."

Mooney nodded, preferring to let her misjudge entirely the intention of his visit. "Well, then, if I might just see Mr. Quintius—"

"Well," she continued to watch him charily, "perhaps just for a few minutes. He's really quite tired."

"I understand," Mooney murmured with an air of doglike obedience. "This shouldn't take more than a few minutes."

A grandfather clock intoned deeply from some distant, unlighted area of the house above them. Suspicion flashed again in Mrs. Quintius's eye and for a moment he held his breath, certain she was about to withdraw everything she'd just conceded.

"Helga," she called over her shoulder, "please show the captain out to the greenhouse."

"Yes, madame."

"Thank you, Mrs. Quintius."

"Wait here, please," the little German lady whispered to him. "I'll get my coat."

Mooney nodded gratefully.

"Remember." Isobel Quintius had once again recovered her icy demeanor. "Ten minutes. No more."

"I understand," Mooney replied and watched her turn and quickly vanish between the Coromandel screens.

72

She'd left him off at the front door of the greenhouse and told him to go right on in. He was to follow the big center aisle, then turn right and go to the very end.

Mooney watched the woman move off across the powdery snow. Waiting outside in the chill blasts gusting off the Sound, he huddled in his overcoat and peered into the greenhouse through one of the wide panes. Then with a sigh of resignation, he stepped in, closed the door behind him and waited there, listening to the sound of his own breathing in the gloomy half-light.

The place had the feeling of a hot moist cave. A light glowing from some point deep within the structure poured through the thickish air, casting a mottled greenish sheen like that of underwater light against the glass walls.

In the next instant he was aware of the foliage, the sheer profusion of it—plants, trees, vines, fronds, flowers, of every imaginable shape and color, the size of them magnified threefold in that strange demi-light. The fragrance of it all, thousands of huge, extravagant blooms, breathing in the warm moist shadows, was overpowering.

Mooney leaned against the wall, almost dizzy from the suffocating sweetness of it. Then he heard the snipping. He glanced up instantly like some predatory creature hearing the telltale sound of its quarry. It was a clicking sound—rapid, metallic.

Mooney started to walk toward the light. The sound of his own footsteps banging rudely over the wide-planked floors struck him as the desecration of a kind of holy place.

Where the big center aisle branched, Mooney veered sharply right as he'd been told. He was confronted at once by a long, tubular structure, a glass tunnel at the end of which he descried a broad white circle of illumination. At roughly the center of that stood a figure. It was that of a man who appeared to be working over a long bench.

As he strode up Quintius recognized him at once. "You're the fellow who was with that crazy man who came to my gallery."

He removed a pair of mud-streaked rubber gloves, taking the hand that Mooney proffered. There was no trace of surprise or alarm in his face. Not so much as even a hint of uneasiness. It crossed Mooney's mind with some disquiet that his visit there was not entirely unexpected.

"I take it your being here has something to do with that person [his pronunciation of the word conveyed disdain] who showed up here the other day."

Mooney reflected. "I just heard about that from your wife. Too bad, isn't it. He's a very sick man."

Quintius chuckled lightly. "You don't have to tell me."

The blade of Quintius's trowel glittered momentarily, then plunged deep into the potted soil. He'd been thinning out some of his bushier, more extravagant roses. He had a number of fresh shoots he was repotting. A stream of water drummed hollowly from a tap into a steel basin as he deftly spaded dark rich humus into big terra-cotta pots. "You mind if I just go about my work here?"

"Sure. Go ahead. Don't let me interrupt."

Quintius took up his trowel again and furrowed deeply into one of the big pots. "Just go on talking. I'm listening." He spoke with his eyes riveted to the design of new cuttings he was planning for one of the clay pots. "Just what is your connection with this—man?"

"That's a long, complicated story," Mooney said. A sharp little grin darted at the edges of his lips. "It has something to do with the fact that he says he once shared a hospital room with you."

"Yes. I know."

"At Beth Israel. Two years ago."

Quintius's huge rubbered fingers tamped a squirming shoot into the rich soil.

"And obviously," Mooney continued, "there are some good reasons to believe that you did, or I wouldn't be here. . . ."

Quintius's trowel never missed a stroke. "Then what?"

"Then it would be my duty to tell you that you're a prime suspect in the deaths of six people and to advise you of your rights."

Quintius completed tamping, then glanced up, seemingly unperturbed. "I'm aware of my rights, thank you. What six people?"

"Six people who died as a result of objects dropped from rooftops over the past seven years. Another man has been crippled for life."

Quintius grew pensive, then took up his trowel once more. Mooney had to give the man credit. If he was playing a part, he was doing it to perfection. There was no discernible lapse, no self-betraying sign of protest or alarm. Not even any attempt to defend himself. Quite the contrary, he now appeared solicitous, even helpful.

"Haven't I read something about that recently?"

"You probably have. A man by the name of Holmes confessed to the killings. At present he's in a mental institution up in Wingdale. Too whacko to stand trial."

"Then why bother me? May I have those shears, please."

Mooney continued to speak as he passed the shears across the potting table. "I'm bothering you because Holmes is innocent. His confession, I'm sorry to say, was pretty much wrung out of him."

"I see. And you believe I'm guilty. What evidence have you?"

"Only circumstantial, but in time I'm convinced I can prove it."

In truth, Mooney was convinced of no such thing. Even if he could establish beyond doubt that Quintius and Watford had shared a hospital room, it was quite a leap from there to prove in the absence of eyewitness testimony that Quintius was the Bombardier.

"By chance, can you tell me your blood type?"

"AB-positive," Quintius replied at once. "Anyone who's served in the army knows that. But that's hardly evidence."

"Only of a minor sort. What's a bit more disturbing is that you registered at the hospital in a name other than your own. And while you were there recovering from surgery, you confessed to Charles Watford that you'd just killed a man by dropping a cinder block on his head from a rooftop."

Quintius's shears snipped on with no perceptible break in rhythm. "Did Mr. Watford tell you that?"

"He did."

"And you believe this poor, admittedly"—he cast about for Mooney's word—"whacko creature?"

"Poor, yes. Unstable, yes. But not entirely whacko." Mooney watched his expression for the slightest reaction.

Quintius thumbed a fresh young cutting into the rich black humus. "A matter of degree, then, his lunacy?"

"It wouldn't be hard to puncture his credibility as a witness in a court of law, if that's what you're driving at."

"Exactly." Quintius nodded. "Is there anything further I can do for you?"

"As a matter of fact, there is." The detective smiled back directly level into Quintius's eyes. "Would you mind dropping your trousers so I can see if there's any recent surgical scars on your butt."

Quintius was neither flustered nor surprised. If anything, he seemed amused. "I'm afraid it's getting late, Captain. You'd better get back to the city before this snow gets much worse."

"If you're innocent," Mooney pressed harder, "there's nothing to hide."

"I have nothing to hide, but you're quite beyond your authority coming out here. This is the jurisdiction of Suffolk County."

"If you prefer, I can request that the Suffolk police ask you to drop your trousers."

Quintius disregarded the facetiousness. "Let me give you my attorneys' number. Take the matter up with them. In the meantime"—he rose, extending his hand—"my best to Mr. Watford. And good night."

"You'll make it easier on all of us if you confess."

Once again there was the wry, likable smile, made even more so by a kind of noble fatigue. "I wish I could, Captain, if only to get you and Mr. Watford off my back. But if I did, I'd be just as crazy as Mr. Holmes. I'm not a murderer. I'm quite well respected in my business, in this community. And, frankly, I don't know what you're talking about. That's why I'm suggesting that you take the matter up with my lawyers—the way any sensible man would who suddenly found himself accused of murdering six people."

The calm, unruffled affability of it rattled Mooney. He'd been expecting something else. He couldn't say exactly what, but patient, good-natured indulgence was certainly not it.

He had just about played his last card when he happened to glance around at some of the larger potted plants surrounding Quintius. Just behind him, in the uttermost branches of an eight-foot succulent, he noted an enormous white bloom. Easily twelve inches across, the flower nodding from the burden of its own weight appeared to have just bloomed.

"May I ask what that flower is?"

Quintius turned and gazed up at it. "Hyalocereus Grandiflora. More commonly known as nightblooming cereus."

It was as if Mooney had been punched in the stomach. The fact that he was still able to smile astonished him. "That's what I thought it was."

"Are you familiar with nightbloomers?"

"Not really. But I know someone who has one just like that. By any chance do you know a Mr. Anthony Boyd? From Wilmette? He's an authority on the subject."

Up till that moment he had failed to get any sort of a rise out of Quintius; this time, however, he knew he'd succeeded. Something appeared to pass across the man's eyes. It was like a film or a shift in light. So fast it was, so slight, as to be nearly imperceptible. But this time it was there and he'd seen it. For that moment alone it had been worth the trip.

Footsteps echoed hollowly behind him. He turned to see Isobel Quintius materialize out of the shadows. She had tossed a trench coat over her shoulders; the blue of the peignoir trailed well below the hem of it. On her head she wore a yellow rain wimple tied beneath her chin. Beads of melting snowdrops glistened on its broad, floppy brim. She looked apprehensively back and forth from one of them to the other.

"I'm just on my way, Mrs. Quintius." Mooney buttoned his overcoat and tucked his collar up around his ears. "Afraid I kept him a bit beyond the ten minutes I'd promised. We just discovered that we have a mutual passion for flowers." Mooney smiled at her, and nodded at Quintius. "Don't bother to show me out. I can find my way."

73

"Nightblooming cereus. Are you familiar with nightbloomers?" Mooney's voice rang in the cold vacancy of the car. He had a vision of Jeffrey Archer belted into a motorized wheelchair; a pencil for writing stuck between his lips, a potted plant beside his bed; a small white card skewered onto its topmost branches; BEST WISHES, A. BOYD. "Son of a bitch. Gotcha, smartass. Wriggle and squirm all you please. You're mine."

Driving through the eerie muffled silence of the snow-covered countryside toward the expressway, Mooney gloated. "His eyes— that thing in his eyes when I said Boyd. Up until that moment he was perfect. Not a false note. Then Boyd, Wilmette and bang. That slight wince as if he'd been nipped. Son of a bitch. Two'll get you five, when the judge orders that bastard to drop his pants there'll be suture scars. A fuckin' railroad track runnin' from the back of the thigh right up into his can."

"What did he want?"

Quintius had begun to rinse off his potting tools and sponge the mud droppings from the aluminum sink top down the gurgling drain.

"Was it something to do with that awful business last week? That dreadful man?"

"In a manner of speaking."

Isobel waited, expecting more.

Quintius gazed up from the sink, cold water from the tap streaming down his mud-streaked hands.

"Well?"

"That man," Quintius went on. "What's his name?"

"Watford."

"Yes. That's it—Watford. He claims I shared a hospital room with him two years ago."

"Two years ago? You weren't in any hospital two years ago."

"I know." Quintius smiled oddly.

She watched him dry his hands with a wad of paper towels. Her face wore a petulant expression. "How odd. When two years ago?"

"May."

"Where was I?"

"London—Ruth was having the baby and you went over to help Freddy."

"Oh, yes. Of course." Her distress lightened momentarily. "But even if you had shared a room with him? What's all that supposed to mean?"

Quintius spun the spigot off and shrugged. "That detective, Mooney. The fellow who was just here. He seems to feel it implicates me in murder."

Her brow arched and she stared at him a long moment. "Murder? You?"

"Not just one, Isobel." Quintius laughed oddly. "A whole series. Six people. I'm accused of dropping cinder blocks from rooftops onto people's heads. Me? Can you imagine?"

In the next moment they were both laughing wildly. Tears streaked down Isobel's flaming cheeks.

That night at Beth Israel Hospital, Watford began to hemorrhage. His leukocyte count had nearly doubled to the point where his white blood cells so outnumbered the red that there was real danger that he would suffocate. Massive transfusions were ordered and he was immediately put on oxygen. Dr. Ramsay was called at home. Watford was not expected to last the night.

300

74

"You have no case."

"And I'm telling you I do." Mooney's face was red. He thrust a trembling finger at the district attorney, then swung it about in a half-arc to include Commissioner Dowd and Captain Mulvaney. "You're all scared. You're frightened that if this thing is opened again, you're all gonna look like jackasses. Well, you are. You've got the wrong guy."

"You haven't proved a thing by me, Mooney," Dowd thundered. "Not a goddamned thing."

"What have you given us that's new?" the district attorney asked. He was a sallow figure with bad skin, and when he spoke it was with an air of earnest but infuriating commiseration. "Let's be realistic, Frank. You don't really expect me to bring new charges with this kind of evidence?" He held up the sheaf of reports and depositions Mooney had filed over the past five years. "A man shares a hospital room with another man. Incurs injury to his thigh. Happens to cultivate exotic cactuses that bloom one night a year. The other man, a known drug addict and admittedly a kook, accuses Mr. Thigh-injury of being the Bombardier. To add to all this our key witness is presently at death's door. Now I don't mean to make light of what you say or sound facetious, Frank, but doesn't all this strike you as just a bit airy, possibly insubstantial?"

As the DA had just described the facts, it certainly did. Mooney was not about to admit that, however. "No more airy than some feebleminded retard who was railroaded . . ."

"Now just a minute . . ." Mulvaney sprang to his feet. "Railroaded."

301

"That's right. Railroaded." Mooney thumped the desk top. "I oughta know. I spoke to the poor, dumb son of a bitch."

Dowd rose to his feet. "I will not sit here and . . ."

"Sit down, Phil," the DA thundered.

"I won't sit here and be a part of this."

"Sit down, for God's sake, and let's try to act like reasonable people."

"Let him be reasonable." Dowd wagged a finger at Mooney, then slumped back into his chair. Sighing, the DA turned back to Mooney. "Now, Frank, let's hear exactly what you have to say."

"I've already said what I have to say. I say they extracted this confession from Holmes. They grilled that poor dim bulb for forty-eight hours straight. He'd have confessed to anything. The mayor's blowtorch was up your collective asses and you needed a quick patsy."

A sharp yelp went up. Mortified, the DA sprang from one to the other. "Quiet. Be quiet, for God's sake. This is a municipal office. The walls have ears." He waved his arm wildly at the bookshelves and the door leading to the anteroom beyond. "Come on, Mooney. You know that's unfair. Holmes wasn't railroaded. I was there too. I spoke with him. Simpleminded, yes. But perfectly capable of comprehending his actions. Medically sane according to the law's definition. Yes, he was questioned for a long period of time, but he had court-appointed attorneys with him every minute. You know that as well as I do. Now, you don't call that railroaded, do you?"

Mooney grumbled something and sank deeper into his chair. The DA continued: "And when the cinder block was found in the guy's apartment . . ."

"That was a setup," Mooney interrupted. "Holmes planted that there himself. The guy wanted to be indicted."

Dowd groaned and flung his hands up. "Howie, don't bother. You're talking to rock."

The DA disregarded the commissioner, continuing instead to bear down on Mooney. "I said it before, and I'll say it again, Frank. You've got no case. If you did, I'd be the first to admit my mistake and take my lumps. You ask me now to petition the Suffolk county police to physically examine Quintius for surgical scar tissue, but so far you haven't given me a scintilla of hard evidence. Not a witness. Not a fingerprint. I'm not going out to Suffolk and make a jackass of myself."

Mooney gazed around and took a last desperate fling: "What about Quintius's own confession?"

"You mean to Watford? In the hospital? That's Watford's word against Quintius's." The DA tossed his head back and laughed. "Given everything you know about Watford's history, would you

302

have the guts to bring a word of his testimony into court with you?" The DA sensed wavering convictions. He probed now for the soft points. "So what am I supposed to go back into court with—a bit of circumstantial evidence? Some mildly diverting coincidences, and Frank Mooney's gut feelings? I'm sorry, Frank. I'm afraid I have to agree with the commissioner and the chief. Unless you can bring me something more substantive than you have, I'm not going to reopen this can of worms."

Mooney sat smoldering in his chair under the collective gaze of his adversaries. He stared straight ahead, declining to meet their eyes. When at last he spoke, his voice was ominously quiet. "What about Mr. Holmes up there in Wingdale? What about him?"

"What about him?" Dowd asked. "You haven't proved the man's *not* guilty. And even if he isn't, like you say, Wingdale's probably the best break the poor bastard's had his whole misbegotten life."

"Beats sleeping on roofs," Mulvaney added.

Mooney swung his gaze round to each of them. There was a sly, suddenly defiant expression in his eye. "What if I go to the press myself? Tell my side?"

The DA leaned forward on the desk, clasping his palms before him. When he spoke again the room was very still. "You go to the media with this story, Frank, and you're all alone. Peter Quintius is a highly respected businessman with gilt-edged credentials, and a triple-A credit rating. When they hit you for libel and defamation of character, don't look this way for help. You're all by yourself out there. And this time there's no coming back in with a raise and a promotion. This time it's for keeps. Finis." He studied the effect of his words on the detective. "Believe me, Frank. Finis."

JANUARY–MAY/'83

75

Winter in New York along about the end of January is an ungodly thing. The November fun of wool socks and heavy overcoats pales quickly. Snow, once white and purifyingly beautiful, takes on a grim, used look. Sub-zero temperatures, icy blasts, and the harsh, unremitting gray of daily life in the city will break the spirit of all but the heartiest.

It was now mid-February and though spring was a mere month off, winter showed not the slightest inclination of relenting. The inclement weather continued to come, rolling vengefully down out of Canada and the Northwest. The streets outside East Seventy-third Street were coated with a brown dirty slush, surmounted by innumerable pyramids of dog droppings. All day and night mephitic steam swirled out of the sewers and up into the gloomy avenues and byways. The pavements, indifferently shoveled by reluctant building porters, glistened with small archipelagos of lethal ice that had to be negotiated by the wary walker at risk of shattered limbs.

If cold weather had disheartened Mooney, his encounter with Dowd, Mulvaney and the district attorney had just about demolished him. Torn between certain conviction that the wrong man had been charged with the cinder-block killings, and his desire to hold on, by the fingertips if need be, for the two more years that would afford him graceful retirement, he had swallowed pride, kept his mouth shut and crept back into his corner.

But winter and loss of self-esteem had taken its toll. Fritzi recognized the symptoms and without bothering to consult packed a small bag for each of them and reserved a pair of seats on an American Airlines Friday-night flight to Barbados.

When Mooney came home that evening, she huddled him protesting and muttering into a cab and off they went to Kennedy Airport. Several times he tried to get out of the cab, citing the pressing nature of his work. But Fritzi had all the answers, having first confirmed with the department that he still had several weeks of unused vacation left over from the year before.

They were in Barbados by 11:00 P.M., stepping off the plane out of February into the moist velvet warmth of a tropical night.

As they cleared customs the airport bustled with traffic. Outside, the Barbadian cabdrivers in shirt-sleeves scurried about, shouting destinations and hustling for customers.

Fritzi hailed the fellow who was piping "Discovery Bay." He was an immense, Buddha-like figure with a high voice and a glistening black moon of a face framed in the most cordial of smiles. He escorted them to his car outside, loaded them courteously into the rear, then raced back with their tickets to redeem their luggage.

They drove across the island from the airport with the windows down, through winding narrow roads lined with sugarcane and shanty villages. The soft night full of the shrill piping of tree frogs and drenched with hibiscus and oleander flooded in upon them.

In forty minutes they were at the hotel. Discovery Bay was a sprawling colonial plantation, a broad expanse of white porticoes and immaculate stone verandas, set amid the dark shadows of encroaching foliage.

Their room, a private cabana, opened directly onto the beach. In another twenty minutes they had changed clothes, swam in the warm turquoise water of an illuminated pool and were having a nightcap at the outdoor bar.

Mooney glanced over his shoulder. He looked about disparagingly but she could see that he was impressed. "They got a racetrack here?"

"For dogs, not horses."

"To bad." Mooney drained his rum punch. "Don't care much for dogs."

"Rudy and I used to come here every winter."

"Baumholz was a sport. We all know that."

"There, there," Fritzi frowned. "Do I detect a note of nastiness?"

"Well, it's true, isn't it? Think he'd approve of me?"

"Probably not. He hated cops."

"Can't say I blame him."

"And he'd certainly take a dim view of our living arrangements."

"A puritan, was he?"

"In a manner of speaking. But it never prevented him from having a good time. Rudy loved good times and woe unto the poor devil who'd try to get in the way of his."

Mooney cocked an eye at her. "That how come you shanghaied me down here? You figured I needed a good time?"

"That and a few other reasons. Number one, you look tired; and number two, you deserve a rest. I don't want to hear anything more about Mr. Quintius or Mr. Watford, or Dowd or Mulvaney or any of that lot. We're here for a week and, by God, we're going to rest and enjoy ourselves. Understood?"

"Understood." They clicked their glasses. "Now what say to another noggin of rum before bed?"

"They're about four hundred calories apiece."

"But they sure do put you in the proper frame of mind for relaxation."

She gazed at him merrily out of the corner of her eye. "Well, since it's the first night of vacation, we'll make an exception. However, let's resolve something right now. You came down here at 175 pounds and you're going back home at 175 pounds. Not an ounce more. Understood?"

"Understood." Mooney flagged the waiter.

When their drinks came they toasted each other. The warm evening, the swim and the rum had already had a salutary effect on Mooney's color. He had indeed begun to forget Quintius, Watford and all the rest. He suddenly noted how pretty Fritzi's red hair was when it was wet.

76

In the days that followed they swam, snorkled, ate moderately and gambled indifferently at the hotel casino. When they were not down at the beach, they were crisscrossing the island in a rented red Peugeot.

One day they drove north out over the Chalk Mountains up narrow, tortuous little roads slicing across the cane fields and down through little parishes dotted with ancient stone kirks and pink and green shanties, enclosed by neat white picket fences, swathed in bougainvillaea. Hens, goats and cows munched plantain and ginger lilies beside rickety porch railings. In the little villages children in immaculate blue-white uniforms straggled in column formation along the road to school.

The Peugeot climbed higher into the steep green hills, plunged down precipitous slopes, winding its noisy way through dark forests of gnarled mahogany and writhing banyan trees.

They were on a long, seemingly endless ascent now out of a damp gloomy canyon, Fritzi radiant beneath a floppy sunbonnet and Mooney, tan and beachy in faded denim Bermudas and a straw plantation hat. Cresting the hill, the engine whined in second gear. Then, suddenly, like a door opening, a wide expanse of sea loomed up ahead. They'd crossed from the Caribbean to the Atlantic and come down on the stormy northern coast of the island in the ancient parish of Bathsheba.

The days were all like that—a long unbroken succession of perfect cloudless skies, the invariable noontime shower, followed by the bright benevolent sun that browned their flesh and baked the February ache from out of their bones. After three days they had the leathery, bleached and salted look of the inveterate islander. At night they slept naked in each other's arms, the sliding glass doors opened to the flagged terrace where their bathing suits dried on the rail. The tree frogs piped and silken breezes rising off the softly lapping water murmured through the feathery branches of the pine overhead.

. Each morning on their terrace the island sparrows hopped up boldly on the breakfast table, darted at toast crumbs and dipped their beaks into the cream pitcher. Fearless, brazen, they plundered crumbs of pastry and French toast directly off the plates. At dusk, the same birds would hop about the pool, lively and playful, occasionally tipping their heads sidewards at a ninety-degree angle to drink from a thin puddle left in the tiled wake of some recent bather's dripping instep.

The Barbadian bartender who confected their predinner swizzles greeted them with a sly conspiratorial smile. He knew all about them but insisted upon calling them Mr. and Mrs. Mooney. His name was Patrice, and when they got married, suddenly, inexplicably (even to themselves), the next day, Patrice was their best man.

He came to the stone kirk in Saint James in a fresh white tropical suit and a faded blue shirt with a black tie. He carried a huge bouquet of island calla lilies, and his shiny black face beamed with wicked amusement. "I know all along. I know the moment I see you, you would do something foolish like this."

Mooney gazed in helpless wonderment at his elegant best man.

310

Standing there in the rector's office of the little kirk, he had a queer vision of the old apartment on 161 Street, with its unmade bed and the suitcases of unlaundered clothing lying all about the floor. In the space of milliseconds a multitude of images reeled off before his eye, then passed forever— Mostly they rose from the squalid wreckage of his past—police squad rooms, all-night hamburger joints, the terrifying clatter of El trains running past the windows in the frozen winter nights, cold suppers taken by himself in the stale, unventilated air of a roachy little pullman kitchen. Oddly enough, there was a sense of loss. It had been a life. It had gotten him through. Now sixty-three, he looked at Fritzi, radiant in the simple white dress she'd bought that morning in Bridgetown, and resented whatever happiness she'd known before him. Patrice laughed and strode before them while all the hurtful, angry ghosts of times past retreated sullenly from the field.

For the occasion of his marriage, Mooney wore jeans and a navy brass-buttoned blazer. The preacher who married them was a crisp slightly reproving octogenarian in black tunic and starched white dickey. His voice intoned the ancient service in a high singsong, and as Mooney slipped his old police academy ring onto Fritzi's trembling finger, the old man pronounced them man and wife.

That evening at the hotel the management laid on a wedding banquet—champagne, roast pig, okra, christophine, shrimp creole, banana cream pie and liqueurs. Hardly a Spartan regimen for a self-denying, youth-pursuing middle-aged couple, who measured out their calories each day with gram scales and coffee spoons. So it came to pass. Fritzi and Mooney were at long last one.

That night as they lay in each other's arms, he said to her, "All that crap about my health and all. You lulled me with warm weather and rum. You seduced me."

"Nothing is forever, Mooney," she murmured into the warm crook of his neck. "Anytime you want to go, you go. No lawyers. No problems. That goes for me, too. Understood?"

"Understood."

There seemed nothing further to discuss. That night, however, Watford returned to him in the form of dreams, though in what connection he was never quite sure.

The dominant image was a bubble of molten sun hanging low in the sky. Something like a mote or a fleck of dust appeared in the sun's upper-right-hand quadrant, then seemed to hurtle toward him, growing larger and larger. The scene repeated itself over and over again—that infinitesimal spot of black zooming toward him at a frightening velocity, growing, multiplying in size like some rapidly approaching meteor until it threatened to crush him.

He awoke, sitting bolt upright in bed, dazzling spokes of sun thrusting through the bamboo louvers, the sparrows and killdeers peeping and foraging on the terrace, clamoring for their breakfast.

When they departed, Mooney was a different man from the one who had arrived several days earlier, pale and harried, on a night flight from New York. Tan, almost lean, dressed in the navy business suit he'd worn down, the muscles in his face were strikingly taut.

The hotel management had presented them with a farewell bottle of French champagne. When the taxi had come to take them to the airport, Patrice pinned an orchid corsage to Fritzi's lapel. After they'd taken off, the flight attendant, who called them Mr. and Mrs. Mooney, chilled their champagne, then came back and served it.

They drank several glasses, chatting easily as the plane droned smoothly along with the white-hot tropic sun reflecting off its aluminum wings. Mooney turned and stared out at the fleecy white cumulus clouds hanging motionless in the limpid sky. Behind him he watched the green line of shore receding in the distance and had an intimation of impending misfortune. He was unaccountably sad. Fritzi had no wish to violate his privacy, but in an instant she had divined the source of difficulty.

"Quintius?" she murmured softly.

He turned and gazed at her in quiet surprise.

It was the first of March when they got back to New York. The weather was unseasonably warm and humid.

Reporting to the squad room at Manhattan South the following day, Mooney found a message from Dr. Ramsay on his desk. He called Beth Israel and was put through at once to the doctor. Watford had disappeared from the hospital. Just got up one evening and walked out. They were trying desperately to locate him. Without his daily medication, he would surely die.

Ramsay had called the sister in Pittsburgh. She had no idea where he was. She was busy and appeared to resent the call. Ramsay asked her to come to New York to help find her brother. She hemmed and hawed, was embarrassed and apologized. In the end she cried, but still she would not come. She tried to explain something about her husband, but then just hung up.

Mooney promised to get on it at once. Ramsay was grateful and offered one last detail. Watford had left Mooney a message in a sealed envelope. Should he mail it up to the precinct? No, Mooney said, he'd drop by that evening and pick it up on his way home.

It was nearly 5:00 P.M. when he arrived. Ramsay was not there, but the floor nurse recognized Mooney at once. She waved him over to the desk and handed him an envelope with his name scrawled across the front. "Dr. Ramsay left this for you."

Once again Mooney experienced that premonition of impending

misfortune as he tore open the envelope. Inside was a message written in a faint, wavery hand, so slight it appeared to be receding along with its author into time and trackless distance.

It had been written two days before, and to Mooney's great disappointment turned out to be scarcely revelatory. Just an exhortation cast in a wry, slightly ghoulish tone.

"Happy summer solstice and greetings from the grave," he said. "Don't quit now. You're ever so near."

That night and for several weeks after, squads of handpicked men went out from Manhattan South, pouring through the underbelly of the city for some clue to the whereabouts of Charles Watford.

77

Green sepals, sliver thin. The calyx clenched tight as a fist. A shudder. The sense of momentous turmoil underneath. A tremulous quake within the pod. Waves of shock radiating outward through rubbery aerial stems. A pause, as if for rest. The action resuming. The breathless exertion of birth. One of the calyx whorls pops. The seam along it starts to tear.

Shortly, the plant, nearly four feet tall, nods as if some unseen presence had just brushed past. The motion is hesitant, barely perceptible, belying the great torsion of natural forces at play behind it.

The tear along the seam descends, followed by another, then a new sepal rips along the line of the calyx. From within its loosening fist, a gash of white flashes, followed by a faint, yet vivid exhalation of something lemony, acrid. Shortly a thin fissure appears along the length of the pod. The long aerial stems appear to sway and brush past each other, then resume a kind of quivering stasis.

From within the slowly widening fissure an expanse of dazzling white is stirring. Pristine white—the white of snow before the dese-

313

cration of earth. Fringes of that white poke their unruly way through the tearing wound, forcing the side of the calyx to rupture with an audible snap. The tight white bloom within uncoils slowly through the break as though a length of silk wrapped tight as a ball were suddenly released.

The outer sepals had been green; those on the inner side were of a delicate lavender and gold. Spent and drooping, the two dangle open, then fall away.

The new bloom itself, extravagant, gleaming white, is fully thirteen inches in diameter, its petals damp and still unfurling, panting from its recent labors. The air is suddenly suffused with something heavy, overpowering, almost cloyingly sweet.

Suddenly there is a burst of applause. The flash of cameras. Cheers and laughter. The popping of a champagne cork.

"Bravo."

"Fantastic."

"Mystical. Almost religious."

"Creepy, I'd say. Something dark and awful about it. I don't like it."

"Have you never seen a foaling? It's just like that. Mysterious. Terrifying. Downright beautiful, too. How the hell did you know exactly when, Peter?"

"When? By God, he had it timed right down to the second."

"He always knows. He has it rigged. I've always suspected some hocus-pocus. Come on, Peter. Fess up."

More laughter. More uncorking. More wine. People crowding about the large terra-cotta pot where the succulent, with its extraordinary white bloom, glowed with a strange, unearthly translucence.

Peter Quintius basked in the glow of approval generated by the assembled company.

"Valuable secrets are intended for transmission only at precisely the right moment," he remarked sententiously. A wan, troubled smile played about the edges of Isobel Quintius's mouth. As friends and relatives flocked around, she sipped champagne with an air of amused distraction.

Quintius continued to answer questions evasively. Enjoying the pose of being cryptic, he preferred to create intriguing puzzles rather than shed light. He had raised the startling cactus from infant shoots, nurtured it tenderly through its first two or three uncertain years, ministered to it daily, until now it stood several feet tall, its rubbery, tentacle branches arching toward him.

The fact that his family was there to share the glory of the moment made it all that much better. Amid wife and children, brothers and nieces, nephews and grandchildren, Peter Quintius was a revered, hence deeply resented figure. The undeclared but tacitly acknowl-

314

edged godhead of the great tribe of Quintius, there were many who felt an obligation to be grateful to him.

As patriarchs go, he looked the part perfectly. Tall, whip-thin, erect as the spar of a schooner, with a rich mane of undulant white hair, he was an arresting presence. On Madison Avenue in New York, on Curzon Street in London, on the Quai D'Orsay in Paris, his prestigious Quintius Galleries, where one could purchase a Vermeer or a Van Gogh as readily as a priceless French impressionist, were unmistakably the hub of the international art market.

His work itself demanded that he live a life of conspicuous privilege. A Sixty-second Street town house in New York, an apartment in London and, of course, the ancestral seat—a seventeenth-century farmhouse high on a breeze-tossed bluff above Long Island Sound on the North Shore at Cold Spring Harbor.

The first generation of Quintiuses had come to the New Land on the earliest wave of Dutch migration in 1680. Quintius's great-great-great grandfather, Henryk, had built the farmhouse in 1683, paying at that time twelve cents an acre for each of the 130 acres he'd purchased from a Pequot chieftain called Bilbahhot. One of Quintius's most prized possessions was the original, now crumbling parchment deed that lay in the family vault at the Morgan Guaranty Trust.

Since Henryk's time generations of Quintiuses had inhabited the house, each adding to it something architecturally consonant with the original structure. Quintius himself had added porticoes and pergola-covered flagged verandas, gardens and topiary and the huge, stone and glass greenhouse cantilevered out from the rose-brick north wing built by his grandfather during the Federal period.

It was in this very greenhouse bursting with blooms of every conceivable sort—camellias, hybrid roses, row upon row of orchids—that the Quintius family had gathered shortly before midnight to observe the one-night-a-year appearance of the nightblooming cereus. The single bloom, born just before midnight, all dewy and quaking with new life, would be dead before midday tomorrow.

Each year since he'd grown it, Quintius celebrated the one-night-a-year blooming with a family party. How he was able to select the precise night of the blooming, what intuition and special affinity he enjoyed with the strange cactus, no one could say. When pressed on the subject, Quintius would nod sagely, but he would offer nothing in the way of concrete answers.

Later that evening Quintius awoke abruptly from his sleep, consumed with the notion that he'd been summoned. It was somewhere near 3:00 A.M. A thick mist came rolling in off the Sound and a foghorn boomed mournfully like some lost and stricken creature out on the water.

The wind was afoot that night. It swept in off the Sound, growling and sobbing about the corners of the house, like some sad, fretful thing full of a deep grievance it was intent upon correcting.

Quintius peered into the dark—into a room he did not at once recognize. The bed, the dresser, the small divan with a silk robe thrown across its back, the skylight above him, showing a broad expanse of star-filled sky, were all, for a fearful moment, part of a landscape utterly foreign to him. And the small delicate figure deep in sleep beneath the quilts beside him was that of a person he'd never seen before. Like a man who'd stumbled inadvertently into some stranger's world, he was frightened.

Slowly, his orientation returned. The robe across the divan he recognized as his own, and the measured breathing rising from beneath the quilt gave off the comfortably familiar scent of Isobel's nighttime creams and lotions. He was aware that his mouth seemed unnaturally dry, parched even. Then he recalled that he'd been dreaming and that it was doubtless the dream that had jarred him from sleep.

Lying in bed listening to the wind buffeting about the eaves, he tried to recall the content of the dream. The substance of it remained shadowy and elusive, but shreds and tatters of it still clung about him. The dream, he knew, involved a box. It was a plain, unpainted wooden box three feet square and three feet deep with a hinged lid. He knew nothing about the box, only that it contained something living and that whatever it was smashed and flailed about inside trying desperately to get out. Sharp cracks and fearful rending noises issued from within it. The wood shrieked and groaned, and at one point so violent was the energy thrashing about inside that the box scraped horribly over the floor and the hinges of the lid stretched to the point where the hasps holding it seemed on the verge of being ripped away.

Quintius had no idea what was in the box. At one point in the dream he threw himself across the top of the lid, using the weight of his own body to bear down upon it. The struggle continued for hours, but despite all his efforts he knew he was losing. Slowly, inexorably, the lid rose. It was at that point that he awoke.

Slightly breathless, as if from his struggles, he stared down at Isobel. There was something unspeakably sad about her there. Like a doll in a child's crib, she appeared to have been sleeping for thousands of years, just waiting there for someone to come and wake her from a spell that had been cast upon her.

The breeze had turned round into the west, causing the slats of the vertical blinds to tremble at the sill. They clicked against each other with a light hollow sound.

Outside beyond the windows, the large gardens sloping down to the water lay swathed in curling mists. The night was almost preternaturally still, an anticipatory stillness as if all life for that mo-ment—all time and even the earth's ancient rotation—were held in some breathless abeyance.

Quintius felt a sense of suffocating weight on his chest. There was within him a sense of dread, combined with a strange exaltation. Something was about to happen, he knew. Something within him was bursting to get out.

An owl hooted in the trees outside. The foghorns boomed and the long slat blinds clicked hollowly against each other. The sense of suf-focation and unspecified rage swelled once again in Quintius's chest. In the next moment he was up, moving about in the chill damp of the room, slipping into a robe and slippers, then stepping out into the cold corridor. Once up and going, Quintius moved with remarkable purpose, like a man governed by strong inner directives which under no circumstances were to be denied.

On the bar in his library one of the magnums of unfinished cham-pagne sat in a bucket of melting cubes. Standing there in the close-muffled dark, a tremor rippled up the length of his right leg as he poured a glass for himself by the light of the moon. It was a full moon—white as rime and ringed with a ghostly halation. A hunter's moon, Quintius thought, lapping tentatively at the wine which had grown tepid and flat.

In those gray, slowly shifting shadows, he gave the impression of a thirsty dog refreshing itself at a pool of brackish water. Then, refill-ing his flute with the dregs of the bottle, he maundered through the wide French doors of the library and out onto the flagged terrace. Old rattan chairs and chaises stood about in the shadows beneath a pergola thatched with the dry lacy stalks of unbloomed clematis.

Turning his robe collar up against the mizzling predawn chill of the hour, he sipped the flat, sourish wine, and stared down over the expanse of sprawling gardens toward the Sound. Though the water was not visible through the fog, he could hear its sound lapping at the pylons of the dock several hundred feet away. Farther out, a buoy bell tolled somewhere out on the dark water.

Quintius tipped his flute back and drained the warm, sour fluid. Grimacing slightly, he set the glass down on a marble table and stepped down off the patio flags onto the cold damp grass.

His tread, stiff and unhurried, cut a slurred trail through the misted grass. The path he was carving at the moment led unswerv-ingly to the low, sprawling greenhouse up ahead where an image of the moon hung trapped in huge plates of skylight glass.

Once inside Quintius felt better. The sweet, dizzy fragrance of lush growth, the earthy smell of peat moss and manure all had a salutary effect upon him. They had the power to subdue the querulous, bickering voices that had beset him all that day. Suddenly his expression appeared more relaxed, more reconciled. Moving through the orangery to the area where his huge collection of succulents were housed, there was no longer the unrelenting gnaw, that vexing sense of doubt and incompletion.

Here in the moon-dappled shadows of the greenhouse, his huge collection of cactus grew, virtually every species known to man. Over the years Quintius had collected and cataloged them all—the large *Euphorbia candelabras,* the *Opuntias,* some twenty-five species of Noto Cactus from South America, the gnarled Lithops from southwest Africa, almost forty-four species of *Kleinia tomentosa, Echinocactus,* and a grandly awesome *Cereus peruvianus monstrosus* thrusting upward thirty feet so that it brushed the greenhouse ceiling. Then Aloes, some three hundred species, and *Agaves,* and finally, above all, his beloved climbing, throbbing, pulsing nightbloomers.

Cryptocereus anthonyanus, Anthony's rick-rack; *Hylocereus undatus,* the Honolulu queen; *Selenicereus werklei,* moon goddess—it would bloom in another night or so, he judged. Then *Selenicereus urbanus,* moon cereus—it would burst its calyx late in the month— Then his own special favorite, now fully bloomed, quivering, radiant, dominating all others by its sheer extravagance, but its life already half over—queen of the night, *Selenicereus grandiflorus,* night-blooming cereus.

Standing before it, Quintius closed his eyes and inhaled deeply the sweet, slightly citrine breath. He gulped it, ingesting the essence of the plant as if he were partaking of special magical properties. Shortly his eyes closed and he rocked slowly back and forth as if in prayer.

78

All was not well between the Quintiuses. In the nearly five months since the snowy evening of Mooney's visit, they had quarreled incessantly. The crux of contention was the charge the detective had leveled at Quintius. Mrs. Quintius was unable to grasp why her husband had failed to answer the charge or even to seek advice from his attorneys. Quintius maintained that he was reluctant now to reopen something which appeared to have quietly closed of its own accord. Quite reasonably, he had an absolute horror of dragging the gallery and the family name through the mud.

At first Mrs. Quintius was puzzled; later she was angry and thereafter, a little frightened. When the situation between them had become intolerable, they agreed that she would go to London for a few weeks in May with her son Frederick on a buying trip. It would give them both a breather—time to think. Later, when she returned, they would decide on a course of action.

Before leaving she made Quintius promise that he would see their lawyers the moment she got back.

The morning of her departure he drove her out to the airport. When they kissed good-bye, she seemed worried and preoccupied. She couldn't bring herself to tell him how sad it made her to see him look so distraught. She knew he had not slept well for weeks and that he no longer enjoyed food. She knew that he dwelled morbidly on the senseless death of their elder son, Billy, blaming himself for everything that had happened, and then this wildly outrageous charge. And that awful man Watford and the detective.

Alone back at the house (he'd given the elderly German caretaker

319

and his wife two weeks' paid vacation), he sat down to wrestle with the problem himself.

Isobel would be home in a fortnight. As far as seeing their attorneys, he knew, she could not be put off much longer. The fact that he had already delayed so long only served to arouse greater suspicion.

Somewhat more ominous was the fact that several times during the past month or so, as the weather had steadily warmed, he had seen the detective. Twice in the area of the gallery as he'd gone out to lunch; twice on the rush-hour platform as he boarded the Huntington express, and then once again while returning to the gallery from an estate auction on the Upper East Side. Taking no special pains to be furtive, the detective was there, presumably shadowing him, watching and waiting, dogging his steps, flaunting his presence as if he could bluff Quintius into making some ultimately incriminating move.

"The dominant suit is Pentacles."

"Is that good?"

"It's masculine."

"Thank heavens for that."

"It's the money suit. High finance. Industry. Enterprise. Progress. That sort of thing."

"Not artistic?"

"Not remotely."

Laughter and chatter. The clink of glasses. The quiet orderly hum of dinner being served. The young couple seated at the table across from Quintius appeared to be lovers. Though the restaurant was Japanese, the fortune-teller was not. She was not even Oriental. More probably Middle-European.

Glancing at her incuriously, Quintius judged she might be on the sunny side of forty. He frowned at the kerchief and bangles, the multiple rings on her fingers, the absurd little panatela tossed in for effect as she shuffled the tarot deck around the tabletop.

"Shall I continue?" she asked.

The young man laughed. "By all means."

Quintius plucked up a sea urchin with his chopsticks, dipped it into a mixture of soy and wasabi and ate, washing it down with hot sake. All the while his anger mounted.

"Your significator is the King of Pentacles," the irritating singsong of the tarot reader drifted back upon him. She held up the card for the young man to see. It had a picture of an aged patriarch, a crown on his head and a scepter in his lap. He was seated on a pig, and in his right hand he held aloft a pinwheel or pentacle. "His number is sixty-four in the deck," the reader trilled. "He's what is called a 'dark man,' meaning mysterious."

"Oh, is he?" the young woman laughed.

"But it's not mystery in the ordinary sense," the reader shook her head, causing her silver loop earrings to tinkle lightly. "It's mystery in the sense of ambiguity. For instance, the 'dark man' is associated with courage and success, but also passions of a dangerous and ungovernable sort."

The slightly mocking smile on the young man's face appeared to droop. He had gradually begun to fall under the reader's spell. So had Quintius, who, all the while he plucked with his chopsticks at the slivers of raw fish, had fastened almost hungrily on her voice.

"Your suit cards," the reader continued, "are the Six of Swords, Four of Cups, Knight of Scepters, Five of Pentacles."

The reader squinted through a whorl of thick smoke from her panatela and shuffled cards once more about the table. "Ah, now you see your trumps—Il Bagatto, the juggler, and . . . Il Motto, the fool."

The girl began to laugh, caught something in the reader's eye and then thought better of it.

The reader flashed her quick, mirthless smile. "The Four of Cups, reversed here, stands for new acquaintance. Not necessarily desirable, I would judge from this suit. The Knight of Scepters is a sad card. It means disunion, rupture, discord. Conceivably tragedy."

Quintius's ears pricked. His jaw slowed. He sipped more sake, feeling the hot astringent fluid at the back of his throat as he strained forward to hear the reader.

"Your Five of Pentacles suggests a deep sense of loss, of grieving, some center of sorrow you have as yet been unable to resolve. Something you deeply regret? The Knight of Scepters here indicates some dark, unhappy destiny."

The young couple stared back at the reader, baffled and a bit surprised.

"What do the picture cards mean?" the young man asked.

The reader seemed reluctant to discuss them, but then sighed and resumed. "They represent dominant personality traits. "Il Bagatto, the juggler, symbolizes will, often of an immoral sort. Il Motto, the fool, impulsiveness. The total picture is that of a highly successful man, in the temporal sense, of course, but one whose feelings, whose deepest emotions are blocked, thereby transforming themselves into something destructive. In this man are violent tides of passion. Ungovernable rages. Dark, unfathomable depths which he himself is unwilling to plumb."

The reading concluded simultaneously with Quintius's dinner. His red lacquer box of raw fish and rice was empty, his sake flask drained.

He sat back now as the waiter poured steaming green tea into his cup.

After the young couple had paid her, the reader rose and left them. She started toward the opposite side of the room, then paused and stared hard at Quintius as if taking his measure. Even before she'd made a move in his direction, he knew she would come. Beneath the table, his hands clenched.

"Is there anything I can do for you this evening, sir?"

Quintius stared fixedly down into his empty red lacquer box. When at last he looked up, he found himself gazing into the smiling, hooded eyes of the fortune-teller, the panatela poised between her jeweled fingers. "A card reading? Perhaps a palm?" From across the narrow table he caught a blast of her smokey breath.

Quintius shook his head from side to side. "No—I think not." He tossed a wad of bills on the table and stalked out.

It was too late to go back to Cold Spring Harbor. He decided instead to stay overnight at Sixty-second Street. He felt poorly. The pain above his eyes he took to be the result of too much sake. Also, he was now troubled with a faintly oppressive sense of fullness in his chest. A walk, he felt, would have a salutary effect.

It was a balmy spring evening and the air along the river had a thick, scorched feeling, the result of incinerators and fog. The hour was roughly 10:00 P.M., the hour of panhandlers and dog walkers. People strolled with their pets up and down the avenue, pausing to chat with neighbors around hydrants and sewer openings.

Quintius walked fast, a man with a mission, bound for some special destination.

At one point he turned to look over his shoulder as though he were certain he was being followed. When he reached the fashionable brownstone at East Sixty-second Street, he didn't go directly up. Instead, he continued to walk at a brisk clip along the river, attempting to exorcise through physical exertion his sense of vague, unspecified dread. On the river promenade he stood by the dilapidated railing and watched the barges slip noiselessly over the inky black water. Their green-red running lights had the look of something phantasmagoric. Attempting to focus his vision on those fleeting, wraithlike lights, they ceased to be fixed points of illumination, changing instead into huge daubs and splashes of paint in the process of chaotic application.

He turned quickly from the railing and hurried off the promenade, away from the barge lights and the lambent flicker of streetlights dancing on the inky water.

Back again at East Sixty-second Street, he bounded up the front steps, then stood outside the door rummaging in his pockets for a key. At that hour lights still streamed warmly out onto the street from nearby apartments and town houses. But his house, its full three stories plunged in darkness, reeked of something ominous and vaguely inhospitable.

Opening the front door he peered into the thick shadows of the small foyer as if listening for something. For a moment he hovered on the threshold, uncertain whether or not to go in. Something made him turn to see if he were being observed. It was at that moment that he saw in the light of a streetlamp across the way the big, rumpled silhouette of Francis Mooney.

He stood there in a wide circle of illumination, brazenly regarding Quintius. For a time, Quintius stared back, half-inclined to go out and confront him. But instead, with a shrug, he stepped into the stale hush of the old town house and locked the door behind him.

Once inside, he undressed quickly and got into bed. But he was too rattled to sleep. Instead he lay in the dark, staring at the strange play of lights on the ceiling.

Ghosts and chimeras swarmed through his fevered brain. Fantastic speculations he played out to their most catastrophic extremes. Then, unaccountably, there in the mottled pattern of light and shadow on the ceiling, the face of his dead son materialized slowly like a photographic image wavering in a bath of developing fluid. It was he unmistakably, not as a grown man, but as he looked as a boy—glowing, vibrant, full of mischief and goodwill, all the world before him.

Quintius turned and buried his fevered face in the pillow. Alone in the vacant, airless shadows of the old town house that had been in the Quintius family for well over eighty years, he could hear Billy's laughter ring out and the ghostly, plangent sound of a Scarlatti sonata played on a harpsichord by his grandaunt Mathilde. Now Mathilde was gone and Billy was gone and the harpsichord, unplayed for decades, gathered dust in the library.

79

The building he'd selected was 356 West Forty-eighth, between Eighth and Ninth avenues. It was ·a vintage twenties, seven-story walkup, built out of grimy brown brick with rows of rusty fire escapes facing out onto the street. Though its occupants were mainly welfare recipients, there was still a hard core of blue-collar Italian-Polish tenants whose families had been in residence there for decades. The building clung doggedly to some notion of clean, albeit shabby, respectability. Geranium pots flourished on the windowsills, and refuse cans, lined up neatly on the curb out front, awaited the trash collector.

There was an Italian bake shop at the corner. Just in from there was an electrical contractor whose storefront windows were decorated austerely with no more than a parched and badly wilted leopard plant. Cheek by jowl to a storefront palmist and fortune-teller was a junk consignment shop with a dilapidated Morris chair squatting forlornly out front.

In the middle of the block the street boasted four small restaurants known to theatergoers for good, moderately priced food and fast service. One was French, one was Greek, one was Cuban and the other was a landmark New York City steakhouse. On any night of the week the lights burned late in the vicinity of 356 West Forty-eighth, and one could depend upon there being people in the streets well up until 2:00 A.M.

The roof of 356 was a typical tar-topped affair with glass transoms, sooty chimneys and a cluttered maze of wash lines and TV antennas. Several of the lines sagged beneath the burden of drying wash. Stepping out on the roof he smelled at once the combination of starch and strong soap wafting across at him from the gently billowing sheets.

There was an elevator but he had taken the precaution of walking up the seven flights to the roof so as to preclude the possibility of encountering anyone. Once up there he pushed the badly scored metal door open and stepped out onto the tar. Having lugged the forty pounds of mortar up with him, he was winded, but at the same time he experienced that keen exhilaration he invariably felt at such moments, not unlike the sort of itchy anticipatory excitement one associates with making love.

It had grown somewhat cooler. A gusty wind barreled in off the river, making the sheets and undergarments rise and fall eerily on the washlines.

He stood for a time with his back to the brick wall beside the roof door. Propping the shopping bag against his leg, he waited for his eyes to adjust to the dark. Off to the east, the glowing sky above the theater district had darkened to a pale cinnabar, like dying ingots. At this elevation the distant rumble of traffic moving up and down Eighth Avenue sounded strangely like the sea. Just ahead of him and coming from beyond the low concrete coping, voices wafted upward from the street. There were laughter and people emerging from restaurants. A taxi horn blared. The sounds carried upward with a vivid, ringing clarity.

He stood there awhile longer, the weight of the shopping bag leaning against his leg like something living and sentient. He waited, as if for some special signal certifying that conditions were precisely right.

The wind gusting in off the river smelled of fish and carried with it a faint hint of sewerage. Closing his eyes, it made him think of Holland, his beloved Terschelling. Across the spate of years he could see the little Frisian village where he was born, the green, foam-marbled sea rolling up the long, pebbled strand, the windmills like tall sentinels staring silently out toward the gray horizon. Inhaling deeply, gulping air, he sensed his respiration quicken, and when he reached down to grasp the handles of the shopping bag, it occurred to him that he was transcendentally happy.

He had not even been aware of it when he'd taken the first few steps, pushed off as it were from the secure anchorage of the wall behind him. It was as if something infinitely benevolent had transported him these first few critical steps of his journey. Some twenty yards ahead, the white concrete coping that ran along the top of the parapet gave off a faint luminescence. Just forward of him and to the right an incinerator shaft rose some fifteen feet into the air. In the darkness it had the squat primitive look of something ancient, wrought from rubble and boulders, like a druidical monument around which dark rites had once been celebrated. Sparks and cinders crackled upward out of its mouth, indicating that it had recently been fired. Even at forty feet he could feel the heat of its scorched breath on his cheek and feel in his stomach its deep chthonic rumble.

Moving toward the strangely glowing white line of coping, the weight of the sack pulled his shoulder down so that he appeared to walk slightly hunched and off-kilter. But his head was light and he was suffused with a growing sense of imminent, almost transfiguring, joy. The shaft, however, as he came closer to it, gave him pause. The rumble from deep within it grew louder and a haze of some indefinable stench encircled it. It made him think of a large animal that had just fed.

As he approached the shaft, moving on that undeviating path toward the parapet, something appeared to detach itself from the shaft. It was as if a part of its dark silhouette had suddenly broken off, rolled out of the shadows directly into his path and stood there awaiting him. It was a man. Or at least it seemed to be a man. He couldn't be certain, but the appearance of it stopped him dead in his tracks. The figure stood just on the perimeter of the shadow of the shaft, the only illumination the sparks rocketing sporadically above it.

He was not in the least frightened. But the unwelcome sudden appearance of this impediment annoyed him. Why was it there now? Why did it block his way?

"What do you want? What are you doing here?" he demanded, as if the person were an intruder on the roof while he himself had every right to be there.

The figure remained silent.

"Who are you? What do you want?"

The figure never moved. They stood there, the two of them regarding each other. He could hear the faint high whisper of the person breathing in the shadows.

The sack in his hand grew heavy. The heat and ashen stench from the mouth of the shaft became increasingly unpleasant. "Who are you? What are you doing up here?"

Still the figure did not move. He made a move toward it, then heard suddenly a kind of deep, muffled groan from the shadows. It was then that some of his elation began to pall. A burst of laughter and departing voices wafted upward over the parapet. Car doors slammed. He started to withdraw, moving backward toward the roof door. It was then that the figure also began to move, as if tethered to him on a line, following him slowly out of the shadows.

"What do you want? You want money?" He took his wallet from inside his jacket and tossed it at the figure. It glanced off him and fell to the floor with a dull thud. But the figure didn't stop to pick it up. Still he could not see the person, only the outline of someone quite large.

Moving backward toward the door, he nearly stumbled but quickly regained his balance. It all had an air of something preordained—as if the figure stalking him had been doing so for years and now at last their paths had finally intersected. The burlap sack in his hand grew heavier, but he would not put it down. He intended to use it as a weapon for defense, if need be. Still, he was not frightened.

"Look, I don't want trouble. But if you come near me, I'm going to start shouting. The police will be up here in a minute."

It all sounded a bit hollow, even to him. If, indeed, he did shout and the police were to come and find him up there with the shopping bag and the cinder block, what then? Shouting for help was simply out of the question.

In the next moment he turned and bolted for the door. A scuffle of steps grated over the tar top behind him. Something like a wind brushed past and ahead of him, then placed itself squarely between himself and the door. His heart pounded wildly and for the first time that evening he had a premonition that something awful was about to happen to him.

Light streamed onto the roof from several apartments across the way. In the thin shaft of one he saw the topmost fire escape from the apartment just below the coping and lunged for that. The moment he did, the feet came scurrying behind him, chasing him with a sound not like human feet, but rather like something padded, swift and strangely feral.

He wheeled sharply and hefted the shopping bag above his head. Threatening his assailant, once again he started back toward the illuminated area where the fire escape still offered a way out.

"Leave me alone," he snarled. He kept inching backward toward the white line of coping, not daring to take his eyes off the figure moving inexorably closer. "Leave me alone. Do you hear? What do you want? You want money? I have a wristwatch. Here." He yanked the sterling silver expansion band off his wrist and flung the watch hard at the man. It glanced off his chest and fell to the tar with a dull chink. Still he kept coming.

He was within five feet of the roof's edge when the figure suddenly entered a pale crescent of light cast from one of the nearby apartments. A cat squealed from somewhere and scurried off. Then he saw him, or it, or whatever it was, for he never actually saw the face of his assailant. All he could make out was a tall, rangy figure, its rippling muscularity emphasized by a black, skintight rubber surfing suit. The costume was finished off with white sneakers and a white baseball cap. Incomprehensibly, the face was covered with a vintage World War II gas mask, giving the appearance in that pale blue half-light of a skull. The mask still had its nasal hose and canister attached. The large cellophane lenses in the eyeholes regarded him

327

with a blank, pitiless expression. In his hand the figure carried a pike, easily six feet, at the end of which the blade of a bayonet or large machete glinted in the dark.

A sort of muffled grunt, like nothing human, issued from behind the mask, and suddenly he felt a cold sting where the blade had flashed up and nicked his cheek. He staggered backward toward the parapet, dabbing incredulously at the warm trickle of blood that had started to flow from the area below his eye.

The head tilted at an odd angle, the blank expressionless face of the mask appeared to regard him inquisitively. Then the pike flashed upward and the figure lunged again. The blade glanced with a loud ping off the shopping bag which he held up before him like a shield.

The figure lunged again, driving him closer to the edge. In an effort to avoid the low coping, he wheeled sharply and bolted. The figure sprinted after him with a loping, almost balletic, grace, all the while goading him back toward the edge with the pike.

Again the blade caught him, this time on the wrist, then in rapid-fire succession, opening a thin gash on the other cheek. A quick, cold flick like an adder's tongue, and at once he felt something wet and warm leak into his collar.

Several times he attempted to maneuver himself away from the edge, but each time the blade at the end of the pike flashed and his cheek or hand were laid open at another point. He tried vainly to evade each thrust, but the cinder block he held up before him had grown excruciatingly heavy and the person wielding the pike was far too agile. In a matter of moments, while the two of them moved round each other in that fatal dance, his hands and cheeks were quickly scored with blood.

Shortly, the weight of the block and the effort to fend off the pike had taken its toll. He was being remorselessly worn down. Slowly, methodically, the masked figure maneuvered him toward the brink of the parapet. Jousting, locked in fatal combat like a pair of pugilists, no word passed between them. Only the grunts and panting beneath the sooty, indifferent sky.

The back of his calves grazed the coping. He stumbled and suddenly sat, kicking out, catching the dark figure on the shin. Something like a yelp issued from behind the mask and the figure faltered, went down on one knee. For the space of a moment the path to the roof door was open. But he was far too spent to rebound. Instantly the figure was up again, moving back at him with a slurred, ponderous strike, like a person trying to wade fast through high water.

He struggled to his feet. In a single leap the figure bounded at him close enough for him to see the eyes, not like anything recognizably human, behind the plastic lenses. The blade flashed, and he whimpered as it caught his throat, then sliced down through the collar of his shirt. His legs buckled momentarily. He leaned forward, grasping the shaft of the pike with his one free hand, pushing it against the chest of his assailant. Locked hard against each other, he could hear those strangely muffled grunts from behind the mask. At one point their faces were so close that he could feel the warm, meaty breath of the man against his cheek.

Exhausted, he fell backward, watching warily the pike inscribe a wide swooping arc as it descended like a bird through the half-moon of illumination at the roof's edge. The blade, however, made no contact. It only served to drive him back farther against the coping. The mask peering at him appeared to reflect, for a fraction of a second, an odd pity, as if the individual behind it had no more love for the task it was there to perform than the victim upon whom it was to be inflicted. The figure, lithe and pantherine, came on remorselessly, forcing him ever backward toward the edge.

The weight of the cinder block in his arms grew agonizing. Intending to smash it down on the man's head, he stepped backward and up onto the coping for maximum purchase. Wobbling unsteadily, he caught a quick glimpse of the yellow roof of a parked cab and then the dimly lit abyss of Forty-eighth Street looming up from below.

Suddenly the skull-like face of the mask was very close.

"I'm sorry," he addressed it directly, unaccountably apologetic. "I never meant . . ." The pike flashed. He felt himself goaded ever so gently as he stepped over into the air, watching the bright yellow roof of the cab racing upward toward him.

80

Mooney was there moments later. Searching frantically up and down back streets in the area, he'd heard the sirens of patrol cars rushing to the site where already a small, hushed knot of spectators had gathered.

Even before he'd gotten close enough to verify the fact, he knew perfectly well what the humped and twisted thing lying in the mound on the pavement was. What he finally saw was quite badly mangled. The roof of the cab where he'd struck it and bounced off onto the street was crumpled. If Mooney himself had not seen Quintius shortly before, leaving his town house, hailing a cab and dressed in the same gray pinstripe and sea-green tie, there would have been no chance that he could ever make an identification from what remained of the face. Where the parietal quadrant of the skull had been shattered, that part of the face directly beneath had collapsed inward. A bubble of gray, quivering cortical matter extruded itself through the rupture, while the lower half of the face was splashed with clots of gore. There was an irony, Mooney thought, in such an impeccable man terminating in such an untidy fashion.

Incomprehensibly, the cinder block, still in the burlap shopping bag, lay canted up against the right side of Quintius's head. Though it seemed inconceivable, it appeared that his head had been smashed beneath one of his own concrete bombs. Since Mooney himself had seen him carry the very same shopping bag out of the town house, there was little doubt he'd taken it up onto the roof with him. The question remained, How had it landed on his head? Had he himself either jumped or accidentally fallen from the roof while still holding the package? In either case he'd held onto it all the way down. The other possibility was that someone had thrown it down after Quintius had bounced from the roof of the cab and miraculously scored a direct hit. The latter explanation Mooney discounted as highly improbable.

It was only after the radio officer from the 33rd Precinct had thrown an old rubber slicker over the body that Mooney noted the hands. They stuck out from beneath the edge of the slicker, palms opened, facing upward, arms extended wide like an ancient icon in a gesture of supplication.

Both hands were smeared and running with blood. As one might expect from the massiveness of the head injuries, there was a great deal of blood splashed liberally about. To the casual observer, bloodied hands might not have signified anything in particular. But it was the pattern of bleeding on the hands that had caught Mooney's eye—not splashed randomly as is generally the case, but striated— long, even streaks as if the hands had been clawed. When the forensic people arrived, Mooney asked pointedly to have those streaks checked out during the autopsy. He also gave instructions that the lower torso of the cadaver be examined for recent surgical scars.

Later, when the body had gone off in the morgue van, Mooney went up to the roof with several of the men from the 33rd. They

330

found the wallet immediately and the wristwatch shortly after. The wallet lay open, several hundred dollars and all credit cards still intact.

Mooney scoured the area directly above the point where Quintius's body had been found. On the white coping it was easy to see the fresh spatterings of blood. So he was bleeding before he hit the earth and that appeared to suggest that the cuts on Quintius's hands were self-inflicted. But after a search of one hour, they were unable to find the knife or weapon with which the wounds had been made. There was no sign of foul play. Quintius's wristwatch and wallet with all valuables intact discounted the possibility of robbery.

To Mooney's facile detective mentality, it seemed almost too clear that Quintius's death added up to suicide. Despondent over the death of his son, haunted by guilt and the knowledge that he was now a prime suspect in the rooftop slayings, had driven the man to that desperate act. Jumping with one of his own "bombs," making it the instrument of his own destruction, Mooney reasoned, was Quintius's twisted way of seeking some kind of poetic retribution.

Leaving the roof with the first gray streaks of dawn, Mooney cast his eyes round once more for a final look at the scene. After nearly six years, the case of the Phantom Bombardier appeared to be at an end. Still, Mooney was filled with a troubled sense of incompletion, of questions unanswered.

Across the way a sheet on one of the laundry lines rose gently and billowed outward. The sparks from the incinerator shaft had ceased to fly upward and its sooty brick walls had cooled now in the fresh morning breeze.

Epilogue

The content of our dreams is mostly a by-product of our unremark-able daily struggles transformed by night and electrochemicals into the terrifying shape of nightmares. In fretful sleep Mooney dreamed often of Watford, seeing the sad, puzzled boyish smile behind which lurked the treacherous schemer.

Now he was dead, having expired peacefully in a Bowery flop-house euphemistically called the Ritz. With no family or any next of kin willing to claim the body, it was sent directly to the morgue. Aside from the usual mortuary staff and the drab city functionaries hovering like crows above the open grave in potter's field, Mooney was the only person to attend the last rites who'd actually known him.

He'd been identified from photographs sent pro forma from the morgue to all city police precincts, along with the requisite set of prints for purposes of identification. Mooney recognized him the moment he saw him even though the eyes in the photo were closed and the face covered with a heavy beard. The name given on the cir-cular was Walter Denton. Having lived virtually all his life as some-one else, running true to form right up to the end, Watford chose to die that way. He clearly found the promise and hope of a different identity—any identity—preferable to his own. Camouflage and mas-querade were perhaps his truest colors.

In waking life, however, Mooney thought a great deal about Quin-tius, whose violent ending had posed more questions for him than it had resolved. A puzzle within a puzzle.

Responding to his query regarding the curious pattern of slashes he'd observed on Quintius's hands, the medical examiner not only verified the slashes during autopsy, but at the same time also discovered at least sixteen additional such wounds in the area of the face and throat.

At the time of the incident Mooney had not seen the face. Much of it, of course, had been shattered from the impact of the fall and covered with blood. "Light superficial scratches," was how the ME protocol described the wounds. "A millimeter in width, and probably two millimeters in depth. Barely deep enough to draw blood. Inflicted by a sharp, thin-bladed instrument. Possibly a razor. Probably self-inflicted. Cause of death, probable suicide," the medical examiner concluded.

All well and good for the medical examiner, Mooney brooded, but no one had ever found the "thin-bladed instrument," although a concerted effort had been made to recover it from the area. Nor had such an "instrument" been found on Quintius's person. If this were suicide, where, then, had it gone?

Still uneasy with the ME's report, Mooney sought out the advice of his old friend, Dr. Baum, the police psychiatrist, who concurred with the medical examiner's determination of suicide. He characterized the strange pattern of slash marks on Quintius's hands and face as part of an elaborate "ceremonial self-castration." Mooney smiled wisely and a bit wearily to himself and left.

At that point the detective was content to let it ride, though he had many doubts about what had transpired in those final moments just before Peter Quintius fell, jumped or was pushed from the roof. Had it not been for the wounds on his face and hands, Mooney might have gladly put his mind at ease with a finding of suicide or possibly accidental death. To the detective, at least, the self-inflicted cuts made no sense whatever. They were precisely the type of wounds consistent with those generally seen on a man trying to defend himself from an assailant's knife. Mooney knew quite well the small subculture of outcasts, mostly harmless, but occasionally dangerous, who were known to inhabit rooftops above the city. Quintius might very well have had the misfortune of a chance encounter with one of the latter. If such were the case, what an irony indeed. It certainly did not look like suicide to Mooney.

For a fleeting moment the notion passed through Mooney's mind that it might have been Watford with whom Quintius had his fatal encounter on the roof. In much the same way he had tracked Quintius to Cold Spring Harbor, why could not Watford in his final days have shadowed the art dealer until their paths converged on the rooftop?

But, of course, that was impossible. Mooney had in his desk drawer a medical examiner's report that set Watford's death several days before that of Quintius. What had truly transpired that night would probably remain a mystery forever. Several times Mooney's detective's curiosity half-tempted him to go back to the area and question the neighbors. At last he did, only to discover that over recent weeks residents of the building on several occasions had reported to the police the appearance of a strangely attired man on the rooftops. Some described him as large and in a leotard or possibly a jogging suit. A woman claimed to have been threatened by him while hanging her laundry. All reports had apparently gone unheeded.

The most satisfying news of all, however, was a simple two-line disclosure buried deep within the ME's official protocol revealing the fact that a surgical scar nearly six inches long and approximately two years old had been found in the upper area of the right femur just below the buttock.

At last Mooney was able to accept the closing of the books, overjoyed at all the embarrassment it brought to Dowd and Mulvaney. In the days immediately following Quintius's death, numerous accounts appeared in the newspapers and on TV. The demise of so notable a figure under such bizarre circumstances could not fail to provoke a great deal of attention. What was a man of Peter Quintius's lofty station doing on a rooftop in such an improbable area and at that hour? No one seemed to know. Furthermore, the matter of the cinder block that had either made the trip down with him, or followed shortly thereafter, immediately resurrected the specter of the Phantom Bombardier.

During that fateful week both Dowd and Mulvaney were subjected to grueling interviews by the press. Potentially embarrassing questions were asked. Time and time again the police insisted that no link existed between the death of Peter Quintius and the activities of the Bombardier. Only once did a reporter, a brash and impolite young man from *The Village Voice* suggest that Quintius and the Bombardier might be one and the same.

The commissioner discounted at once such a fanciful notion, maintaining as he had all along, that the Bombardier who had terrorized the city for five years and had been responsible for the death of six people and the permanent crippling of another, was now tucked safely away behind brick and mortar in a maximum security ward of the state facility at Wingdale, where he would undoubtedly spend the rest of his life. Quintius was a separate and wholly unrelated matter. If, indeed, he was the victim of foul play, the cinder block found beside him was probably a crude copycat attempt or, possibly even someone's warped idea of a joke. If it was, it was a particularly ghoulish one.

The dossier of circumstantial evidence Mooney had compiled over the years in the Bombardier case, along with the incontrovertible fact of the shattered cinder block found beside Quintius the night he died, were discreetly impounded in the police archives and never made available to the press. The district attorney drove a final nail into that coffin by impounding the records for a period of seventy-five years. Since no one was going to leap to Gary Holmes's defense, the matter, to all intents and purposes, was closed.

In any event, Mooney no longer cared. To his mind, the job was done. Fritzi and the Balloon and Gumshoe were more than enough to fill his days. They filled, in fact, far more. He had carried about emptiness for so long, had grown so accustomed to the daily sensation of inner vacancy, he couldn't fathom that life might ever be anything other than that until, that is, Mrs. Baumholz had come along and shown him otherwise.

Cornet fanfares. Horses surging at the post. A bell rings. The gates bang open with a loud clash. The stands rise to a tumultuous roar.

Mooney and Fritzi stood down on the field amidst a number of other horse owners. Gumshoe had been running route races lately, somewhat unevenly at the beginning, but with a nice and steadily improving consistency. His PP's showed that he had won two out of his three previous starts at three-quarters of a mile. At the six-furlong mark of his last race he was ahead three lengths. At today's six fur-longs he appeared to be right up to the mark.

The Mooneys had carefully studied the field. The only horse that might trouble Gumshoe was Anthropos, who'd earned an 87 in his next-to-last start at this length.

Gumshoe looked like a prime bet that afternoon. Trained by a good if not stupendous trainer, he was in outstanding condition and would pay no less than $6.40 to win, a price that wouldn't break the bank at Monte, but was nothing to sneeze at.

Breaking smartly from his post position of number 5, with several speed horses inside of him, he was not quite fast enough to get the lead on the rail. But he was running well in third position and had it in him to run beautifully in the stretch.

Fritzi resplendent beside him, Gumshoe down front going flat-out in full panoply—the bright little Spanish jockey Sanchez, florid in green Irish silks, holding third position and closing on second, life seemed a dream to the detective. The race was a dream. A distant roar and clash—one he'd run often before and invariably lost.

As the field thundered past, the roar behind him was deafening. At the quarter pole Gumshoe had fallen back to fourth position, running 12^7. Now at the half he was at 26, having regained third position. Mooney and Fritzi were on their feet, shouting at the top of their lungs.

The blood punched along Mooney's veins just as fiercely as it did in those of the wonderful yearling streaking up the course. Pounding past them, Gumshoe closed the gap between second and third position, coming up fast on Anthropos. A big dapple-gray filly called Spanish Main was running third, a ghostly white blur eating up the track with terrifying piston strides.

Suddenly, the yearling was astride Anthropos, running for a full furlong nose to nose, the proud, graceful sweep of their necks conforming with the track's curve. A voice on the crackling loudspeaker screamed above the din, and it seemed to Mooney that the stands behind him were about to buckle and crash down upon their heads.

He didn't dare turn or look back for fear he might break the eerie state of communion he'd established between himself and the noble creature racing its heart out for him. An unearthly sensation—the horse and himself, suddenly one. He could feel something palpable between them, an invisible tether born of some mutual sense of shared loneliness within all those who have contended.

Tail streaking, legs rising pistonlike, puffs of powder flung backward like cannon shot off his hind hooves, the horse came out of the second turn neck and neck with Anthropos and turned down to face the grinding 1300 feet of the final stretch, the jockey Sanchez flailing madly with his crop.

The once fat man who could only move with great effort felt suddenly light on his feet and fleet as the beast striding free out there on the track, all by himself. Gumshoe blazed under the wire, tail streaking. Sanchez in green silk humped forward, rose in the stirrups, bringing the horse down gradually to a pounding gallop, lovingly stroking the great heaving withers.

Fritzi jumping up and down, waving winning tickets. Crowds roaring. Pennants flying. Voices shouting over the crackling PA. Numbers pulsing big and white on the tote board. The rest of the field thundering in after the winner. Judges streaming down onto the field behind them. War colors brilliant in the bright, late afternoon of lilac spring. The pageantry. The spectacle. The race of races. The proud, vain, empty game. A race that begins and ends at the same point and runs on forever. Mooney smiled as a new field moved into the gate.